Patricia Duncan was born in Asheville in 1961 and raised in Black Mountains, Swannanoa, and Shelby, North Carolina. She holds a BA in Journalism from the University of North Carolina at Chapel Hill and an MA in English/Creative Writing from North Carolina State University in Raleigh. She lives in Graham, North Carolina, where her good neighbours watch out for her, and is at work on a second novel.

PAMELA DUNCAN

M○○N
WOMEN

PIATKUS

Copyright © 2001 by Pamela Y. Duncan

First published in Great Britain in 2001 by
Judy Piatkus (Publishers) Ltd of
5 Windmill Street, London W1T 2JA
email: info@piatkus.co.uk

First published in the United States in 2001
by Random House, Inc.

The moral right of the author has been asserted

A catalogue record for this book is available from the British Library

ISBN 0 7499 3271 6

Book design by Lynn Newmark

Printed and bound in Great Britain by
Mackays of Chatham Ltd, Chatham, Kent

For
Eloise Davis Price
Patricia Yvonne Price Duncan Eaton
Tracy Joanna Duncan Henderson
Elizabeth Joanna Duncan

and for

Lisa Lynn Barrett Rogers

"Who will tell the tale of a family, its love, its heartache? Who will recognize the struggles for dignity and importance, and through the telling of them, make them important to others? Who will remember this time, this minute, this moment? Who will remember us?"

—Christopher R. Baker (Dramaturg)
(from a program description for the
Horton Foote play *The Death of Papa*)

PROLOGUE

July 1973

Ruth Ann wasn't one to cry over nothing, but dang it all if tonight didn't feel worth crying about. A.J. was late coming home again, Angela and Alex had fought all day, the washing machine broke down, she burnt her arm ironing A.J.'s shirts, and to top it all off, she was eight and a half months pregnant with what felt more like a whale than a baby. This kid swam and leaped and butted constantly, grinding against her spine one minute and wringing out her bladder the next. Her whole focus in life had narrowed to survival, counting down to D-day—drop day, dump day, delivery day, thank-you-Jesus-I'll-never-do-that-again-as-long-as-I-live day. Hallelujah!

But if it come down to survival of the fittest, Ruth Ann wasn't sure she'd win. Becoming a mother in her thirties was a whole lot different than having babies in her twenties. It'd been ten years since she was pregnant with Alex, ten years of working full time and raising them two pretty much by herself, and now here she had to start all over again. A good cry didn't seem like too much to ask.

So when the kids was finally asleep, she took her cigarettes and a big glass of seven and seven—heavy on the Seagram's, light on the 7-Up—out to the front porch to cool off. It was July, sticky hot, and they couldn't afford an air conditioner. The bricks of the porch steps felt cool and sharp against the backs of her legs when she sat down. She chugged the seven and seven in one long drink, then took a big drag off her Kool and blew smoke at the sky. It was pitch-black out, except for a slice of light from the open door. No moon, and more stars than she could stand to look at.

Ruth Ann felt like another drink, but resisted. If her mama knew she'd took up drinking occasionally, she'd have a pure-t fit. But with A.J., drinking just seemed to come natural, nothing wrong with having one every now and then. And sometimes, like tonight, it took the edge off, kept her from getting in that car and driving till she run out of gas, then getting out and walking till she couldn't walk no more, going and going till she was just as far from here as she could get.

Her back spasmed and she leaned forward, trying to straighten the kink by stretching over the hump in her belly. The baby rolled over, pressing against her diaphragm so she couldn't catch a breath. All right, you little shit, Ruth Ann said, and straightened her spine. The baby rewarded her with a kick, then went back to sleep. Ruth Ann finished her cigarette and reached for another, aware on some level that smoking and drinking wasn't supposed to be good for pregnant women. But honest to God, she just didn't believe she could make it without a little help from somewhere.

That's all it took to get her started, thinking about how alone she was in all this, with A.J. gone all the time, the kids too young to do much, and her mama busy helping her daddy on the farm. The crying always built up slow, trickly tears and sniffles at first, then the lump in her throat, then the hard, silent, open-mouthed wailing. Her hand automatically went up to cover her face, even though it was dark, and nobody there to see even if it wasn't.

After a while, when the crying eased up, she moaned to herself, making soft whimpering sounds like the kids made when they finished crying about something, right before they fell asleep. Now she understood why they did it. It was a comforting sound and made her feel less alone.

She sat staring at the empty dark yard, her eyes burning and her brain fuzzy-feeling. What in the hell was she going to do? She pulled Kleenex from the pocket of her nightgown and blew her nose. It was just about impossible to keep up with the kids she had, much less one more. The move to this new house, with little or no help from A.J., had just about done her in, and on top of that her pregnancy—well, it was all just too much.

Out of the emptiness in her mind left by the crying, a word began to form, and it grew and grew until it popped out before she could stop it.

"Goddammit!" she said. She said it again, pronouncing each syllable slow and loud. Her voice sounded strong and controlled, not at all the way she felt. Ruth Ann had never said that word aloud before, though of course it had gone through her mind at times, just like other words she'd heard her brothers say but was too afraid to say herself, words like fuck and cunt and cock. Why was it so many of the bad words, the four-letter words, had to do with sex? All the things that had got her in this mess in the first place.

She said fuck, tasting the word. No thunder rumbled, no lightning struck, no stars fell from the sky. She got slowly and unsteadily to her feet and picked up the empty glass she'd been drinking from. It was one of a set of twelve iced-tea glasses Cassandra give her for a wedding present—real crystal with two little doves etched on the sides, each bird holding one end of a ribbon that had *forever* wrote on it in curly letters. Cassandra was just a kid then and had saved her nickels for months to buy them glasses, so Ruth Ann never told her little sister how ugly she thought they was. Some things you had to try and learn to love.

She raised the glass high over her head and hurled it against the sidewalk. With a satisfying crash, it splintered across the concrete and into the grass. Immediately Ruth Ann's hand flew to cover her open mouth as she stared, horrified, at the mess. She'd have to sweep all that up before the kids come out in the morning or they'd get cut to pieces.

A chill crawled down her arms, puckering her skin into goose bumps. Why was she the one always having to clean up everybody's messes, and nobody ever returned the favor? She decided it was time to stop worrying about tomorrow, about everybody else's tomorrows, while her own slipped by.

"Fuck," she said again. "Fuck, fuck, fuck." If this was what losing her mind felt like, Ruth Ann was beginning to enjoy it. "Fuck this shit," she said. She went in the kitchen and pushed the step stool close to the high cabinet over the refrigerator. She kept her special dishes there so the kids couldn't get at them. She'd got one of Cassandra's glasses down earlier because she felt like doing something special for herself. Now she felt like doing something real special for herself.

She climbed up and down, breathing hard, setting the glasses in the dish drainer. When she had the other eleven of the crystal set, she carried the drainer full of glasses out to the front porch. The glasses clinked as she let the screen door slam behind her. She worried for just a flash about waking up the kids, then remembered they could sleep through an explosion. She giggled, feeling suddenly like somebody had sliced off the top of her head and her brains was floating out.

"Now," she said. "Now we can get down to business." She lit another Kool and sucked smoke into her lungs, exhaling up into the night, breathing out whatever it was that had been clogged inside her.

She clamped the cigarette in the corner of her mouth and reached for a glass. "That first one was for ugly wedding presents," she muttered under her breath. "Number two here's for unplanned pregnancy." It shattered on the sidewalk near the first. Ruth Ann picked up another glass. "And three. For bratty children. And four. For piles of laundry. And five. For unwashed dishes. And six. For stretch marks. And seven. For swollen ankles. And eight. For ironing boards. And nine. For houses with no air-conditioning or shag carpet. And ten—"

Ruth Ann, standing with arm upraised in her white cotton nightgown, got caught in A.J.'s headlights as he pulled his truck in the yard. She hadn't even heard the truck coming or she would've quit, but it was too late now. "Ten. For husbands who come home late or not at all. And eleven. For sperm strong enough to overpower birth-control pills."

Ruth Ann stared into the lights and felt her brains begin to sink back into her head.

A.J. cut the engine, opened the door, and jumped to the ground. He stood staring for a minute, then stepped up on the running board and reached in the window to kill the lights. "Goddamn, Ruth Ann," he said. "What's going on?" His boots crunched on the gravel driveway, then across the broken glass on the sidewalk. He stood at the foot of the steps and stared up at her.

"Stop." Ruth Ann held up a warning hand. "One more and I'm done."

"Have you been drinking?"

"I said stop." Like a quarterback, she held the last glass in her right hand, her left hand keeping him away as she looked down at him. He looked pretty small at that moment.

"Honey, I can see your panties," he said.

Her nightgown, which had nearly reached her knees four months ago, now swirled around the tops of her thighs. "Back off, A.J. You had all of me you going to get. No more babies, you understand? No more." She watched his face change, saw relief flood in. She knew exactly what was going through his little mind. Answer Man had found the answer for what was wrong with her tonight. Pregnancy. Hormones. Hadn't he been through it twice before? She wanted to fling herself off the porch and crush him with the combined weight of her and the baby.

"All right, baby, whatever you say." A.J. smiled a little bit.

"That's what you said after Alex, asshole. I want you to get fixed. I want you to call that doctor tomorrow and make an appointment. If you don't—"

"I said all right." A.J. held up his hands in surrender. "I promise. Please, will you calm down?"

"No I will not!" Ruth Ann said. "I may never be calm again." She sucked a big lungful of air in through her nose and blew it out her mouth. "But I'll tell you one thing. I am not going to be like my mama. I am not having no twelve young'uns. I ain't even having four. This is it. Do you hear me?"

"I hear you, baby." Ruth Ann saw A.J. look at the glass in her hand. She saw him wonder if it was about to hit him instead of the sidewalk. Good. Let him worry for a change.

She took a last drag off the cigarette, flicked it in the yard, and took a deep breath. "All right then, just one more." Ruth Ann kissed the glass and held it high. "Twelve. For doctors and husbands and men in general, all the men in the world who lie, lie, lie." She watched A.J. jump back as the glass splintered around his feet. He looked up at her like she might really be crazy. Hell, wouldn't she have to be crazy to stay in her life? A cheating husband, two little kids and another on the way, a full-time job at the plant and another at home. She must be out of her ever-loving mind. When did she choose this life for herself anyway? She didn't remember doing that.

She laughed, then the laughter strangled into sobs, and she slowly lowered herself to the top step. She rocked back and forth, hands on her knees, staring straight ahead.

A.J. tiptoed across the glass and sat on the steps next to her legs. His hand cupped the back of her calf, rubbing and squeezing.

Ruth Ann jerked her leg away. "Don't touch me!"

He clasped his hands together and stared at his feet. "It'll be all right. I'll call the doctor about it tomorrow if that'll make you feel better."

"About a vasectomy. It's called a vasectomy. It's not like they're going to cut your nuts off, A.J."

"I know, baby. Take it easy. Your hormones is all stirred up right now."

"I knew it." Ruth Ann heaved herself to her feet. "I knew that's what you'd say. You leave my hormones out of this." She went in the house and come back out wearing a pair of old loafers, carrying the broom, dustpan, and plastic kitchen trash can. She flipped the porch light on so she could see what she was doing.

"Here. I'll do that." A.J. got up and wrapped his hand around the broom handle, but she snatched it against her stomach.

"Go to bed," she said, her voice hoarse. "I'll clean up my own mess. I always do." She glared at him until he let go.

"Damn, Ruth Ann." He shook his head, went in and got a beer, then come back out to watch her sweep. He sat on the top step and gulped half the beer in one swallow. "Doing a damn fine job, honey," he said.

She ignored him.

"Good thing it's dark. Neighbors be getting quite a show."

"Don't you think you ought to go to bed now?"

A.J. leaned back on his elbows. "I don't have to work tomorrow. I get to sleep late."

"It must be nice." Ruth Ann emptied the dustpan in the trash and studied the edges of the sidewalk. "Damn! I can't get the glass out of the yard with a broom." She stomped past A.J., into the house, and dragged out the vacuum cleaner.

A.J. laughed, a high-pitched hee-hee sound. "What the hell you up to now, baby? You going to vacuum the yard?"

"Well, I got to get this glass up somehow, or else I'll be picking it out of your children for the next six months."

Ruth Ann took the head off the vacuum and stuck the silver pipe into the grass. Bent over because she couldn't squat and still reach the yard, she vacuumed along both sides of the sidewalk twice. When she finished, she hit the off switch and straightened up, massaging the knot in her lower back.

A.J. laid on the steps, laughing like he couldn't quit if he wanted to. "Oh, baby, don't stop. I think you missed a piece over there." He pointed with his toe.

Ruth Ann stood in front of him with her hands on her hips, or the place where her hips used to be. "Shut up!" she said. He kept laughing.

Her whole head felt hot, like it might shoot off her neck any minute. And A.J. still laughing like a hyena. Real slow and careful, she said, "I said. Shut. The fuck. Up."

A.J.'s whole body got real still and his mouth fell open as he stared back at her. His mouth actually fell open. Amazing, she thought, the power of a four-letter word.

"What did you say?" A.J. said. "You just said fuck."

Like she was too stupid to know what had just come out of her own mouth. "Yes," she said. "Do you have a problem with that?" Calm eased down over and around her like a force field. She crossed her arms and rested them on top of the baby.

A.J. stared a minute longer, then shook his head. "No, ma'am, I don't have a problem."

"Fine. Now, would you like to tell me what was so damn funny a minute ago?"

He looked confused. "Huh?" he said. Then, "Oh," and he smiled, looking at her from under his eyebrows in that way he had. "Nothing. Just that big old white moon of yours floating across the yard."

"What moo—" Ruth Ann clutched her butt with both hands, which pushed her belly even further out. "Oh, good Lord. I'm wearing underwear, A.J." She looked left, then right, but the neighbors' windows was dark. She'd made a fool of herself, though, and didn't even do it in the house where nobody could see. And how did she know them people wasn't hiding behind their curtains watching her right now? She pulled at the hem of her nightgown, but it was as low as it was going to get.

A.J. leaned forward, grabbed her hand, and pulled. "Come on, baby," he said, patting the step beside him.

She resisted at first, then finally let him pull her up the steps. The brick felt cold against her butt when she sat down.

"It's all right, baby," A.J. said. "Nobody but me out here to see it, and I done seen it all before." He put his arm around her back, then started rubbing her shoulders. Against her will Ruth Ann relaxed little by little until finally she slumped against him, exhausted. A.J. held her, kissed her sweaty temple, gently stroked the wet hair off her forehead. "It's all right, baby," he said, and held her while she cried into his neck.

August
1992

A dump truck full of red dirt roared by, going the same direction she had to go, shaking the ground under her as it passed. Ruth Ann decided to sit in the driveway a few more minutes, let that truck get way ahead of her before she got on the road herself. She read a story in a magazine about a dump truck accidentally dumping a load of rocks on a car behind it, killing both passengers in the car, a mother and her little girl. Stories like that just tore her nerves up. She didn't know why she read them, except what else was there to do in the checkout line at the grocery store? Of course, that truck only had dirt in it, not rocks, so if it did fall on her she might have a chance of surviving. But it just wasn't worth the risk, and anyway, she wasn't in no rush. Ruth Ann put the car in park and started opening her mail. Bills, that's all it was. Phone bill, gas bill, magazine bill. That was twenty dollars a year she didn't need to spend, but at least *Family Circle* give her something to look forward to in the mailbox besides bills every month.

There was a postcard too, from Alex. He was working in Dallas for two weeks and wouldn't be able to come for the weekend. She could just smell the relief in his handwriting, that he didn't have to spend a day or two with his family. He could've called, but she knew how much easier it was to write, to not hear the disappointment in her voice. Well, at least Angela would show up Sunday with the boys. That was better than nothing.

Ruth Ann slid the mail in her pocketbook and put the car in drive. She looked both ways one more time, then pulled out on the road. Seemed like a lot longer than four months she'd been making the trip from Davis to Asheville, a trip that never got any easier, especially not today. It wasn't so far distance-wise—only sixty-five miles—and took her only an hour and a half to two hours, depending on the traffic and whether or not she had to stop to use the bathroom, which she almost always did. Her bladder had been shrinking ever since she had her first baby, and she figured by now it couldn't be much bigger than a peanut. No, what really bothered her was all that long time in the car alone, too much thinking and worrying to do between here and there.

As Ruth Ann drove past Cassandra's house, she noticed the van was gone. They was probably at the mall getting their supper at the cafeteria. Cassandra wasn't never big on cooking, and their mama had got to be a real danger in the kitchen lately—bad to leave a pot on the stove and forget about it until it caught on fire and set off the smoke alarm.

At the Davis city-limits sign, she slowed down to thirty-five. Town was empty this time of day, nobody on the street. All the stores closed at five o'clock, except the florist. It stayed open until six. Ruth Ann let the car come almost to a standstill as she stared in the window of Cox's. One great big arrangement in the front of the window had caught her eye. It had birds of paradise mixed in with orange carnations and baby's breath. White roses in there too. Good Lord, what was they thinking? Didn't they know birds of paradise don't need no other flowers to keep them company?

Somebody come up behind her and honked. Ruth Ann looked in the rearview mirror, but she didn't know whoever it was, so she sped up and went on down the street. At the edge of town she slowed down again and studied the parking lot at Ruby's Hot Meals. She didn't see A.J.'s big old red truck in there nowhere. The man must be sick. Every time Ruby cracked the door, he was in there eating. It was a wonder he hadn't got fat in the two years since Ruth Ann kicked him out.

A little farther on she slowed down again, at the duplexes where A.J. rented an apartment. There was his truck, impossible to miss since the thing was near about as big as a fire truck. He'd probably be paying on it for the rest of his life. For just a second, Ruth Ann thought about stopping to see if he wanted to go to Asheville with her. He'd only been once, the first week Ashley was up there. Ever since then he'd been too busy to go, which was a lie. He was retired. What else did he have to do? No, he just couldn't take it, that was all.

Ruth Ann put her foot down on the accelerator. He probably didn't even remember Ashley was coming home today. The selfish bastard.

She sped up to forty-five around the curve where Cleveland Yarn sat, wanting to get past it. It still made her mad that she'd had to work on a Saturday. They always called her when somebody got sick, and now it'd be way past dark before her and Ashley got home. She was supposed to have picked her up that morning. Maybe it was for the best though. At least she'd been so busy at work she hadn't had time to think, and now they could just come home and go to bed and not have to sit and stare at each other, wondering what to say.

After she passed the mill, she set the cruise control to fifty-five and settled back in her seat. She could relax a little the twenty-five miles to I-40. Nothing between here and there but corn and cows and convenience stores. She enjoyed this part of the drive. It was the interstate tore her nerves up.

She passed a little white store with two old men in overalls sitting out front. Every time she rode by, there they sat in that same spot, and they always threw up a hand and waved. She didn't wave back. She didn't even know them. And besides, she didn't feel like waving. It wasn't like she was out for a pleasure cruise.

Ruth Ann slid a hand inside her pocketbook and felt for the shape of a cigarette pack. Then she remembered for about the millionth time that she'd quit. She snatched her hand out and put it back on the wheel.

Hands at ten and two. That's what Mr. Howard taught in tenth grade. Now, that was somebody she hadn't thought about in a while. Ruth Ann had been in love with him all through driver's ed. He was a real gentleman, and a gentle man. A.J. could've taken lessons from Mr. Howard.

She twisted the radio tuning knob and picked up some staticky music, then stopped when she heard a familiar tune—*our d-i-v-o-r-c-e becomes final today*. Lord, Tammy Wynette. She hadn't heard her in years. Normally Ruth Ann didn't like country music—too twangy—but that song said it all.

She'd almost forgot about it being the first anniversary of her divorce from A.J. Now, wasn't that something? One whole year, two years since the separation. Something to celebrate. She should've took off for Daytona Beach, or maybe even Atlantic City. Anywhere but where she was right now. That was the story of her life, though, never being able to cut loose because she was too dang responsible.

As she headed up the on ramp to the interstate, Ruth Ann cut the radio off. She put Ashley and A.J. and everything else out of her mind in order to concentrate on driving. When the kids was little and bounced around the car like basketballs, making all kinds of racket, she'd had to train herself to tune everything out. The thought of killing one of them in a car wreck give her nightmares, even still. She kept the cruise control on fifty-five, even though the legal limit was sixty-five.

By the time she got to Old Fort, traffic thinned out some, and Ruth Ann relaxed a little bit as the car downshifted for the climb up Old Fort Mountain. She didn't even look to her left like most people done, to see the view. She'd been looking off at them mountains and valleys ever since she could remember. It was about as familiar to her as the road from her house to the mill. Her mama and daddy used to take them up to Madison County to visit at least twice a year, more if somebody got married or died. None of them had been back up there in years though, not since her daddy died. Her mama never acted like she wanted to go after that.

It was strange how a road and some scenery could bring back so many memories. Her and Cassandra and their brothers used to hate going to Madison County, because it was such a long car ride and Clark used to always get sick and throw up in the backseat. He had to hold a big old pickle jar on his lap the whole way, and it was usually full by the time they got where they was going. Ruth Ann had always wondered why her mama never brought the lid to that jar. It might've saved them shivering in the cold with the windows rolled down because of the smell.

Once they got up there to Slatey Knob, they had fun running loose on top of that mountain with their cousins. But then it was back in the car, back to Davis, and Mama always in a bad mood, picking at Daddy's driving all the way home. Her mama didn't like going, but she didn't like leaving even more. Ruth Ann had always known there was something troublesome between her mama and daddy, and she knew it had to do with Madison County. Whatever it was, though, they kept to themselves.

The car topped the mountain and picked up speed down into the Swannanoa Valley, past the Blue Ridge Assembly and the sign for Black Mountain. It hit Ruth Ann all of a sudden that this really was the last time she'd have to make this trip. She didn't know whether to feel relieved or not, because she still didn't know what in the world she was going to do with that girl once she got her home.

Why couldn't Ashley have just finished high school and gone on to college like she was supposed to, like Angela and Alex did? Then Ruth Ann's biggest worry right now would be coming up with tuition money and spending money. She could handle that. But Ashley had never done what Ruth Ann wanted, not from day one. Her whole problem was she was too much like her daddy, never thinking about consequences—selfish, really.

Then again, Ruth Ann thought, maybe it was her fault. Maybe Ashley heard all that crying and carrying on she done nearly the whole nine months she was pregnant. Doctors nowadays was saying how babies in the womb know exactly what's going on around them. Angela's doctor told her to read to Bryan and Jonathan while they was still in her, and look how smart they turned out. Both boys was in accelerated programs at school, so they must be something to it, though Ruth Ann would hate to think of some of the things Ashley heard. She loved Ashley, but that didn't change the fact she was an accident. Of course, she'd be lying if she said the other two was planned.

Back in May when Ashley called out of the blue, Ruth Ann had been tempted to hang up on her. No word from the girl in nearly a year and suddenly she decides she needs to talk to her mama? But then Ashley started crying and said she was in jail in Asheville and could Ruth Ann please come? Ruth Ann's heart nearly stopped when she heard that, and her stomach just drawed up in a knot. She'd been so afraid it would eventually come to jail or worse, but she reckoned nothing could prepare a parent for something like that when it actually happened. She prayed Ashley hadn't killed somebody, and felt such relief when it turned out she got caught shoplifting at the Asheville mall. Ruth Ann had told Ashley she'd come that afternoon and hung up the phone. All she could think at the time was how things didn't seem to have changed much since the last time they talked.

The last time was right after Ashley turned eighteen, right after Ruth Ann and A.J. signed their final divorce papers, right after her mama had started going downhill so bad. That was the first time in her life Ruth Ann thought she understood what a nervous breakdown must feel like. Almost exactly a year ago to the day, what she had wanted most in the world was to run away, get as far away from Davis and her family as she could possibly get. It was all too much for one person to handle, and it wasn't fair. Life just wasn't fair, which was another one of her mama's favorite sayings, only she always said it like it was something you get used to.

Ruth Ann had felt alone a lot in her life, but never more than that day Ashley run away for the last time. Ruth Ann had got home from work and there was the back door standing wide open and nobody home. At first she didn't notice anything unusual. She put her pocketbook down on the kitchen table and headed to her room to change clothes. But on the way down the hall she got a funny feeling and went back to the living room. Something wasn't right. She turned around in a circle in the middle of the room, then stopped and realized the TV was gone. And the VCR. She went to the kitchen and the microwave was gone too. What in the world? She'd been robbed? She hollered for Ashley but got no answer. She was a little bit scared to go through the rest of the house, but then figured whoever it was must be long gone. She checked her room and nothing seemed to be missing there. Ashley wasn't in her room, but everything looked okay there too. Until Ruth Ann noticed the closet door was open and Ashley's suitcase was gone. She opened drawers and saw that half Ashley's clothes was gone too.

It took a minute to sink in. Her own child had robbed her and then run off? Ruth Ann sat down on the bed and just stared. How could this be? How had she raised a child that would do such a thing? About that time the little white princess phone on Ashley's night table started ringing and Ruth Ann picked it up.

"Mama?" It was Ashley.

"Yes."

"Mama, it's me."

"I know." All of a sudden Ruth Ann felt tears coming on. No, sir, no, she would not cry now. She cleared her throat. "Where are you?"

"Mama, it wasn't me, I swear."

Ruth Ann didn't say anything. She couldn't think of anything to say.

"Mama, I didn't take the TV and the other stuff. It was Rusty. It was him that done it. I should've stopped him, but I got scared. I was afraid he'd do something crazy, maybe hit me or something. Please don't be mad at me."

Ashley got quiet, but still Ruth Ann couldn't think of anything to say.

"Mama, I know you got to call the police, but I swear it wasn't me. I told him I was breaking up with him. I don't want nothing else to do with him."

"Then why did you pack a suitcase?"

Ashley got quiet again, then said, "I figured I'd leave before you threw me out."

"Where are you now?"

"I'm staying with a friend. A girl friend. I mean it, Mama, I'm done with Rusty."

It dawned on Ruth Ann then that she did need to call the police. A crime had been committed right here in her own home and she knew who had done it. She sat up straighter. The tears was going away and now she was getting mad.

"I'm swearing out a warrant for that boy's arrest," she said. "And I ought to have you arrested too. It was just as much you as him. You let him in this house. And it probably wasn't the first time either. You could've at least shut the door on your way out instead of leaving the place wide open for somebody else to come in and rob me, or maybe even kill me. What was you thinking? You let that no-account criminal in my home, after me and your daddy told you and told you he wasn't no good, after he's done been in jail for stealing and selling drugs and Lord knows what else. And still you wouldn't listen. And don't tell me you didn't help him. Don't you dare say that. You helped him just as sure as if you carried that TV out to his car yourself. That was a brand-new TV too. I let your daddy take the old one."

There was more silence on the other end of the line. Ruth Ann could tell Ashley was crying, and that just made her madder. "You might as well save the salt and quit that crying, Ashley. It ain't no use. You made your bed and now you can lay in it. You're eighteen years old, so you go on and go wherever you want to. Me and your daddy are not going to scour the countryside for you like we done the last two times. You're on your own, young lady."

Ruth Ann listened to the dial tone for a minute after Ashley hung up on her, then hung up her end. What should she do now? Call 911, she reckoned. 911. That was something you seen on TV, not something you done in your real life. Only this was real life, about as real as it got. Maybe she ought to call A.J. first, get him over here. But no, he wasn't her husband no more, and this wasn't his home that had been broken into. He was still Ashley's daddy, so she'd tell him about all this, but tomorrow, not tonight. She couldn't deal with him tonight. He'd be wanting to run out and find Ashley, find that sorry Rusty Pruitt, find all their things. All her things. And at that very moment she didn't want none of it back, especially not Ashley. Right then she didn't care if she never seen that girl again. It scared her to feel that way about her own child, scared her worse than anything else that had happened. She picked up the phone, but instead of 911, she dialed Cassandra's number. She'd wait for her sister to come over, then call the police. She had to have somebody. She couldn't do it alone. She just couldn't.

The interstate began to curve around the half of Beaucatcher Mountain still left after the state blasted a highway through the middle of it. Half a mountain. How could that be? Mountains was one of the few things in this world could be counted on to last. Or so Ruth Ann had always believed.

Didn't they know they wasn't supposed to mess with things like that? Her mama said the only constant is change, and damn if it still didn't make her mad to realize her mama was right.

She found her exit and headed through downtown Asheville, thinking as she turned up the long winding hill to Appalachian Hall that it was too beautiful a place for what it was. Tall trees and pretty homes lined the road, and at the top of the hill Appalachian Hall sat like a big mansion or hotel or something, which it probably was before they turned it into a hospital. If she hadn't seen it for herself, it'd be hard to imagine that beautiful old building full of wild kids trying to come off dope and alcohol.

At least Ashley was safe here and getting help Ruth Ann didn't know how to give. But once they got home, Ruth Ann didn't have a clue what to do with Ashley then. Her mama had told her they'd just have to figure it out as they went along, just like everybody else. Easy for her to say. She didn't have to live with Ashley and put up with her mess and fight all the time.

Ruth Ann reached the top of the hill, pulled the Buick around the circle drive, and stopped at the front where it would be easier to load all Ashley's stuff. She checked her makeup and put on a little more lipstick, then closed the mirror and stared through the glass doors. Maybe it would be all right. Ashley wasn't stupid. Maybe she'd learned something, or at least had time to think and realize she didn't want to spend the rest of her life in a trashy trailer park, or in jail, or in an institution. She'd said all the right things in the therapy, but Ashley was like her daddy that way. Them two always knew what to say to get what they wanted. Of course, saying and doing was two different things altogether.

The first floor of Appalachian Hall could almost pass for a hotel, an elegant but shabby old hotel with high ceilings and archways connecting the large sitting rooms. It made Ashley think of the mall, all that space, and she felt comfortable in it. She sat down on a couch facing the front door. She'd see her mama before her mama seen her.

She put her feet on the coffee table, enjoying the sound her boot heels made against the wood. Tanya stared at her from the reception booth. I'll put my feet on the goddamn table if I want to, Ashley thought. I'm getting out of this place in a few minutes anyway. She checked her watch, then tilted her head back against the cushions and closed her eyes.

From the other end of the building she heard dishes clink and silverware ping and clang, then the whoosh and flap of the swinging kitchen door. She could still smell the bacon from supper. Groups of them took turns cooking on the cook's day off, and the breakfast and lunch groups had it easiest. Just cereal for breakfast and sandwiches for lunch. Supper had to be a hot meal, and breakfast-for-supper was the easiest and safest thing to make. It reminded Ashley of spending the night with Cassandra and Granny, how they'd make breakfast-for-supper sometimes when they didn't feel like cooking a big meal. She couldn't remember the last time they done that.

Cassandra hadn't been to visit in a couple of weeks, but Ashley had been so preoccupied with Keith and what to do about him that she hadn't had time to miss her aunt much. Or anybody else. Of course, her mama come twice a week, just like she was supposed to, and never said a word unless somebody asked her a direct question. Chuck said Ruth Ann was a real stoic, hiding her feelings even from herself. But then, Chuck was a shrink, always overanalyzing everybody. He was a pretty good guy and had helped her figure some things out, but Ashley still didn't appreciate him saying things like that about her mama. It might be true that Ruth Ann stayed clenched so tight you couldn't drive a toothpick up her ass with a sledge-hammer, but that wasn't none of Chuck's business. Ashley was reminded of how Alex used to tell his friends that he could beat the crap out of his little sister if he wanted to, but nobody else better not touch her. That was how she felt about her mama when Chuck pressured her about talking more.

Mostly Ashley did all the talking though. She'd found that Appalachian Hall was not the place to hide anything that resembled a feeling. They wouldn't let you. She'd been stoic too, at first, but eventually Chuck had wormed the whole story out of her. How she started sneaking her parents' cigarettes when she was eleven, then started sneaking their liquor when she was thirteen, then started hanging out at the mall and cruising and drinking with some older kids when she was fifteen. That was when she met Rusty and got into smoking pot and sometimes doing other stuff. She didn't do much of that heavy shit though. That stuff scared her. She didn't want to end up frying her brain before she was twenty like some of those idiots she hung out with. All she wanted was to have some fun and to get the hell out of that dead house where her parents sat night after night, smoking cigarettes and watching TV.

Now she was ready to get the hell out of this place. Four months was long enough. Enough talking, enough listening, enough waiting. She didn't want to think about her life no more. She just wanted to live it for a change. The only time she felt any kind of freedom at all in this place was with

Keith. He just let her be. Of course, he could also piss her off worse than anybody, except maybe her mama. What made her the maddest was how, when her mama and Cassandra was here, he paid more attention to them than he did to her, and any time she said something against her family, he always took up for them. It drove her crazy how he always made sure he got the last word and it was always the same: At least you got a mama and daddy that cares if you live or die.

She reckoned she couldn't blame him though. Considering the trash he come from, her family must look pretty good. His mama come one time to visit and she looked like the raggediest old whore Ashley had ever seen, a walking skeleton with bleach-blond hair and way too much eye makeup. Keith said she was living with some drug dealer in Asheville and stayed strung out on something all the time. He didn't know where his daddy was. That son of a bitch left when Keith was six. If it hadn't been for his granny and his uncles, no telling what would've happened to Keith. They took him to live with them and he done all right for a while, but then he went and fell in love with this girl that was just like his mama, and she got him into drinking and drugs. But as soon as his uncles found out about it, they dragged his ass straight to Asheville, said they wasn't going to let him end up like his mama and daddy, that they raised him to do better than that.

The first time she seen him, Ashley couldn't take her eyes off him. For a week or so, she just watched him, watched him eat alone, watch TV alone, walk alone. The only time he was with people was when he had to be, in group therapy, and even then he looked alone. The fact that he was an Indian made him seem even more separate from the rest of them. But that's what Ashley liked about him. He didn't need nobody.

She started talking to him at lunch one day, just sat down and started a nonstop monologue about something she'd seen on TV the night before, the weather, whatever come into her head. She didn't ask him any questions or give him any opportunity to shut her down. He didn't get up and leave, which she took as a good sign. And eventually he started talking back, and it wasn't long before they had got in deep with each other. They wasn't supposed to have sex, but hell, what else was there to do in that place? The nurses watched them pretty good, but two people with enough incentive could always find a way.

Ashley didn't know if she believed in love at first sight, but whatever it was between her and Keith had started that very first day and never let up the whole time. It was something she never felt with Rusty or any boy. She'd made one other friend here, Peri, and that was nice, but with Keith it was way more than friendship. He was a man, almost twenty-one, and the feelings she had for him made her feel like a woman, not a little girl anymore. It wasn't just that she liked him or wanted him. She needed him, and that scared the ever-living shit out of her.

That might be part of the reason she didn't feel too bad about being apart from Keith now. She needed to be away from him for a while, see how she felt when she wasn't with him every day. It was too bad they'd had that big fight, and over nothing really. She'd been so mean to him the last few weeks, but she couldn't seem to stop herself. She couldn't blame him for trying to get back at her with Cindy. He hadn't really cheated on her, she knew that, but pretending he had made it a whole lot easier to say good-bye. Actually, she hadn't even said good-bye, because they was still mad at each other when he left. His Uncle Bill come and got him early one morning and he was gone before she even woke up, and she hadn't heard a word from him since. Considering he was the father of her baby, she'd thought he might at least call and see how she was doing, but no, he was too stubborn. Well, she could be just as stubborn. He knew she was going home today and he knew where to find her.

God or somebody must be having a good laugh, because after all the talking and analyzing, Ashley had finally figured out that all she wanted was to go home, the very place she'd been running from, the very place that had got her here. She had no clue what she'd do once she got there, just that it was where she needed to be right now. She was so tired, and most of the time felt a whole hell of a lot older than nineteen. You can't go home again though. She didn't have to read the book to know that. Her and Peri even skipped the tour the day their group visited the Thomas Wolfe house. Instead, they bought Cokes and smokes and sat on the front porch watching people go in and out of the high-rise Radisson in old Tom's front yard. No way he could or would call the place home now. Watching all the tourists going in and coming out, Ashley felt like she'd taken a little vacation herself, a four-month vacation from the real world. And scared as she was about going back, she was ready to give it a shot. If her mama would let her.

"Hey, Ash, when's she coming?" Peri flopped down beside her, then leaned forward and pulled her hair over one shoulder. It fell across her chest and between her legs almost to the floor. If she hadn't been so sweet, Ashley would've hated her for being perfect, blond and petite and almost too pretty. Definitely too thin. That's what heroin had done for her—heroin and her father.

"Who the hell knows." Ashley closed her eyes. "What you up to?"

"Nothing. I just come down to keep you company. I see our lovely receptionist from hell is here tonight." Peri flipped her middle finger at the reception booth and laughed when Tanya slid the window shut. "Don't worry, Tanya," she yelled. "I ain't going to cut you. Tonight." She sat back and crossed her legs and arms. "That is one uptight bitch. So, have you talked to Keith yet?"

"No."

"He didn't fuck Cindy before he left, Ash."

"I know that."

"She said all they did was kiss. And he only did it to get your attention." Peri looked sideways and raised her eyebrows at Ashley. "I guess it worked."

Ashley didn't say anything.

"Maybe you ought to call him when you get home," Peri said.

"Maybe he ought to call me. You sound like you're taking his side."

"You're my friend, Ashley. The only one I got in this goddamn place."

Ashley put her arm around Peri. "I'm sorry," she said. Peri scooted closer and laid her head on Ashley's shoulder. There was only four years difference in their ages, but sometimes Ashley felt more like Peri's mama than her friend. "I wish me and Keith could get a trailer and live on our own and just say the hell with all the rest of them, Mama included. Then you could come live with us when you get out."

"You're lucky. At least you got a mama to take you back."

"Yeah, but she makes it so fucking hard. She can't just be quiet and let me work things out on my own. She's always got to tell me what to do, and how to do it, and she's got this look, like she's crucified every time she sees me."

"Jesus," Peri said. "Maybe it'll be different this time."

"It better be." Ashley rested her hands on her belly. "I got a baby to think about now, don't I."

"You going to keep it?"

"Well, yeah," Ashley said. "I love Keith, even if he is an asshole sometimes." She leaned her elbows on her knees and pushed her hands through the long black curls Keith loved so much. Cher hair, he called it. "God. I got to figure something out. I ain't had a drink or nothing since I got here, but I'm scared. And I'm worried about the baby. I don't know if it'll be messed up from all the shit I done. And I don't know what I'll do if Mama kicks me out."

They sat quiet for a minute and Ashley could almost hear Peri's mind working. The girl's mission in life was to make everything work out for everybody else, like working a big puzzle till all the pieces fit and made a happy picture. She didn't understand yet about missing pieces or that some puzzles took a lot longer than others.

"Well," Peri said. "She told you you could live at home till you get a job and get your act together. She won't change her mind just 'cause you're pregnant, will she?"

"You don't know her." Ashley looked at the chipped polish on her long nails. "She says she expects me to work and save up so I can get a place of my own, and if there's any more foolishness like before, my ass is on the street."

"I bet she didn't say ass though, did she?"

Ashley laughed. "Oh, yes, she did. Maybe it's all coming back to her now. Angela and Alex said Mama used to cuss like a sailor when she was mad, but then I reckon she decided to clean up her act for me."

Peri laughed too. "By the way, your mascara's all to hell, Ash. You look like a raccoon."

"Thanks, bitch."

"And just remember, when life gets you down, all you have to do is re- cite the Serenity Prayer one hundred times a day and everything will be okay."

"Yeah, right," Ashley said, and made a face. "God grant me the divinity to change the things I cannot accept . . ."

Peri added in a high-pitched voice, "The legal age to drink the things I can . . ."

Ashley finished with, "And the wisdom to hide the evidence. Amen!" They fell back against the couch, laughing.

When they'd calmed down, Peri said, "You'll be all right, Ash. You're strong, and you know how to take care of yourself, and most important . . ."

"What?" Ashley said.

"You got people in the world care if you live or die."

"That's what Keith's always saying."

"Well, he's right. You work things out with your mama. And if you fuck up, I'm coming to personally kick your ass."

"Yeah, like you could, scarecrow."

Ashley looked up then and watched as her mama came through the glass entrance doors and stopped in the middle of the foyer. Ruth Ann Moon Payne. The only person in the world that ironed her blue jeans till they had permanent creases in them. The only person in the world that could strike the fear of God just by walking in the room. Ashley stood up and looked down at Peri. "This is it, girl. Wish me luck," she said. They high-fived, then Ashley turned away and walked over to Ruth Ann.

"Hey, Mama." She gave Ruth Ann a quick hug, then they turned and walked toward the elevator.

"You ready to go?" Ruth Ann said.

Ashley knew her mama meant more than just packing. What she meant was, are you ready to act like a human being and live in my house without stealing from me, lying to me, or running away?

Ashley said, "I guess."

"Well, you better do better than guess." Ruth Ann pushed the up button and they waited for the elevator without speaking.

"How you doing today, Mrs. Payne?" Joan, the floor nurse, said as they signed in on the hall. "You ready for this girl to come home?"

Ruth Ann didn't answer, just followed Joan into the office. Ashley took one last look around the nurses' station. God, it was depressing. The fluorescent lighting glared off the gray tile floor and the white walls covered with memos and room assignments. Ashley didn't see what Joan had to be so damn perky about.

"Why don't you go get your stuff while your mama finishes up this paperwork, and then Chuck wants to see you in his office before you go, okay? Thanks, hon." Joan smiled that fucking fake Miss America smile of hers and turned back to Ruth Ann.

Sure, hon, whatever you say, hon. Ashley knew better than to smart-mouth Joan though. She might be only five feet tall, but that bitch was strong. On more than one occasion Ashley had watched her wrestle freaked-out kids into solitary with no help from the male staff.

She went down the hall to her room and stood in the middle of it, staring around at the naked walls. When she closed her eyes, the room spun and she was free-falling, floating, with nothing solid or real to grab on to. She didn't belong anywhere. Not in Murphy with Keith and his granny and his uncles, not in Appalachian Hall, not with any of the guys she'd been with before Keith, not even home with her mama, not really. But it was her only option until she figured out what she needed. Hell, she wouldn't know how to go about getting what she needed even if she knew what that was. She'd just have to do like that story Chuck told her, the one about driving at night. It's dark as hell and you can only see as far as the headlights, but you get to the end of the headlights and then you can see a little farther and so you keep going that way and before you know it, it's daylight. She hoped to God that was a true story.

Ashley crossed to the window and stared through the bars. She breathed in wild onion and fresh-cut grass, surprised as always that the smell made it up this high. Over beyond the treetops, the mountains rested hazy and blue in the August heat, like old humpyback women leaning against each other in a circle, surrounding her, surrounding everything, hemming her in. Her granny come from somewhere over there in Madison County, but Ashley couldn't remember exactly where. After all the stories she'd heard all her life, how could she not remember? She turned away from the window and took one last look around the room, then picked up her suitcase and headed down the hall to meet her mama.

She left her bag for Joan to watch while they went in to talk to Chuck one last time. It amazed Ashley that him and Ruth Ann got along as well as they did, in spite of him being about twelve years younger, black, and a psychiatrist. Ruth Ann never completely relaxed in his office, but at least she showed up, which was more than Ashley could say for her daddy.

"How you doing, my dears?" Chuck said. He perched himself on the edge of the coffee table across from where they sat on the couch and pushed his glasses up on his nose with his thumb. "You feeling ready to go?"

Ashley had always thought he looked like a fuzzy-headed owl, especially when he cocked his head to one side like that. What was she supposed to say? Hell no. I'm scared shitless. "Yeah, I guess so."

Chuck leaned forward and smiled, crinkling the corners of his owly green eyes. "You'll be fine." He tapped her hand to get her attention. "You listening?"

Ashley looked up at him. "Yes, sir."

He turned to Ruth Ann. "How about you, Mrs. Payne?"

"I'll be fine as long as she behaves herself," Ruth Ann said.

"Okay." Chuck took off his glasses and polished them with the hem of his shirt. He always wore these long shirts that he said he got in Jamaica. That's where he was from. They had embroidery down the middle. He put his glasses back on and squinted at Ruth Ann. "But listen. You both need to remember how important it is to be open to the possibility for change, okay? And I really encourage you both to go to the twelve-step meetings."

Ruth Ann glanced at Ashley. "I guess her granny's right. The only way to get through this is by figuring it out as we go along."

"God, Mama, you don't have to act like it's some kind of punishment or something." Ashley crossed her arms over her chest and slouched down on the couch.

"Listen, my dears," Chuck said. "Living with people is never easy. You both know that. But you're family and you love each other, and that's a good place to start." He slapped his hands against his thighs and stood up. "Okay, that's it, then." He shook hands with Ruth Ann, then hugged Ashley. "Good luck, my dears," he said as they left the room together.

Ashley looked over her shoulder and Chuck raised his eyebrows and gave her the thumbs-up. That was it? Good luck and thumbs-up? Holy shit. She was going to need a lot more than that to get through the next few hours. Days. Weeks. Months. Years. She was going to need a fucking miracle, divine intervention, something. Something to show her the way. The big saying around here was always "Let go and let God." Okay, God, she thought, here's your big chance. Let's see what you can do.

Only once did Ashley look back up the hill toward Appalachian Hall as Ruth Ann drove them away. All she could see were trees and the road behind her. Ahead lay the real world, with her mama and her family and especially this baby she was carrying. She faced forward and wondered again where she would get the courage to tell her mama. She'd practiced the conversation with Peri, but Peri was a lot less intimidating than Ruth Ann.

Ashley asked if she could turn on the radio, and they listened to oldies for a while because Ashley knew her mama hated heavy metal. Setting the mood for this discussion was very important, and she knew that Guns n' Roses would not leave her mama in a good mood. They rode for almost an hour listening to the Carpenters, Bill Haley and his Comets, Bobby Darin, Connie Francis, and a bunch of others before Ashley asked her mama for a rest stop. Her bladder wouldn't hold as much now, and besides, she wanted to get this confrontation over with and she figured it'd be safer for both of them if she did it when the car wasn't moving.

Ruth Ann stopped the car next to the door of a Hardee's and kept the motor running.

"Don't you have to go?" Ashley said.

"No, you go on," Ruth Ann said. She looked at her watch. "Do you want to get you some supper while we're here? It's after seven o'clock."

"No, I'm not hungry."

Ruth Ann hesitated, then reached in her purse for some money. "Well, I want you to get me a Coke and some french fries, so you go on and get you something too, but I want some change from this." She handed Ashley a ten-dollar bill.

"I'll be right back." Ashley hurried to the rest room, then stood in line to order Cokes and fries. She practiced breathing deep. It's all right, she told herself. She's not going to kick you out because of the baby. And if she does, then you can go to Cassandra's until you figure out what to do next. Be calm, be calm.

"That was fast," Ruth Ann said when Ashley got back in the car.

"Supper crowd's already been, I guess," Ashley said. She set the cardboard drink tray on her lap and handed Ruth Ann her change and fries.

"Mama," Ashley said. Her voice was shaky. "Mama, can you pull in a parking place while I drink my Coke?"

"What? No, you can drink it while we ride. I want to get home. Hold my fries for me."

Ashley ignored the carton of fries Ruth Ann held out. "Mama, please. I need to talk to you about something." She looked down at the Cokes and felt her mama staring at the side of her face.

"Well," Ruth Ann said. "What you done now?"

Ashley felt the tears building in her throat and looked sideways at Ruth Ann. That was it, the look and the voice that made her feel lower than dirt. "Mama, will you please?"

Ruth Ann hesitated, then drove to the parking space farthest from the Hardee's, facing the highway. She left the motor running.

Ashley leaned forward and turned down the radio, then tore the paper off two straws and stuck them in the cups. She handed one to Ruth Ann, then sipped her own. The cool fizz going down made her feel more normal somehow, like she was not trapped in some old black and white movie playing Joan Crawford's or Lana Turner's rotten daughter. Her and Cassandra and Granny used to love to stay up late and eat popcorn and peanut butter fudge and watch old movies on TV. Back then she always identified with the good girl.

"Mama," she said. "I'm pregnant." There. It was out now. No turning back, as if that was ever an option. Ashley stared out the windshield at the Taco Bell across the street. Nothing but a bunch of gaudy neon signs and fast-food places clumped around the interstate. What a wonderful setting for a mother–daughter chat.

"What?" Ruth Ann said with a fry halfway to her mouth. She dropped the fry and grabbed Ashley's arm and jerked her around. "Look at me, young lady." She stared for a long time, then dropped Ashley's arm like it was hot and turned away, shaking her head.

Here we go, Ashley thought. Fat tears popped out and slid down her face. Damn, why do I always have to cry? Why can't I just for once face her and talk to her without crying? She got a Kleenex out of the glove compartment. Still keeps them in the same place, she thought. Nothing ever changes much with old Ruth Ann.

She blew her nose and wadded the Kleenex up in her hand. "Look, Mama, it was an accident. It just sort of happened."

Ruth Ann snapped, "I'm sure of that. Do you even know whose it is?"

"Oh. That's sweet."

"Well?"

Ashley considered not telling her, but figured she'd better. Her mama had liked Keith, or acted like she did, so maybe if she knew he was the father, she wouldn't be as upset. "You remember Keith?"

"That Indian?"

That Indian, like he wasn't even a real person. "Cherokee, Mama."

"Well, I don't see how you and him could've done anything in that place."

Ashley figured her mama didn't really want to know the details of how they managed to get together, so she kept quiet.

"How far along are you?"

"About three months."

Ruth Ann set her fries on the dashboard and leaned back. "What are you planning to do?" she said without looking at Ashley.

"Mama, I love Keith. And I want to have this baby."

"What're you going to do with a baby? Are y'all getting married? Or are you going to keep slutting around?"

Ashley felt her face go hot, and the words jumped out before she could stop them. "Mama! Why don't you keep your damn mouth shut!" She stopped and took a deep breath. Cool it, girl, she thought. You need her. Mama's the only one you got a chance with, and you can't afford to blow it, no matter how much of a bitch she is. You can do this. Just calm down. "Mama, don't you even remember what it was like to be my age, to make mistakes?" Still no response. "Oh, that's right, I forgot, you're perfect, you never make mistakes."

"This is not about me, young lady."

Ashley waited to see if Ruth Ann would go on, but she didn't. "Mama?" she said. "Is there something you'd like to say?" She waited again. Still nothing. "You think you're being so strong and in control, but I know you're just dying to ream me out. Well, go ahead. Anything's better than watching you have a stroke over there."

Ruth Ann's lips twitched like she might cry. Ashley could just barely hear Tom Jones singing *why, why, why, Delilah* on the radio. Her mama loved Tom Jones and used to watch his show all the time back in the 70s. Ashley had seen him on MTV a couple of times recently, and he could bump and grind pretty good for an old man. She looked at Ruth Ann again.

"Mama?"

Ruth Ann clutched the steering wheel, ten and two, and stared through the windshield. "I just don't know what to do with you, Ashley. I've tried everything I know."

"Mama. You don't have to do nothing with me. Just listen to me. Look at me."

Ruth Ann raised her head but would not look at Ashley.

"See, Mama. You can't even look at me. Even when you do, it feels like you're looking through me and not at me. Like you wished I wasn't even here. Is that it? Do you wish I'd never been born? Because I can tell you, I've wished it myself a few times."

"Don't say that."

"Why not? As Keith always says, the truth will set you free."

"Why do you want to hurt me so bad?"

It took Ashley a minute to think of something to say to that, she was so stunned. "Hurt you? Mama. I ain't trying to do nothing to you. All I'm trying to do is tell you what I'm feeling, and trying to get you to do the same. Is it that hard? I'll go first. I feel like shit. I'm scared what's going happen to me, I'm scared to have this baby, I'm scared to not have this baby, I'm scared to be going home with you again, I'm scared you don't love me, I'm scared I don't deserve to be loved. That ought to do for starters." She sat back, exhausted, and fumbled around in her bag for a cigarette. She was afraid to look at her mama.

Ruth Ann let out the breath she'd been holding and relaxed her grip on the steering wheel. "Oh, Lord, Ashley," she said. "I love you. That's not the problem."

A minivan pulled into the parking space next to Ruth Ann, and she turned her head to watch the family of four get out and head into Hardee's. The children squealed and ran while their daddy called them back. They ignored their parents and kept running. When they got to the door it was too heavy for them to open by themselves, so they stood there waiting, grinning, knowing Mama and Daddy would take care of it. The mama and daddy looked at each other and shook their heads. Ruth Ann knew exactly what was going through their minds, because she'd been there. They was thinking, do you believe these hardheaded young'uns of ours? And they was thinking how cute they was standing there grinning. Couldn't that mama and daddy see how what was cute today could be dangerous tomorrow? Right then they didn't seem much older than their young'uns.

Damn, Ruth Ann thought. It didn't seem all that long ago Ashley was a happy little two-year-old that thought her mama was the queen of everything, the little girl who liked dress-up and make-up and doing anything Mommy did. And now look at her.

She studied Ashley out the corner of her eye. She'd put on a little weight recently, and Ruth Ann didn't know if it was the pregnancy or just having regular meals again. They gave people plenty to eat at the rehab to make up for not having the other stuff, drugs, alcohol, whatever. Of course, not all the people up there was addicts. Some of them was just plain crazy. They kept that bunch on the top floor to make it harder for them to get away.

At least Ashley wasn't crazy. That was one blessing anyhow. At least she could change if she put her mind to it. Ruth Ann wondered if Ashley understood that, appreciated how lucky she was to keep getting second chances. Ruth Ann had never had that luxury.

"Ashley," she said finally. "I guess the problem is I just don't like you very much right now." She rolled her head to the right and watched Ashley cry. "What I mean is, I don't like the way you been acting. Give me one of them cigarettes."

"No, Mama," Ashley said, and wiped away tears. She rolled down the window and threw her cigarette out, blew smoke out after it. "You been quit a long time. Don't start back now." She blew her nose and looked over at Ruth Ann. "I need to quit too. It's bad for you. It's bad for the baby."

It was true. Everybody knew that now. Ruth Ann never thought she'd be able to quit herself, but two years ago she'd just out of the blue decided to give up two bad habits at once, cigarettes and A.J. She wasn't sure which one she missed the most. Probably the cigarettes. Even with the bad cough, they was still less aggravation than A.J.

Ruth Ann started the car and concentrated on backing out of the parking space. As she pulled forward toward the exit, she looked over at Ashley. "I should've quit when I was pregnant with y'all," she said.

"Mama, don't start, okay," Ashley said. "Let's just go home."

2

Marvelle peeked around the bedroom door at her forty-two-year-old, two-hundred-fifty-pound daughter propped up against pillows in the bed, asleep, TV blasting, an empty pint of mint chocolate chip ice cream on the night table beside her. That gal needs a man, she thought as she closed Cassandra's door. She moved down the hall and through the kitchen without turning on a light, then eased out the back door as quiet as she could considering she had arthritis, a walker, and a ten-pound pocketbook to contend with. When she got to the bottom of the back steps, she stopped, tied her pocketbook to the top rail of her walker, and set off down the driveway toward the road. The gravel made walking tough, especially since her pocketbook banged against the walker every time she moved. She wished again they'd had the money to get the driveway paved last year. But gravel was expensive enough these days. Lord, them big rocks did hurt her feet right through her shoes though.

When she reached the end of the driveway, Marvelle stopped and looked back toward the house. She could see the flickers of the TV light against the window shade in Cassandra's room. She shook her head. M–m–m. Yes, Lord, might be if that gal had a man she wouldn't need no sweets, nor television neither.

Marvelle faced the road and looked both ways before turning right toward Ruth Ann's house, about a mile away down Stamey Dairy Road.

Couldn't afford no sweets when I was a girl, she thought. Maybe I wouldn't had to get married if I'd had me some sweets. She laughed. That Jesse was a sweet one though. When it suited him.

Walking was easier on the pavement and she settled into a steady rhythm: lift the walker, set it down, take two steps. It was slow going. At one time Marvelle had thought she'd get around faster with one of them walkers on wheels, but when she tried it at the store, the dang thing raced right out from under her and she nearly broke her back. No, this way was slow but steady and certain. She'd get where she was going. She always had before.

After a while she stopped to rest. Standing in the middle of the two-lane blacktop, she cocked her head and listened to the summer night sounds— crickets, owls, the far barking of dogs. She squinted and made out the dark humps of cows in the pastures on both sides of the road and the darker stands of cedar and pine growing along the fence lines.

Funny how them same trees seemed to grow in most every pasture she'd ever seen in North Carolina. Riding down the mountain on the train with Jesse and the young'uns, into the foothills and right down to nearly flat land, the trees was the only things that didn't seem to change much. She left the only home she ever knew in this world to follow that man, and so had to take comfort from any little thing that reminded her of home, even trees.

Moving away from Madison County had been like tearing off a piece of herself, and after fifty-some years she still felt like an outlander in Davis, especially with Jesse gone now. But Davis was her children's home, and so it would have to be her home too. She'd thought about moving back to Madison when Jesse died but decided she was too old to make such a change. She had to settle for what she had, though the pissy little hills around Davis would never measure up to Madison, weren't big enough to amount to nothing, not even high enough to see any distance, certainly not enough to rest her eyes against, make her feel surrounded.

Eh Lord, it was a mystery, the way a woman could love a man and despise him at the same time, need him as much as breathing, and still sometimes wish the fool was dead. Heaven knows that Jesse led her a chase nearly sixty years. Didn't seem like it could've been that long though, long time to be married. But the time she'd been without him, eleven years now, seemed even longer. Lord, Lord. Time had a way of slipping past without telling a body.

Suddenly a breeze carrying sharp onion scent blew across the highway, washing away the sour meaty smell of cow shit. Oh, that smell! So many nights as a girl, she laid on the hill behind her house, wrapped in a scratchy horse blanket to hold off the chill, the wild onion like perfume, the night sky sparkling like God's own tin punch lamp. She dreamed dreams then about climbing up and looking over the mountains into the faraway places, never going, just looking. But them dreams never took into account a flat-lander from Davis come to Madison County to work the talc mines.

Marvelle first laid eyes on Jesse when he got off the train at Barnard one Saturday morning. She was waiting on her mama to get back from vis-iting her sister in Asheville. Jesse stepped down from that train like a young Abraham Lincoln, only handsomer, tall and clean-shaven, eyes sharp as an eagle's. Marvelle had sat up straight and blinked her eyes to test him. When he stopped, turned, and lifted a hand to help her mama down from the train, Marvelle knew he was real.

Her mama spoke to him, looking up into them eyes and smiling kindly, and like a dream he followed her over to where Marvelle waited. When he got closer she could see them eyes was silver-gray as the rocks she sat on and twinkled a little bit when he smiled, like mica. He was a smiling man, always looking like he was in on a great big joke didn't nobody else know about. Quiet he was, but with a way about him that made Marvelle pay at-tention.

Jesse and her mama had struck up conversation on the train from Mar-shall. Turned out he needed a place to stay, and her mama told him about Velda running off and them having the empty room. That was how he was brung to her, like a gift somehow. Her mama brung him and told him, this here's Marvelle, the one I told you about, the one stayed.

Marvelle had locked eyes with Jesse and hadn't been able to break a-loose. Even when they walked up the road home, him alongside her mama and Marvelle following behind, she couldn't forget them eyes. She studied the back of his head, a nice-shaped head with smooth clean hair. The clothes needed some work though. Marvelle figured it wouldn't be long before she'd find a way to take needle and thread to them. Jesse couldn't be going around in them raggedy overalls, not living under their roof. They was poor, but they was always clean and decent. All except Velda.

But she'd run off with some stranger, a traveling man, and even though Velda was her twin, Marvelle didn't much care if she ever laid eyes on the girl again. She'd had a bellyful—sixteen years' worth—of Velda's nonsense and living in Velda's shadow and she was tired of it. Marvelle felt like Jesse was a sign, something new and good coming in the house right after something bad went out.

As she stood in the door of Velda's room, it bothered her for just about a minute to think of Jesse in her sister's bed, and she thought of switching rooms, but instead she drug Velda's feather tick outside, slung it over the porch rail, and whaled the tar out of it. She beat the dust out, beat a few feathers out, beat all trace of Velda out, beat it till she set in to sneezing and had to quit.

Once the bed aired out, Marvelle took down Velda's curtains and scrubbed the walls and the floor and the windows. She brung the tick back in and made up the bed with sheets white from bleach and hanging in the sun, inhaling the clean smell as she flung them over the bed and tucked them in. She took and put more feathers in the pillows and plumped them up and got her own good candlewick spread out of her hope chest.

Marvelle stood smoothing the bedspread over the pillows, brushing her hands back and forth across the nubby material, tickling her palms. The room seemed brand new, like nobody ever slept there before. She didn't hear Jesse until he dropped his suitcase on the floor. Her head jerked up and her face went hot when she seen him standing there in the door, just standing there watching her. He smiled that slow smile. Didn't set foot inside, but somehow he filled up the whole room.

Marvelle got so hot she thought she might swoon over. They was a funny feeling in her chest, and a funny feeling kindly like a itch in her woman's parts. She watched Jesse studying the room, taking it all in before he looked at her again. Then she remembered how dirty and sweaty she was, her hair all stringy and hanging around her face. She jerked her hands off the pillow and run to the door where Jesse stood. He didn't move to let her pass, just stood there, looking. Her breath come fast like she'd been climbing. After a minute, he reached out a hand like he might be fixing to touch her cheek, and her heart went flippety right down to her belly and then up to her throat. She ducked under his arm and run out the house, out the yard, up the mountain just as fast as she could go.

She run till her legs quit and her breath give out, then flopped down in a laurel slick where she couldn't see or be seen. Her breathing got slower and slower and she began to be amazed at herself. What on earth had possessed her? The same thing that made Velda do what she done? Marvelle laid on her back with her arms behind her head and stared up at the waxy dark green leaves blocking out most of the sky. It was hot under that laurel, hot and still. She found herself praying for Jesse to be gone when she went home, wishing that he'd never come, but then all of a sudden she was thinking what it would be like if he was there with her, hot and sweaty together under the laurel. What would happen if he was to come up there and find her? She closed her eyes and felt the whole world spin. Something had shifted, and life would never be the same again. He would be there when she went home, and already she could tell there would not be much waiting. Already everything had speeded up faster than she ever dreamed it could.

And now here she was, an old rip, couldn't run even if she wanted to, much less do any of the other things she used to do. Marvelle stopped again to catch her breath and leaned on the walker. What did she know about anything back then? Lord God, that girl was just a fool, a fool over a man— a boy, really. She hawked and spit and cleared her throat good. Seemed like she'd passed in a blur from that hot-faced girl to a dried-up old woman, with all the years and the children and the living in between just shadows now. She used to wonder how it must feel to grow old, watching first her granny, then her mama, but now she knew firsthand, and mostly she didn't like it. She used to think a body got used to the idea as years went by, maybe even welcomed age, or at least the wisdom that come with it. But she didn't feel one bit smarter now than she did at sixteen. And they was times she hated her own wrinkledy, saggy face in the mirror. She'd long ago stopped trying to understand how the days and years can sometimes drag so slow while you're living them, but once they're gone, seems they went real quick, too quick.

Marvelle sniffed, then sniffed again. That was one thing about this flat-land she'd never got used to in all the years since Jesse brung her there in nineteen and forty-two—the smell of cow shit in the summer. Maybe it was due to the heat down here. It stayed cooler in the mountains and didn't stink as bad. Cows must have a poor sense of smell, else they'd never be able to gag down a bite with that stink clogging up their heads. She'd never liked cows the way Jesse did, even after working with them forty-some years. They just wasn't interesting creatures, not like dogs or pigs or chickens. Or people.

She picked up the walker and set off down the road again toward Ruth Ann's. She knew they'd be needing her, Ruth Ann and Ashley. Now, there was a pair if ever they was one. Both hardheaded as the day is long and bound to fight every chance they got. They was too much alike, that was their trouble. They needed somebody to step in from time to time, and who better than her? Hadn't she lived long enough to know a few things about raising children?

She stopped, looked up, and squinted. Seemed like she must've passed Ruth Ann's house by now. It'd never took her this long to walk a mile before. None of this part of the road looked familiar at all. Suddenly, Marvelle seen lights in the distance.

"Lord," she said. "Looks like Ruth Ann's got every light in the house on." She started walking again, then stopped as the lights grew brighter, blinding her. She meant to yell for Ruth Ann to open the door and let her in, but the brightness confused her so she couldn't think what to say.

"Well, I'll just wait right here," she thought. "Sooner or later somebody's bound to see me standing here and come open the door."

Snap decisions, Ruth Ann hated making snap decisions, and this time was no exception. Of course, this didn't have to be a snap decision. She had a whole half a second to decide. Should she slam on the brakes and hope they caught before she hit her mama, or swerve off the road and risk killing herself and Ashley? Maybe it was a hot flash that made her wonder if, either way, she herself might survive, while tragically both Ashley and Marvelle would be killed—Ashley in the collision with a tree, Marvelle of heart failure.

"Mama!" Ashley said, and put her hands on the dash to brace herself.

Ruth Ann clenched her teeth and put both feet on the brake. While she waited for the big silver Buick to rock to a stop, she flashed back on the white smile and manicured hands of the good-looking car salesman who spent a whole afternoon convincing her to pay extra for antilock brakes. Thank you, Rolly Gates, she thought, you slick, smooth-talking son of a gun.

"Lordy mercy," Ruth Ann said, staring at her mama. Marvelle's mouth worked like she was trying to blow a bubble with bubble gum. Here lately she'd got in the bad habit of running off without telling nobody. It worried Ruth Ann and Cassandra to death, not so much her running off, but her not being able to find her way back again.

Ashley pushed Ruth Ann's arm away from her chest and looked at her kind of disgusted. Ruth Ann couldn't help it. She guessed mothers had been throwing their arms across their children since the invention of the automobile. You're welcome, she thought as she watched Ashley lean forward and squint through the windshield.

"Well, goddamn, it's Granny!" Ashley said. "She looks like a deer caught in headlights."

Ruth Ann opened the door. "Ashley, will you please get out and help me?" she said.

Ashley got out of the car, ran to Marvelle, and gave her a quick kiss on the cheek. "Hey, Granny, how you doing?" she said.

Marvelle eyed her up and down suspiciously, then barked, "I thought you was dead."

"Well . . . no . . . Granny, I ain't dead."

"Too damn bad. You caused a hell of a lot of trouble for this family."

Ruth Ann watched the grin slide off Ashley's face. It was almost worth heart failure to see that.

"Mama!" Ruth Ann said, and slammed the car door. She went over and grabbed the walker and tried to pull Marvelle's hands loose. "Come on now, let's get you in the car." She felt the sweat running down the sides of her face, probably smearing her makeup. It had to be ninety degrees still and it nine o'clock at night. "Mama, let go!" she said, and yanked the walker away.

"Don't speak to me like I'm a child." Without the walker for support, Marvelle swayed as she pointed at Ashley. "She shouldn't never have come back."

Ruth Ann pushed the buttons that made the sides of the walker fold in so it would lay flat in the trunk. "Ashley," she said. "Grab her before she falls and help her in the backseat."

Marvelle jerked away when Ashley reached for her. "I'm telling you, Velda, you better watch yourself," she said. "You stay away from me and Jesse."

Ruth Ann's head snapped around. She hadn't heard that name in years.

Ashley dropped her arms at her sides and looked at Ruth Ann. "What the hell is she talking about?"

Ruth Ann stared at Marvelle a minute longer. She'd always wondered if the stories about wild, crazy Velda was true. If so, maybe it had skipped a generation and hit Ashley. Maybe Ashley was crazy after all and couldn't help herself. Maybe Marvelle was crazy too. One thing for sure, they was both driving her crazy. Which would be worse, Ruth Ann wondered. To be crazy and helpless to change it, or to be in your right mind but too sorry to try and live like a decent human being?

"She's just having one of her spells where she don't remember right, that's all," Ruth Ann said. "Now, help her in the car."

"I don't need no help," Marvelle said.

"Fine," Ashley said. She opened the back door of the car and left it standing open, then got in the front seat and shut the door.

Ruth Ann watched as Marvelle reached out and held on to the body of the car and worked her way down its length. She practically fell into the backseat and then reached out to pull her legs in one at a time. Ruth Ann stowed the walker in the trunk, made sure her mama was buckled in, then locked and closed the car door. When she finally slid into the car herself, the air-conditioning began to lift the hundred-pound weight of humidity off her and she relaxed against the seat. "Lord, I need a cigarette," she said.

"Give me one of them cancer sticks, Velda." Marvelle unbuckled her seat belt and leaned over the console between the bucket seats. "I ain't had me a cigarette since they put me in that hospital."

Ruth Ann blotted the sweat off her face with a Kleenex and then started the car. She looked over at Marvelle. "Cassandra's house is not a hospital, Mama," she said. "And you know I quit smoking. I ain't got no cigarettes." Ruth Ann put the car in gear and headed down the road past her own house to her sister's place, a mercifully short trip, she thought.

"I wasn't talking to you," Marvelle said. She poked Ashley's shoulder with a knobby finger. "They got me locked up in a hospital now, Velda. You know about that?"

"Well, that's a coincidence. I been in a hospital too." Ashley turned in her seat a little bit to face Marvelle.

"The bad thing is it's a children's hospital," Marvelle said. "Little young'uns running around screaming and hollering all day long. They's never a minute of quiet, and that big nurse makes me stay in there with them, so she can watch me, she says, like I ain't old enough to watch myself."

Ruth Ann slowed the car and pulled into Cassandra's driveway. The tires crunched gravel as the headlights swung across the grinning yellow crescent moon on the sign in the front yard: *Moon Child Day Care Center, Cassandra Moon, Director.*

"You're home, Mama," Ruth Ann said.

"This world is not my home," Marvelle said. "I ain't no child, and that big nurse is mean, and ugly as gouge."

"Cassandra's not a nurse, Mama. She's your daughter, remember?" Ruth Ann looked at Ashley. "I'm going to get Cassandra," she said. "Maybe she can get Mama to go in." She got out of the car and walked around the back of the house.

When Ruth Ann was out of sight, Marvelle leaned toward Ashley and whispered, "Well, she looks like a big, ugly nurse to me, and she smells like piss."

Ashley laughed. "All nurses smell like piss, Granny. It's the ammonia."

"I wish you'd quit calling me Granny, Velda. You're older'n I am by two minutes."

"Sorry, Marvelle, I forgot," Ashley said.

"That's all right. You forget things when you get old, I know. But it's important to remember if you can." Marvelle placed her hands on the seat tops. "I remember so many things. Do you remember all the names, Velda? Like Mama used to tell them to us? Remember her telling how Ann used to be a man's name way back in the old days, the name of a king? But now it belongs to the women. Isabel Ann, Elizabeth Ann, Amanda Ann, Dorothy Ann, Sally Ann, Myrtle Ann, Glory Ann, Velda Ann, Marvelle Ann. Then Ruth Ann. Then Ashley Ann." Marvelle sat quiet for a minute. "Ashley Ann," she said again, like she'd just found something familiar in an unfamiliar place. "Ashley Ann. Me and Velda was twins, you know, so Mama give us both the middle name of Ann. Wouldn't been right to give it to one and not the other."

"I didn't know you had a twin sister," Ashley said. "Whatever happened to her?"

A door slammed and Ashley turned to watch Ruth Ann coming toward the car. "Granny," she said, turning back to Marvelle. "Where is she? Is she dead?"

Ruth Ann got in the car. "Is who dead?" she said.

"Velda. Velda's dead." Marvelle closed her eyes. "Velda's dead."

Velda again. Ruth Ann wondered why Velda was on her mama's mind all of a sudden. She stared out the windshield, watching the TV light flash bright then dim at Cassandra's bedroom window. The flashes seemed almost violent, the way they kept coming and kept coming, the beating of light against dark. Funny how she'd never noticed that when she was actually sitting in front of the TV. Cassandra was in the bed, dead to the world, and Ruth Ann had decided not to wake her up. She'd call and leave her a message when she got home. Cassandra was always letting that machine pick up anyhow.

Marvelle pushed her upper body between the two front seats so she could face Ashley. Her left side bumped against Ruth Ann's shoulder. "Ashley Ann," Marvelle said. "Ashley Ann, I bet if your baby's a girl, you'll name its middle name Ann, won't you? Your sister's just got them two boys, and don't look like that brother of yours'll ever marry, so it's up to you."

Ashley's mouth fell open. "Granny," she said. "How did you know I was pregnant?"

"Don't say pregnant," Marvelle said, and smacked Ashley on the hand. "That's a ugly word."

Ashley looked at Ruth Ann. "Mama, how'd she know?"

"Lord, I don't know. She probably thinks you're somebody else."

"No, she don't. She just called me Ashley Ann."

"Well, I guess she's psychic, then." Even in the dimness of the car, Ruth Ann could see that Marvelle's head needed a good washing, but she felt too tired to deal with it. Hair washing could wait, she decided.

"Ashley Ann," Marvelle said. She pulled on Ashley's arm to get her attention. "You'll name your baby girl's middle name Ann, won't you? Not like your mama here, who don't go in for tradition."

Ruth Ann took a deep breath and let it out slow. It was an old argument, one of the oldest in the world between her and her mama. Ruth Ann was supposed to name her oldest Angela Ann because Marvelle was afraid there wouldn't be another girl child. She badgered Ruth Ann to death, telling her, "Just look at me, having only the one girl in a houseful of sons for so long. Sure, Cassandra come along, but I had no way of expecting another child, much less a girl child. You'll not likely get another chance to pass down the name." But Ruth Ann had prevailed. All she had to do was point out that Marvelle was the fifth and last girl child in her family. Why did her mama wait? That shut her up for a while.

Of course, Ruth Ann could've also said something about her sisters, Rachel and Rose, the twins that died before she was born. Why didn't Marvelle name one of them Ann? But she didn't care enough about winning to use that kind of ammunition on her mama. Her aunt Martha had told her about the twins, about how they looked like two little angels with golden hair and dimples in their little cheeks and had the sweetest natures of any children she'd ever known. She said when they was four years old, they come down with the diphtheria, which they didn't have a vaccine for back then. Rose died first, and she hadn't been dead but a day or two when Rachel said she was going to go play with her little sister and the next day she died too. They was the light of Marvelle's life, and it like to killed her to lose them. She sometimes talked about her other young'uns that had died, Mason and Peter, but she never talked about the girls. Ruth Ann figured it must be too painful, so she never brought it up, never asked why her mama didn't call them Rachel Ann and Rose Ann. Probably she was like most women, never thinking about running out of time to do things, have more children, pass on the name.

What Ruth Ann wanted to know was, what was so great about the name Ann anyhow? Ann was so plain and cut-off sounding. Ann, like half a name, a fraction of a real name. Same with Ruth. Instead, Ruth Ann called her daughter Angela Juliette because she liked the sound of it. Angela Juliette, a name that rolled out of her mouth like poetry. Then Alex, Alexander James—she didn't have to worry about naming him. He got named after his grandpas, Alexander Jackson Payne and Jesse James Moon. Then Ashley come along as a complete surprise, leaving Ruth Ann too tired to argue anymore. Plus, she was so mad at A.J., she didn't want to give another child his initials.

"Mama, I named her Ashley Ann, didn't I?" Ruth Ann said. "Now, come on, let's get you in the house so you can go to bed. It's getting late."

"I'm not going in there, I told you. I want to go to your house."

Ruth Ann groaned, paused a minute, then said through her teeth, "Fine." She could not face any more arguing tonight. She backed slowly out of the driveway, careful to avoid the ditch. "I'll just call Cassandra when I get home and tell her to come get you in the morning."

Marvelle held on to the front seats as the car picked up speed for the short drive down to Ruth Ann's. "You know, Ashley," she said, "I wanted your mama to name you Queen Ann, like Queen Anne's lace, 'cause it's so pretty even though it's got chiggers on it. But some people always got to have their own way about everything."

Ruth Ann looked over just in time to see Ashley mouth the words *thank you, Mama.*

Ashley hauled her suitcase out of the trunk and set it down to wait for her mama to find the right key. Ruth Ann opened the door wide and went ahead into the kitchen, and Ashley picked up the suitcase and followed her. She dropped the suitcase on the kitchen floor and watched her mama turn on lights as she moved through to the living room, then down the hall, and then she disappeared into her bedroom. Ashley shook her head, then reached for the suitcase again.

"Will somebody come get me out this car?" Marvelle said. She had rolled down her window and had her head hanging out. Ashley sighed and put the suitcase down again. Her mama had apparently forgotten about her own mama. Ashley stepped to the back door and stared out at her granny.

"I can't get this door to open," Marvelle said.

"Well, Granny. Can't you even get out of a car no more?" Ashley went and pulled open the door and waited for Marvelle to swing her legs out. She looked at the car door and said, "No wonder. Mama's got the child-proof lock on."

"Get me my walker, girl."

Ashley pulled the walker out of the trunk and set it in front of Marvelle.

"Now," Marvelle said as she took hold of the walker and pulled herself up. "I don't need you no more. I can do it myself."

"Whatever you say." Ashley went back in the house and carried her suitcase to her room. She flipped on the light, then stood there, stunned. Her room was gone. Her canopy bed and matching dresser and chest of drawers—gone. Her pink ruffled curtains, bedspread, and table skirt—gone. Everything that said this is Ashley's room—gone. Ruth Ann had turned it into some kind of guest room. There was twin beds covered with white candlewick spreads, a little night table and lamp in between, and a mismatched chest of drawers and dresser. White miniblinds covered the windows, and there was a dark blue valance over each one.

"What the hell?" Ashley said. She kicked the suitcase over and crossed the hall to knock on Ruth Ann's door.

"Mama?"

Ruth Ann snapped through the door, "I'm putting on my nightgown."

"Mama, where's all my stuff?"

The door opened and Ruth Ann held on to the doorknob with one hand and had her gown in the other. It was the same old ratty cotton nightgown she'd been wearing for ten years, practically see-through by now. Ashley had given her new ones for Christmas and her birthday, but she liked the old one best. "That ain't your room no more. You left, remember?"

"Mama."

"Don't Mama me. You and your granny can sleep in there just fine."

"Well, what about Alex's old bedroom? Can't one of us sleep in there?"

"There ain't another bedroom no more. I had the wall knocked out to make this room bigger, and added a bathroom in here." Ruth Ann shut the door in her face.

Ashley turned and went back to her room. A guest in her own home. Un-fucking-believable. She plopped down on one of the beds and bounced a little bit. Mattress was too soft. She'd have to put a board under there. Her reflection looked back at her from the mirror over the dresser, showed her pouting and spoiled-looking. Well, hell, didn't she have a right to be upset? This was her home. Of course, she'd left of her own free will and hadn't told anybody where she was going or whether she was coming back. Nearly a year since she'd been in this room. Even the walls was different. No more pale yellow wallpaper with pink ribbons and roses. Now the walls was painted off-white with a blue willow border near the ceiling. All traces of Ashley Payne gone or covered over, like she'd never been there.

"It like to tore your mama to pieces ever time she come in this room after you left," Marvelle said. She stood in the door, hunched over her walker.

Ashley stared at Marvelle, tears in her eyes.

"Ain't no sense crying now, honey. What's done is done."

"She just wiped me out though, Granny. Where's all my stuff?" Ashley sniffled. "She probably burned it."

"They Lord, honey, that wouldn't have helped nothing. No, your things is all stored out in the building, just waiting for you to come home again and get them." Marvelle sat beside Ashley and patted her hand. "You hurt your mother more than you know, honey. It'll take time to make things right. She still loves you, but there's more to it than that."

"Like what?" Ashley flopped on her back and rested her hands on her stomach.

"Well, you got to prove you're serious, prove you're trying to grow up."

"I am grown-up. Don't you think a person's grown-up that's about to have a baby in six months?"

Marvelle laughed. "They Lord, honey, it don't take nothing to have a baby. It's raising one that's hard." She shook her head. "Why, I had my first young'un when I wasn't but seventeen and thought I knowed it all too, just like you. But I had no idea." She took off her glasses and wiped them with her shirttail. "And maybe that's all right. Maybe that's how it's got to be, else nobody'd never have children. Lord knows, if a woman knowed ahead of time the grief children bring." Marvelle put her glasses back on and patted Ashley's knee.

Ruth Ann opened her door and stopped at the sight of Ashley and Marvelle side by side on the bed. She stared for a minute, then waved a hand toward the lamp. "I'll get a bulb for that. It's been burned out a month now." She went off down the hall.

"She acts like we're company or something," Ashley said.

"Well, I reckon we are, girl, so we better start acting like it. Get up from there and I'll help you unpack."

Ruth Ann came back as they opened Ashley's suitcase. She changed the bulb in the lamp, then stood watching them for a minute. "Well," she said finally. "I've got to call Cassandra, and then I'm going to bed. Angela and David and the kids is coming to dinner tomorrow. They're stopping on their way home from Dollywood. Angela wants to see Ashley."

"Yeah, right," Ashley said.

"You go on now, honey," Marvelle said. "We'll be fine." She waved Ruth Ann away, then sat and took off her shoes. As Ruth Ann's bedroom door closed again, Marvelle lost her balance and fell backward on the bed. "I hate these goddamn soft mattresses," she said as she tried to sit up again.

Ashley pulled Marvelle to her feet. "Granny, you're a hoot," she said.

"Cassandra. This is Ruth Ann. I just wanted to let you know that Mama's over here."

Cassandra picked up the phone and said, "Hey, I'm here."

"Why do you always let me talk into that dang machine before you pick up?" Ruth Ann said.

"I'm screening my calls."

"You don't get that many calls. Who calls you besides me?"

"Well, you could've been somebody calling to sell me lightbulbs or something. Did you say Mama's over there? When did you come get her? I didn't hear you."

"I could've murdered you in your bed. The back door was standing wide open and you in there sawing logs while Mama run off down the middle of the highway. It's a wonder I didn't run over her myself. She'd got all the way past my house and was nearly to the intersection. Me and Ashley had to put her in the car and bring her home with us."

Ashley, that's right. Cassandra had forgot about Ruth Ann going to get Ashley today. "How'd it go?" she asked.

"Well, she's here. We'll just have to see."

Didn't sound too good so far. Sounded like they probably already had a fight. Cassandra wondered how in the world the two of them would ever work things out. "Did she say anything?"

"Yeah, she said something. She said she's pregnant."

"What!"

"As if we ain't got enough troubles already."

"Pregnant. How in the world did that happen?"

"Well, if you don't know, I ain't going to tell you."

"You know what I mean."

"I didn't ask for details. She said that Indian boy, Keith, is the father."

"Keith. He seemed nice." Cassandra remembered Ashley telling them how quiet he was, what a loner, but whenever they come to visit, he set with them and acted just like one of the family.

"Nice enough to make my daughter an unwed mother. Now I got to go. I can't talk about this no more tonight."

"Well, all right, but how's Mama?"

"She's fine. She's going to stay over here tonight and you can come get her tomorrow. Don't forget now."

"I won't forget." Cassandra hung up the phone feeling kind of huffy.

Dang her sister for being so bossy and trying to make her feel guilty. It wasn't Cassandra's fault Mama had decided to take off in the middle of the night like that. Cassandra looked at the clock. Well, maybe not the middle of the night, but ten o'clock was late enough for both of them to be in bed asleep. She was allowed to sleep, wasn't she? Was she supposed to keep her eyes open twenty-four hours a day? It was so easy for Ruth Ann to act all high and mighty about it, but she didn't have to live with Mama, be insulted day and night, make sure she didn't run off or set the house on fire.

The house was so quiet. Cassandra knew it didn't make sense, but she missed the sound of her mama's snoring. She missed knowing another living creature was in the house with her. She went back to bed and found an old movie on TV.

She only half watched it, the other half of her mind just drifting, floating, until she fell asleep sitting up. She woke up a little after midnight, wide awake. She hadn't stayed up this late in a long time, probably not since the last time Ashley spent the night. They used to have such a good time, her and Ashley and Mama, making popcorn, watching movies, laughing and listening to Mama's stories. It wasn't that long ago, really, just a few years. And now look at Ashley, grown and pregnant. What a mess. But maybe now Ruth Ann would find out for herself how hard it was to live with somebody that needed watching all the time. Maybe she wouldn't be so quick to judge from now on.

Cassandra didn't know if it was being awake so late when she was usually sound asleep, or if it was having the house all to herself with nobody to look after, but all of a sudden a wild idea come into her head and would not go away. She had Mama, and now Ruth Ann had Ashley. Mama and

Ashley had always got along pretty well. Maybe the two of them could look after each other. Maybe they'd even be good for each other, the older and the younger generation. Of course, Ruth Ann would throw a fit if Cassandra suggested it. As far as she was concerned, Cassandra and Marvelle was roommates for life.

If she had it to do over again, Cassandra thought, would she do anything different? Probably not. What could she do? Mama and Daddy had give her the land and made the down payment on this house for her. So in a way it was as much their house as it was hers, even though she'd been the one making payments all these years. And she couldn't turn her own mama away, could she?

Cassandra understood her mama not wanting to stay at the homeplace after Daddy died. Too many memories. What she couldn't understand was why she ended up being the only one to volunteer to take Mama in. None of the rest of them said a word, just acted like the natural thing would be for Mama to move in with her since she was the only one, besides Clark, that wasn't married. She hadn't been living in that house a year, not even long enough to finish decorating. It took her till she was thirty years old before she even thought about getting a home of her own, and look what happened when she did.

Sometimes she wondered if Daddy knowed he was dying and built that house for Mama more than for her. That'd be just like him, killing two birds, he'd say. He always liked it when he could get something for nothing. That old man. Cassandra still missed him, even after eleven years. Her and Ruth Ann had always been more their mama's young'uns, but their daddy was the one made them feel safe in the world somehow. They always knowed he'd kill anybody tried to harm them, even if it was their brothers. Anytime the boys got to worrying them, all the girls had to do was say, "I'm telling Daddy. . . ." It was good having somebody to take care of you if you needed it. She missed that feeling.

She wished her daddy was here now to take care of things, to take care of Mama so she wouldn't have to. If her daddy was still alive, him and Mama would still be living over at the homeplace and she, Cassandra, would be . . . what? Living here alone? Maybe. Maybe not. Maybe she might've got married and had young'uns of her own instead of always taking care of other people's. She might've done anything. Moved to the beach, dyed her hair blond, and become a surfer girl. Cassandra had to laugh at that, the picture of her big old self up on a surfboard. But Lord, who knew what she might've done with her life? And now she'd never know, because she was stuck with her mama and six little young'uns all day, and sometimes she felt like she'd go out of her cotton-picking mind.

This is not my life, she thought. Not my real life. My real life is waiting for me out there somewhere, only I can't get to it because I've got to take care of Mama, and by the time she dies, it'll be too late. Cassandra covered her mouth with her hand even though she hadn't said the words out loud. What a thing to think, sitting there almost wishing her mama was dead. She didn't mean it, she didn't mean it. Not that way. She didn't want to lose her mama. It was just that she felt so lost herself, lost and desperate to do something about it before it was too late. She'd be an old woman herself soon. Hell, she acted like an old woman now, acted older than Mama sometimes.

Cassandra's brain was too busy working and she couldn't sleep, so she got up and carried the empty ice cream carton to the kitchen. She didn't bother turning on a light, just threw the carton away and put the spoon in the sink, then got herself a Coke and sat down at the table. There was enough light from outside that she could see her shadow on the wall. It looked like a big blob. That's what she felt like, a big blob of nothing. But she wasn't nothing. She might be big, but she wasn't nothing. She worked hard, worked her ass off and always had, first at the plant and now at the day care. She worked just as hard as Ruth Ann or her brothers, and it paid off, at least at the plant it did. The plant manager promoted her from office assistant to office manager in just six years.

Ruth Ann and the rest of them had thought Cassandra was getting above herself, taking that office job when she got out of high school. They acted like a desk job wasn't real work. Cassandra knew how their minds worked, even though they never said anything right to her face. They thought she didn't know what real work was, that she was the baby and had always had it too easy. They made jokes, saying that's why her ass was so wide, from sitting on it all day at that pie job. That was part of the reason they didn't think it would be no hardship on her to take Mama. But at the time, Cassandra didn't care. That job made her feel good about herself, and she was happy she could help the family too.

And then when Lance come there to work, that was probably the best time of her life, that five and a half months when he come to set up their computer. Being the office manager, she had to work with him every day, explaining their procedures, helping him figure out what their needs was, learning the new system.

When she first seen him, her only thought was, *nerd*, and then she forgot he was even a man. He had black plastic frame glasses and wore jeans and T-shirts to work everyday, and he was so absentminded, sometimes he wore his shirt inside out. But she found out the first day that at least he was funny and had a good sense of humor. They got talking about old TV shows and songs and had a good time. It went like that for months, and Cassandra got to where she looked forward to going to work everyday because she had so much fun with Lance.

And then one day she turned around and seen the back of his head and fell in love with him. How could the back of a man's head make you fall in love? But it did. Them beautiful silver blond curls growing wild all over his head. And then he turned around and she noticed the blue eyes inside them black plastic frames, then he smiled and she noticed them white straight teeth, and that was it for her, the end of a perfectly good friendship and the beginning of a terrible crush. Every night she agonized over what to wear the next day, how to fix her hair. She went on a diet, which put her in an even worse mood. When she was alone with him, she couldn't relax, she stayed so worried what he thought of her, did he like her, was he attracted to her, did he want to date her. Being in love with a real man was hell, just hell. It was much easier having a crush on Elvis Presley or Mel Gibson.

She didn't tell nobody about it, not even Ruth Ann, although she figured Ruth Ann knew when she kept making cracks about how much time Cassandra and Lance spent alone together in the office. Cassandra had said something to her mama one time about Lance, about how nice and attractive he was, but all Mama said was, "Lance? That ain't a name. That's something you do to a boil."

There was nobody to ask what to do, and she was too afraid to talk to Lance directly. So when the job was done and he told her he had to go back to Charlotte, she just let him go. Not that he would've stayed if she'd asked him to. He probably would've laughed in her face. But at least if she'd tried then, she'd know for sure now. She wouldn't be spending her days wondering, her nights lonely. That's what stung, having been face-to-face with somebody she actually knew and cared about and not having the guts to admit it to him and see what happened. Gutless wonder, that's what she was.

Her daddy used to say, "Almost only counts in horseshoes and hand grenades," but Cassandra did give herself a little bit of credit for almost calling Lance. That last night he was in town, she'd known she had to do something, no matter how it scared her. She'd wanted to call him so many times before, had always intended to, but never got her nerve up. But that night was his last night, her last chance, and she remembered saying to herself over and over that she was really going to do it this time, she was really going to call him, she really was, she really was, she really was.

She'd worked it all out in her head, what she'd say and what he'd say back. Of course, she could only imagine what he'd say, but hers she'd written down because she knew she'd get flustered once she heard his voice, and all her practiced words would fly right out of her head. With the paper in front of her she could do it, she could make it through.

But when she'd reached for the phone, she noticed her hand was shaking and got distracted by that. Lord, why was she getting so nervous? This was Lance, good old Lance who she'd been working with and eating lunch with everyday for five months. He wasn't scary. And hadn't he given her his number, told her to call if she needed anything? What would he say if she called up and said Lance, honey, I need something. I need you. I love you and I want to marry you and have your children. He'd probably head for the hills, thinking she was some crazy stalker.

But of course she'd never say anything like that. She wouldn't make such a fool of herself. But hadn't she already? Hell, everybody at the plant knowed she was crazy in love with Lance. Everybody except Lance. Although Ruth Ann said a man can always tell when a woman's interested in him. She said men are so cocky they think most every woman they meet falls instantly in love with them, or at least wants their body. They're not like women, she said, always doubting themselves and agonizing over every little thing. Men all think they're God's gift, and all they got to do is nod at one of us and we'll fall all over ourselves running to kiss their feet. Ruth Ann and A.J. was having troubles then, and Cassandra just couldn't believe her sister really believed all men was like that. She didn't believe it. She definitely didn't think Lance was like that. He was different from all the men she'd ever known, which she reckoned wasn't saying a whole lot since most of the men she knowed was kin to her.

Lance was something else. He was smart, and real funny. That first day he come to work in the office he made her laugh, and they'd been laughing ever since. She'd never laughed so much with a man before. Laughter seemed like such an intimate thing when it happened between a man and a woman like that, like they was connecting deeper than the laughing somehow. Or maybe that was just wishful thinking on Cassandra's part. Some days she swore Lance felt it too, that connection, but other days she felt like he only seen her as a coworker and nothing more. She didn't understand how they could spend so much time together and enjoy each other's company so much and him not feel something too.

But if he had felt something, why hadn't he never asked her out? She knew he was single, didn't think he was gay since he'd mentioned old girl-friends, said he hadn't been dating anybody since he broke up with his last girlfriend in Charlotte right before he come to Davis. So that left a couple of possibilities. One, he was just real shy and afraid to ask her out. Or he just wasn't attracted to Cassandra that way, and who could blame him? He wasn't no Tom Selleck, but he was nice looking and built good and made good money. He could have anybody he wanted, so what made her think he'd settle for a big old heifer like her?

It was the not knowing that was killing her, tearing up her nerves, mak-ing her feel all hopeful one day and depressed the next. But this night would tell the tale. It was his last night in town, so what did she have to lose? His job in Davis was done and he was heading back to Charlotte. He was supposed to come by the plant to say good-bye in the morning, but Cassandra could not, would not, try to say what she wanted to say to him at the plant, where somebody else might walk by and hear. She didn't even know if she could say it in person. The phone seemed like the safest way.

She'd call and tell him she'd really enjoyed working with him, and that she was really going to miss him, and did he think they could maybe get to-gether sometime? Charlotte wasn't all that far from Davis, only a couple hours. They could meet halfway. That felt safe enough to say out loud, and it opened the door for him to say something to let her know how he felt. And if he wasn't interested and she was humiliated, then she'd call in sick to work tomorrow and never have to see him again. Everybody at the plant would figure she laid out because she couldn't stand to see him go, but so what? Let them think whatever they wanted to. They would anyway.

Cassandra couldn't help hoping he'd declare his undying love and come tearing over to her house and grab her up and kiss and hug her till she squealed like a pig. That's what she hoped for, but she'd prepared herself for disappointment. She imagined what would really happen was that he'd be embarrassed at her putting him on the spot like that, putting him in the uncomfortable position of having to let her down gently. That's one thing she knew for sure though; he was a nice man and he would be kind.

She took a deep breath and reached for the phone again. This was it. She was really doing it. She was being an 80s lady and calling her man. She giggled, then jumped when the phone rang. Oh, Lord, what if it was him? What if he'd called her? Wouldn't that be something, them on the same wavelength like that? She picked up, and when she said hello, she could've sworn her voice sounded all breathless and curious, like Marilyn Monroe wondering who could this be calling me tonight? John F. Kennedy? Joe DiMaggio?

A woman's voice said, "Cassandra."

Cassandra's mind went blank for a minute. It wasn't him. It wasn't Lance.

"Cassandra? Are you there?"

She caught on then that it was Ruth Ann, and she sounded like she'd been crying. "What's wrong?"

"Cassie, can you come over here?"

"What's wrong?"

"It's Ashley. She's gone."

"What do you mean gone?"

"She's run off. She took some of her clothes and she's gone. A.J.'s out looking for her now."

Oh, Lord, Cassandra thought. Lordy mercy, she'd probably run off with that no-account Rusty Pruitt. Ruth Ann and A.J. had told her not to see him no more, so she started sneaking out at night, then got grounded when they caught her. "All right, honey," she said. "I'll get Mama and we'll be over there in a few minutes."

It wasn't until right after midnight, when she finally got into bed so tired she couldn't sleep at first, that she remembered Lance. Remembered the phone call she never made. She'd got so caught up helping Ruth Ann call Ashley's friends, then calling the police, then going through everything in Ashley's room looking for clues, then getting Mama home and calmed down, that she hadn't had a minute to herself to think about Lance.

She turned the light out and rolled over on her side. Maybe it was for the best. Maybe it would've been a big mistake anyway. He was leaving town, and a man didn't leave town if there was a woman he wanted there, did he? No, she was better off just letting him go and getting on with her life. She had enough to worry about right here, with Mama and Ashley and Ruth Ann and her job at the plant running that office by herself. She was a busy woman and didn't really have time for a man. Anyway, the phone worked both ways. He could've called her. He could've called and left a message. As a matter of fact, he should've been the one to call, since he was the one leaving. Why should she have to do all the work?

The shadow of the Indian cigar tree outside her window fluttered on the wall, and Cassandra watched the big leaves waving. She could hear the wind picking up. Must be a storm coming. Tomorrow would be the first day without Lance, and she'd better go on and get used to it. No more lunches, no more laughing together, no more nothing. Maybe she was just one of them people that was never meant to marry. There was people like that in the world, although the majority of people seemed to have no trouble at all getting married, a lot of them more than once. Love just didn't seem to be in the cards for her, and she had to accept that.

Them words, which she must've said to herself a million times over the years, this time made her feel like all of a sudden her heart would bust. This time was different. This time she was in love. Her heart was so full of loving him, wanting him, that she couldn't hold it all, but it had nowhere to go. He didn't want her. She thought her head would split from wanting to know why why why, why didn't he want her? What was wrong with her? She didn't want to be one of them women that never knew how it felt to be loved by a man. She didn't want unrequited love. She wanted Lance. She wanted him to love her. She wanted him to want her. She wanted, she wanted, she wanted.

Cassandra turned her face in to the pillow so her mama wouldn't hear and cried for a long time, cried so hard the pillow got wet and she had to turn it over. She cried that side wet too, cried until she couldn't feel anything anymore.

In the time since then—only a year, but for some reason it seemed longer—Cassandra had cried herself to sleep many a time, cried over Lance, over lost love, over all the regrets she had about things left undone. Seemed like the regrets lasted a whole lot longer than any embarrassment she might've felt if she'd taken the chance and called him and maybe got rejected, maybe made a fool of herself. If she ever got another chance, she promised herself she wouldn't waste it this time. She wouldn't be left wondering what if for the rest of her life.

After she hung up from talking to Cassandra, Ruth Ann brushed her teeth, took off her makeup, washed her face, patted on moisturizer, and crawled into bed. She felt guilty about not flossing, but she was just too tired. Murmurs and occasional giggles seeped into her room from across the hall. Ruth Ann rolled on her side, turned off the bedside lamp, and lay still in the comfort of dark. Gradually she relaxed and let the tears come, her face hot against the cool percale pillowcase.

What had she ever done to deserve this? Hadn't she always done what she was supposed to? Always took care of business. And look where that got her. Stuck here with no husband, and her mama and her wild daughter and an illegitimate baby on the way. It was too much. To have her daughter, her baby, back home again was a blessing in one way, because at least now Ruth Ann knew where Ashley was, knew she was safe and not laying dead somewhere, or cold or hungry, or drunk, or among strangers who didn't care for her. But what was she supposed to do with her? And a baby. And her mama.

The Kleenex box on her night table was empty, so Ruth Ann had to go to the bathroom and blow her nose. She always felt better after a good cry, and as she crawled back in the bed, she remembered that her mama would go back to Cassandra's tomorrow, so that would take care of her. As for Ashley and her baby, well, Ruth Ann decided to just wait and see how she felt as the days passed. But she'd done made up her mind that the first time Miss Ashley took a drink, or stole anything, or stayed out late, or even looked at Ruth Ann crossways, she was out the door, baby or no baby. It was time for Ashley to do some getting along for a change.

Ruth Ann didn't like feeling so hardened to one of her own children, but A.J.'s petting and spoiling had not helped Ashley one bit. It was time for her to face some hard facts of life, just like Ruth Ann had had to face them, just like everybody in this world had to face them. There ain't no free ride; you have to earn your way. And they's lots of things you got to do in this life that you don't want to do, and you don't always get what you want, just because you want it.

Ruth Ann smiled into the pillow. She remembered hating her mama for saying them very words and vowing never to speak them to a child of hers. Lord, how times did change.

Well, Mama, she thought, you got your wish. When I married A.J., you said you hoped I'd have children who'd cause me as much grief as I caused you. Probably every mother ever born says that to her child at least once in life, and means it too. Somehow, though, Ruth Ann couldn't compare her teenage rebellion to Ashley's. At least she got married as soon as she found out she was pregnant. Ashley hadn't even mentioned marriage. Maybe reverse psychology would work. Ruth Ann could tell Ashley that getting a job and getting married was the last things in the world she should be thinking about doing right now. It had sure worked on Ruth Ann.

Marvelle grunted and rolled over, trying to get comfortable. Lord knows, she'd slept on worse beds, corn-shuck mattresses and pallets on the floor, but this one was about to get the best of her. She could hear Ashley's heavy breathing coming from the other bed and knew the child was deep asleep. She shifted again, and after the springs quieted, laid still and listened hard. From across the hall, she could just make out the sound of Ruth Ann blowing her nose. Something clutched tight inside Marvelle's chest at the sound of her crying, the sound of her girl hurting.

Though she was almost fifty-one, Ruth Ann was still her girl, and witnessing her suffering was ten thousand times worse than facing her own. For how could she ease pain that Ruth Ann kept to herself? That gal was determined to do it all her own way, with no help from nobody. She'd always been hardheaded, no matter how Marvelle scolded or whipped or whined or pleaded. Ruth Ann must always go her own way, even if it was the hard way.

Even when she was little, Ruth Ann was bad to slip off. She'd just go out in the woods and play or go by herself a-visiting. She didn't care that the closest neighbor lived a quarter mile off. Wasn't scared of nothing. She'd set them little fat legs a-walking till she got to Miss Annie Tate's farm, where she'd always get a cookie before Annie picked her up and carried her home. Marvelle tried everything to keep that young'un in the yard, even tied her ankle to the fence post with a long strip of an old sheet. Nothing could keep Ruth Ann home if she didn't want to be there. And nothing embarrassed Marvelle more than hearing Miss Annie call her name from the yard and going out to see her baby girl, naked as a jaybird, in that old colored woman's arms, a half-eat cookie in her hand and a big grin on her face, her little overalls and shirt in a pile next to the front gate. Yes, Lord, that Ruth Ann and Ashley was cut from the same cloth and didn't even know it.

It was a good thing Cassandra didn't need her no more, because them two surely did. Cassandra was plum busting to get out somewhere and do something on her own, and Marvelle knowed she would if everybody'd leave her alone long enough to figure it out. Yes, Marvelle was right where she could do the most good, and Miss Ruth Ann had another think coming if she thought she was going to get rid of her old mama.

Marvelle thought about the baby Ashley carried inside her. A little girl, she'd bet on it if she was a betting woman. They needed her help now, all of them, and they needed the stories. Well, they'd be plenty of time to tell Ruth Ann and Ashley now, and then they'd tell the new baby, and she'd tell her babies. That was how it had always been, and always would be if the world went along the way the Lord designed it.

The narrow mattress bucked as Marvelle rolled again, first to her left side, then to her right. Finally at last she settled on her left side and folded the foam pillow in half under her neck. It kept popping out every time she moved. She let the pillow stay flat and laid her head on her arm. What Ruth Ann needed in here was some new beds and some nice feather pillows. Contrary to Ruth Ann's opinion, foam pillows did not make for better support. That gal didn't seem to understand how feather pillows was a whole lots easier to mash into the right shape for your head.

It was the same train, the one brung Jesse to Madison County, carried us to Marshall to get married. Didn't tell a soul we was a-going, just planned for a Saturday morning in June and off we went. I wasn't but sixteen, and Jesse, he was twenty, but oh, we was in love then. I remember holding his hand all the way there. I wore the prettiest yellow dress I'd made for myself, and Jesse brung me some daffodils to hold. Now, you know I can't abide the smell of them things, but it sure was sweet of him, and they did go with my dress.

Well, we got to Marshall in about twenty minutes and went right straight to the courthouse and got our license. The justice of the peace married us in front of two folks standing in line to pay their taxes. I remember Jesse's hands was shaking when he signed his name, but I wrote Mrs. Marvelle Moon *just as bold as you please. I was a Dockery before I married, but I got used to being a Moon that first day.*

When we walked out that building married, oh, honey, the world ain't never dazzled me so before or since. They was a little breeze stirring the river, and the sun so bright it bounced off the water and the walls, shimmering and sparkling so we was nearly blinded. Oh, it was pretty! And for just a little while it was all our own, our secret. We could pretend like they wasn't nobody else in the world but us. We strolled down the street to the station to wait for the train home, smiling at everybody, creating quite a spectacle, I'm sure, for everybody knowed us and wondered at us being there in town together like that. But I reckon they figured it out right quick when they seen that ring on my finger. It wasn't much. Jesse didn't have no money. But it was gold-plated and sparkled like it was gold all the way through.

It was only after we was on the train, watching the trees pass by all blurry, that I thought of the future at all. Jesse, I says, where in the world we going to live? Don't you worry, he says, I rented us a house, Treadway's old cabin. Treadway, I says. Why, that old place ain't fit for a goat. And he says, now, darlin', we'll fix it up. It's all I can afford right now. Don't you want you a home of your own?

Yes, oh, yes, more than anything I wanted my own home. I wanted to be my own boss, away from Mama and Papa and my brothers and sisters telling me what to do, and how and where and when. The only way to get any independence then was to get married, but that's not the only reason I married Jesse. I loved him too.

Mama wasn't none too happy about it, thought I should've waited, but when I reminded her she got married at fifteen, she says, all right, girl, you'll do what you want anyhow. Always have. Which is true. I reckon I was spoiled.

It's a hard lesson to learn you don't always get what you want, especially when you don't learn it till after you're up and growed and married. Makes it hard to settle down and get on with the business of living if one thing don't go your way and you spend all your time lamenting that, instead of moving ahead.

First thing didn't go my way, I lost my first child. And blood, oh, the blood was awful in this world. I thought I was a-dying. Then when I found my baby gone, I wanted to die. Tore me up something awful. Me and Jesse'd already done picked the names. Jude for a boy and Lena for a girl. But I reckon it wasn't meant to be. The good Lord knows when the time is right and when it ain't, but I'll tell you, I argued it with Him. I didn't think it ought to be up to Him to decide my babies for me. What does a man know about a woman and her children?

Of course, Mama was horrified at me for that, but I believe she understood. She lost five that way herself. So she didn't hold it against me, and I don't believe God did neither, 'cause He soon blessed me with Mason, and from then on my babies was all born healthy. Now I done outlived five of them, and had my share of trouble with the others, but when all's said and done, they have been the joy of my life. You'll see, Ashley Ann, when yours is born, you'll see how it changes everything.

3

Cassandra pulled into Ruth Ann's driveway, turned off the headlights, and sat for a minute looking out over the pastures behind the house. She never could get over the pretty view from the driveway, especially this time of day when that little bit of light before sunup give everything a kind of a blurry outline, like a glow. The whole world was still asleep in shadows, everybody except Cassandra, and she loved that feeling of being the only one awake in the world. It thrilled her and terrified her at the same time, like riding the roller coaster at the fair with her daddy when she was little. She rolled the window down and listened to birdcalls and cows and the wind playing in the trees.

She was reminded of an episode of *The Twilight Zone* she seen once about the world after a nuclear holocaust and only one person left alive. The scene that stuck in her mind was that one person—she couldn't remember if it was a man or a woman—sitting on the steps of the New York City Public Library surrounded by piles and piles of books and bricks and pieces of fallen-down buildings. Cassandra wondered then, and still, if a person could be happy with nothing but books for company. Books could teach a person most anything they needed to know to survive in a post-apocalyptic world: how to drive a bulldozer, wire a room, sew up a cut. But could they keep you from going crazy without nobody to talk to, without no kind of living companionship?

Sometimes she felt crazy when she got thinking about things like that, her mind going in circles, working on the details. It did help her fall asleep though, letting her mind work on puzzles, like ways to survive worst-case scenarios. Or thinking about stories where people give up their own lives for loved ones or sometimes even for total strangers. When she was younger, she used to wonder if she'd ever be able to do that if she had to, give her life for another, say take me instead, knowing it meant death. Now she was older, she knew the answer, knew without hesitation if it come right down to life or death, her answer would be easy as pie: Take me. For family, even for a stranger.

She made the mistake of telling Ruth Ann about that one time, asking her what would she do, and Ruth Ann looked at her funny and said don't be so damn morbid, Cassandra. Was it morbid to give your life for another? To make the ultimate sacrifice? It just didn't pay to tell people nothing, especially not about the workings of your mind.

The lines and corners of Ruth Ann's house began to show up sharp out of the dark—neat and perfect, just like her. Cassandra could still remember the very day they found this house. Her and Ruth Ann had been driving around one Saturday morning looking at FOR SALE signs in yards when all of a sudden Ruth Ann seen this one, slammed on brakes, and hollered, there it is, that's my house.

"God, Ruth Ann," Cassandra said. "Don't do that. You scared the life out of me."

"Look at it. Look," Ruth Ann said.

To Cassandra, it was nothing outstanding, just a little brick ranch with nandina and holly bushes planted all around it, and a two-car carport. It wasn't red brick, though, like the houses to either side of it. This brick was white, with the shutters painted forest green. It almost looked like a little fairy-tale house, really, especially with them green bushes that showed up real good against that white brick. On second thought, Cassandra decided it was right cute.

"It looks like a Christmas card, don't it?" Ruth Ann said.

Cassandra looked at the house, then at Ruth Ann, then at the house again. Well, she thought. It was cute, but she didn't know if she'd go quite that far. Maybe if there was some snow around it, or maybe a Christmas tree in the window, or Santa Claus on the roof. But the ninety-five-degree heat and humidity made it hard to imagine Christmas right then.

"Let's go look," Ruth Ann said. She backed up the road and pulled in the driveway. "Look at that view," she said. "Beautiful rolling hills, no neighbors in front or behind, just one on either side, and not too close." They sat and enjoyed the pastures, the black and white milk cows, the stands of cedar marking the fence line in places.

"I don't believe I've ever paid attention to the property from this side," Cassandra said, though she knew she'd been down this road a hundred times if she'd been once. If she had X-ray vision, she bet she could look right through that hill and see the homeplace, maybe even see Dwight and Betty in the kitchen.

When they got out of the car, the sour smell of cow shit hit them like a wave.

"They Lord, if that ain't the stinkin'est stuff!" Cassandra put her hand over her face. The cow pasture run along the back of the property. "You'll have them cows right in your backyard," she told Ruth Ann. "Just like Dwight."

"I don't care," Ruth Ann said. "And you know it ain't always this bad. They must've just sprayed the fields or something. Come on."

Ruth Ann led the way to the carport and tried the back door. Locked. They went to the front door, but it was locked too. Then they tried all the windows, but the house was shut up tight and they had to be satisfied standing on crates, peeking in the windows with their hands cupped around their faces to keep out the glare. The house wasn't new, but it looked well-cared for, and the carpet, from what they could see, did look clean.

Ruth Ann was pregnant with Ashley then, and Cassandra had to help her down off the crate, then stood and watched her waddle around the front yard. It was one of the few times in her life Cassandra didn't feel like an elephant around her sister.

Ruth Ann stopped in the middle of the yard, put her hands on her hips, and turned around in a circle. "I bet A.J. would love this place. Just look at the size of the yard! He'll have a ball mowing, and planting trees and all."

Yeah, Cassandra thought. I'm sure he'll just love that. He never mowed the grass they had now.

Ruth Ann got her new three-bedroom house, and A.J. got his new half-acre yard, and they'd worked so hard to keep it up. The place was still in good shape, better than when they bought it. Too bad Ruth Ann and A.J. had not come through as well.

Something thumped against the side of the van and Cassandra jumped, then turned her head to look in the side mirror. Elmer Jones's black

Mustang went racing away around a curve. The little snot. She hadn't even heard him coming. Sixteen and already driving a vehicle like that. What was his parents thinking?

She got out of the van and picked up the fat Sunday edition of the Davis *Daily News*. The boy had an arm on him, she had to give him that. It was a good sixty yards from where he threw the paper to where it landed, and the thing was heavy. No wonder the high-school baseball team done so good last spring.

She tucked the paper under her arm and yawned real big and stretched. A second later, A.J.'s truck come cruising up the road. Cassandra watched him slow down, then stop in front of the house, the engine idling at a low roar. She waved. A.J. lifted three fingers off the steering wheel in her direction, then sped off around the curve behind Elmer.

Cassandra shook her head and turned toward the house. It was the saddest thing in the world to her that A.J. and Ruth Ann hadn't been able to work things out. She knowed all the times he cheated on Ruth Ann and hurt her so, but Cassandra couldn't help still loving him. He was like a daddy and a uncle and a big brother all rolled up in one. Him and Ruth Ann started dating when she was about nine, and that first month or so, Marvelle made Cassandra ride with them on their car dates, which always had to take place while there was still daylight. Lucky for them they met in the summertime and had plenty of daylight to work with.

Cassandra reckoned her and Ruth Ann fell in love with A.J. together, and she'd always felt like together they brung out the best in him. She took a lot of credit for getting them together. Why, if she hadn't quit going on their dates with them, Ruth Ann might never have got pregnant and they might never have got married. And even though they ended up divorced, at least they had three children to show for their life together. That made it all worth it, to Cassandra's way of thinking.

As she walked toward the house, a soft breeze blew across her from the direction of the pasture, and she wrinkled her nose at the smell. Yes, Ruth Ann, she thought, it does smell that bad all the time, at least in the summer. She headed for the carport and the back door, her keys jangling on the bracelet key ring on her arm. At the door, she stopped and looked at her watch. Six o'clock. Her mama'd be up any minute, wanting coffee. Cassandra found the right key and let herself in.

Even after two years, A.J. couldn't seem to stop himself from slowing his truck and staring every time he drove past what he now had to call Ruth Ann's house. It was as automatic as it used to be for him to swing in the driveway and head in the back door. He was glad to see she was keeping the Buick clean, but he bet she took it to Super Suds instead of doing it herself. He'd always took care of the cars when they was married. Matter of fact, A.J. had maintained Ruth Ann's vehicles ever since they started dating, and Cassandra's too, once she got old enough to drive. Before that, their daddy always done for them in that area. Neither one of the Moon girls had ever been good at practical things. That was why he sometimes thought of Cassandra and Ruth Ann as Can't and Won't.

He made sure his girls learned how to pump gas and change a tire and change the oil and check the battery, your basic auto maintenance that most women never grasped. Oh, they whined about it the whole time, but they learned. He didn't want them depending on some strange man for help if they ever broke down on the side of the highway. And he didn't want them calling him to come pick them up neither. Of course, Angela made David do all that now. Wouldn't even pump her own gas, made her sorry-ass husband fill up the tank once a week, regular as clockwork. That girl was just like her mama, born to boss.

Ashley, on the other hand, was more like him. She definitely had inherited his love of the road. The girl had run away from home the first time when she was only two. Ended up at the store half a mile from the house, trying to buy a piece of candy with a penny. It made A.J. laugh his ass off every time he thought about Ed Carter trying to explain one-cent tax on a one-cent piece of candy to a two-year-old with a penny in her hand. When A.J. walked in and found her, he was so relieved, he bought her a whole sack of candy, which of course made Ruth Ann mad, but he didn't care. He didn't think it was right to punish a young'un for taking a little initiative, going after what she wanted.

He noticed his truck had practically come to a stop in front of the house, then seen Cassandra waving. He waved back and sped off. He didn't want the rest of them looking out the window and seeing him loitering in front of the house. Wouldn't they make a meal out of that. Poor old A.J. couldn't stay away but didn't have the guts to come in his own home. Damn.

He drove across town to Ruby's and went in for breakfast. Toni, his regular waitress, followed him to his regular booth, handed him a menu the minute he sat down, then trotted off to get coffee. She come back and poured him a cup, then stood there grinning like a monkey, waiting for his order. The girl obviously had a thing for him, even though she was young enough to be his daughter—hell, maybe even his granddaughter.

Toni cleared her throat and jiggled a pen between her thumb and forefinger like she was in a hurry. A.J. knew if he made eye contact again the girl would flutter around him all morning, and he just didn't feel like worrying about her feelings right now. Without looking up, he asked for country ham, two fried eggs, two biscuits, and orange juice.

He waited for her to go away, and when she didn't, he waved the menu in her face and said, "That's all."

She stared for a minute, then said, "Yes, sir!" all huffy, snatched the menu, and walked off.

Now, a couple years ago, A.J. would've been all over her like white on rice. But ever since Ruth Ann divorced him, seemed like he'd lost interest in girls. And now he was retired, the time just crawled by with nobody to spend it with. He leaned back against the red vinyl and stared at the tabletop like he might see his future there in the scarred Formica.

He wasn't sure when he'd come to the realization he wanted Ruth Ann back. It wasn't like a sudden lightbulb coming on kind of idea, but a gradual creeping on of misery until he finally realized what it was he was missing. It wasn't girlfriends, or sex, or any of the things he used to think he couldn't live without. What he missed was his partner, somebody to come home to, eat supper with, watch TV with, play with the grandchildren with, take weekend trips to Gatlinburg or Myrtle Beach with.

A.J. looked around the restaurant. He was the only one there besides two old ladies over in the smoking section. He knew it'd start filling up soon though. Ruby always done good business on Sunday. He liked having the place mostly to himself for a while. He liked hearing people's voices in the same building with him, without being interrupted by them. It was the same reason he kept the TV on when he was home.

Toni come back and just about flung the plate in front of him. She refilled his coffee and said hope you enjoy it in a voice that meant I hope you choke on it.

He looked up and took inventory: the pouty pink mouth, the wide blue eyes just begging for attention, the pretty blond curls pulled out from her tight ponytail to frame her face. He shook his head and smiled like he would at one of his own daughters having a temper tantrum over some little nothing. Her face turned red and she twirled away. A.J. smiled at the twitch of her skinny hips in that short pink skirt. He bet she wouldn't waste no more time looking for a daddy with this old man. He felt suddenly, sincerely hopeful of having another chance with Ruth Ann.

Ruth Ann's kitchen, like the rest of her house, was always perfectly neat and tidy, everything in its place behind a door or in a drawer somewhere, even on the weekend. Nothing showing. All the dishes was washed and put up, no potato chip bags on the counter, not even real fruit in the fruit bowl in the middle of the kitchen table. Wooden fruit didn't rot and draw bugs, according to Ruth Ann. Cassandra believed a few fat oranges and apples and bananas brightened up a kitchen, even if she didn't always get around to eating them. It was worth the extra couple dollars at the grocery store.

She hung her pocketbook on a chair, laid the newspaper on the table, and opened the refrigerator to take stock. By the time Marvelle come in at six-fifteen, Cassandra had coffee dripping and bacon frying in the skillet.

"I thought I smelled something," Marvelle said, and eased down onto a chair. "Fix me a cup of coffee, and don't put nothing in it. I like it black."

Cassandra turned from the stove with a fork in her hand. "Well, good morning to you too, Mama," she said. "You want some breakfast?" She watched Marvelle yawn and rub her face. Trying to get her to eat was getting harder every day. Seemed like nothing pleased her no more.

"I don't want none of that mess. Just coffee." Marvelle snapped the rubber band off the newspaper, unrolled it, and separated the sections into piles. She picked up a section, licked her thumb, and turned straight to the obituaries.

Cassandra swallowed a smile and poured coffee in the blue If Mama Ain't Happy, Ain't Nobody Happy cup. Some things never change, she thought, and set the cup in front of her mama. The woman wanted to see who was dead every living morning of the world.

"Lord, Eustace Farrow died. Poor old soul. Remember him? Used to sell shoes uptown at Foster's before it burned down?"

"Yes, ma'am," Cassandra said. What she remembered was a little man with bad teeth, which she noticed because he always smiled so much while he tried shoes on them every fall before school started. Her and Ruth Ann didn't like him because he always held on to their feet a little longer than necessary. "What'd he die of?"

Marvelle leaned into the paper and searched the column. "It don't say here. I wish they would tell."

Cassandra turned back to the stove to watch the bacon.

"Why don't you eat a little something, Mama?" she said over her shoulder. "I'm making some eggs in a minute."

"Hush." Marvelle slurped her coffee, then made a face and flapped her tongue in and out of her mouth.

"Is it too hot?"

"No, it tastes like gunpowder."

Cassandra rolled her eyes and went back to cracking eggs in a bowl. When she had six, she beat them with a fork, watching the hand holding the fork. She liked to see how fast she could go, and the motion felt good, like she was doing something useful. It struck her how pretty the yellow of the eggs looked against the blue of the bowl.

Ruth Ann's central air kicked on with a moan, then settled down and blew cool air through the room. Cassandra could hear Marvelle behind her, turning the pages of the newspaper. A feeling of peacefulness settled in the room with them, a nice change from the rush of every day. Cassandra hummed a tune, the way she always did while doing something mindless, recognizing after a minute that it was "Sweet Sweet Spirit." That had always been her favorite as a child, one of the few hymns that didn't focus so much on dying. Marvelle started humming along, then sang the words. Cassandra kept humming so she could listen to her mama's voice.

"There's a sweet, sweet spirit in this place, and I know that it's the spirit of the Lord."

Marvelle carried a tune well, despite the gravel in her voice now. She sung every word like she meant it too. It amazed Cassandra that her mama couldn't always remember what she had for supper last night or what you said to her five minutes ago, but she could remember every detail of her first day of school seventy-some years ago, and all the words to every song she'd ever sung.

When she was a little girl, Cassandra remembered how surprised she was to find out other kids' mamas didn't sing and tell them stories at night before they went to sleep. She felt sorry for them kids. Her mama's voice, winding through her mind like a dark water creek, narrow and near about invisible, always making a low music behind the noise of the world, well, she reckoned it would be with her always.

After "Sweet Sweet Spirit" they got quiet again. Cassandra put bacon on a paper towel to drain, then got another pan for eggs. She liked her eggs cooked in butter, not bacon grease. The pan banged down on the burner loud, and Marvelle told Cassandra to quit making such a racket. While she

was talking, her voice got hung up in her throat and she commenced coughing and spent three or four minutes clearing her throat. Cassandra was
relieved when she went back to reading the paper. For such a clean little
old woman, Marvelle sure could make some disgusting noises. While the
eggs cooked and the bread browned in Ruth Ann's little toaster oven, Cassandra set four places at the table, moving around and reaching over
Marvelle.

"I told you I don't want nothing," Marvelle said, leaning to the side as
Cassandra set her place.

"You don't have to eat it, Mama." Cassandra put eggs, bacon, and toast
on two plates and set them on the table. Before she could sit down, she
heard footsteps and Ashley shuffled in, wearing an oversize Myrtle Beach
T-shirt.

"What's going on?" She stood in the door scratching her stomach, eye-
ing the table. She sniffed. "Oh, God," she said.

"What?" Cassandra loaded a third plate and put it on the table.

"I hope that ain't for me." Ashley turned away from the table and
poured herself a cup of coffee.

"Oh," Cassandra said. "Morning sickness. They's cereal in the cabinet if
you're hungry."

Ashley eased down on a chair and groaned. "Uh-uh. It's the smell of
that bacon making me queasy. Just let me drink some coffee and see what
happens." She spooned sugar and powdered creamer in her coffee and
stirred, clinking the spoon loud against the sides of the cup. She quit when
she seen Marvelle staring at her, then ran her hands through her hair and
pulled it back off her face. "I guess Mama told you last night," she said.

"Yeah," Cassandra said. Didn't seem that long ago Ashley was a baby
herself. She noticed her mama was completely ignoring her plate. "Mama,
please eat some of them eggs before they get cold." Cassandra brought the
coffeepot to the table and refilled her cup.

"I'll not tell you again. I don't want none of that mess." Marvelle turned
to Ashley. "How long you staying?"

"I don't know." Ashley yawned. "I guess it all depends on Mama."

"Well, I need to know now," Marvelle said.

Cassandra studied her face. What would make her say that? she wondered.

"What depends on Mama?" Ruth Ann said as she came in the kitchen
and went to get a cup from the cabinet. She looked at Cassandra, then
poured coffee and sat down.

"You want some breakfast? I made eggs and bacon and toast." Cassandra started to get up.

"Sit down. I'll get it in a minute." Ruth Ann reached for the Sunday magazine section of the paper and flipped it open, then sipped her coffee, black like her mama's. "What are y'all talking about?" she said.

"Mama wants to know how long Ashley's staying," Cassandra said.

"I'd kind of like to know that myself," Ruth Ann said without looking up from the paper.

Cassandra didn't like the look on Ashley's face, and she certainly didn't feel like having a nice peaceful Sunday morning messed up with a fight. "What time's Angela and them getting here today?" she said.

"Probably dinnertime," Ruth Ann said. "I told them we'd cook something here."

"They bringing the young'uns?" Marvelle said.

"Of course. What else would they do with them, Mama?" It startled Cassandra sometimes, how fragile her mama looked. She seemed to have shrunk just in the past year or so from the big, laughing woman she used to be into this tiny bird lady.

"Good. I ain't seen the boys in a long time. They don't never come see me no more, ever since that one there brung all them other young'uns on the place."

"Oh, Lord, here we go." Cassandra carried her empty plate and cup to the sink, then went back to the table. "And here I thought you was going to stay with us today, Mama."

"I'm right here and I ain't going nowhere, you hear me? I'm here to stay. If I need any help, Ashley can do it, and you can go on back to your hospital."

Ruth Ann choked and reached for a napkin to wipe her mouth. Coffee dripped on her pink cotton nightshirt, and she rubbed it with the napkin. "Shit. Look at that."

"Mama said a cuss word! Mama said a cuss word!" Ashley got up, wet a rag, and handed it to Ruth Ann.

Ruth Ann scrubbed at the coffee stain, then put the rag down. "Ashley, what ideas have you been putting in Mama's head this morning?"

Here we go, Cassandra thought. Never fails.

"Me?" Ashley said. "I didn't do nothing. But of course you immediately assume I did because I'm the bad seed, right?"

Ruth Ann's head come up and she glared at Ashley.

Ashley looked away first. "I'm going to take a shower," she said, and left the room.

Cassandra shook her head at Ruth Ann. "As you can see, Ashley and Mama are being their usual cheerful selves this morning."

"Oh, yeah, I'm a barrel of monkeys." Marvelle's hands held tight to the edge of the table as she pushed herself up. She stood a minute to get her balance, then turned and left the kitchen.

"Ah, Mama, don't get in a huff. Mama, come on back now." Cassandra watched her shuffle like an old possum trying to get out of the road.

After she was out of earshot, Ruth Ann said, "She's so sensitive lately."

"She's getting worse. Them spells used to come on her about once a week, but it's getting to where it happens every day. She'll forget where she is, thinks it's a children's hospital and we've all gone off and left her there. Half the time she can't remember my name, or her own. And if I dare try and tell her anything, well, Lord, she bites my head off. And now she's run off twice here in the last few weeks. That worries me more than anything."

"We need to take her to the doctor again."

"Won't do no good. She'll just sit in the backseat like she did last time and refuse to go in." Cassandra picked up a fork and started eating from Marvelle's plate.

"Well. He examined her in the car one time, he can do it again."

"We got to do something. What if we can't find her next time she runs off?"

Ruth Ann rubbed her temples, then started stacking sections of the paper in the middle of the table. "I never thought Mama'd get this way. She's always been so strong."

"She's still strong, but now she's crazy too." Cassandra put the fork down. "I didn't mean that. Mama's not crazy. I know she can't help it, but I swear, sometimes . . . sometimes I just don't think I can take it anymore. Watching after Mama and them young'uns all day—well, it might look easy, but it ain't. And Mama's a twenty-four-hour-a-day job. She gets up and wanders around the house at night, and I'm so scared she'll go outside and get lost that I can't sleep. Sometimes I wonder . . . I just wonder if staying with me is the best thing for Mama right now. That's all."

Ruth Ann didn't say anything, just stared out the window next to the kitchen table. The grass looked like straw, it was so dry. Ever since A.J. left, the yard had gone to pot. That had always been his job, even though she had to practically beat him to get him started.

Down the hill, Dwight's cows crowded up close to the fence, and the tall ones lowered their heads over to Ruth Ann's side, trying to eat the weeds growing there. When Ashley was little, she'd go down all by herself and pet them cows while they ate. It got to the point they'd wait for her every day, just like dogs. Nobody could call cows stupid, at least not when it come to human affection. They knew Ashley loved them. Ruth Ann could still see her little arms reaching up toward them animals so much bigger than her. What had happened to that little girl?

Now, though, the problem of Ashley took a backseat to the problem of Marvelle. Ruth Ann never imagined having to decide her mama's life this way. The possibility of her losing her right mind just never come up. Marvelle Dockery Moon had too much going on to lose her mind. Ruth Ann's nose stung and she knew she might be about to cry, so she turned away from the window and watched Cassandra finish Marvelle's breakfast.

Her sister had always been a little on the chubby side, but these last few years, she'd really packed it on. Ruth Ann knew she wasn't one hundred percent happy, even when she quit the mill and opened the day care center, which was what she said she'd always wanted to do. The family all knew she done it to be able to keep an eye on their mama, and they was all relieved when she volunteered, because it meant they didn't have to.

Cassandra never did take to mill work, though she never worked in the mill itself. She took Office Occupations in high school, which they didn't even have when Ruth Ann was coming up, and got a job in the office doing payroll. Cassandra acted like it was hell on earth, but it always seemed like a pretty cushy job to everybody in the winding room who come out soaked in sweat and covered with cotton fibers every day. They had air-conditioning in the office.

Ruth Ann figured it must not have been work that was bothering Cassandra in the first place. Something else was going on, but it was probably as much a mystery to her as it was to everybody else in the family. Angela thought it was repressed childhood trauma, but Ruth Ann, being nine years older than Cassandra, had witnessed her entire childhood, and nothing worth repressing had ever happened to the girl. Of course, everybody had their own idea of trauma.

Maybe Cassandra just needed a man, like her mama said. Ruth Ann didn't think a man was the answer to any woman's troubles though. Maybe the cause of them.

Her life was a lot calmer without A.J. around, that was for sure. It didn't make sense how she found herself missing him sometimes, not after all he done. But there was something about him she missed, especially in the night. Not sex. Him. Laying there in the bed beside her. She'd know A.J. anywhere in the world, even blindfolded, by his breathing when he was asleep. He didn't snore or nothing, just breathed in and out real slow and deep and steady. Just hearing him sleep so good, taking such long, slow breaths, one after another like that, on and on all night long, seemed to say to Ruth Ann, lay back now, lay back and sleep, baby. Everything's going to be all right. I'm here. Anybody like that was bound to be a comfort to sleep next to.

"What you looking at?" Cassandra said.

Ruth Ann blinked. "Nothing."

"Well, I can't stand somebody staring at me while I eat, so quit." She put her fork down and took a drink of cold coffee, swished it around in her mouth before she swallowed.

"I'm sorry. I was just thinking." Ruth Ann reached over and took a piece of bacon. She loved that salty crunch in her mouth.

"You'll draw back a nub next time you reach for my food," Cassandra teased, then pushed the plate over to Ruth Ann. "What you all serious-looking for?"

"Nothing. Just Mama. And Ashley. And A.J. And you."

"Didn't you leave somebody out of that list?" Cassandra left the table to start the cleaning up. She poured grease from the skillet into an old lard can Ruth Ann kept under the sink.

"What are you talking about?" Ruth Ann said. She watched Cassandra wipe bacon grease off her fingers.

"Mama and Ashley and A.J. and me. What about you, Ruth Ann? Don't you figure in there somewhere?"

Ruth Ann stacked the plates and carried them to the sink for Cassandra to rinse. "I don't know what you're talking about. I'm not the one needs help."

Cassandra dropped a handful of forks and spoons into the utensil basket in the dishwasher. "Oh, and I do?"

"No. You know what I mean. I'm talking about Mama and Ashley."

"Uh-huh."

"You're as bad as Mama sometimes, you know that?"

"Well, Ruth Ann, seems to me it's about time you started wondering about yourself for a change."

Ruth Ann clammed up then and went back to the table, just like Cassandra figured she would. Cassandra finished loading the dishwasher, added soap, and turned the machine on. She could hear water splashing inside and wondered again exactly how that thing worked. It never got the dishes clean enough to suit her, and the dishwasher soap made the glasses smell funny. Nothing beat sink-washing, as far as she was concerned. She leaned back against the counter and looked at Ruth Ann, sitting there so straight and perfect. Even in her nightclothes, she didn't have a hair out of place. Hard to live up to perfection like that, so Cassandra never even tried. Her sister was the pretty one, so what did that make her? The troublemaker, she reckoned. No, looked like Ashley stole that one. Her and Marvelle together. Who could say if it'd work or not? But it was worth a shot.

"I know you're doing right taking Ashley back in," Cassandra said. "Family's supposed to help family if they can, just not at the expense of your own life."

"Have you been reading them self-help books again?"

"All I'm saying is, I'd hate to see you sitting around here worrying yourself into the grave, like you done before Ashley went to Appalachian Hall. You went to work, you come home, you worried. You got to get you a hobby or something."

"Like you?" Ruth Ann put down the paper and started raking crumbs off the table into her palm.

"I know I ain't got no room to talk. But I will. I'm going to do something." She would too, she would do something as soon as she figured out what it was.

Ruth Ann didn't answer, just kept wiping the table.

Instead of filling the silence by changing the subject to work or Mama, Cassandra decided to wait it out and see what Ruth Ann would do. She squirted some dish soap on a rag and washed the sink. After a minute, the silence got comfortable, like it was with her mama earlier. Cassandra hummed and wiped the ceramic tiles Ruth Ann had on the wall above her sink. No matter how pretty they looked—Williamsburg blue with geese— Cassandra still wished there was a window instead. It just didn't seem right standing at the sink without a window to look out. Of course, Ruth Ann used her dishwasher most of the time anyhow, so it probably didn't matter to her. Cassandra, however, liked to watch the world go by.

"What are we going to do, Cassie?" Ruth Ann said finally. "About Mama."

"Lord, I don't know." Cassandra took her watch off and rubbed her wrist where the stretchy band left its imprint. She sort of did know what to do about her mama, but she had to talk Ruth Ann into it first, had to ease into it just the right way. She sat down at the table again.

"You know," Cassandra said, "she's not always ornery or living in the past. A lot of the time she remembers exactly who we are and where she is. There just ain't no telling what'll set her off. That's the bad part, not knowing when or how long her spells are going to last."

"I don't see how you've stood it."

"Well, you do what you have to. But I don't think I can much longer." Cassandra wound the watch and put it back on. Her Granny Moon give her that watch when she was a little girl. It was Cassandra's favorite possession, even though it nearly cut off the circulation in her arm. One of these days, she'd get a new band for it.

"Ruthie," she said. "Sometimes I think I'm going crazy too. Not just because of Mama. Sometimes I feel like I'm not in this world, like I'm hiding somewhere watching me take care of kids, and take care of Mama, and go to church, and go to the grocery store, and go to the video store, go, go, go."

"I know what you mean," Ruth Ann said.

"I'm tired, Ruthie. I'm tired of being busy. I want to sit still for a while and just look at something. I think that's why I watch TV so much. It's the only thing relaxes me."

Ruth Ann laughed a little bit. "I seen a bumper sticker the other day that said *Kill Your Television!* Can you believe that?"

"Ruth Ann, what would you think about Mama staying with you for a while?" There, she'd said it, no taking it back. Cassandra almost laughed at the way Ruth Ann's head whipped around so fast.

"What?" Ruth Ann said.

"Now, don't get all in a huff," Cassandra said. "It's just a suggestion."

"Good."

"Well, I was just thinking that since Ashley'll be here all day with nothing to do, then maybe she can keep a eye on Mama and we could just see how it goes like that for a while." Cassandra stared at a point just over the top of Ruth Ann's head. There was a little crack in the wall, right near the ceiling there.

"I don't think so." Ruth Ann shook her head like the conversation was over already. "Besides, Ashley's got to get a job."

"Couldn't taking care of Mama be Ashley's job, at least for a while?"

"I don't think so," Ruth Ann said again.

Cassandra's whole body went stiff. Ruth Ann always thought she had the final word on everything, just because she was older.

"Wait a minute here," Cassandra said. "Do you think you're the only one with any say in how the world is run?" She pushed her chair back from the table and stood in front of Ruth Ann. It was a move to a power position. She'd seen it on Oprah. "Now you listen to me. I been living with Mama forty-two years now and I'm tired of it. I want to get out on my own before I get too old, and I think it's high time the rest of this family stopped taking me for granted and pitched in and helped out just a little bit. It won't kill you to have her here. Your precious peace and quiet is already messed up by Ashley being here, so what difference will one more make?" Cassandra knew she ought to be making eye contact to get her point across, but Ruth Ann kept looking out the window like she wasn't even listening.

"Well?" Cassandra hovered for a minute, then sat back down.

"What do you want me to say?" Ruth Ann looked down at her hands, fiddling with her rings.

"I don't know," Cassandra said. She put her hands around the salt and pepper shakers and twisted them nervously.

"I guess I don't have a choice," Ruth Ann said.

Cassandra watched her. Ruth Ann appeared to be moving from the bossy stage of her argument to the martyr stage.

"I ain't doing this to make trouble," Cassandra said. "Or because I don't love Mama or nothing like that. It's just I'm burned out. I used to always like it that I was the one Mama lived with instead of y'all. Made me feel like I could do something y'all couldn't. But she don't need me. She needs to be somewhere she believes she can do some good. And Ruth Ann, I think she can help Ashley. I really do."

"You'll say anything right now to get your own way, won't you?"

Cassandra didn't answer. She wasn't falling for the guilt trip neither. That was Ruth Ann's specialty.

"Well," Ruth Ann said. "I don't seem to have much choice here. All I can say is, better Ashley than me. Lord knows I can't do nothing with neither one of them."

Cassandra didn't know she'd been holding her breath till it whooshed out. She took a few more deep breaths. Ruth Ann must be losing her touch. This was the first time Cassandra could remember winning an argument with her. "Look," she said. "You work hard and you can't be here to watch Ashley every minute of the day, but maybe if Mama's here they'll keep each other out of trouble."

"What if she lets something happen to Mama though? What do we do then?"

"Ruth Ann, if anything happens to Mama, it'll be because Mama lets it happen, not Ashley. Y'all think she's so frail, but you ain't lived with her lately. She may not look big and healthy, but inside she's the same ornery old woman she's always been. At least when she remembers who she is."

"I guess she can at least stay here till Ashley's baby comes," Ruth Ann said, and Cassandra could almost see her mind working. "By then we should have some idea of what to do with both of them."

Cassandra shook her head. "You talk like they ain't got no say in it, Ruth Ann. You better remember who you're dealing with. We don't even know if either one of them will agree to it."

"I know, I know. I'll talk to Ashley later, and you can talk to Mama." Ruth Ann looked up at Cassandra. "If you don't mind."

Cassandra nodded. "You heard her in here a little while ago. She's ready now."

"It just ain't fair," Ruth Ann said. "I guess Mama was right all them times she told me ain't nothing about life fair and we got to make the best of what we're given to work with. Lord, I used to hate it so bad she was always right about everything. And now look at her. I can't stand it."

"You know the only thing makes me able to stand it? Mama knows something's happening to her mind, and I know it scares her to death, but if she can act like nothing's wrong, then so can I. She told me the other day she thought I was the one with the mental problem because I couldn't seem to remember that she was the mother and I was the daughter and I better quit telling her what to do. I believe that's when she decided to pack up and come over here to stay. I guess she figured you'd be gone all day and she'd have the house to herself."

"She didn't count on Ashley," Ruth Ann said. "I don't know which one I feel sorriest for, Ashley or Mama. Can you imagine the two of them here together all day long?"

Cassandra laughed. "I'd rather go back to the plant than live through that."

Usually Ruth Ann enjoyed the fact that she didn't have to drive anywhere on Sundays. The last few weeks felt like she lived in her car, so staying out of it was a good thing. But today, with a house full of people and more company coming later, she needed out. It'd been only one day, but already her mama and Ashley was getting on her nerves. She got a list together to go to the grocery store, then had to tell all of them no, they couldn't come with her.

It was ten-thirty by the time she got ready, and the store closest to the house didn't open till one o'clock, so Ruth Ann drove across town to the Winn Dixie. She didn't usually get out that way on the weekend since the only reason to go in that direction was to get to work. Ruth Ann slowed down a little bit as she drove by the plant. Cleveland Yarn was the only mill in the county that closed every single Sunday, and seeing the parking lot empty, no trucks pulling in and out, made her feel lonesome somehow. She never realized how dead the place looked without all of them there.

Hard to believe she'd spent the last thirty-three years of her life in that place. Thirty-three years. A long damn time, and a great big chunk of her life. It'd never been her intention to stay so long. All she wanted was a job somewhere besides the farm to earn her spending money until she got married. That was all she could think about back then, getting married, although she never expected to find a husband at Cleveland Yarn.

That first summer she worked there, when she turned eighteen, Ruth Ann worked in the winding room, and A.J. drove a truck for one of their vendors. They met one hot summer day when she went to the canteen for her afternoon break. A.J. was in there slamming the top of the cracker machine with the flat of both hands, trying to make his Nabs drop. That was his whole approach to life—if something don't go your way, hit it head-on and force it, or else get something better lined up and then turn your back and walk away from the old thing that wasn't satisfying you no more. That particular day, he'd just got tired of slamming and was about to walk away, when he seen Ruth Ann.

"Here," she said, wiping her sweaty forehead with one hand and digging for change in her pocket with the other. "I was just about to get me some Nabs too." She put in a dime, pulled the knob, and watched both packs of crackers fall, one behind the other. They reached for them at the same time, and A.J.'s face was so close she could see down his pores. He grinned and dug for more change when she snatched her crackers.

"Here, let me get you a drink since you got me my crackers," he said, and put change in the soda machine. When he looked at her with one eyebrow raised, Ruth Ann said, "Co-Cola, please." She could feel the blush creeping up her neck, making her even hotter than she already was from working in the hundred-degree heat of the winding room. Ruth Ann figured she sweated off about a pound a day in there, but she didn't mind, she could take it. They put the younger ones like her on day shift in the summertime, so the older employees could work the cooler night shift.

She carried her snack to a table and A.J. come over. "You mind?" he asked, halfway to sitting down.

"No," she said, pulling Nabs out of the crackly package.

"Hey," he said, popping the top on his Pepsi. "You shy or something?"

"What?" Ruth Ann said.

"Shy. You seem awful shy compared to most of the women in this place." He smiled when she didn't answer. "That's all right. I don't care for girls who come on too strong myself. My name's A. J. Payne, Jr."

"I know that," she said, irritated.

"You do? Well, well."

"I seen you. Everybody knows who you are." At least the women in the mill did. A.J. had a reputation. Not only was he the best-looking thing in town, he was the horniest. Behind his back, folks called him Hanky Panky.

"Well, well, well. I sure wish you'd tell me your name."

"Ruth Ann Moon."

"Hey, you kin to Frank Moon in the warehouse?"

"He's my brother."

"Boy, he sure is ugly. How'd he end up with such a pretty sister?"

Ruth Ann grinned. Frank was no more ugly than A.J., and just as cocky about it. This was just A.J.'s way of easing into asking her for a date. Ruth Ann didn't have five brothers for nothing.

"You married?" he asked.

She held up her bare ring finger.

"All right. I don't mess with married women no more. Like to got myself shot one time doing that." He waited to see if she was impressed, then, when she only stared at him, he popped a Nab in his mouth, slurped his Pepsi, and swallowed hard without chewing. Ruth Ann thought it was like watching a snake swallow a frog.

He squinted at her and lit a cigarette. "You want to go out sometime?"

"Where to?"

"Oh, drive-in, or maybe the Ponderosa."

"I can't go in there. My mama don't allow us to drink or go to places where it's done."

"Do you always do like your mama says, little girl?"

"Yes," Ruth Ann said.

"Well, Frank must've been gone the day she made that rule, 'cause I can't tell you how many Saturday nights I seen him down at the Ponderosa drunk as a cooter."

"Frank's grown."

"You look pretty grown to me." Ruth Ann watched his eyes flick down to her bosom, then back to her face again. "How many of y'all is there?" he said.

"Twelve—seven boys and five girls, but only seven of us living now."

"Damn!" A.J. laughed dirty. "I guess I know what your mama and daddy did to keep warm on cold winter nights."

Ruth Ann stood up. "I don't think you ought to be talking about my mama and daddy's business, do you?" She put her cracker wrapper in the trash and walked away.

"Hey, now, don't get in a huff." A.J. put his hand on her arm and stopped her at the door. "I didn't mean no disrespect, baby." That was the first time he ever called her baby, though by no means the last. She kind of liked it, but she didn't let on. He took his hand away when she just looked at him. He stood there looking back. The blush came up Ruth Ann's neck again and she turned away so her profile was to him.

He sucked in a deep breath. "Lord, you sure are a pretty one."

Ruth Ann pulled open the door and immediately his voice was drowned out by the roar of the winding machines. Feeling safer in the noise outside the canteen, she turned to A.J. "What?" she yelled. "What'd you say?"

He put his lips next to her ear, sending shivers over her bare arms. "I said, I'm going to talk to your brother about getting together a double date, you and me, him and his girl."

"Frank ain't got a girl," she yelled.

"Well, I reckon he can get one. I've seen him with one or two."

They grinned at each other for just a second, then she turned and hurried away. When she got to her backwinder, she looked over her shoulder, then jerked her head around when she caught him still looking. A.J. was whistling as he headed for the warehouse.

Ruth Ann should've known from that first meeting, when A.J. told her about fooling with a married woman and almost getting shot, that he couldn't keep away from other women. She found out right before their wedding that she was the last girl he got around to dating at the plant, and he only married her because she was stupid enough to get pregnant. But Ruth Ann couldn't blame their divorce on a shotgun wedding. A.J. asked, and she accepted, and they both went down the aisle of their own free will.

Maybe in his heart he wanted to be faithful, but his problem with fidelity wasn't in his heart, it was in his pants.

When A.J. left Ruby's, he headed over to the Winn Dixie to buy his weekly groceries. Even though he ate out most of the time, he liked to keep a few things in the house—cereal and milk, bread and baloney and mustard, and of course Pepsi. He got hooked on that stuff when he was eighteen and drove one of their local routes for a while. Whenever he felt like it, he'd sneak a bottle and nobody ever knew. That's when he got hooked on trucks too.

In the deli meat section, trying to decide between beef, chicken, or turkey baloney, a familiar shape lodged itself in the corner of his eye. His head come up and he froze with a pack of beef baloney in his hand. He hadn't seen Ruth Ann since their last fight about Ashley three weeks ago. Strangely enough they'd managed to avoid each other even in a town the size of Davis. A.J. watched her push her cart up the soft-drink aisle in his direction.

Ruth Ann had her head down as she picked up a bottle each of Coke, Diet Coke, Caffeine Free Diet Coke, and Sundrop. That was another difference they never reconciled. He was Pepsi, she was Coke. They'd had a couple of fights about that too in their years together, but they usually ended up laughing about it. Couldn't stay mad when it was just little things they argued over. It was the big things that come later was what split them up.

But the last time, right before she kicked him out, she throwed a full two-liter bottle at him. She missed, but the bottle hit a little cuckoo clock she'd bought in Gatlinburg, one he never liked because of the noise it made, and he was glad to see it laying on the floor at his feet. He walked on the pieces to get to Ruth Ann, meaning to hug her and say sorry, but she run out of the room crying, locked herself in the bathroom, and told him if he wasn't gone by the time she come out, she'd call the law.

A.J. waited for her at the end of the aisle. She didn't see him until she was almost on top of him.

"Hey, baby," he said. She'd said to quit calling her baby when they separated, but it was as natural as breathing to him.

"Hey yourself. What you doing here on a Sunday morning?" She pushed her buggy on around to the next aisle and A.J. followed.

"Ah, I just needed a few things," he said. "What you doing?" He pushed his buggy alongside hers and looked into it. "Cokes and pickles, dinner rolls and paper plates. What y'all having for dinner, a picnic?"

"No. We just needed a few things and this was the only store open."

"I seen Cassandra's van in the driveway a little while ago. Her and Marvelle eating with you?" He watched the side of her face as she studied a row of soup cans.

"Yeah. Mama run off again last night and ended up staying with me," Ruth Ann said. "By the way, you might be interested to know Ashley's home." She dropped two cans of cream of mushroom soup in the buggy and moved on down the aisle.

A.J. stood there a minute, taking it in. He had a bad feeling he must've done something wrong, but he didn't know what. "She's home? When did she get home? I thought she'd be up there longer than that. I thought she was supposed to stay up there longer than that."

Ruth Ann stopped her buggy and faced him. "I swear, if you ain't the most self-centered creature I have ever known, not to mention deaf. I told you about Ashley coming home. I told you three weeks ago. Did you not hear one word I said?"

A.J. rocked his buggy and watched the cans of frozen orange juice roll around the bottom and bang against the baloney. He didn't know what to say.

"And another thing." Ruth Ann leaned close to him and whispered, "She's pregnant."

A slow burn started somewhere in A.J.'s gut and spread up his chest, his neck, his head, down his arms. He held on tight to the buggy, so tight a tingling started in his fists and burned up through his wrists. He wanted to slam something, slam it hard.

"Did you hear me? I said Ashley's pregnant." Ruth Ann hissed the words at him like a snake. She looked like she was almost enjoying how hard it was for him to hear that his baby girl was knocked up when she wasn't married and nobody in the family even knew the boy. Or at least he didn't think they knew him.

"Do you know who the father is?"

"Yes."

A.J. looked at Ruth Ann. "Well? Who is he? What's his name?"

"Keith something. I don't remember his last name."

"Damn." A.J. shook his head. "Damn. I never expected this."

"Well, do you think I did?" Ruth Ann said.

"No, baby." A.J. patted her hand where it clenched around the buggy handle. She pulled her hand out from under his, sniffed, and pushed on down the aisle.

A.J. watched her go. He had to give her credit. At fifty, the woman could still fill out a pair of jeans better than any female he'd ever seen. "Hey," he said.

She stopped and turned toward him. "What?"

"How about if I come over?"

She stared for a long time like she was thinking about it. She looked so tired, he wanted to take hold of her and squeeze her. She sighed. "You might as well come and get it over with. Just come on at dinnertime. Oh, Angela and David and the boys'll be there too." She turned the corner and was gone.

Angela and the kids? Why the hell didn't he know about that? Or Ashley coming home? They never told him nothing. And what did she mean, get it over with? Did she think he was out to make some kind of trouble? All he wanted was his family. Was that too much to ask? He shook his head at himself. Well, maybe it was too much to ask after all he'd done, but he had to try anyhow. Aim high, like his daddy said, aim high and even if you fall short, you probably won't fall all the way back to where you started from.

He wished sometimes now he could go back and change the past, but if he was honest about it, he wasn't sure exactly how he'd change anything. What women like Ruth Ann couldn't seem to understand about men, especially men like A. J. Payne, was that they had to be free while they was young. When he was home, he wanted to be with his wife and kids, but on the road he forgot for a little while. He always thought she ought to be glad he never done no messing around at home, saved all of that for out of town.

But Ruth Ann didn't see it that way. She thought he should be man enough to control himself at home and on the road. She said him screwing anything that'd hold still long enough in eight or nine different states was not an improvement over him staying home and maybe drinking, maybe fighting like his daddy had been bad to do. Big maybes, she said, and at least if he was home, she'd know where to leave him if he did start acting like his daddy. But on the road, he could be dead in a ditch or having a big time in Atlantic City with a hooker, and they'd still be sitting home like always eating fried chicken and drinking iced tea and thinking they had a perfect family. Ruth Ann said he was selfish, that all men had a real deep and wide selfish streak that at one time was essential, for some reason, to the survival of the human race but now was just a damn pain in the ass for all the women of the world.

Ruth Ann clenched her hands around the steering wheel while she waited for the air-conditioning to cool her off. She had it turned up as high as it would go, but it was taking forever to get cold. She pulled a Kleenex out of the glove compartment and looked in the rearview mirror to make sure her mascara didn't smear when she dabbed under her eyes. She didn't know if this hot flash come on by itself or if seeing A.J. triggered it, but it was a strong one. As she walked away from him in the store just now, she had an almost overwhelming urge to stab him repeatedly with something sharp.

For the last six months, Ruth Ann had been having the craziest fantasies about killing people. Sometimes a family member or acquaintance came to mind, but anybody would do—mailman, Avon lady, preacher—whoever come within a thirty-foot radius during a hot flash was doomed.

They wasn't mild murders neither; they was flashes of rage, uncontrollable and wilder than Ruth Ann ever allowed herself to feel in real life. But there was no allowing to it, no permission, no justification. Pure and simple, every damn body got on her damn nerves. She didn't use to cuss so much either, but the hell with that.

It was menopause, Ruth Ann knew that much. Hormones. Her periods stopped coming nearly a year ago. Cassandra said she was lucky to be getting it over with. Cassandra didn't know yet about the hot flashes, the chills, the headaches, the joint aches, the little mustache that had to be bleached a couple times a month. And she especially didn't know about the rages.

The first time it happened, Ruth Ann was buying groceries and run into Myra Jenkins, somebody she'd disliked since elementary school for no reason except she was always dirty-looking. Myra had been halfway cute in high school, for an albino, but she'd let three pregnancies turn her body into a little barrel-shaped blob.

"Well, hey there, girl! I ain't seen you in a coon's age!" Myra hollered loud enough for the whole county to hear. Ruth Ann put on her fake smile and focused on Myra's lipstick, which was a terrible shade of pink that clashed with her beady rabbit eyes. Ruth Ann had always despised white rabbits because of their evil-looking pink eyes, and that's what she always thought of when she looked at Myra—a fat, evil rabbit. The hot flash started up in her throat and spread across her face and chest, scorching like sunburn. Ruth Ann pulled out her pocket calendar and fanned so hard her hair moved.

"Hot flash?" Myra said with a sadistic grin. "Getting them myself these days. Lord have mercy, sometimes I got to get up in the night and walk around the house naked till I cool off." She threw a box of tampons in her buggy.

"Well, Myra," Ruth Ann said. "It's been good to see you, but I got to go now. My frozen yogurt's starting to melt. Bye-bye." The bye faded and drifted back over Ruth Ann's shoulder as she pushed her cart past the feminine hygiene, past the diapers, past the baby formula. Why did I even come down this aisle? she thought. If I'd been paying attention to my list, I wouldn't even had to run into that woman.

"Oh, Ruth Ann!" Myra jiggled up next to her. "I meant to ask if you'd like to come to a Country Interiors party I'm having next week. Just some of the ladies from church. They got some great new figurines in this catalog you might like."

Ruth Ann's fingers curled hard around the cart handle. Country Interiors. That was the last thing she needed, to sit around with a bunch of women looking at knickknacks and doodads, spending money on crap like that. And worst of all, Ruth Ann knew they'd somehow work around to asking about Ashley, or Marvelle, or something else that was none of their damn business. Suddenly, in her mind's eye, there was Myra, naked and swinging from a meat hook in the walk-in freezer of the grocery store, eyes bugging out and her whole body blue as a cornflower.

Ruth Ann shivered and closed her eyes. She had to shake it off. It wouldn't do to have a fit in front of somebody like Myra, in front of anybody. It wouldn't do to have a fit at all. She turned on her automatic smile, the one reserved for salespeople—"No, thank you, I'm just looking." It was very similar to the one she used for Reverend Bob Padgett and other uninvited visitors—"Of course you're not disturbing me, come on in." Either way, it would do for Myra Jenkins.

"Why, Myra," Ruth Ann said. "I'd just love to come. But I can't. Bye now." She escaped the sound of Myra's "Oh, that's all right, honey," rounded the corner too fast, clipped the edge of a shelf, and knocked a whole stack of Starkist on the floor. The cans rolled around the wheels of her cart, but Ruth Ann kicked them out of the way and kept going. When she got to the produce section, she pushed her nearly full buggy behind the cut-flower display and got the hell out of there.

That was just the beginning, and the hot flashes and everything else just kept getting worse. Now her mama and Ashley come to live with her, and what could she do? Just like Myra Jenkins in the grocery store, they sprung it on her too quick, one after the other in what seemed like a conspiracy. There was no time to think it through, and she couldn't say, "I'd love to, but I can't," this time. She couldn't say, "No, Ashley, you cannot come live with me until you have that baby and decide what to do with the rest of your life, and no, Mama, you cannot come live with me just because you don't like Cassandra's day care."

Ruth Ann took a deep breath and relaxed a little bit as the air finally turned cold and blasted her face and neck. It was probably messing her hair up, but she could fix that later. As she pulled out of the parking place and headed for the exit, she noticed A.J.'s truck parked way away from all the other cars. Typical. Had to make sure nobody touched his precious vehicle, even if he had to walk half a mile in stifling heat to get where he was going. If he'd took that much care with his home life, maybe they wouldn't be divorced now.

Before she pulled out on the highway, she caught sight of A.J. in her rearview mirror, coming out of the Winn Dixie with a sack of groceries. In the mirror he looked like a different man, little and lonesome-looking. She didn't want to stab him anymore, and that was a relief, but neither did she feel like eating dinner with him. Still, he did want to see his children, and that was reason enough to put up with him for a couple hours. As long as he behaved. There hadn't been any sharp objects at hand in the grocery store, but she had a whole drawer full of knives at home, not to mention scissors, an ax, knitting needles, screwdrivers, and an ice pick.

"Honey, you must be crazy," she said out loud to herself, and whipped the car out of the parking lot. She turned the radio way up, a country station. Country was growing on her here lately. She recognized the song and started singing, really belting it out. So what if she looked like a crazy person talking to herself all alone in her car? Public opinion be damned, that was her new motto.

It was after one o'clock when A.J. pulled into Ruth Ann's driveway and stepped down out of his truck. With any luck, he'd timed it so dinner was on the table and he wouldn't have to sit around waiting to eat, wondering what to do with his hands and wondering what to say to Ashley, to Marvelle, to any of them. He stood and studied the house he'd left just a little over two years ago and hadn't set foot in since. He hadn't even seen what the inside looked like since Ruth Ann had the wall between their room and Alex's knocked out and a bathroom added. Things on the outside looked pretty much the same. The bushes was bigger and needed trimming, and a few places needed going after with the weedeater, but he could see she'd had somebody out to paint the trim and fix the roof. That was good. If she ever sold the place, he wanted his half of the profit to amount to something.

A.J. felt pretty confident, though, that Ruth Ann would stay in their home until they carried her out feet-first. She'd worked too hard on the place to give it up, and she'd hate the thought of strangers living in the house where she raised her children. Not to mention the fact that Ruth Ann hated change, hated it way more than most people. That's probably the main thing kept them married so long.

Lucky for him Ashley was home, so he had a good excuse to come over now, and keep coming over. No way Ruth Ann wouldn't allow him to visit his child. Angela hardly spoke to him since the separation, except to say hey and bye, and he never seen Alex except Christmas, and sometimes not even then, but he knew Ashley would be on his side.

The front door opened and Ruth Ann pushed out the storm door. "Well. Are you coming in or not?" she yelled.

He headed down the sidewalk toward the front, but she waved in the direction of the carport. "No, no," she said. "Go in the back. I don't want you tracking across this living room carpet. I just cleaned it." She let the storm door swing shut, latched it, and closed the front door. A.J. stared for a second, then did a ninety-degree turn toward the carport. He didn't knock or wait to be invited in.

Everybody was already settled at the table in the middle of eating ham, green beans, corn, mashed potatoes, and fresh sliced tomatoes. Angela sat there with the boys on one side and David on the other, looking like just what she was—a prim and proper schoolteacher—even in jeans and a T-shirt. He couldn't get over how much the boys had grown. Last time he seen them was Easter, he reckoned. How old were they now? Bryan must be eleven, so that would make Jonathan seven, although he still had that baby look to his face that made him seem younger.

Ashley looked about ready to cry right there in front of everybody. A.J. couldn't tell she was pregnant, not from this angle anyhow. He studied her belly when she pushed her chair back and come over and hugged him.

Nope. Couldn't tell at all. Maybe it was a mistake. He went and sat between her and Ruth Ann. As luck would have it, he sat right across from Marvelle, and one look at her face told him he was in deep shit.

Marvelle barked, "I'd like to know what in the hell he's doing here," and pointed a crooked finger at him.

Oh, Jesus, here she goes. A.J. knew he wouldn't get to eat a bite until she'd had her say, so he didn't even bother loading up his plate, even though the ham smelled so good and them mashed taters looked just right, smooth and creamy.

"Mama, please don't start." Ruth Ann looked at Marvelle, then back at her plate, like maybe if she ignored her Marvelle would quit. Fat chance, A.J. thought.

"Mama, don't you want some more bread?" Cassandra waved the bread basket under Marvelle's nose. Marvelle smacked the basket out of Cassandra's hand and rolls bounced across the table. One fell in A.J.'s lap and he put it on his plate for later. It might be the only one he got.

"Alexander Jackson Payne," Marvelle said.

Oh, hell, there she went with that finger, like the finger of God, only knobby and swole up with arthritis. A.J. half expected to see lightning shoot out the end any time it was pointed at him.

"What are you doing in this house again?" she said. "Did she not tell you to get your sorry ass out and never come back, you lowdown, slackjawed, two-timing son of a bitch?" Marvelle slapped her hands down on the table so hard the silverware rattled.

Damn if the woman couldn't still put the fear of God into a man. If looks could kill, he'd be mortally wounded right now. A.J. felt his face go hot and looked over at Ruth Ann. She wouldn't look up from her plate. She never had took his part over her mama, not even when she still loved him.

Ashley stood up and glared down at Marvelle. "Granny, this is my daddy, and this is our house, and if you don't like it you can go back where you come from." She didn't back down an inch when Marvelle stood up too and told her to shut her mouth.

"No, you shut yours," Ashley said. "That ain't no way to talk, especially on Sunday. Now, you leave my daddy alone!"

Whooeeee! Looked like old Marvelle had met her match. This could get interesting real quick. A.J. folded his hands across his belly and watched.

The staring contest went on a minute longer, then Marvelle looked at

Ruth Ann. "Fine," she said. "I'll be the one to leave, then, 'cause I ain't breaking bread with the likes of him!" And with that she stomped off in the living room and turned up the volume on the TV.

Everybody sat real quiet, looking anywhere but at each other, listening to John Wayne in what sounded like a war movie. Ashley got up and shut the door into the living room so John Wayne only come through when he yelled or blew something up.

A.J. wanted to tell Ashley she done good, but he knew the rest of them would jump on him like a duck on a June bug, so he kept his mouth shut. He eased his hand across the table and slid a piece of ham on his plate, then another. The way he seen it, it was good for them to get all that pent-up stuff out of their systems. Ruth Ann's family had always been bad to hold things in, and they suffered for it later with strokes and heart attacks and intestinal problems. Not A.J.'s kin. No, sir. They let it all hang out and didn't care who was there to see it, and most of them lived well into their nineties, the ones that didn't get shot or die in car wrecks.

"Ashley," Ruth Ann said. "I don't want you talking to Mama like that ever again. She's my mama and your granny. Do you hear me?"

Ashley said, "Mama, are you going to let her get away with acting like a bitch just because she's old? If that's so, then why don't I get away with it because I'm young, or you because you're middle-aged?"

"Ashley," Angela said. "Why don't you just keep your mouth shut altogether?" She glared over her boys' plates at Ashley.

A.J. noticed Jonathan and Bryan hunkering down in their chairs, trying to be invisible. Their daddy leaned back and stared at the ceiling like he didn't need to watch the fight, like he'd seen it all before, which he had. A.J. didn't envy David his lot in life with a wife like Angela, a throwback to Marvelle if there ever was one.

Angela kept on. "All you do is upset Mama and Granny and everybody else in the family. That seems to be the one thing you're good at, making trouble."

"You prissy bitch!" Ashley said. She grabbed a roll off her plate and threw it at Angela. It hit her jaw with a soft pop and fell on the floor. "You think you so goddamn perfect. Well, you ain't. Nobody can even stand to be around you because you're so stuck-up. Daddy's right. You better not let yourself get caught out in the rain. Your nose is turned up so high, you might drown."

Oh, hell, A.J. thought. Why'd Ashley have to go and tell that?

Angela didn't even look at him though. She focused on her sister. "That is not true! You're the one nobody can't stand to be around. Do you think Mama wanted you to come back? After all you done?"

Ashley pushed her chair back and stood up, then Angela did too. They faced each other, about ready to draw blood. "You shut your mouth or I'll shut it for you!" Ashley said.

"Oh, I'm really scared now," Angela said.

"Angela!" Ruth Ann said. "You two quit it right now."

David jumped up and come around the table. He wasn't stupid enough to get close to either one of them. He stood behind the boys' chairs. "Both of you hush!" he said. "Ain't it bad enough we're all sitting here pretending to get along, without you two trying to kill each other? And in front of the young'uns? Look at the boys. They're practically under the table."

"Shut up, David," Ashley said without taking her eyes off Angela. "This is between me and Bird Legs here."

"Don't you be telling my husband what to do, Miss High School Dropout," Angela said. "That's my job." She give David a hateful look and opened her mouth to say something else, but then she looked and seen Bryan and Jonathan slid down to where they was practically sitting on their necks, their fingers in their ears. She shut her mouth and her lips started twitching a little bit, like she was trying not to smile.

Cassandra was trying not to laugh, but then she snorted and out it come, that big belly laugh of hers. Ashley looked at the boys and got tickled too. That set Ruth Ann and Angela off, and all of a sudden seemed like the four of them was laughing so hard they was crying, while A.J. and David stared at them like they was crazy. The boys took their fingers out of their ears and sat up, and in a minute they started laughing too. Relief pumped through the room like oxygen, and by the time Angela and Ashley sat back down, David was the only one left that still looked mad. Nobody paid him any attention though, because a pissed-off David wasn't nothing this bunch worried about.

A few little giggles snuck out as Angela put more mashed taters on the boys' plates and Ashley passed the corn. When the bowls got around to him, A.J. loaded up. Cassandra got the young'uns talking about Dollywood, and pretty soon everybody forgot about the fight. A.J. figured it was finally safe for him to eat. He crammed his mouth full with a big bite of taters and ham and corn, then started chewing. It all tasted so good, he closed his eyes and just enjoyed it. Now, Ruby's food was fine and sure beat cooking himself, but couldn't nothing compare with Ruth Ann's cooking, the one good thing she learned from her mama.

Before starting his fourth piece of ham, A.J. sat back to unsnap his britches and caught Ruth Ann giving him a mean-assed look. He let go the snap and acted like he just meant to tuck his shirt in. Wouldn't do to piss her off now. He was too full anyhow, so he pushed the plate away. He'd wrap up what was left and take it home for supper. No sense letting it go to waste.

A.J. caught Bryan staring at him and give him a wink. Bryan grinned back. Dang if that young'un wasn't the spitting image of him at that age, except for that red head. Good-looking boy too, if he did say so himself. A.J. looked over at Jonathan, watched him cram a big old spoonful of mashed taters in his mouth. To be so little, that boy was one hell of an eater. No doubt about it, they was Paynes through and through. Until they come along, it never entered A.J.'s mind that grandchildren could make you feel so good. But just looking at them, knowing they was in the world, satisfied him like nothing else.

Now he figured all he needed was a little girl grandbaby to spoil just like he used to spoil Ashley. He sat up straight all of a sudden and looked at her, sitting there talking to Cassandra so innocent. In all the excitement, he'd forgot about her being pregnant. What the hell was she doing having a baby? She was just a baby herself.

"Daddy, what are you staring at?" Ashley said.

"What?" A.J. said. They all stared at him. "Nothing. Just thinking about whether or not I wanted me some more taters." He pulled the bowl across the table and slapped a spoonful on his plate. The waistband of his britches was cutting him in two, the potatoes was cold, and nobody was looking at him now, but still his elbow kept bending.

Fat and dead of a heart attack, that was how he'd end up if he didn't quit. He slid his free hand under the table where Ruth Ann couldn't see and unsnapped his pants. There, that was better. At least he could breathe, as long as he didn't look at Ashley. He took one more bite, then pushed the plate away. He'd do a lot of things to get his family back, but killing himself with taters wasn't one of them.

4

Ashley groaned and rolled over, then sat up, listening to the crying getting louder and louder. Who the hell could that be? Marvelle's bed was empty, but Ashley couldn't imagine her making such a racket as that. It was after seven o'clock, so her mama should've already left for work. Ashley couldn't imagine her making that racket either. She got out of bed and followed the sound to the living room.

"Granny?" She walked closer and patted Marvelle's arm. "What's going on? Hush now. What's the matter? What you doing up so early?"

"Oh, Jesus, take me now, Jesus, Jesus." Marvelle's head thrashed back and forth on the headrest.

Ashley knelt down by the recliner and held Marvelle's hand. "Come on now, Granny, what's the matter?"

"I can't remember nothing no more, Ashley. I might as well be dead. I'm about as much use as tits on a boar hog." Marvelle thrust her shoulders forward, grunted, tried to sit up, then fell back again. "That's why I been left here in this chair to die."

"Granny, for heaven's sake." Ashley pushed on the footrest and the chair buckled back into an upright position. "Nobody left you here to die. Next time you sit in this chair, don't push all the way back."

"Won't be no next time. Ruth Ann's shipping me back to that hospital."

Ashley put a hand on Marvelle's back and gave her a push to help her stand. "Hospital? You mean Cassandra's day care?"

Marvelle swayed on her feet, then grabbed Ashley's arm: "I'm tired of looking after all them young'uns," she said. "I done raised my young'uns. I got other things to do."

"Like what?" Ashley said. She held Marvelle's arm with one hand and run the other hand over Marvelle's hair. She shook her head, wiped her hand on her T-shirt, then headed for the kitchen.

"I read my Bible, play solitaire, watch my stories," Marvelle said. "I'd have thought by now I could do what I wanted instead of always doing for my children." Her bare feet squeaked against the linoleum as Ashley steered her around the kitchen table toward the sink.

"Granny," Ashley said. "Why don't you just stay here with us?"

"Us who?"

"Me and Mama."

"Well, I guess anything'd beat that big nurse."

Ashley laughed. "Why you keep saying that?"

"She is a nurse. She's always got on that white suit and them white nurse shoes."

"Them ain't nurse shoes, they're orthopedic shoes 'cause she's got bad feet. And she just likes to wear white, don't ask me why. Makes her look that much bigger. But just because somebody wears white don't make them a nurse." Ashley turned on the faucet at the kitchen sink and held her hand under the water until it got warm.

"You think what you like. I've lived with her, I know. Now, what you doing?"

"We're going to wash your hair, Granny. It looks like it ain't been washed in a month. I'll be right back." Ashley went to the bathroom and brought back shampoo and conditioner.

"That nurse tried to wash it the other day. Like to killed me too, scrubbing my head with them big hands of hers."

"Granny, she ain't no nurse." Ashley stood Marvelle in front of the counter and pulled her head over the sink. She used the spray nozzle to wet Marvelle's hair, then poured on shampoo and started scrubbing. "Has Cassandra ever tried to give you a shot?" she said.

"She better not." Marvelle's voice sounded hollow from inside the stainless steel sink.

"Has she ever took your temperature?"

"No."

"Has she ever give you medicine?"

"My blood-pressure pills."

"That still don't make her a nurse." Ashley rinsed Marvelle's hair, rubbed in conditioner, then rinsed that out. When she was done, she tapped Marvelle's shoulder. "Come on now and raise up so I can wrap a towel around your head.

"Goddamn, Granny!" Ashley said as Marvelle swung her head away from the sink, slinging water across the kitchen and Ashley. She brushed water off her neck and chest, then grabbed a towel and wrapped it turban-style around Marvelle's head and pushed her shoulders back so she stood upright. She used a dishrag to catch the water running down Marvelle's face and neck, then stood back and looked at her good. "I know what you need, Granny," she said. "You need a makeover."

"A what?"

"You'll see." She led Marvelle to Ruth Ann's room and settled her at the vanity table. "You want some breakfast first?"

"Just coffee. I ain't hungry."

Ashley brought a cup of coffee and set it in front of Marvelle, then started combing her hair. "I'm getting my cosmetology license once this baby's born," she said. "I can go to school right here in town, and it'll only take me a year."

"A year. I'll be. I didn't even finish tenth grade."

"I remember you telling us that." Ashley parted Marvelle's hair down the middle. "How come you quit school?"

"Had to get married when I was sixteen."

"Had to?" Good Lord! Her granny had to get married? Ashley didn't remember hearing that part of the story. She'd just assumed Granny and Pawpaw done things in legal order—first marriage, then young'uns. It occurred to her for the first time that they was young once too, young and carried away with each other just like her and Keith.

"Had to. Wanted to. Little bit of both, I reckon." Marvelle stared at Ashley's reflection in the mirror like she was daring her to say a word.

"Well, I for one know what it's like, Granny, so I ain't saying a word. Listen, I'll have to use these sponge curlers on you. Your hair's too fine to hold hot rollers. Then we'll set you under Mama's old helmet dryer for a while." Ashley pulled pink curlers from the drawer and started rolling Marvelle's hair.

"You know, Jesse's been dead eleven years now. Eleven years is a long time to be dead. A long time to be without a husband too. Ow!" Marvelle slapped Ashley's thigh. "Don't yank it so hard."

"Sorry. Your hair's so thin it's hard to get it to stay. Now, hold still."

"I used to have beautiful long thick black hair, straight as a stick. My great-grandmother on my mother's side was full Cherokee."

"Well, mine's straight as a stick too without a perm in it." Ashley let go Marvelle's head so she could take a drink of coffee. "What was her name again, your great-grandma?"

"Her white name was Josephine Miller. Her Cherokee name was something with clouds in it. I can't remember exactly."

"My boyfriend Keith, he's half Cherokee."

"Where's he at now?"

"He stays with his granny in Murphy."

"Is he the daddy of your baby?"

"Yes."

"Are you sure?"

"God, Granny, I'm not a slut. At least, he's the only one I been with in a long time. Long enough I'm sure he's the daddy."

"Do you love this boy?"

"I don't know, I guess so."

"Oh, honey, they ain't no guessing about it." Marvelle stared into the mirror, but it was obvious she wasn't seeing her own face. Ashley could tell her eyes was looking far away inside somewhere.

"When Mama brung Jesse home to board with us while he worked the mines, I knowed he was the one for me. I felt like I'd done got a wish granted without even knowing I wished. Course, Mama ought to have known she couldn't keep us apart, living under the same roof like we done, but she needed the rent money to help feed us all. They was too many of us to live just on what Papa made."

"What did he do?"

"Worked for the railroad. He was gone a lot."

"So," Ashley said. "Y'all was carrying on right under your mama's nose."

"Well, I don't know what you mean by carrying on." Marvelle twisted her wedding band around and around her finger.

"Come on now, Granny."

"My first baby was the price I had to pay for my recklessness then, honey."

"What?"

"That baby died afore it could even come into this world. Even after me and Jesse done the right thing and got married."

"You mean you had another baby before you had Uncle Mason?"

"I would have if she hadn't a come too soon."

"I guess back then it was a big disgrace."

"It's still a disgrace." Marvelle eyed Ashley's belly. "They ain't nothing we can do but live with it."

"Why is it such a disgrace?" Ashley said. She knew she sounded whiny but couldn't seem to help it. "Wouldn't it be worse if me and Keith got married and then it didn't work out?"

"I just can't believe you let yourself get that a-way in the first place, what with all the things you girls have nowadays."

"What are you talking about?"

"Why, honey, if they'd invented any of that birth control when I was young, I'd a never had all them young'uns."

Ashley's fingers stopped in the middle of wrapping hair around a curler. "But, Granny, if you hadn't had all your children, you wouldn't have had Mama, and she wouldn't have had me."

"Well, honey, you don't miss what you never had." Marvelle laughed low in her throat.

"Granny! That's like wishing we was never born."

"Now, I didn't say no such of a thing! I said you don't miss what you never had. Honey, raising children in the Depression wasn't easy. I ain't saying I wish my life had been easier, but I do wish it'd been better for my young'uns. You'uns got it a lot better now. When your baby's born, you might worry about it getting sick or getting hurt, but you won't never have to worry about feeding it.

"I remember this one time, I'd just made a dollar for doing a lady's washing, and I took that dollar and took the young'uns and went down to the store and bought a loaf of bread and some canned milk to make gravy and bread for their dinner. We didn't have a thing else in the house to eat. Well, this Mrs. Levy was in the store—she was a rich lady—and she says to me, Mrs. Moon, would it bother you awful much if I bought you and your children some groceries? And I looked her dead in the eye and I said, why, no, ma'am, it wouldn't bother me one bit. But I want you to know, it like to killed me." Marvelle nodded her head. "When your young'uns is hungry, their bellies matters more than your pride."

Ashley waited for Marvelle's head to be still, then went back to rolling her hair. "It was all worth it though, right? All the hard times?"

"Well, hard times do seem to make for good people, but the way them children suffered, Lord have mercy, even if they didn't always know it. It hurts my heart to think about it."

Ashley stared down at Marvelle's pink scalp, the white hair pulled tight over the curlers. She looked up again at Marvelle's reflection in the mirror.

That's what I want, she thought, with the fiercest feeling of wanting she'd ever had in her life. She wanted that look her granny had, that look that told the world here I am, I'm somebody, and here is my life. I been young and old and in between, I loved a man, raised my children, worked, laughed, cried, and, see, even after all that, here I still am.

"I'll be eighty-three in the spring, if I live to see it," Marvelle said. She leaned closer to the mirror and pulled at the skin of her neck. "Lord, I'm old. Look at that. Looks like a turkey wattle. Old and wrinkled and sagging."

Ashley smiled. "Sure beats the alternative though, don't it, Granny?"

"Huh?"

"Getting another year older beats dying, don't it?"

"That shows how much you know. They's worse things than dying."

Ashley snapped the last curler in place and checked for loose hairs. "I don't know about that, Granny." She glanced up and seen Marvelle looking at her real sad.

"You just can't know, honey. And I hope you never do."

"Me too," Ashley said. She stood back and squeezed Marvelle's head with both hands to make sure the curlers was tight. "That takes care of your hair. Now let's work on your face." She opened Ruth Ann's makeup drawer and pulled out foundation, blush, mascara, and lipstick.

"I ain't wore makeup since Jesse's funeral," Marvelle said.

"Why not?"

"What's the point of wearing it if you ain't got a man to wear it for?"

"The point is, there's other fish in the ocean."

"I done give up fishing." Marvelle squirmed. "What's that mess you're putting on me?"

"Just hush, it's foundation." Ashley blotted it on with a damp sponge. "We got to even out your skin tone. You got them age spots all over your face. And now a little blusher." She brushed pink triangles on Marvelle's cheeks, then blended the color toward her hairline.

"Don't paint me up like a harlot."

"Chill, Granny."

"What's that supposed to mean?"

"Chill, be cool." Ashley could tell Marvelle wasn't real thrilled with what she seen in the mirror. "Granny, it means don't worry, be happy."

"They ain't no time to be happy. I got too much to worry about."

"Uh-huh. Hold still now." Ashley chewed on her lip and concentrated on spreading eye shadow across Marvelle's wrinkled eyelids. When she finished, she tilted Marvelle's chin up and turned her face side to side. "I swear, Granny, you're still a good-looking woman."

"Don't sound so surprised."

Ashley let go Marvelle's chin and helped her up. "Let's get you under the dryer now," she said.

"Don't let me miss my story, now," Marvelle said as Ashley settled the helmet over her head.

Ashley looked at Ruth Ann's clock radio. "It's only eight-thirty, Granny. Your story don't come on till one." She plugged in the dryer, adjusted the heat setting, and clicked the on button. The dryer come on with a low whoosh, then settled into a loud whirring noise.

Ashley leaned down and yelled in Marvelle's face, "Is that all right?" When Marvelle nodded, she patted her hand and left the room.

Marvelle sighed and closed her eyes for a little nap. That gal, she thought, had a whole lot to learn, and Marvelle was just the person to teach her a thing or two about life, her being at the end of one and Ashley close enough to the beginning she hadn't started to find her way yet.

One thing I've learned in this life is that love between a man and a woman is a hard thing to hold on to. It always starts out real pretty and nice, and both of you thinks each other's perfect, but then you stay together long enough you start finding out you ain't. Little things that didn't used to bother you begins to get on your nerves.

Like Jesse. I knowed when I married him he chewed tobacco, but I didn't think a bit more of that than nothing, not till after we'd been married nearly a year. We was renting a little house over at Barnard, and Jesse was working for Dr. Miller, taking care of his property, fences, animals, things like that. Anyhow, he'd come home every day from work and the first thing he'd do was set on that porch, fill his jaw full of bacca, and spit all over my nice white porch rail. He'd aim it off in the yard somewhere, but mostly he missed, and that nasty stuff looked like shit.

We'd already been through a lot together, running off to get married, losing our first baby, making ends meet, and so I was pretty caught up in all that, and I was in love, you know, and thought a good wife ought to clean up her husband's messes. But by and by I got tired of it. And he didn't take my hints that he ought to change his habits. He'd set right there and keep a-spitting, with me on my knees in front of him scrubbing them boards. I reckon that seemed like the most natural thing in the world to him, a woman at his feet. Maybe that's every man's secret dream. But let me tell you, I set him straight on a few things real quick one night.

There's two ways to get a man to pay attention, and that's to quit cooking and to lock him out the bedroom. So that's what I done. And do you know he didn't have the first idea what I was mad about? I had to finally at last come right out and tell him, and he acted like it never entered his mind that he was making a mess and making extra work for me when I already had the work of two women to do around that place all by myself. Ooh, I flew hot then. He spent the night outside on that porch, and it nearly November and cold, Lord, it was cold that night. Well, when I come out next morning to fetch eggs, he'd not only cleaned that porch, but he'd whitewashed it too, and he painted the ceiling sky blue, just like Mama and Papa's porch at home. I never did find out where he got paint in the middle of the night.

Now, what can you do with a man like that? When he makes up to you, he more than pays the debt, he puts a little extra in the bank for the future too. Well, I got them eggs and I cooked him a great big breakfast and that's all I'm going to say about that day, but I can tell you it wasn't but about nine months till Mason was born.

That was our first disagreement, but by no means our last. I felt blessed we learned to work things out so well over them first few years together. They was no way to see then that them little storms was nothing compared to what would hit us later. I reckon we was both a little too satisfied with ourselves, so we was took unawares by the trouble come later. That's the way of things though. And just 'cause you see something coming don't mean you can stop it, so I reckon we was better off ignorant.

5

Ashley slid the glass door open and stepped onto the screened porch. The humidity wrapped her up like a warm wet veil and felt almost good after the air-conditioned house.

She was just sitting there, listening to the swing chains creak, enjoying the sun shining on the yard, when she heard the unmistakable sound of Keith's Camaro. It growled up the driveway, stopped, restarted, then sputtered to a stop again. A door slammed. He must've gone around front first, because it was several minutes before Ashley saw him come around back. She stood to latch the door and watched him walk up to the porch.

"What the hell do you want?" she said.

He stopped on the bottom step and looked up at her. "Hey," he said.

"Get off my mama's property before I call the law."

"I come all the way from Murphy just to see you."

"That ain't my problem."

"Damn, Ashley, let me talk to you?" He put his hand on the screen and stared at her like he didn't mean to quit until she let him in.

She made him wait a minute, then unlatched the door and turned away to sit on the swing, arms crossed over her chest. Keith stepped inside and leaned against the doorpost. He put his hands in his pockets and stared back at her, the blue light in his eyes throwing shadows on his cheekbones. Damn, them eyes got her every time.

"Why'd you leave without letting me know?" Keith said. He ducked his head and his hair swung around his cheeks. Ashley loved that hair, loved to squeeze the fat ponytail it made in her fist, loved the way it hung around their heads like a curtain when he was on top of her.

"You know why," she said.

He looked up then. "I said I'd marry you. I love you."

"I seen you and Cindy that night."

"What?"

"I know you fucked her in the laundry room. Probably wasn't the first time either." Ashley could feel herself getting mad all over again at the thought of that little slut with Keith.

"You're crazy."

Ashley jumped up. "No, you are, if you think I'll put up with that kind of shit from you or any man." She turned her back on him and stared out at the cement birdbath, cracked down the middle and empty of water and birds. She felt like she might cry any minute now, and she was damned if she'd let him see. "I think you ought to leave now, Keith. If Mama knowed you was here, she'd have a stroke."

"Ashley—"

"I said leave!" She listened to the long silence behind her and jumped when the door banged shut. She seen the top of his head come around the corner under the porch window, then watched him stomp around the house to the driveway. The car door slammed and the Camaro cranked on the first try. He roared out of the driveway, tires squealing as he pulled off down the road, doing about seventy from the sound of it.

Maybe he wasn't lying. Maybe Peri was right and he didn't mess around. But maybe he did. Watching her mama and daddy through the years, Ashley knew how easy it was for a man to tell a woman what he figured she wanted to hear and how easy it was for a woman to let herself believe it.

Keith was so mad all he could manage to do was drive around real fast for a while on some back roads where he wouldn't get a ticket. He wanted a beer, a lot of beers, pretty bad. But while he sat in the parking lot of the convenience store trying to decide whether or not to go in, he seen an old man in overalls come stumbling out with a six-pack, get in his old beat-up truck, and take off down the road, just a-weaving. It reminded him of so many of the old men back on the reservation when he was a little kid, reminded him exactly what he wanted to get away from.

Finally he went in and got him a Mountain Dew and stood in the parking lot and drained it. It was hot as hell when he got back in the Camaro, so he gunned it to get that two/fifty-five air-conditioning going. He was five miles down the road before he realized he didn't know where the hell he was headed. He stopped the car in the middle of the road to think it over. Probably he ought to go on back to Ashley's house and talk some sense into her. Dang if she wasn't the stubbornest woman he'd ever known. He didn't know how he could make her believe him. He never touched Cindy, in the laundry room or anywhere else. That girl wasn't nothing but a slut anyhow. No telling what all kind of diseases she carried. Keith wasn't dumb. He knew Cindy came on to him more to make Ashley mad than because she liked him, and it sure worked.

On that deserted road, so far from home, green pastures and black and white cows all around him, not a human soul in sight, Keith felt about the loneliest he'd ever felt in his life. He was scared to face Ashley, but he couldn't go back without her either. He had to try one more time. He put the car in gear and, as he swung into a U-turn, noticed a sign nailed to a fence post beside a long dirt road. HELP WANTED, it said, with directions to follow the dirt road all the way to the end and stop at the house. Keith didn't hesitate but a second before turning on to that road.

When he pulled up in front of the house, an old woman in a print dress come to the screen door, looked at him sitting there in the Camaro, latched the door, and then hollered over her shoulder for somebody named Dwight. Keith cut the motor and got out to stand next to the car so they could see him good, see that he didn't have no gun and didn't intend to kill them or nothing. He'd found that a lot of folks got nervous around Indians still, and them two in the house looked worried in case he was just a distraction while the rest of the tribe circled around to come through the back door.

"I seen your help-wanted sign, sir," Keith hollered. "Is the job taken?" There, he'd give them an easy out in case they was too scared to say they wasn't about to hire no Indian.

The old man unlatched the door and come out in the yard. Up close, he looked to be about sixty. He was a little dude, and he squinted up into Keith's face, taking stock.

"Nope," he said. "Job ain't filled yet." The old dude spit tobacco on the ground and shifted his wad to the other cheek. "What's your name, son?"

"Keith Watty."

"You ever done any dairy work?"

"Nawsir, I'm a mechanic. I can fix or drive anything with a engine in it. I'm willing to learn. I just need a job." Keith kept his eyes on the old man's face, waiting to see what his reaction would be.

They studied each other for a few seconds, then the old man started walking toward a barn not far from the house. "Let's look over here a minute," he said, pointing in front of him. "That's the milking barn. They's a place to sleep over top of it with a little kitchen and a bathroom." He spit again. "Now, son, how come you to be out here looking for a job? We don't get many strangers this way, especially none looks like you."

Keith held his breath for a minute. He didn't want to get mad and ruin his chance at a job this close. He looked off at the cow pasture, where about fifty black and white milk cows grazed near a little pond. It was a beautiful spot, and if he had his geography right, Ashley's house was just over that hill there.

"Mister, I'll be honest with you." Keith looked the old man right in the eyes. "My girlfriend lives just down the road here. We're having a little trouble right now, but if I can be close by, we might can work things out." He hesitated, then decided he might as well tell the whole truth. "She's going to have a baby in about six months."

"Is that right. What's this gal's name?"

"Ashley Payne. She's living with her mama right now. Ruth Ann Payne. Do you know them?"

"Uh-huh." The old man stuck out his hand and when Keith took it, he said, "I'm Dwight Moon. Ruth Ann's my little sister."

Keith dropped his hand and closed his eyes for a second. Well, that's the end of that, he thought. He opened his eyes and seen Dwight Moon watching him with his squinty little blue eyes.

"Well, sir, I guess I'll be going now. Sorry to take up your time." He started toward the car, but Dwight Moon called him back.

"Hey, son, where you going? I thought you wanted a job."

When Keith looked back, that old dude was grinning like a monkey and waving for Keith to follow him into the house. He introduced Keith to his wife, Betty, then took him to the apartment over the barn. It was small and clean, furnished with a single bed, a night table, a chest of drawers, and an armchair with matching hassock.

"This is nice," Keith said. "Real nice." He wiped his face with his sleeve. The room was stifling hot.

Dwight raised the windows on opposite sides of the room, and a breeze blew the curtains out. "That'll get you some cross-ventilation going in here," he said. "Ain't got no air-conditioning machine. Don't believe in the things." He walked over to the kitchen area and showed Keith the small refrigerator and stove.

"You don't believe in air-conditioning?" Keith said. He'd never thought of that as something to believe in or not. It just was.

Dwight opened the cabinets and Keith noticed the shelves neatly lined with blue shelf paper. Betty Moon had been busy in here, obviously.

"I'll tell you something, son," Dwight said, and closed the cabinet doors. "The two worst things ever invented was air-conditioning and television. First, the air-conditioning made it so folks didn't want to go out of doors no more. And since they was all cooped up inside their cold houses, they needed something to do, so some other feller invented television. Now, you tell me one good thing ever come from them two contraptions." He paused. "You can't, can you?"

"Well," Keith said. He thought for a minute. There had to be something good, because he couldn't imagine life without them, but he was damned if he could come up with it. He shook his head.

"That's what I thought," Dwight said. "They ain't never been television nor air-conditioning on this place and never will be as long as I live here and pay the bills. Now, come on and I'll show you the barn."

Keith followed Dwight down the stairs, every step taking him further and further out of the world he knew and into something that felt completely over his head. But he needed a job, and he needed to be close to Ashley. It was a perfect setup, although he felt far from perfect at that moment. Mostly he just felt scared.

As they walked back into the sunshine, an idea come over him like a wave. That help-wanted sign back at the road, that wasn't no accident. It must've been meant for him, meant to be. That sign was a sign, and he made up his mind right then and there to trust it.

In the shade beside the water, the air was almost cool, though out in the open pasture the sun blazed so hot even the cows had joined him under the trees. Keith didn't mind sharing with them. Actually, they was there first, so he was the guest, not them. He'd discovered right off that cows was nosy creatures. They must've thought he had some food, because they come crowding around when he started putting up the tent, but as soon as they found out he didn't, they moved away.

It had been a last-minute decision to bring that tent. As soon as Dwight told him he had the job yesterday, Keith headed back to Murphy to pack his stuff. He dumped his clothes in a couple of pillowcases and was about to take off when he remembered his tent. He wasn't sure what had made him think of it, and he had to go rooting around in the shed to find it. But it didn't take up much room, so he threw it in the backseat with his clothes. He left a note telling his granny and uncles where he was going, then headed back to Davis in a hurry because he wanted to start work the next day.

Dwight had looked at him kind of funny when he asked if he could pitch the tent out in the pasture, but he didn't ask no questions, and Keith didn't offer to explain. On the drive back he'd figured out what he meant to do, which was to put that tent as close to Ashley's house as he could get without being on her property. The day before he'd had a sign that he was supposed to stay right here, and he wanted to give Ashley a sign too, something she wouldn't be able to miss. He intended to tell her as soon as he seen her though, just in case she couldn't see the tent for the trees.

When he first went to live with his granny and his uncles when he was eleven, Keith had a hard time getting used to being around people all the time. At his mama's, he stayed alone a lot, and that's what he was used to. His Uncle Bill give him the tent so he could have a place to call his own when he felt like being alone, a little home away from home.

It looked like a little blue igloo parked there next to him—probably did look pretty stupid. But it felt right, and all he had to go by was feel at this point.

Probably his Cherokee ancestors had lived like this—outdoors, near water and trees and animals. He kept meaning to talk to his Uncle Bill about all that stuff, but he just never got around to it. The only stories he remembered was the ones his granny told when he was little, about how the stars got up in the sky, shit like that. He pulled off his T-shirt, then sat on the ground and leaned against a tree. The rough bark felt good against his back, and every now and then he scratched side to side like an old bear. He sat there a while, just listening to the wind in the leaves, smelling grass and cow shit, and pretty soon he started to relax and feel at home. It was almost like camping down by the creek at his granny's house.

He must've slept a while, because next thing he knew, there come a heavy crashing through the weeds and he opened his eyes to find Ashley standing over him, completely out of breath, her face red as a tomato.

When she could talk, she said, "What the hell are you doing here?" She shot a look at the tent, then back at him.

He couldn't help grinning at her, she looked so beautiful standing there with her belly sticking out just a little bit and her black curly hair pulled on top of her head in a ponytail.

"Hey," he said, yawning as he got to his feet. He grabbed her and hugged her before she could stop him, then jumped back when she slapped his arm hard. "How'd you know I was here?" he said.

"Are you crazy? I'm not blind. I come down to pet the cows and I could see you from there." Ashley folded her arms across her chest and glared at him. "It's a good thing you can't see it from the house. Mama's going to kill me if she finds out you're down here. Do you want her to kick me out?"

"She won't kick you out. And if she does, you can just come stay with me."

"In a tent? I don't think so. Where do you go to the bathroom? In the creek?"

"Dig a hole, dummy. Ain't you never been camping?"

"No, and I don't want to start now. God. You beat all I ever seen." Ashley turned her back on Keith, then faced him again. "And in case you didn't know, this is my Uncle Dwight's land and he won't like it one bit if he finds you squatting out here. He'll call the law on you." She bent and looked down in the tent. "That ain't even big enough for you to sleep in."

"Sure it is. I slept in it all the time when I was a kid."

"Yeah, but you're about two feet taller now, dummy. You'll have to sleep all curled up or else have your feet hang out the flap, and then you'll get eat up by bugs."

"Don't you worry about me. I got plenty of bug spray, and besides, I won't be out here all the time. I got me a place to live and a job."

"Yeah, right. Where?"

"Guess," Keith said. When she just stood there waiting, he said, "Your Uncle Dwight give me a job. Looking after these cows. He give me a place to sleep over the milking barn."

"Am I supposed to be impressed here?"

"Well. Yeah," he said, and grabbed her hand. "I'm going to work hard and save up money for the baby. For us."

Ashley pulled her hand away. She still looked mad. He waited.

"What the hell is this tent for then?" she said.

"To be close to you. To prove I'm serious. It's a sign, Ashley."

"A sign? What is that supposed to mean?"

"It's a sign I'm here to stay, that's what it's supposed to mean."

She looked at him then, long and hard. "I want to believe you," she said.

"But I just don't." She walked away, kicking aside branches and vines that come up around her bare legs. She'd be scratched to pieces by the time she got to the fence, but there was no talking to her now. Now was the time to wait. Keith watched her go over the fence but couldn't see her no more when she headed up the hill. That was all right though. In a couple months the leaves would fall and he'd be able to see all the way up to the house, and she'd see too, all the way back to him.

October
1992

6

As cold as it was out on the carport, Ruth Ann couldn't seem to make herself go in the house. She put her hands under her arms and leaned back against the wall with her eyes closed. Ashley and Marvelle had the back door standing open like they was expecting somebody, but she couldn't think who. They must not have heard her drive up or they'd have come out. Ruth Ann shivered and hoped they wouldn't look out the window and see her. They'd have too many questions she just didn't feel like answering right now, like what was she doing home in the middle of the day and why wasn't she at work. If only there was some way to slip past them and get to her room. But that'd never happen, and they certainly wouldn't understand her need to be alone.

She could hear them there in the kitchen, probably fixing dinner, talking a blue streak about some dumb soap opera. Honestly, they talked like the *Days of Our Lives* people lived right down the road and might drop by for a visit.

"Granny," Ashley said. "Marlena didn't really die years ago. They just wanted us to think she was dead. You know they never found her body."

"Huh," Marvelle said. "Seems to me, when most people die, they pretty much stay dead for the duration. Now, I know Doug and Julie ain't dead, and I wish they'd come back. I like to hear that Doug sing."

Ruth Ann would've got a good laugh out of that conversation if she didn't feel so damn close to crying. Okay, what were her choices here? Go in the house and probably end up screaming at Ashley and Marvelle, or else get in the car and drive, drive and drive until she felt better, then come home at her usual time just like nothing happened.

"Hey, Mrs. Payne, how you today?"

Ruth Ann's heart lurched so hard in her chest, the rest of her body jerked away from the wall like it was electrified. Damn the boy for sneaking up on her like that. Keith Watty looked entirely too at ease, slipping his skinny self up on her carport unexpected, like maybe he'd been coming up there a lot when Ruth Ann wasn't home.

"You about give me heart failure!" Ruth Ann whispered so Marvelle and Ashley wouldn't hear. "Where'd you come from? I didn't hear a car."

"I always walk across the pasture. It ain't far." Keith whispered too.

He looked so young, too young to have a job and make a baby. He also looked a little bit nervous, and considering this was the first time they'd been face to face since she found out he got her daughter pregnant, he damn well ought to be nervous. But there was something about his face, the way he held his mouth firm and looked her in the eye, that told her he wasn't as young on the inside as he looked on the outside.

"What do you mean always?" she said.

"I been coming up here to eat dinner with your mama and Ashley about every day," he said. "I hope it's all right. Your mama invited me. She said they always made plenty, and it'd give me and Ashley a chance to spend some time together. Ashley didn't act too thrilled with the idea at the time, but she still lets me come. She's getting to be a pretty good cook too. I think she's making chicken and dumplings today. Her first time."

Keith had got talking faster and faster so when he finally quit, Ruth Ann was too surprised to say anything for a minute. "Well," she said at last. Apparently there was a lot going on here during the day that she knew absolutely nothing about, but she'd have to deal with that later. What difference did it make anyhow? It was clear to her now like it never had been before that everybody in the world was going to do exactly what they pleased and didn't intend to consult Ruth Ann Payne's feelings one bit.

"Are you all right, Mrs. Payne?" Keith said.

Ruth Ann was scared she might cry in front of the boy any minute, and while he might could handle that, she certainly couldn't. "Don't call me that," she said, more hateful sounding than she intended.

"All right," he said, and looked at her with his head pulled back on his neck like he was scared she was fixing to smack him. Maybe she was. She didn't know what she might do from one second to the next.

"Just call me Ruth Ann," she said. "No Moon, no Payne, just plain old Ruth Ann, and if I could change that too I would. I'd name myself something a lot better than Ruth Ann. I'd name myself . . . oh, hell, I can't think of nothing right this minute."

"Gardenia," Keith said.

He looked as surprised as she was.

"I don't know why I said that," he said.

"For me, you mean?"

"Yeah. Probably because you got one at the corner of the house. Ain't that a gardenia back there?"

"Yes," she said.

It was quiet on the carport for a minute, and Ashley's voice carried out to them. "Are you sure that's the way it's supposed to look, Granny?"

"Uh-oh," Keith said. "I hope she ain't ruined them dumplings. You want to go in now?"

"No!" Ruth Ann said, then looked at her watch. The numbers blurred so she couldn't tell what time it was. "I got to be somewhere. You go on in, and don't tell them you seen me." She grabbed his arm. He didn't feel quite as skinny as he looked. "I mean it now. Don't say nothing."

Keith nodded, and Ruth Ann let go his arm and hurried to her car. She could make her getaway while Keith distracted them. Behind her, she heard him knock once, then open the storm door. The boy was obviously pretty comfortable letting himself into her house. She got in the car and backed into the road fast, then stopped and stared straight ahead. Where was she supposed to go now? She hated to just drive with nowhere to go— a waste of gas.

A car passed, blowing the horn, and Ruth Ann jerked her head around, then put the car in drive. Drive somewhere, drive anywhere, just keep moving. She headed toward town, blind to landmarks. Her brain was too busy panicking, so she let her arms and legs and hands and feet do the driving. They knew the way, knew where to stop, where to turn.

She had to get hold of herself. The world wasn't coming to an end, for heaven's sake. It was only a job. Why did it feel like more, then? Maybe because it was so sudden, maybe because it was so damn unfair. After thirty-three years without missing a single day except for maternity leave and her daddy's funeral, thirty-three years of hard work and building her retirement, now suddenly here she was laid off without warning of any kind. This was not supposed to happen. The plant was home. She'd spent more time there than she had with her own family. What did people do when the one thing they counted on to always be there wasn't there no more? Find another job? Where? Who in the world would hire a fifty-year-old mill worker except another mill, and there wasn't any other mills in town.

Ruth Ann took and slammed her fist against the passenger seat, hard. Then again. Damn it to hell, she didn't want to draw unemployment, didn't want another job. She wanted her old job, where she knew everybody and everybody knew her and there was no surprises. Work was safe, and now she had nowhere safe to go.

The sky let go with a light rain and Ruth Ann turned her wipers on intermittent, then noticed she was almost directly in front of Ruby's. It was one o'clock and the parking lot slam full of cars. No wonder Ruby could afford to drive a Lexus. And sure enough, there was A.J.'s truck. Ruth Ann figured he must spend at least fifty bucks a week in that place. Seemed like every time she passed and it was mealtime, there he'd be.

Almost of its own accord, her car whipped into the parking lot. She parked behind A.J. and sat there staring at the back of his truck. His vanity plates said BIG RED. Big Dummy, that's what he should've put, spending that much money on a vehicle. Did she really want to go in there and see him? She sighed, cut the engine, and got her umbrella out. As bad as things got between them, A.J. was the one person in the world she felt understood her, knew her ninety-nine point nine percent and still didn't think she should be locked up.

When she got inside, she spotted him sitting alone in a booth in the non-smoking section. She looked over at the hazy corner of the restaurant where several men that looked like house painters sat talking over cheeseburgers and onion rings and cigarettes. It was amazing how that smoke just hung in the air around them. Ruth Ann noticed things like that now she'd quit smoking herself. For about a second, she wished she could go over there and bum one drag off a cigarette. Just a little nicotine to take the edge off. The way she felt right now, it wouldn't even bother her to smoke a cigarette that had just been in somebody else's mouth. She headed over to A.J.'s booth, studying his profile as she walked toward him. Damn if he wasn't still a handsome man, even with gray at the temples and crow's feet. Why was it men got better-looking with age and women just got old?

He had some kind of papers spread out on the table, studying them so hard he didn't even notice her standing there. She cleared her throat.

"I'm fine, Toni," he said without looking up.

"Do I look like a Toni?" Ruth Ann said.

A.J.'s hands flew down over the top of the papers, then he smiled up at her and said, "Hey, baby!"

Ruth Ann recognized that guilty look right away. What was he up to now? She tried to read between his fingers but couldn't make out any words.

"Sit down," he said, and stood up. He waited for her to sit across from him, then sat back down and stuffed his papers in a manila envelope.

"What is all that?" she said. She waited to see what kind of story he was going to come up with. At least it would take her mind off her troubles for a minute.

"Oh, nothing. Just a little idea I'm working on." He put the envelope on the seat beside him and leaned toward her. "Ain't you supposed to be at work? What you doing out this time of day?"

She didn't know it was coming or she would've gone to the ladies' room. Ruth Ann started to cry. It was so embarrassing, but she couldn't stop once it started. It'd been coming on all morning. She covered her face with her hands and turned toward the wall. A minute later she felt A.J.'s body at her back, then his hand rubbing slow circles under her shoulder blades.

"It's all right now, baby. Ssshhhhhhhhh." He held a paper napkin in front of her until she took it.

A minute or two later the worst of it was over and Ruth Ann reached in her pocketbook for a mirror and a Kleenex to mop up her face a little bit. She shot a quick look around the restaurant.

"Don't worry," A.J. said. "Nobody seen you." He pushed a glass toward her. "Why don't you take you a drink of water and then tell me what's got you so upset. Is it Ashley?"

Ruth Ann shook her head. "No, she's fine." Funny how she'd never thought anything could shake up her world like one of her children, but this sure had done it. She looked A.J. square in the face and told him, "I got laid off today."

"What?"

It gave her some satisfaction to see he was as stunned as she was. "You heard me."

"What for?"

"You know all them rumors about the plant closing down?" When he nodded, she said, "Well, this time it looks like they're true."

"Do you know when?"

"When I'm laid off or when the plant's shutting down?"

"Both," he said.

"I'm laid off effective immediately. So is half the winding room and some of the girls in Quality Control. The plant's supposed to close sometime in December."

"Mary Deal too? Shit, she's less than a year away from retirement."

"They laid her off too."

"Son of a bitch. I can't believe this shit." A.J. put his arm around her shoulders. "Honey, I'm just as sorry as I can be. I know this must be hard on you. I wish there was something I could do."

Ruth Ann let herself lean against him, just for a minute. It felt so good having his arm around her, having him be sweet to her. She needed it so bad right now, just a little comfort. Wasn't nothing wrong with letting him do that, was there? She realized then she must've intended to find A.J. all along. Why else would she come right by Ruby's at his regular feeding time?

"Thank you, A.J," she said. "I just couldn't stand going home and facing Mama and Ashley yet."

"Well," he said. "If the plant's shutting down for good, I reckon this layoff is going to be permanent. Have you thought about what you're going to do now?"

Ruth Ann sighed. "I have no earthly idea," she said. She felt his chest shake and looked up at him. His lips twitched like he was trying not to smile. Was he laughing at her? If there was one thing she could not stand, it was somebody laughing at her. She jerked away and faced him. "Is there something you find amusing about my misfortune?" she snapped.

His face straightened right up. "No, ma'am," he said. "There ain't nothing funny about losing your job." Then he got this real tender look on his face, sort of smiled and shook his head. "It ain't funny funny, but it sure is funny strange, how all this is working out. Working out better than I ever could've planned it."

Working out? Did he really just say that? And did he really have a big smile on his face? God, it was just like him to think her problems didn't amount to nothing, that she could just have a good cry and then laugh it all off. Just like when they was still married and she'd be so wore out from working and taking care of the kids that she wanted to cry, and she'd try to talk to him about it and he'd act sympathetic at first, but then he'd want her to hurry up and get over it and get back to taking care of him. It was just like him.

"What the hell are you talking about?" she said. "Ain't nothing working out. Nothing, do you hear me? First I got Ashley, then Mama, moving in with me, so I got to take care of them. And now I've just lost my job. And you think it's funny? Well, I am just so damn happy I could brighten your day a little bit. Now, get out of my way. I'm leaving." She pushed against him and he scooted out of the booth. He tried to take her arm to help her up, but she jerked away. "Don't touch me," she said. "I must've been crazy coming to you for sympathy." She got out of the booth and reached back in for her pocketbook.

"Ruth Ann. Baby, come on. I wasn't laughing at you. If you'll just sit down and let me talk to you—"

"Go to hell," she said, looking him right in the eye. "Just go straight to hell." She marched out, not caring that the whole restaurant had just heard her and was now watching her leave. That was the last time she'd be fool enough to turn to him when she was in trouble. She must've been out of her mind.

The minute she stepped into the parking lot, the sky opened up and she realized she'd left her umbrella under the table in there. Damn if she'd go back for it though, and damn if she'd let him see her run. She made herself walk. By the time she got in the car, she was soaking wet and shivering and cussing A.J. for all she was worth.

He couldn't help it, he really couldn't, and probably wouldn't if he could. A.J. just let that big old smile ride right across his face and stay there. Damn it all if things didn't seem to be working out in his favor for once. Even watching Ruth Ann get soaking wet and squeal out of the parking lot like a NASCAR driver couldn't shake his feeling that things was looking up. When she was out of sight, he reached for the manila envelope. If he'd been having trouble making up his mind before, it was made up now. Ruth Ann walking in just then had been a sign, the go-ahead from God.

He'd been racking his brain for weeks, trying to come up with some way to make up to Ruth Ann, and it wouldn't hurt his feelings a bit if it also turned out to be a way to get her back. At first all he could think of was little things, like writing letters or sending flowers, but the situation called for something way bigger than that. Then he thought of maybe buying her a car or sending her on a cruise where he just might show up too. Anything could happen on a boat in the middle of the ocean with plenty of good food and liquor to soften Ruth Ann up. But he knew she'd never go on a cruise by herself, which dropped him back to sending flowers. And that's what made him remember.

Years ago, when the kids was still home and Ruth Ann and A.J. was so busy they hardly ever seen each other, they'd got the idea of opening their own business. Really it was a buddy of A.J.'s who was in the florist business that put the idea in their heads. Roger Cox wanted to sell out, and he give A.J. the option to buy, plus he'd stay on and run the place until A.J. and Ruth Ann caught on to how things worked and could do it themselves. It was about the closest they ever got to each other, the hours they spent daydreaming about it and planning. Best sex they ever had too. Ruth Ann was on fire all the time then. As soon as they started talking about the business, something inside her lit up and she started talking about being her own boss and fulfilling her potential and things like that.

It amazed A.J. He'd never realized Ruth Ann was a dreamer. When he married her, he thought she was a girl like all the other girls he'd been with who just wanted to get married and settle down. She was a good housekeeper, a good cook, a good mama, and he always tried to let her know how much he appreciated her keeping their lives running so smooth. Beyond that, he didn't think about what went on inside her head too much, except for the times she blew up at him or went on strike. He figured she had everything she wanted and was happy with the way things was going along.

But he found out different.

There was stuff inside Ruth Ann like he never imagined, things she wanted for herself that had nothing to do with him or the kids. And what made him feel so bad, worse than the fact that he'd never noticed this side of Ruth Ann himself, was seeing how guilty it made her feel. He'd always gone right after what he wanted without a thought in the world for what somebody else might think about it. But seemed like women got eat up with guilt over the least little thing.

Of course, in the end it hadn't worked out. They'd both put in too many years with their other jobs to give up retirement and benefits, and they had the kids to think about. The truth was, they was too scared to try, both of them. For about three months there they rode high on that dream, then they fell off and let it go. The dream had drifted back this week though, and A.J. intended to grab it and ride it out if it killed him.

He'd run into Roger Cox the other day at the gas station, and old Roger was still in the flower business and ready to retire. Seemed he'd chickened out too all them years ago and decided to stick with a sure thing. As long as people died or fell in love or cheated on their wives or had mamas, they'd always need flowers. That's what appealed to A.J. over the other businesses he'd considered at the time. With a restaurant, you always had to worry about people going somewhere else better or cheaper, or even staying home. And a gas station was just too much work. And most businesses, you had to worry about hiring good help, and that was a hassle right there. But a florist, now him and Ruth Ann could run that themselves, no sweat.

With Roger ready to sell out, the same deal all over again, and now with the sign from Ruth Ann, A.J. knew the timing was perfect. He'd have to go careful though, or she'd tell him what he could do with his flowers. He'd have to find a way to convince her it'd work, that she could afford it, that she could tolerate working with him every day. The fact she'd come looking for him today give him a lot of hope. She must need him for something, and if he could just figure out what it was, he could use it to get her back.

Ideas and plans tumbled around his head like laundry so he couldn't concentrate no more. The rain had quit, and the sun made drops of water shine like dimes on his truck. A.J. leaned back in the booth and stretched. Yeah, things was looking up for A. J. Payne, and just to be safe he said a little prayer of thanks to whoever or whatever had decided to help him out. It was about time.

Ashley helped Marvelle out of the taxi and took her arm as they headed toward the mall entrance. The afternoon was cool, but by the time they got inside, Marvelle was sweating and breathing hard and had to sit down to rest on one of the benches in the atrium.

"Honey, I can't do a lot of walking today," she said. "You go on and get what you need and I'll wait here." Marvelle fanned her face with her hand and looked around at the giant ficus trees in pots the size of washing machines. "Lord, this place looks like a jungle in here."

"Granny, I can't leave you here. I'll rest with you till you feel better, then we can go to the bookstore."

"A bookstore? Don't you know it's a waste to buy books when there's a perfectly good library down the road?"

"We're looking for a different kind of books," Ashley said.

"Huh?"

"I thought it'd be fun to get us some puzzle books."

"Are you talking about crossword puzzles?"

"Yes, Granny, and any other kind of puzzles, like find-a-words."

"Huh. Well, you can just go on without me. I'm content to set right here and watch the world go by."

Ashley stood over her for a minute, then realized it was hopeless to try and talk Marvelle out of anything once she'd made up her mind. "Okay, Granny, but I'll be back here in twenty minutes, so stay put, okay?"

Marvelle waved her hand at Ashley, shooing her away. "I can look after myself. Go on now."

Ashley looked back over her shoulder once as she rounded the corner. Marvelle, sitting under the skylight in her blue floweredy dress, looked like some kind of little bird perched on the bench under all them hothouse trees. Sunlight filtered through the leaves and surrounded Marvelle without actually touching her. She didn't look quite real from this distance. Ashley shivered and turned away. She couldn't understand why they kept it so damn cold in the mall, maybe to get people to hurry in and hurry out, make room for the next batch of customers. She walked as fast as she could to warm herself up and to make sure she got back before Marvelle decided to stop watching the world go by and got lost in it instead.

Ashley bought three puzzle books—one with crosswords, one with find-a-words, and one with all different kinds. Then she went in Rose's and bought a couple of thousand-piece jigsaw puzzles and a Chinese checkers game. Marvelle could work the puzzle books on her own when Ashley was busy, and they could play checkers and work jigsaw puzzles together when they had time. That was one thing Ashley did remember about her granny. That woman dearly loved to work jigsaw puzzles. Ashley had already dug out a card table from the storage room so they could set it up and leave it in the living room with the puzzle on it. That way they could go and work on it whenever they took a notion, and it would always be convenient. Even though Ashley had set the table in the corner out of the way, she knew her mama would pitch a fit about having a card table in her living room. Ruth Ann would have the rest of her life to get over it though. This was important.

Earlier in the week, flipping through an old *Life* magazine in the bathroom, Ashley come across an article about a bunch of nuns somewhere in Minnesota, or one of them cold states, who all lived to be about a hundred years old and never got senile or sick or nothing. When they finally did die, it was just from old age, pure and simple. Some guy doing a brain study on them found out that by working around the convent, playing musical instruments, and doing puzzles, they was able to live longer and stay in their right minds the whole time. The work kept their bodies going, while the music and the puzzles expanded their brain connections so that if they did have a stroke or anything like that, they had some extra brain connections up there to make up for the ones they lost. Made perfect sense to Ashley, and she immediately thought that might be the way to help Marvelle.

Of course, she couldn't come right out and tell Marvelle why she wanted her to start doing puzzles. Even though Ashley was positive her granny knew she was not always right in the head, Marvelle got mad as a hornet if anybody tried to talk to her about it. No, Ashley would casually bring them out one day like it was just for fun, and Marvelle'd never know what hit her.

Marvelle sat real still, watching people pass by. She felt almost like she was at a circus, there was so many different things to look at. Lord, the whole place just a-working alive with people, and all of them looking like if they didn't get wherever it was they was a-going, they might bust. Young mothers pushing their babies in strollers, old people in jogging suits walking real fast around and around the mall, old black men sitting on the bench down the way from her, smoking cigars and laughing. She couldn't understand what all these people was doing here in the middle of the day. Didn't they have jobs? Marvelle shook her head. It was sad, it really was, folks just going around in circles wasting time when there was so much to be done in the world.

For a long time she watched two teenage girls that was walking up and down the mall smoking cigarettes one after the other and laughing and punching each other as they went in and out of stores, not buying nothing, just making the salespeople watch them sharp. They had their hair teased up a foot in front and flat as a pancake in back, makeup so thick it'd take a jackhammer to get it off. Them gals ought to be in school this time of day, Marvelle thought. Where was their parents? She wondered if anybody knowed or even cared where they was or what they was a-doing.

Why, when she was a girl that age she already had two young'uns to look after. She didn't have time to gad about shopping and acting a fool all day. And even if she hadn't been married and had young'uns, her mama and papa would've never allowed her to act in such a way as that or go in public looking like a painted-up whore. Marvelle put her hands on her knees and pushed herself to her feet. Them two gals needed a little talking to, and she was just the person to do the talking.

Marvelle held on to the handrail and walked carefully up the steps leading out of the atrium. She got the girls in her sights and headed over to them. The going was tough without her walker, but she hadn't thought she'd need it with Ashley to lean on. She had to get to them two girls though. Up close, she could see they was right pretty little things, a little older than they looked from a distance, maybe Ashley's age, and empty-headed as the day is long. Well, their little heads was fixing to get filled up with something.

"Hey, you two!" Marvelle said.

The girls stopped giggling, turned, and looked Marvelle up and down. "Are you talking to us?" the blond one said.

"Yes, honey, I certainly am. What's your name?" Marvelle faced them, swaying a little bit. She spread her feet wider apart to get her balance.

"Puddintain. Ask me again and I'll tell you the same." The red-haired girl laughed, but she stopped when Marvelle grabbed her arm and held on tight.

"You listen here, missy. Don't be sassing me, neither one of you." She grabbed the blond girl's arm with her other hand. They didn't pull away, just stared at her all wide-eyed like they didn't know what to make of her. "I been watching you two, and you're headed for trouble if you don't change your ways."

Both girls jerked their arms away at the same time and rubbed them. Marvelle's grip had left fingerprints.

"You look, old lady," the blond one said. "You ain't my mama, so why don't you just go the hell on." She looked a little bit afraid as she turned to the redhead and said, "Come on, Brenda, let's get out of here. This old bat's crazy."

"What did you call me? What did you say? Come back here, hussy. I'm not through with you yet." Marvelle was determined to do something for them girls if it killed her. They didn't know how foolish they was being or how much they had to lose, and Marvelle knew she probably didn't have much of a chance of teaching them anything in such a short amount of time, but she had to try. The girls laughed and run a little ways, then stopped and waited for her to come closer. As soon as she'd get almost near enough to grab them, they'd run a little farther. Lord help me, she prayed. Show me the way to help my girls.

When Ashley reached the atrium and found Marvelle gone, her first thought was that her mama was going to kill her. The one thing she'd managed to get pretty good at in the last couple months—keeping up with Marvelle—and she'd done screwed that up too. Then she started to worry about what might have happened to Marvelle in the twenty or so minutes she'd been gone. Ashley run out in the central aisle of the mall and looked toward the Belk's end. Nothing. She turned and looked toward the Dillard's end and at first saw nothing there either, then she heard a commotion and seen a little patch of blue.

Ashley felt like she was running a gauntlet as she passed through people lining either side of the aisle. Then she seen what they was all so interested in. Marvelle looked to be chasing—if you could call it a chase at that speed—two girls down the mall, yelling at them to come back because she wasn't done talking to them yet. Ashley stopped dead and stared. What the hell was she trying to do? Then she seen that the two girls had run back and was laughing in Marvelle's face, taunting her, holding their arms out and then snatching them back. Ashley's face got hot and she stomped over to Marvelle and put her arm around her shoulders. She looked at the two girls, ready to tell them to go to hell, when she realized she knew them.

"Karen? Brenda? What the hell's going on here?"

"Do you know these two hussies, Ashley?" Marvelle was breathing hard and Ashley could feel her trembling all over.

Know them, hell. It was like looking in a mirror.

"Well, hey, Ashley. Where you been?" Karen pulled a pack of cigarettes out of her pocket and lit up. Brenda did the same.

"How do you know these girls?" Marvelle said, and looked up at Ashley.

"From school, Granny. But I don't have nothing to do with them no more."

"Well, I'm glad to hear it. These two been giving me a time today."

"This your granny?" Karen said. "You better get her back on her leash. She's dangerous."

Marvelle's hand squeezing her arm was the only thing that kept Ashley from telling the bitch to shut her fucking mouth. It wouldn't do to get in a fight with these two losers.

"Yeah, Ashley," Brenda said. She took a long drag off her cigarette and stared at Ashley through the smoke as she exhaled. "Whatever happened to you anyway? You sure did drop out of sight. We heard you checked in the nuthouse."

Marvelle stepped in front of Ashley and said, "Well, wherever she's been, she's certainly going better places than the two of you is headed if you don't change your ways."

Ashley put her hands on Marvelle's shoulders. "Come on, Granny, we got to go. Keith's probably waiting on us in the parking lot by now."

"My work here ain't done yet," Marvelle said. She tried to shrug off Ashley's hands.

"Don't waste your breath, Granny." Ashley got Marvelle turned around and they walked toward the nearest exit. She looked back over her shoulder once and seen Karen and Brenda still standing there watching them.

"Hey, Ashley," Karen yelled. "Your granny's fucking crazy! You should've took her to the nuthouse with you." Then her and Brenda laughed and headed down the mall in the other direction.

Yeah, well, fuck you both, Ashley thought. The best thing she could do right now was get Marvelle home and try to forget about the whole thing. There was no forgetting some things though, no matter how hard she tried.

"Are you coming?" Marvelle said.

Ashley hadn't even realized she'd stopped moving. Marvelle pulled on her hand and said, "Come on, let's go before I miss my story."

"Granny," Ashley said. "We done watched your story, remember? It's nearly five o'clock now."

"Oh," Marvelle said. "Well, then, we best get on home and get supper for your mama."

They waited for Keith outside in front of the drugstore, watching people go in and out. Ashley didn't see anybody else she knew, which was a blessing. She felt numb after seeing Karen and Brenda. They'd never been that tight, just partied together, and she didn't care if she ever seen either of them again, really. So why was it still bothering her?

"Them two gals is right pitiful, ain't they?" Marvelle said.

"What?" Ashley looked down at Marvelle. She felt like a giant standing next to her.

"I said they're pitiful. What kind of mama and daddy lets them run wild like that? They're going to end up in a bad way, and nobody to care."

"Granny," Ashley said. "What exactly did you think you was going to do if you caught them?"

"Lord, honey, I don't rightly know," Marvelle said. "Give them a piece of my mind, I reckon."

"Well, Granny, you ain't got none to spare, so from now on you better just keep it to yourself. You might've got hurt."

Marvelle's fingers dug into Ashley's arm. "You look here, missy. I'm eighty-two years old. I've took care of myself at least seventy-five of them years and I ain't about to quit now."

Ashley didn't know what to say. For an old lady that looked like she was about to fall over, Marvelle still had a will that would not bend. She had to admire that, even while she knew that what Marvelle had just done was crazy. At least, it appeared crazy to the rest of the world. After the last weeks together, Ashley was beginning to see how her granny's mind worked.

"I know," Ashley said. "I know you just wanted to help, but they really ain't nothing you can do, unless of course you want to go live with them instead of me." Ashley smiled.

"They Lord, honey, they'll be fifty years old by the time I get done with you. You're a big project all by yourself."

Ashley nearly dropped her shopping bag when a car horn sounded behind them. They turned to look. "Our ride's here," she said. The Camaro idled so loud that people stared as they walked by.

Keith got out and opened the door for them. "Looks like y'all got what you come for," he said.

Ashley set the shopping bag on the backseat, then climbed in after it.

Marvelle held on to Keith's arm until her butt hit the seat, then let go and swung her legs in one at a time. She sighed and laid her head back as Keith slammed the door shut.

Ashley hadn't realized until then that Marvelle was wore out. She leaned up between the seats. "We'll be home before you know it, Granny," she said. She turned to Keith. "Thanks for coming after us."

Keith patted his belly. "Y'all keep feeding me the way you been doing, I'll take you anywhere you want to go. At least till I get too fat to fit behind the wheel."

Marvelle opened her eyes and looked over at Keith. "Reckon you got a tapeworm?" she said.

"What?" Keith shot a look at her, then concentrated on pulling out on the road.

"Must be you got a tapeworm. Or a hollow leg, because I can't see where all them groceries is a-going." Marvelle laughed and closed her eyes again. "Just like Jesse. Eat like a horse, and I'm the one got fat."

"Hey, Granny," Ashley said. "Maybe after you have you a little nap, we can try one of them jigsaw puzzles."

"Honey," Marvelle said. "They ain't no try about it. Either we'll do it or we won't."

"Well, then," Ashley said. "I reckon we will."

Even with the windows of the Buick rolled up, Ruth Ann could hear the young'uns shrieking in Cassandra's backyard. How in the world did she stand that racket all day long, all them young'uns that wasn't even hers?

Ruth Ann got out of the car and walked around the side of the house. Sure enough, there they all were, six preschoolers bundled up in pink and yellow and blue jackets, and Cassandra in her white cotton pants and smock. Their mama was right. She did look like a big nurse in that outfit. Of course, Cassandra's reasoning made sense. The white was easier to clean—just bleach out the jelly and snot and blood and poop and spaghetti sauce. Plus it did make her look more like a professional, like somebody to trust your children with.

Ruth Ann leaned on the chain-link fence. Cassandra was pushing two little girls on the swings, turning every few seconds to watch three little boys fighting for the slide and another little girl sitting by herself in the sandbox playing dolls. No doubt about it, Cassandra was good with kids. She'd always loved to play with Angela and Alex and Ashley when they was little. The thing about Cassandra was, she still remembered what it felt like to be a child.

Ruth Ann said hey and Cassandra looked up, her face first startled, then worried. Ruth Ann knew she had some explaining to do, but somehow it seemed easier with Cassandra, not like with her mama or Ashley. She let herself in the gate and met Cassandra halfway across the yard.

"What's wrong? Is it Mama?"

Ruth Ann shook her head. "No, everybody's fine," she said.

Cassandra looked into Ruth Ann's face for a minute, then put a hand on her elbow and led her over to a bench facing the kids.

"Here. Sit down." Cassandra pushed Ruth Ann down on the bench. "Watch the kids a minute while I get us something to drink." She disappeared in the house and come back a few minutes later with two mugs.

The cup warmed Ruth Ann's hands and made her feel more like she was back in the world again. She blew steam off and watched it drift up and disappear over her head. It was a beautiful fall day, the sky sapphire blue and leaves falling all around. It was funny how the whole world could be falling apart and still look so normal.

The bench creaked when Cassandra sat down and put her arm along the back, behind Ruth Ann's head. Ruth Ann looked over at her and tried to smile. "I lost my job today," she said.

"What?" Cassandra said. "What happened?"

"Laid off. The plant's closing for good at Christmas."

"I can't believe it," Cassandra said. "That's a hell of a birthday present."

Ruth Ann's birthday Monday was the least of her concerns. She'd just as soon forget about it. She sipped the hot coffee and found it had a little whiskey mixed in. She looked over at Cassandra and raised an eyebrow.

"It's just a little bit," Cassandra said. "You looked like a ghost standing there. Like to scared me to death."

Ruth Ann took another sip and sat back with her eyes closed. She was glad she'd worn long sleeves and a sweater today, the air was so chilly. She shivered and held the coffee close to her face.

"What you going to do?" Cassandra said.

"I have no idea," Ruth Ann said.

From a long way away, she heard the kids start screaming, then Cassandra yelled, "Jason! Travis! You quit that right now. Don't make me have to come over there!" They stopped long enough to listen to Cassandra, then started up again. Cassandra sighed and said, "I'll be right back."

Ruth Ann felt her weight leave the bench, but still didn't open her eyes. It was peaceful just sitting, not thinking, not moving. She sipped from the cup, and the whiskey-laced coffee slid sweet and warm down her throat. Happy birthday to me, she thought.

She heard leaves rustling, then soft breathing near her knees. Ruth Ann opened her eyes then and seen a little girl about four standing in front of her, staring. She blinked, not recognizing her at first, thinking only that she looked so familiar. Then Ruth Ann realized she was the one who'd been playing dolls by herself in the sandbox. She was a pretty child, with long dark hair and brown eyes. The little girl come closer, then climbed right up in Ruth Ann's lap and snuggled against her. Ruth Ann sat there stunned, automatically holding the hot coffee away so the girl wouldn't get burned.

In an instant she was pulled away, outside of time to a memory of herself in her mama's kitchen, about the same age as this little girl. All day she'd pestered her mama to let her help cook, and her mama kept shooing her away. Ruth Ann remembered standing by the stove, looking up at the pot handle, reaching for it, watching it fall. Her mama was making chicken and dumplings for dinner, and the broth splashed over the sides of the pot when it landed bottom down on the wood floor. A few dumplings bounced out and slid across the floor, and only a little of the broth splattered Ruth Ann's legs and feet, but it was hot enough to blister. She screamed, lifting first one foot, then the other off the floor, holding her arms up for her mama to get her. Marvelle just stared for a minute, it all happened so fast. Then she got mad, madder than Ruth Ann had ever seen her. She didn't say nothing, just grabbed Ruth Ann's arm and dragged her across the kitchen to the corner where the hutch sat. She pulled a piece of binder's twine out of a drawer and tied Ruth Ann's ankles together, then tied them to the foot of the hutch. Ruth Ann kept screaming and crying while Marvelle put the pot of chicken and dumplings back on the stove and cleaned the floor. Then she stood over the sink with her back to Ruth Ann, just stood there for the longest time, not moving.

A little while later, when Ruth Ann sat crying quietly in the corner, Dwight come in from helping his daddy with the milking. He was nearly sixteen then, and to Ruth Ann the sun rose and set in her brother. He didn't let the other boys pick on her, and he brung her candy when she was good.

He stood froze in the doorway, looking first at Ruth Ann, then at Marvelle. "Godamighty, Mama, what in hell's going on?" he said. He come and untied Ruth Ann and sat down at the table with her on his lap. When he seen where the twine had rubbed raw red circles on her ankles and the little white blisters from the hot broth, he told Marvelle to bring a pan of cold water and a soft rag. She did just what he said and stood watching him wash Ruth Ann's legs. Ruth Ann remembered his face then, how it almost didn't look like him. He wasn't one to get mad easy. He always stayed calm, no matter what might be going on, no matter how upset everybody else got.

"Mama," Dwight said slow and quiet. "I want to know what happened here." He rinsed the rag and spread it across Ruth Ann's legs. The cool wet soothed the burning some.

Marvelle sat on a chair and stared like she wasn't quite sure where she was or who they was. "She pulled the pot down on her," she said. "I told her not to go near the stove."

"Mama, she's just a little girl," Dwight said. "She ain't no animal to be hobbled and left to suffer."

Marvelle blinked then and reached out a hand to touch Ruth Ann's hair. Ruth Ann shrunk back against Dwight, hiding her face in his chest. She remembered his clean smell, like cow and sawdust. He still smelled that way.

Marvelle's hand stopped halfway to petting and halfway to pulling back. "I wasn't even thinking," she said. "I just done it and didn't even know what I was a-doing, I was so mad." She took her hand back and curled it into a fist against her belly. She looked at Dwight then. "It'll not happen again," she said. Ruth Ann remembered them staring at each other over the top of her head.

They just sat like that for a while, until Dwight said, "I smell something burning."

"What?" Marvelle said. "Oh, Lord." She jumped up and run to the stove. The door banged down when she opened it and she reached bare-handed for the smoking pan inside. She screamed and dropped the pan, turned in a circle, then run out the open door, crying.

They watched her run into the trees and disappear, then Dwight got up and set Ruth Ann on the chair. He took pot holders and picked the pan up off the floor. It had landed top down, and pieces of cake stuck to the floor when he lifted it. He picked up the pieces and dumped everything in the slop bucket. "Cake," he said. "Pound cake. Birthday cake, I reckon." He stared down in the bucket a long time.

Finally he come and hunkered down in front of Ruth Ann. He tapped her cheek with his knuckles like knocking on a door, and she smiled. When he opened his hand in front of her eyes, she said, oh, and reached for the silver dollar. "Happy birthday, honey," he said. Then he got up and went out the door. Ruth Ann sat right where he left her, holding her silver dollar and watching the door.

Directly they come back, and Marvelle put Ruth Ann on her hip while she finished fixing dinner, then they made another cake together and covered it with brown sugar icing. Brown sugar pound cake was her favorite then, still was. What remained most vivid in Ruth Ann's memory even now was the sweet, sweet of that cake in the kitchen still smelling of something burned.

The little girl reached up and patted Ruth Ann's cheek so Ruth Ann would look at her. "All better now?" she said. Ruth Ann realized she'd been staring at the little girl without really seeing her. She blinked and nodded. "I'm just fine, honey," she said. It still surprised her this child had come to her. Ruth Ann wasn't the type of woman children just naturally wanted to snuggle with. Not even her own children. Now, Cassandra was a natural-born snuggler, big and soft and slow and easygoing. But Ruth Ann was always too bony, too busy, too something.

The little girl slid off her lap and run toward the house when Cassandra started calling the kids, rounding them up to go in. It was getting late and their lips was starting to turn blue. A young'un would stay outside and play until it froze to death, Ruth Ann reckoned. She felt like laughing suddenly, watching Cassandra. She looked like a big sheepdog, chasing after them young'uns, herding them, barking at them to quit running back to the swings, quit picking at one another, hush up, line up, get in the house. She finally caught the two little boys who'd run from her, grabbed them up and hugged them, then carried them squirming and giggling into the house with the other four following behind, jumping around her and all talking at once.

Ruth Ann sat with her arms wrapped around herself and the empty coffee mug beside her. The empty quiet made her feel lonesome somehow.

Cassandra opened the back door and leaned out. "Come on in the house," she said. "You're going to get sick if you stay out here. The young'uns'll be leaving in half an hour, then we can make us some supper."

"No, I think I'm ready to go home now."

"You sure?" Cassandra said.

Ruth Ann stood up and pulled her keys out of her pocket. "I'm sure," she said.

"Mama? Mama!" Ruth Ann closed the back door behind her and walked into the kitchen. "Ashley?" She laid her keys and her pocketbook on the kitchen table, then took off her sweater and laid it over a chair. Now where had them two got to? They didn't have no car. For a minute Ruth Ann felt panicky, thinking that the bus didn't run out this far, but the ambulance sure did. Then she seen the note on the counter.

Dear Mama,

In case you get home before us, me and Granny went to the mall. There's barbecue chicken in the Crock-Pot, and we'll make supper as soon as we get home.

Ashley

Ruth Ann put the note down and felt herself getting mad. They had no business taking off to the mall like that, one nearly six months pregnant and the other weak as water. She turned and leaned against the counter and seen the Crock-Pot sitting next to the sink. Beads of water clung to the underside of the clear glass lid, and she realized she'd been smelling the chicken ever since she walked in the door. It smelled good.

Ruth Ann decided then and there it was pointless to be mad. Ashley and Marvelle was both adults and could take care of themselves. They'd been doing a good job the last couple of months. It was funny how she got so busy with work and her own concerns, she hadn't stopped to notice that not only was Ashley and Marvelle staying out of trouble, they was running the house, cooking and cleaning and all. The only thing Ruth Ann had to fool with anymore was shopping, and that was just because she was the one with the money and the car.

She picked ten new red potatoes out of the tater box, turned on the cold water, and started scrubbing dirt off the potatoes. She'd roast them with some baby carrots and onions and heat up some rolls and have supper ready by the time everybody got home. Ruth Ann hummed to herself. She couldn't remember the last time she'd stood at this sink making supper. It felt good to be back, like she'd been on a trip somewhere and hadn't even known she was gone until she got home again. Was it just this morning she walked out of the plant feeling like the world was coming to an end?

Well, her life wasn't over by a long shot. She could see that now. There was millions of things she could do, and by God she'd find something. Fifty-one wasn't nearly old enough to sit down and give up. Hell, her mama was eighty-two and she still hadn't slowed down, though Lord knows she had plenty of reason.

When the vegetables was set in the oven to cook, Ruth Ann checked the chicken, then turned the Crock-Pot on low. As she put the lid back on, she heard Keith's Camaro rattling up the driveway. She went to the back door and watched him help Marvelle out of the front seat, then pull Ashley out of the back. Lord have mercy, how in the world did she get herself wedged in that tiny little space? When Keith finally got her out, Ashley laughed as she fell against him, then she reached back in for a big shopping bag. What could they have bought? Ruth Ann pushed out the screen door and held it while Keith took Marvelle's elbow and helped her step up into the house.

"Hey, Mama. Did y'all have fun?" Ruth Ann said as she studied Marvelle's face. She looked tired.

Marvelle grunted and passed on by.

Keith whispered, "She's got to go."

Ashley stepped in behind Marvelle, then leaned back and kissed Ruth Ann's cheek. "Hey, Mama," she said.

Ruth Ann looked at Keith. "Don't tell me. She's got to go too."

"Uh-huh." Keith stood there with his hands in his pockets, looking at Ruth Ann, then turned and ran toward his car. "I forgot something," he hollered over his shoulder. It took him two tries to get the door open. Ruth Ann wondered if he was going to keep driving that monster until all the parts fell off. She started to step back inside and let the door close, but Keith hollered for her to close her eyes.

"What for?" she said.

"It's a surprise."

Ruth Ann closed her eyes, though she was a little concerned about what kind of surprise a boy like Keith might come up with. She just wished he'd hurry so she could quit standing there holding the door. She heard his footsteps and braced herself. He stood in front of her and she heard something crackling like paper or foil.

"Okay," he said.

She smelled the mums before she seen them, and knew somehow they'd be yellow. When she opened her eyes all she could see was yellow, and she opened her arms to it in delight.

Keith leaned sideways and let the door hit his shoulder so it wouldn't bang against Ruth Ann when she let go. "Ashley said your birthday's Monday, but I figured I better go ahead and give them to you now, before they wilt or something."

The flowers swayed back and forth in their pot as she took them from Keith's hands. Oh, she had missed mums, and all her flowers, which she hadn't had time to fool with in years. She looked at Keith over the top of the pot, stared steadily for a good long minute. His face turned a little red, but he stood in front of her and stared back, letting her look all she liked, not trying to turn away or hide.

Dwight had told her last week what a good job the boy was doing, how he was really earning his keep and then some. Only this was no boy in front of her, and she guessed she'd better get used to that fact. She broke the staring contest and looked over his head toward the Camaro.

"Keith, when you going to get you a decent car to drive? That piece of junk out there looks like it's held together with chewing gum."

Keith turned and studied the car too. After a minute, he said, "Well, I'm still working on her. It'll take me a while to save up for parts and make time to do the work myself, but I'm patient, and she's worth it."

Ruth Ann looked down on the top of his black head and noticed how long and clean and shining his hair was. She hadn't noticed that when she seen him at dinnertime. Her hand twitched with the need to smooth it for him, pet his head like she used to do her own children when they filled her heart so she didn't have any words. He looked lonely there on the carport with his back to her, just a skinny young man who wasn't near as cocksure as he acted.

"Come on in this house and eat," she said. "We're having barbecue chicken, and right now I'm starving." She didn't have to ask him twice.

My Ruth Ann was forever and always in love with flowers and beautiful things. I reckon being such a pretty child herself, she was naturally drawn to beauty. Nothing could've surprised me more than to have such a handsome young'un in the family. Not that the Moons or the Dockerys was ugly or nothing like that, mind you. But we wasn't beautiful by no stretch of the imagination. I can't recall anybody truly beautiful in my family or Jesse's for that matter. Some real attractive folk on both sides, tall and lean and sharp-featured on his side, and short and plump and round-faced on mine. Seems Ruth Ann got the best of both sides. Everybody always said she could've been in the movies, she was so pretty, and I reckon she could if she'd took a mind to. She's got them high cheekbones like my great-grandma Josephine had, them Cherokee cheekbones, and that pretty white skin, like milk, and them blue eyes and dark hair. I reckon that gal Elizabeth Taylor couldn't be no prettier than my Ruth Ann.

Lord, we had a time with that one when she got old enough to draw the attention of the fellers, but when she was little, why, she didn't care a bit more for her appearance than nothing. If she'd had her way, she'd have run wild outside all day naked as the day she was born, which she sometimes did when she could slip off without me a-seeing her. When she got old enough to where I could let her play outside in the warm weather without watching her, she'd disappear for hours at a time. I always knowed where to look for her if I needed her though. From April till October, she'd be in them woods hunting things. Not things like her brothers though, not squirrels and bluejays and rabbits. Ruth Ann couldn't bear to see nothing killed. No, she hunted stuff she could bring home and have a little bit of something pretty in the house. We never had no money for pictures or set abouts. Them things was all luxuries back then, not like they are now where you can buy everything in the world for a dollar, seems like. That Ruth Ann though, she couldn't bear living in a place unadorned.

In the spring, Ruth Ann loved the daffodils, but the smell of them things closed up in the house made my head hurt, so she'd just dig up bulbs in the fall and plant them out back. Lord, by the time that girl was twelve or thirteen, I bet she had a acre of them things growing out there.

Course, Dwight plowed them all up after Ruth Ann left and got married so he could plant sorghum for them cows. I hated to see them stinking yellow flowers go. It was a miracle ever spring to look out the kitchen window and see that blazing yellow, like the sun looking at its own reflection on earth.

Things I did let Ruth Ann bring in the house was the forsythia and the quince. She'd cut limbs of them things and put them in a old broke pitcher or something and set them about the house. She liked to bring in ferns and pinecones and pretty little rocks too. She never would cut any of the dogwood limbs though. She said it'd be sacrilege, and I had to agree with her there.

I remember finding her one day in the woods laying under this great big dogwood tree in full bloom. She was just a-laying there, not doing nothing but looking up through the limbs to the sky, and when I come up on her and said hey, she set up straight and I could see she'd been a-crying. I said, why, honey, what's the matter? and set down next to her, and she just shook her head and looked down at her hands. Then she looked back at me and said, oh, Mama, it's so beautiful I can't stand it, that's all. And she laid her head on my shoulder and cried some more, and then I set in to crying too.

Well, that was the spring she started her cycle, and I figured the whole world was beginning to look different to her then, the way it looks different to a woman than to a child, and that's enough to make anybody cry, the pain of being in that in-between place and not knowing where you belong. So we cried a little bit, and then directly we went on home and got supper ready together without saying a word. That day me and Ruth Ann didn't need no words, and let me tell you, that's the closest I think I ever felt to any of my young'uns, as far as just being two equal people together and not mother and child. It's something I wouldn't mind having more of, but don't seem like none of us can ever get to that place again, and I think it's a shame, a durn shame.

We're not going to the mountains today." Ruth Ann switched the phone to her other ear and reached for her coffee.

"Why not?" Cassandra said. Ruth Ann knew she was used to sleeping late on Saturday mornings, and she sounded like she was still in the bed.

" 'Cause my car won't start this morning," Ruth Ann said. "I got A.J. coming over here to look at it, but we might as well wait till another day."

"Well, why can't we just go in my van? There's plenty of room and it's running fine. A.J. just had it tuned up for me a month ago."

"Your van? There's probably so much junk in there we'd never fit the four of us in."

"Well, I'll have you know I keep that van clean. It ain't like my car was. And I just happen to have a full tank of gas."

Ruth Ann sighed. "Okay, get your tail over here quick, then." She hung up the phone. There was no getting out of this one. Ever since Ashley had told her Marvelle wanted to go see Madison County one last time, and Ashley wanted to visit her friend Peri at Appalachian Hall, Ruth Ann had been trying to think of a reason not to go. Ashley had even suggested driving herself and her granny so Ruth Ann could stay home. But even though Ashley had been behaving herself, and she was a big help with Mama and the house and the cooking, it had only been two months and that was not much to go on. Ruth Ann had just now got to the point where she wasn't surprised every day that she come home and found Ashley still there. For the longest time she expected her to run off again, just disappear like she done last time.

She couldn't come up with a good reason not to go to Madison County, so Ruth Ann finally agreed to take them, and she asked Cassandra to go along for moral support. She knew Cassandra would jump at the chance to take what she called a road trip. That was the difference in their outlooks. To Ruth Ann it was an ordeal. Well, hell, she was unemployed now. It wasn't like she had to spend the weekend catching up on chores and resting for the week ahead.

Ashley had already helped Marvelle out of her coat and they was just sitting there on the couch flipping through channels on the television, the volume turned up entirely too loud. Nothing on Saturday morning but cartoons. Ruth Ann watched them for a minute from the doorway. As they leaned back on the sofa, hands resting on their stomachs, legs stretched in front of them with feet crossed at the ankles, they looked like then and now pictures of the same person.

A horn honked and Ruth Ann jumped, surprised that Cassandra got there so quick. "Hey!" Ruth Ann hollered over the sound of the television.

Ashley and Marvelle turned their heads at the same time and looked at Ruth Ann.

"Get your coats back on. Cassandra's driving us in her van."

"All right!" Ashley flicked off the TV, rocked forward, and rolled to her feet, then turned and pulled Marvelle up.

"What? I thought the car was broke." Marvelle hiked her skirt up, adjusted her slip, then let her skirt fall back around her legs.

"It is, Granny. We're going in Cassandra's van."

"She ain't bringing none of them young'uns, is she?"

"No, Granny, it's Saturday. They're all home today. It'll just be us chicks." Ashley bent to tie her shoe, grunting as she leaned over her belly to reach her feet.

"Well, that's a relief. I don't want to be chasing after no young'uns at the cemetery, having to keep them off the graves and out of the road."

Ashley straightened slowly and rubbed the small of her back. "What cemetery you talking about, Granny? I thought we was going to see your homeplace."

"We are, but I want to show you'uns where I want to be buried."

"Well, Granny, you'll be buried right here next to Pawpaw, won't you?" Ashley lifted Marvelle's coat from the arm of the couch and held it open.

Marvelle slid first her right arm then her left into the sleeves, then shrugged the coat around her and buttoned it up.

"Lord," Marvelle said. "I believe I must've had this old coat fifty years. They don't make them like this no more." She rubbed her hands down her sides, over the navy wool, into her pockets. She thought for a minute, then looked Ashley in the eye. "This was her coat, you know. Velda's. It's the only thing of hers I kept, this and a lock of our hair that's all mixed together from the first time Mama ever cut our hair. They ain't no way to tell now which ones is mine and which ones is hers."

Ashley was fumbling with the zipper of her jacket, but she looked up suddenly and studied her granny's face. She didn't have that vacant look she got when her mind left her. No, this was just a sad memory like anybody in their right mind might have on the day they're going home for the first time in a long time.

"You miss your sister, don't you," Ashley said.

"What?" Marvelle's head jerked up. When she finally focused on Ashley, she said, "I mean what I say about being buried in Madison County. I want to be buried right next to my mama and papa, and if I have to get a lawyer to write it down so you'll do it, I will."

"Are y'all coming or not?" Ruth Ann hollered. Ashley knew it wasn't a good time to contradict Marvelle, so she kept quiet and steered her down the hall.

They come in the kitchen just as A.J. come through the back door.

"Oh," Ruth Ann said. "I thought you was Cassandra."

"Hey, baby," he said. "What kind of car trouble y'all having?"

"The engine won't even turn over," Ruth Ann said. Another horn sounded. "That must be Cassandra." She picked up her jacket and pocketbook and followed Ashley and Marvelle to the back door. "Keys is in the car. We'll see you later."

"What's your big hurry?" A.J. followed them out the door, onto the carport.

"We got to get on the road." Ruth Ann waved to Cassandra, then watched while Ashley slid the panel door open and pushed Marvelle up into the van. After Ashley got in, Ruth Ann slid the door shut, then opened the passenger side door. A.J. kept standing there fidgeting like he wasn't quite sure what to do next. Ruth Ann didn't get in, just waited for him to say whatever it was he had to say.

A.J. put his hand on the van door. "I need to talk to you," he said.

Oh, Lord, Ruth Ann thought. "About what?" she said.

"Hey, Mama, do you have any sunglasses I can use?" Ashley called from the backseat.

Ruth Ann sighed. "I think I got some in the house. Come on, then, A.J., talk fast." She shut the van door and A.J. followed her inside.

He just stood there watching as Ruth Ann went through the junk drawer in the kitchen. She pulled out coupons, pot holders, pens, a sponge, toothpicks, an ashtray with a lighter in it, jar lids, pliers, an old picture of Angela and Alex and Ashley as kids, a salt shaker, bread ties, a shoehorn, toenail clippers. No sunglasses. She dropped the ashtray and lighter in the trash, then raked the rest of the junk back in the drawer. "I ain't got all day," she said, noticing that A.J. was rubbing his hands on his jeans. Sweaty palms, a bad sign.

A.J. cleared his throat. "I got a little proposition for you."

"Uh-huh, a proposition. What kind of a proposition?"

"Well, uh, I'm thinking about buying a business and I need me a partner."

Ruth Ann slammed the drawer shut and faced A.J. with her arms crossed over her chest. "A business? What kind of a business?"

A.J. crossed his arms over his chest and leaned his hip against the counter. "Roger Cox finally sold out."

"Roger Cox? Well, I'll be durned." Ruth Ann turned to lean against the counter next to A.J. "It's been a long time."

"I know. Me too. I was at the gas station the other day and me and Roger got to talking and he mentioned he was retiring. That's when it hit me."

"Hit you? What? To start yourself up in business just like that? A.J., don't you never think about nothing before you act on it? You don't know the first thing about flowers or business."

"Yeah, but you do."

"Flowers, maybe, but not business."

"Baby, you took that class at the community college."

"Yeah, but, A.J., that was fifteen years ago. I done forgot all that now." The horn honked twice and Ruth Ann straightened up and started digging in her purse for sunglasses. "And another thing." She paused and looked at A.J. "What makes you think I want to be your partner?"

"You need a job, don't you? Well, I'm offering you one. Only this way you'd be your own boss. Of course, you'd have to kick in a little money for the partnership. It'll be fifty–fifty all the way."

"Yeah, except when it comes to the work."

"I said fifty–fifty. I'm not a silent partner."

"That's probably the truest thing you've said all day." The horn honked again and she threw her stuff back in her pocketbook. "Hell, I can't find them sunglasses. It's cloudy anyway. She won't need them." She slung her pocketbook over her shoulder and headed toward the door.

"Ruth Ann," A.J. said.

She stopped with her hand on the doorknob and turned back. "How much money are you talking about here?"

"Up front, about three thousand."

"Three thousand!"

"Well, Ruth Ann, you got to put something in before you can expect to get anything out. I was going to get the loan all on my own, but I knew you wouldn't want to work for me." A.J. pulled an envelope out of his back pocket. "Just read over this stuff and think about it. I done talked to a lawyer."

Ruth Ann took the envelope and dropped it in her pocketbook. She knew she needed to get going, but the way he looked, there was something else, something she wanted to hear.

A.J. walked over to the window and looked out. "I'll be honest with you," he said. "I need something to do. I don't like being retired, and I don't want to be one of them men that retires and a year later dies of a heart attack 'cause they're too useless to live."

Ruth Ann stared in front of her, not really seeing anything. It was just like him to do this, spring this on her. She jumped when the horn honked a third time. "I got to go," she said.

"Yeah," he said, and looked over his shoulder at her. "But think about it."

She knew he could tell by the look on her face that she was already thinking about it, thinking hard. He knew her too well, dammit.

"There's some muffins in the microwave if you want something to eat," she said. "We'll be home by dark." She left him standing there with that look on his face, that look like a little boy waiting on his mama to tell him he can go out and play.

From underneath Ruth Ann's car, all A.J. could see was a narrow slice of yard, grass turning brown, leaves blowing around. It was a gray day and cold as hell on his back on the cement of the driveway. It hadn't occurred to him to put on a jacket.

He hoped they wouldn't get any snow in the mountains. He'd hate to think of Ruth Ann and them being stranded up there somewhere, especially when he had reason for wanting her home. It wasn't good she had all that time to spend thinking in the car either. If she thought about it too hard, Ruth Ann might think herself right out of it.

What he'd do, when she got home, he'd take her for a little ride and show how good her car run with the new starter. They could talk in the car. Hell, they could do a lot of things in the car. He turned and focused on the engine again, then sneezed three times fast. Damn, he better not be taking a cold.

At the sound of footsteps, A.J. rolled his head and watched a pair of muddy black boots coming across the pavement toward the Buick. They stopped next to the right front tire.

"Mr. Payne?"

Shit. It was that boy, Keith. A.J. scooted out from under the car and stood up, wiping his hands on a rag hanging out of his pocket. "Hey," he said. "What can I do you for?" He felt stupid saying that, like some service-station attendant. The boy threw him off balance. It was bad enough seeing Ashley big with a baby without having to look at the boy got her that way.

"Nothing, sir. I mean, I just seen Ruth Ann's car and wondered if anything was wrong, since they was supposed to go to the mountains today."

"They went in Ruth Ann's sister's van. I'm putting a new starter in the Buick." A.J. leaned his hip against the front bumper and crossed his arms over his chest.

"Oh." Keith took a step back, looked down at his feet, glanced around the yard. "Well, I guess I'll leave you to it, then."

A.J. faked a smile and nodded. "All right." He waited for the boy to go.

Keith just stood there, staring at A.J. "Look here, Mr. Payne," he said finally. He cleared his throat. "Look here," he said again.

A.J. straightened away from the car, keeping his arms crossed. This ought to be good.

Keith focused on A.J.'s chin as he spoke. "I just want you to know I mean to do right by her and the baby, is all." He made eye contact for a second, then looked at A.J.'s chin again. "I mean, I'm going to marry her."

"Is that right." A.J. studied Keith's face. The boy's eyes looked scared as he looked up from under heavy eyebrows—like he was looking up at A.J., even though Keith was a good four inches taller. A.J. wasn't so old he couldn't remember being in Keith's position, but his reaction had been a little different. Oh, sure, he'd married Ruth Ann, but he hadn't taken any of it as serious as Keith seemed to. Maybe if he had, he wouldn't have to work so hard now to get it back.

"Well, I'm glad to hear it. Ashley thinks a lot of you, I know." He put the emphasis on Ashley so the boy would know A. J. Payne was still waiting judgment.

Keith relaxed a little. "That's good to know, because I sure am having a hard time convincing her we should get married."

"What have you got to offer that she'd want?"

Keith looked down at his boots, then back at A.J. "Well, I got a job, and I'm saving up for a place to live."

"Do you even have a car?"

"Yes, sir."

"What kind?"

"A 1987 Camaro."

"Does it run?"

"Yeah. It don't look real good, but I'm fixing her up."

"Well, you're going to need something besides a Camaro once that baby comes. You've got to start thinking about these things. You can't drag a wife and baby around in a Camaro. You need you a family car."

Keith looked confused. "You trying to sell me a car?"

"Hell, no. I'm just trying to see if you're really thinking about what all's involved in having a family. But I guess you'll never understand it till you're in it. I know I didn't."

They stood quiet for a minute or two. A.J. didn't know what else to say to the boy.

Finally Keith spoke up. "Guess I better get on back."

A.J. leaned against the car again and stared down toward the cow pasture. "Is that your tent? Ashley told me about that."

Keith turned toward the cow pasture too, then stuck his hands in his jeans pockets and leaned against the Buick beside A.J.

"I don't live in that tent, if that's what you mean. I just like to spend time outdoors, is all. I got a room over the milking barn."

"Mmmm. Yeah, I never was one for the outdoors myself."

A dog ran from the neighbor's yard toward the pasture, stopping just a second to look at A.J. and Keith before it run off, crawled under the barbed-wire fence, and headed across the field.

"That's the mutt been chasing them cows, I bet." Keith watched the dog disappear over the hill.

"That's Speed. He belongs to them damn Spiveys next door. They're crazy as hell."

"Well, Dwight's going to have to pay them a visit, I reckon, and tell them to keep their dog off his cows."

"Won't do no good. They'll just tell him to go to hell, it's a free country. I tell you what, the neighborhood went downhill the day them people moved in."

"When was that?"

A.J. thought for a minute. "About fifteen years ago, I reckon. Ashley was about four, and they had a little boy the same age. Them's some of the meanest damn young'uns you ever seen. Fought all the time, with each other and with my kids. And the parents ain't no better. They never set foot out of that house except to come over here and complain about something. Our kids was making too much noise, our dog was running through their yard. One year they tried to get a court order to have all the trees on that side of our yard cut down because we wouldn't come over there and rake the leaves up in the fall. Me and Ruth Ann told them we'd rake as soon as they all fell, but they wanted every leaf picked up the minute it hit the ground."

"What happened?"

"The judge laughed his ass off and run them out of his courtroom. Of course, that started a big grudge on their side and they ain't spoke to none of us since. I don't think they understand I planted them trees between our houses for a reason."

Keith laughed. "No wonder Dwight's been putting off talking to them."

"Yeah, he knows what they're like. He'll probably have to shoot that animal to get it to quit. I remember he had to one time before. Tore him up too."

"You can't let dogs run your cows though. It'll make them so nervous their milk dries up. I've found that much out already."

A.J. sneezed again and reached in his pocket for a handkerchief. "How you like working for old Dwight?" He blew his nose loud and shoved the handkerchief back in his pocket.

"I like it. He's easy to work for. I do my work and he does his. I like his wife too. She's a good cook. She's got me taking breakfast and supper with them now."

"Yeah, they're good people. They never had no young'uns themselves, and they always loved ours. Spoiled them to death. That's why Ashley likes them cows so much. She was always following Dwight around."

"She used to talk about that, back at Appalachian Hall. She said he was like— Well."

"I know," A.J. said. He knew Dwight had been more of a daddy to his kids than he had. And now it was coming home to him.

"What does your daddy do?" A.J. said.

"Don't know," Keith said. "Don't even know where he is."

"What about your mama?"

"Don't want to know."

"You got people somewhere, don't you?"

"My granny raised me, her and my uncles. They live up in Murphy."

"Right. I been through there one time, driving a truck to Tennessee." A.J. paused. "So," he said, "what's the story with you and Ashley now?"

Keith looked sideways at A.J., then back toward the pasture. "I can't figure it out," he said. "Ashley used to talk to me all the time at Appalachian Hall, but she won't have hardly nothing to do with me now. I mean, we eat dinner together about every day, but we don't talk much. I feel like she's waiting on something, and I can't figure out what it is."

"I hate to be the one to break it to you, but the majority of your women is always going to be high maintenance," A.J. said. "No matter how sweet and pretty they are, or how good they might be at certain things, they're always going to be a lot of work."

"It ain't women. It's one woman," Keith said. "Ashley."

"Right," A.J. said. "Glad to hear it."

Keith stepped into the yard, picked up a stick, and started scraping mud off the soles of his boots. "I don't know why I'm doing this," he said. "I got to go right back through the mud." He dropped the stick and stood, wiping his boots on the grass. "I don't understand her," he said. "Why does she have to make it so hard?"

"Well, I'll tell you, you got to understand how these women work." A.J. spit across the driveway onto the grass. "I been studying them for thirty-some years, and I can't say I got them figured yet. These Moon women is special—quare, really. And make no mistake about it, Ashley's last name might be Payne, and she might marry you and become a—what's your name again, son?"

"Watty."

"Watty? What kind of a name is that?"

"Cherokee, I reckon. It's my daddy's name, and that's what he is."

"Cherokee. Huh. Well. Anyway, even if Ashley marries you and becomes a Watty, even if she gets married a hundred times, at the heart of her she's a Moon like her mama and her granny, and them women will give you trouble all your life. I seen it with Ruth Ann's daddy, and I can vouch for it myself."

Keith quit wiping his feet and come back over to stand by A.J. "So what makes you stay? Or come back?" he said.

A.J. shook his head. "Son, I have no idea. All I know is, once I got tangled up with Ruth Ann, that was it for me. Looks like it'll be the same for you."

"You think Ashley'll give in eventually?"

"Hell, no. Them women don't never give in, even when they know they're wrong." A.J. looked sideways at Keith and smiled. "She might marry you though. And you'll probably live to regret it many a day."

"But it's worth it, right?"

"Hell, I don't know. Just don't make the mistake I made. Don't take nothing for granted. What'd you do to make her mad anyway?"

"Nothing. That's just it. I didn't do nothing. She thinks I messed around with another girl up in Asheville, but I didn't."

"It don't matter whether you did or not. She thinks you did and that's what you got to work with. Tell her you're sorry."

"I ain't going to confess to something I never did. I ain't going to lie to her."

"I didn't say confess or lie. Just tell her you're sorry. You don't have to say what for. Just say you're sorry. That's all they care about."

"Well, I'm sorry, but I don't believe that."

"Try it and see. I'm telling you, a well-timed apology can get you a long way in a marriage." A.J. reached out and rested a hand on Keith's shoulder. "You take my word on it. Now I got to get back under this car and get it running before Ruth Ann gets home, or I'll have some more apologizing to do myself."

"Can I help you? I'm pretty good with cars."

"That's all right. I'm about done."

"All right then." Keith held out his hand and A.J. shook it. "Thanks, Mr. Payne. I appreciate it."

"Ah, hell, my name's A.J. Mr. Payne was my daddy."

8

The two-lane road to Marshall run straight and narrow between the mountain and the river and the railroad track on the left and the mountain on the right. Talk about being between a rock and a hard place, Ashley had never seen any place so closed in and crammed together. It was like the land had opened up just a crack, just wide enough for the river, the railroad, and the road, and then threw up walls to keep everything else out. She didn't understand how Granny could love it so.

Ashley leaned her cheek against the cool glass of the window and watched the river go by. Dark wide water rippled over rocks and logs, past steep banks of laurel. Pretty soon she started seeing little houses on the riverbank, houses that probably got flooded every time it rained, they was so close to the water. She raised her head up. Looked like they was almost to Marshall now. Probably the town was as tiny and cramped as everything else, having to be squeezed into such a little bit of flat land. It was frustrating not to be able to see any distance. Ashley figured if she ever had to live up here, it'd have to be right on the top of one of them mountains, with nothing blocking her view of the world.

She yawned and glanced at the backs of Ruth Ann's and Cassandra's heads. They just sat up there in front, not saying a word, staring straight ahead like robots, like two crash-test dummies on TV. They'd seen all this before, and Ashley figured it wasn't nothing to get excited about anyway.

Granny was excited though. She'd been fidgeting ever since they turned off the interstate.

"I wish the sun was shining," she said. "Ain't nothing so pretty in this world as that river in the sunshine." She leaned back again and sighed. "I wish Jesse was here with me. I wish it so bad."

Ashley patted her hand. "You got us, Granny."

Ruth Ann looked around the seat at Marvelle. "We're about in Marshall now, Mama. Where is it that we turn to go to Walnut?"

"Keep on a-going and I'll tell you when we get there." Marvelle tried to lean forward and look between the front seats, but the seat belt held her back. She pulled at it, then sat back and started pointing out buildings. "Up yonder's the courthouse." Marvelle glanced at Ashley. "That's where me and your pawpaw got married. And there, that used to be the hotel, and now look, it's about to fall in. There's the funeral home. That's where my body'll be laid out for the viewing."

"Mama!" Cassandra and Ruth Ann said at the same time.

"For heaven's sake, Mama, don't talk like that." Ruth Ann rolled her window down a crack to get some fresh air.

Ashley studied the block of one-story buildings they passed, the big silver dome on top of the courthouse, the tiny car dealership that had about ten cars on the lot. "Well, hell, Mama," she said. "What should we talk about on the way to the cemetery where Granny wants to be buried?"

Marvelle spoke up again. "Now here comes the road—turn right here. Turn, I tell you."

"I'm turning, Mama, I'm turning," Cassandra said.

The road immediately began to climb up and around another mountain, twisting back and forth in long slow arcs. The snaking two-lane went on for several miles before they reached the turnoff for Walnut. Cassandra put on her signal and waited for a truck, covered in mud, to pass before she turned.

Ashley looked up the hill, trying to see something. All she saw was woods and what was left of a corn patch.

"That's Jewel Hill," Marvelle said.

Cassandra made the turn and started up the hill, doing about twenty-five. They passed a couple of houses, rounded a curve, and the first thing Ashley saw was a graveyard, then the little white church.

"Is that it, Granny?"

"Yes, ma'am, that's Walnut Methodist, and when we get to the top of the hill, we'll see the store and the schoolhouse, and the place where

Mama's boardinghouse was, but it ain't there no more. It burnt up in nineteen and thirty-three. And you can see Marthy's house, and Kate's."

"I mean," Ashley said, "is that all there is to it? I didn't know it'd just be a wide place in the road. I thought there'd at least be a post office and a bank and a Hardee's or something."

The look on Marvelle's face told Ashley she better be careful what she said as long as they was on Marvelle's turf.

"Just pull in next to the church, honey," Marvelle told Cassandra. "Right here, right here! Just park right there next to it in the dirt."

"Mama, quit hollering! I know how to park." Cassandra made a sharp left into the patch of rocky ground next to the church, bumped across some ruts, and stopped the van.

"Thank God," Ruth Ann said. "Now let's get this over with." She got out and opened the sliding passenger door for Marvelle and Ashley.

"Well, Mama," Cassandra said as she come around the van to join them. "Don't look like nobody's home." The only car in sight was parked in front of the little convenience store across the road.

"They ought to call this place Mudville," Ruth Ann said. "Every car and truck I've seen up here is just covered in mud. I'd have thought all the roads'd be paved by now." She lifted her feet and checked the bottoms of her shoes.

Marvelle grunted at them and started toward the graveyard. Markers of all shapes and sizes spread out behind the church, covering every flat foot of ground up to where the land dropped off suddenly into a little hollow about a hundred yards back of the church.

Ashley started to follow them, then stopped and studied the store across the street. She had to pee bad, and that might be her only hope of relief.

She told Ruth Ann where she was going, then headed toward the store, noticing another graveyard, or maybe more of the same one, running up a hill directly across the road from the church. And another graveyard on a hill behind the store. Seemed like there was more dead people than live in this place.

When she walked in the store, a couple of good-old boys turned from the window where they'd been watching the goings-on at the church and stared at her. She said hey and smiled, and the one behind the counter smiled back and said, "Help you, ma'am?" while the other one just kept staring.

"Do you have a bathroom I could use?"

"I'm sorry, ma'am, we sure don't."

Uh-huh. Like hell you don't. Ashley rested her hands on her belly and rubbed it. "I don't know what I'm going to do. This baby's putting so much pressure on my bladder I feel like I'm about to bust. Are you sure you don't have a rest room I could use? I promise I'll hurry. Please."

The two men looked at each other, then one guy pointed toward the back of the store. "Go around the magazines and straight back to the door that says *Employees Only*."

"Thank you so much. I really appreciate it." Ashley hurried off before they changed their minds.

It didn't hit her until she sat down to pee that she was stalling. She didn't want to go out there and walk around looking at graves, and she certainly didn't want to think about her granny being in one of them. She couldn't understand why her granny wanted to either. But that old woman had been determined to come up here for weeks, and Ashley knew it was about more than picking a place to be buried. It was to visit her home one last time, to say good-bye.

Ashley couldn't imagine ever getting to that point in her own life, where she felt ready to say good-bye to everything and everybody forever. It didn't even bear thinking about. Did it scare her granny as bad as it scared her? Did something happen when a person got to a certain age, something that made you not be so afraid, something that made you ready to die? Her granny didn't act afraid, just tired. Or maybe she just didn't show she was scared. Maybe she didn't want them worrying about her.

Sometimes at night, Ashley would look up into the darkness above her bed and force herself to think, Someday I'll be dead. I'll be dead and gone, not here on this earth no more. Her heart would start to racing and the fear would seize hold of her mind so that she felt all in a panic and couldn't think anything except, No, no, no! But, then, seemed like it wasn't long and her mind would settle down and the panicky feeling would leave her. And in its place would come this curiosity, this wondering what it was going to be like wherever it was you went when you died. It was like her mind could only stand so much of the fear before some kind of switch flipped over and, instead of thinking about the end, she started thinking about a new beginning on the other side of the end. It was like a circle that way, somehow.

Maybe that's where her granny's mind was now, on that same wheel, only she'd got further around than Ashley, that was all, that was the only difference. Granny was just on the other side of that circle that they was all going around and around. That made her feel some better, thinking of it that way, made her feel like she could go out there now and not bust out crying at the thought of her granny being gone from this world.

Anyway, she couldn't hide forever, and the boys outside must be wondering if she fell in. Ashley washed her hands and hurried out, saying a quick thank you as she passed the two men. She'd been meaning to buy a Pepsi on her way out of the store, but no matter how thirsty she was, dang if she'd buy a drink from somebody who didn't even want to let her use their bathroom.

Cassandra and Ruth Ann was walking one on either side of Marvelle when Ashley reached them, and Marvelle was reading names off grave markers as she passed. She showed them where her mama and papa was buried, then her sisters and brothers and their spouses and even some of their children.

"I was the youngest of fourteen," she said. "I'm the only one left now." She stopped at one stone where the writing had worn completely away, leaving only a flat, grayish-brown rock the size of a book.

"That's Marthy and Jim's boy Jody, died of typhoid when he was just three years old. I remember the day we buried him there. I was just a little thing myself, no more than six, and I used to play with Jody all the time. I kept asking Mama and Papa, where did Jody go, where did Jody go, and Mama just cried and cried."

"Marthy, Martha, was your oldest sister?" Ashley knelt down and pulled some weeds away from the marker, then rubbed her hand across the stone. The surface was smooth, cool, and blank as the sky overhead. Ashley shivered. Once Marvelle was gone, who would remember this?

"Yes, she was like a second mother to me, and oh, I was so jealous of Jody when he come along. But Marthy said Jody was my little brother and I had to take care of him and be a good sister and teach him things, and that made me feel better. I thought Mama would never get over it when he died though. He was her first grandchild, you see, and it like to have killed her. She's the one had to wash his little body and make a gown for him to wear, 'cause of course Marthy was in no shape to do it, and Papa made the box to bury him in. I remember it didn't take them long to dig that grave, and back then they didn't do all that embalming and stuff they do now. You had to get them in the ground quick."

Marvelle took hold of Ashley's arm and looked in her face. "I'm telling you right now." She stopped and looked at Ruth Ann and Cassandra to include them. "And you two as well. I want a plain pine box and none of that fancy stuff, and no shooting me full of chemicals. Just put me in the box and put me in the ground."

"Now, Mama," Ruth Ann said. "We went through all this when Daddy died. You know good and well it's against the law to bury somebody without embalming them first. Would you rather be cremated?"

"Yeah, Mama, and besides, you don't need to be worrying about all that stuff now. When the time comes, we'll take care of it, won't we, Ruth Ann?"

"Cassandra's right, Mama."

"Oh, yeah, I know just how the two of you'll take care of it. You'll do it all your own way just like you always do, without a care in the world for what I want. You'll have me burnt down to a little pile of ashes and stick me in a drawer somewhere. Well, we'll just see about that."

Ashley stepped in front of Marvelle to block her view of Ruth Ann and Cassandra. "Listen, let's talk about that later, okay? It's too cold to stand out here arguing." She took Marvelle's arm and pulled her toward a big double monument a few feet away. "Come on, Granny. Let's go over here. Who's buried over here?"

As they got closer, Ashley could see that the marker was made of beautiful pink marble and stood close to four feet high. Birds and roses was carved all around the front, and two little angels sat on top, one on each side, with their little feet dangling just above the place where the names and dates went. On the left was the name *Harvey Roberts, 1901–1977*, but the right side was blank and rough-looking, like something had been there once and then been scraped away.

"Whose grave is this, Mama?" Ruth Ann turned and moved aside so Marvelle could see the headstone. When Marvelle suddenly started laughing, they all stared at her like she was crazy. Then it struck them a little funny too and they started grinning and making eyes at each other. When Marvelle finally caught her breath and wiped her eyes, Cassandra said, "Mama, what is so dang funny?"

"Oh, Lord, girls. That's my grave there. Or at least it was meant to be."

"What?" they all three said at once.

"Yep, that spot next to Harvey was reserved for me. To think I could've spent eternity resting under such as that."

"Mama, what are you talking about? Who's Harvey Roberts?" Ruth Ann walked around the back of the monument to see if anything was written there, then stared over at Marvelle.

"Oh, honey, that was just a man I knowed a long time ago, before any of you'uns was born." Marvelle took a Kleenex from her pocketbook and blew her nose. "Eh Lord, he thought he was my feller, and nothing I said or did could convince him otherwise. Why, he used to come courting every Sunday evening, and he'd set out there on the porch with Papa and Mama even if I refused to come out. Sometimes I think he courted me just because he liked my family so much."

"Didn't you like him?" Ashley said.

"Oh, he was a nice enough feller, real sweet, but didn't have much going for him up here." Marvelle tapped her head. "Or here." She touched her face. "Back in them days, I was a fool for a man with a pretty face."

"But what about the grave?" Cassandra said.

"Well, when he seen he couldn't impress me the usual way, walking and talking, why, he set out to spend money on me. Now, he wasn't rich by no means, but his parents had left him his own home and he had a good job on the railroad. Anyhow, he'd go off on the train to Asheville and come back with something for me just about ever week. Course, Mama always made me give it back since I wasn't intending on marrying him."

"What kinds of things?" Ashley sat down on the grass and looked up at Marvelle.

"Here, Mama, come lean up against this headstone. You might as well use it for a while since it's yours." Ruth Ann and Marvelle leaned against the marble while Cassandra sat next to Ashley on the grass.

"Well, let me see. I remember one time he come in with a jewelry box made out of silver stuff. It wasn't real silver, but it was shaped like a heart and real pretty. I didn't have no jewelry though, so I had no use for it. Then another time he brung me a book about flowers 'cause he knowed how much I loved flowers. And a hairbrush, and some perfume, and I think even a framed picture of himself one time. The last thing he ever brung me was this thing here." Marvelle kicked her heel against the tombstone.

"What in the world made him think you'd want a tombstone?" Ruth Ann asked.

"Well, he come and asked me to walk with him one evening and I said no, but then he said if I didn't like this one last gift, he'd never bother me again, so I figured I'd just go on and get it over with. Jesse had come to Madison County by then, you see, and I was so much in love with him I couldn't see straight. Harvey was harmless, but he irritated the fool out of Jesse. I knowed I'd have to get him to stop courting me or Jesse might hurt him."

Marvelle turned and pointed toward a tangle of trees and bushes and weeds about a quarter mile away, close to the school. "See that little patch of woods there? Our house was right behind there. One evening it was getting close to dark—what we always called the gloaming, my favorite time of the day, especially in the summertime when everything's cooling off and the light gets soft and the lightning bugs come out. Well, anyhow, Harvey come and got me and we set out walking. That road wasn't paved then. It was soft dirt that kind of puffed up when you walked on it. Made terrible mud when it rained. I reckon Harvey thought he was about to win me over, because he was so excited he fell down before we even got here. I had to pick him up out the road and brush him off, and I couldn't keep from laughing. He didn't seem to mind though. Just kept on.

"Of course, I had no idea this was where we was headed. I just thought we was walking to be a-walking. Harvey says, Oh, the grass is so green and cool, let's walk through the graveyard, over to the church, so we do, and he starts in to talking. He tells me how beautiful I am and how he's loved me for so long and how he'll never stop loving me even if I marry another, even after death, and to prove his undying love for me, he had something real special sent all the way from Knoxville. He puts his hands over my eyes, turns me around, takes his hands away, and says, Surprise, darling!

"Well, you can imagine, it being about dark, I opened my eyes and didn't see nothing at first but this big pink rock, and then all of a sudden I made out my own name joined with his, *Marvelle Dockery Roberts, 1910–*, with a blank place where my death date would go. I tell you, I let out a scream to curdle the blood, it startled me so, and poor Harvey turned white as a haint and fell over right there under his name. I run home fast as my legs'd carry me, and it took Mama a long time to get that story out of me.

"Of course, we all had a good laugh over it later, but when Jesse got wind of what Harvey'd done, he come down here himself in the dead of night with a pickax and took my name right off of there. Then he went to Harvey's and I don't know what all happened, but the next week Harvey moved away and we never heard tell of him again. And I reckon that was just the push Jesse needed, for he asked me to marry him the very next day." Marvelle leaned down and touched a finger to the *1977* on Harvey's side. "Poor old feller, I never thought he'd go ahead and have himself buried here. I reckon he never married."

"Well, Granny," Ashley said. "I hope this ain't where you want to be buried. Although it is paid for." She rolled to her knees and got to her feet, then turned and pulled Cassandra up.

"Lord, no, honey. I didn't want to sleep next to him in life, and I certainly don't want to spend eternity with the fool. Although looking back now, I should've been more grateful to have somebody love me so. Harvey wasn't a smart man, but he was good and would've treated me right."

Ashley noticed Marvelle's eyes had got swimmy with tears. "Yeah, but you had Pawpaw, and he loved you more," she said.

"Oh, yes, honey, Jesse was a good man, and he did love me, I know that."

Ashley looked back at Ruth Ann, but Ruth Ann was walking away, back toward the church. "Mama, where you going?" Ashley called after her.

"I'm going to sit in the van. I'm cold."

Cassandra came and stood close enough to Ashley that their arms touched. She was shivering.

"Why didn't you wear a coat, Cassandra?"

"I don't need one. We're not going to be here that long. Let's get Mama to do her business and go on back to Asheville. We've still got to stop and see your friend, don't we?"

Ashley looked at her watch. It was ten-thirty, and they'd told Peri they'd pick her up at noon. She hollered, "Granny, we got to go soon."

Marvelle had wandered off to the edge of the graveyard and stood looking toward the mountains. Ashley and Cassandra followed and stood on either side of her, staring in the same direction. The wind whipped around them, blowing their hair back and chapping their cheeks, but Marvelle kept staring. Ashley wondered what she saw that they didn't.

"How in the world?" Cassandra said.

Ashley saw that Cassandra was looking down into the little holler below them where, somehow or other, people had got a trailer down there. Apparently they was living in it too, because a truck and a car was parked next to one end, and clothes flapped on the line.

"I bet they can't get to work when it snows, even in that truck," Cassandra said. "How do these people stand it up here?"

"No telling," Ashley said. It was then she noticed a square gray stone almost directly in front of Marvelle's feet. "Is that a grave, Granny?" she said. "Looks like a grave, but it ain't got nobody's name on it."

"Would you just look," Marvelle said, her voice hoarse. "I believe I could stand anything for the sight of that every morning of the world."

The mountains seemed to go on and on in layers, like waves in the ocean, like they never ended. For just a minute, Ashley saw how small they all was in comparison, and it made her feel lonesome, and made her glad she wasn't alone.

Marvelle pulled her coat tighter around her, rubbing the material over her arms. "I should've wore pants," she said as she turned back toward the graveyard. "That wind's whipping up my skirt and my butt's froze. Come on, girls, let's go." She stopped at a bare spot by a double tombstone. "This is where I want to rest," she said. "Right here by Mama and Papa."

"What's this?" Ashley said, stopping beside a big pointy piece of white quartz that come up to her knees. It stood on the other side of the bare spot where Marvelle was.

A look come over Marvelle's face such as Ashley had never seen before and hoped never to see again. Her face twisted up for just a second like a washrag being wrung out, then she got hold of herself and started walking to the van.

"That's Rachel and Rose," Cassandra said. "Mama's first two girls that died when they was four."

Ashley run her hand over the rock, feeling the jagged surface of it against her palm. "What'd they die of?" she said.

"Diphtheria."

"What's that?"

"I don't know," Cassandra said. "One of them diseases they didn't have no cure for back then."

Ruth Ann watched as Marvelle, followed by Ashley and Cassandra, made her slow way to the van. Lord, what a picture they made there among all them graves, with the ashy blue mountains and gray sky behind them. She wished suddenly she'd brung her camera to capture that moment, for it might never come again. She had a feeling next time they come to Madison County would be to say good-bye to Marvelle. She turned her head away from the window and reached in her purse for lipstick. The wind had chapped her lips something terrible. She pulled down the visor and opened the mirror to put on lipstick and check her hair. Ruth Ann watched in the mirror as Ashley slid the van door open, helped Marvelle in, then got in herself. She closed the mirror and pushed the visor back in place. Cassandra walked around the front of the van, got in, and started the engine.

"Y'all look froze to death, and your hair's all over the place," she said, turning to look at Ashley and Marvelle.

"Thanks, Mama," Ashley said.

"Okay, where to next?" Cassandra said.

Ruth Ann looked at Marvelle. "Mama? Where else you want to go?" She saw that Marvelle had that faraway look in her eyes. "Mama?" She put her hand on Marvelle's arm and shook her a little bit. Marvelle pulled her arm away and leaned back in the seat. Ashley buckled her seat belt for her, then said, "Granny, do you want to go anywhere else?"

"I want to go home," Marvelle said. "I'm tired."

Ruth Ann locked eyes with Ashley for a second, then turned to face front again.

The van lurched as Cassandra backed into the road. "Is everybody buckled up?" she said as she pulled her own seat belt on. She yanked at the shoulder harness to get it comfortable across her chest, then reached for the radio buttons.

"Want me to do that?" Ruth Ann said. Cassandra had a bad habit of taking her eyes off the road for long periods of time trying to find just the right radio station or admiring scenery. The woman needed a chauffeur.

"Nah, I got it."

Cassandra had a little grin on her face that Ruth Ann understood as soon as she recognized the song coming on. It was "Stay" by Maurice Williams and the Zodiacs. Summer 1960, Cassandra was nine years old, Ruth Ann was eighteen and dating A.J., and Marvelle would send Cassandra with them when they went riding in A.J.'s Chevy. Cassandra would sit up front between Ruth Ann and A.J., and he always let her control the radio. They called her Cassie back then. She loved that song, loved to sing that falsetto part, and she'd flit from station to station looking for it. Whenever she found it, she'd crank it up and sing at the top of her lungs and they'd just howl.

Cassandra wasn't singing now, but Ruth Ann knew she wanted to. She closed her eyes and felt a rush of summer and heat and memory wash over her mind. She hadn't thought about those days for a long, long time, hadn't let herself think about it. It wasn't all good, but that was okay too. She was starting to get used to the fact that nothing was all good or all bad. Finally, at almost fifty-one, she was learning.

She'd put A.J.'s proposition out of her mind once they got to Madison County, but she'd thought about it all the way up the mountain and it came back to her now. What had possessed him to go and do this thing? She knew A.J. well enough to know he wasn't doing it out of the kindness of his heart. No, he had an ulterior motive. Ruth Ann just wasn't sure what it was. Maybe another plan to get himself back in her life. Lord knows he'd made it clear he wanted back in. But with A.J. the hunt was what mattered most, the chase, the challenge. The minute she took him back, he'd be right back to his old ways, hunting and gathering anything in a skirt that was dumb enough to think he meant what he said.

Still, if they had a legal contract. Doing something she'd always had an interest in, and she'd be her own boss, and his too, though he probably didn't know that yet.

Roger Cox had always made a profit with that business, since it was the only florist in town. And whatever water was under her and A.J.'s bridge, she did feel comfortable with him. As scary as this was bound to be at first, it'd be nice to have something familiar around as a sort of cushion. A.J. wouldn't like that at all, being thought of as a cushion—comfortable and safe and convenient, but not necessary—which made Ruth Ann like it even more.

By the new year, she could be in business for herself and the hell with the mill. Her stomach jumped at the thought. That was what excitement felt like. She hadn't felt it in so long she almost didn't recognize it, and it was so close to fear, it was hard to tell the difference.

Ruth Ann took a quick look in the backseat. Ashley and Marvelle was sound asleep, their heads against the windows.

"They're gone," she said.

"Good," Cassandra said, and turned the radio up a notch. The song had changed but they both knew the words.

"And then there suddenly appeared before me," they sang. "The only one my arms would ever hold. I heard somebody whisper please adore me . . ."

Jesse could always make me laugh and see the brighter side of things, even when the day was gloomy, like now. That man did love to laugh, didn't seem to take nothing serious, on the surface anyhow. But once I got to know him, I begun to realize how all that laughing and cutting up was just to hide how serious he took everything. Yes, Lord, he took things so much to heart. Everything touched him a whole lot deeper than I ever guessed.

I reckon that's why he was always so trusting of anybody that was in trouble. He couldn't bear not to help them, even if we was in the poor-house ourselves. They was times he give the very shirt off his back and the food off our table to strangers that come to the back door begging. Now, this was during the Depression, and I didn't mind helping nobody, but not when it meant taking food out of our own mouths and the mouths of our children. I believe if everybody takes care of themselves and their own, then won't nobody have to be on welfare or go about tramping and begging. It's just too bad everybody in the world don't have decent family to help them out when they're in trouble. I reckon Jesse thought the whole world was his kin.

If I had to choose between a too generous man and a too stingy man though, I'd have to go with the over-generous one. Either way, they're trouble, but at least the generous man includes his own family in his generosity. My sister Kate was married to a stingy man, and it amazes me to this day she never starved to death. He was so stingy he never even give her no young'uns. I always had my doubts as to whether he was even a husband to her. Kate was a big healthy woman when she left home and should've had twenty children. It was the sorrow of her life, and it turned her skinny and sour by the time she was thirty-five, and she up and died before she was fifty. She couldn't bear it no more, is what I think.

If it'd been me, I never would've stayed with such a man. Now, I had my trials with Jesse, but he did give me beautiful children and that'll make up for a lot. Though there is some things a man'll do that a woman just can't forgive. Oh, she can get over it and go on and keep a-living with him, and even still love him in a way, but the old love is dead and gone and can't never be got back. And of course, the man knows that, and it always makes him mad before long, mad that there's something in the world he can't do nothing about. But I learned early on from watching Mama and my sisters that I had to make out the best I could with what the Lord give me to work with. Ain't no use getting frustrated with things you can't change. It's best to go on and take care of your family and set aside the things that grieves you.

It's only in the night sometimes, or when it's quiet and I'm by myself, that I can't forget. I wonder how things would've been different if I hadn't never found out what he done. But I can't complain. I've had a good life, and I got children that take care of me, sometimes more than I want them to. And I think Jesse will understand about me wanting to be buried between Mama and Papa and our little girls, instead of in Davis next to him. I don't think he'll be mad, for I stayed by him all his life, and all my life, and I like to think when I'm dead I can finally do what I want.

9

"I don't see her," Ashley said. "I figured she'd be out here waiting on us."

"Well, go in and get her. We'll wait out here," Ruth Ann said.

Ashley crawled over Marvelle, trying not to jiggle her as she got out of the van. Marvelle jerked awake when the cold air hit her. "Where are we?" she said.

Ashley stepped out of the van, then turned back to Marvelle. "We're in Asheville, Granny. I'm going to get Peri. Remember my friend I told you about?"

"Your boyfriend?"

"No, Peri's a girl."

"What kind of name is that for a girl?"

Ashley looked at Ruth Ann and rolled her eyes, then slid the van door shut.

"Turn up the heat, Cassandra," Ruth Ann said. "It's cold in here."

Listening to the sound of warm air rushing through the vents, Ruth Ann watched the tops of the trees bending in the wind and wished Ashley would hurry. It seemed so lonely and empty up here, nothing but bare trees and that cold gray building to look at. She hadn't thought she'd ever come back to this place. She flipped down the visor and opened the lighted mirror.

After she checked her lipstick, Ruth Ann adjusted the mirror so she could see Marvelle's face behind her. She'd gone back to sleep, her chin resting on her chest. She looked so little and old back there, too little to have ever been somebody's wife or mother.

Ruth Ann closed the mirror and glanced at Cassandra. She looked like she was asleep too, just like Marvelle, with her chin on her chest. Ruth Ann shook her head and looked toward the entrance of Appalachian Hall. While she watched, the door opened and a man came out. It was Chuck Trent, Ashley's counselor. He hurried over to the van, and Ruth Ann could tell by the look on his face something was bad wrong. She got out of the van and shut the door behind her.

"Mrs. Payne." Chuck put his hands in his jacket pockets and huddled in front of her. "I guess I better just say it straight out." He cleared his throat. "Peri Morgan's dead. She killed herself."

"Oh, my God." Ruth Ann's fingers felt like ice as she pressed them over her mouth. That little girl couldn't be dead. She was only fifteen. No, sixteen. "Where's Ashley?" she said.

"Upstairs in Peri's room with Joan."

Ruth Ann's body slowly slumped back against the van and rested there. She could see Peri's face plain as day, that beautiful girl laughing with Ashley while they smoked cigarettes after lunch on Sundays when Ruth Ann come to visit. She'd known they was laughing about her sometimes, but she didn't mind. She was just relieved Ashley had a friend, somebody else to help her, so Ruth Ann didn't worry as much. Ashley never seemed to have friends in school like Angela and Alex did, and Ruth Ann didn't remember her ever having a best friend. But for some reason her and Peri had clicked that first week, maybe because they was both so wild, and maybe because Peri needed somebody to give a damn about her, and Ashley needed somebody to give a damn about.

Chuck leaned against the van beside her. "The night watchman found her early this morning, on the pavement behind the building. We still don't know how she got up there." He stuffed his hands deeper in his pockets and stared up toward the roof. "Her dad called yesterday to say he was coming to get her today, and she got real upset when she found out she wouldn't be able to see Ashley. We called and asked if he couldn't wait till tomorrow, but he refused."

Ruth Ann couldn't imagine what she would do in that man's place. It made her mind slam shut just to think about it. "Sweet sixteen," she said.

"What? Oh, that's right," Chuck said. "Her birthday." He put his fingers over his eyes for a second, then looked at Ruth Ann. "Listen, it's too cold to stay out here. Why don't y'all come on inside?"

Ruth Ann looked in the van. Cassandra was watching them, but Marvelle was still asleep. Ruth Ann motioned for Cassandra to get out, then told her what happened.

"Don't tell Mama, okay?" Ruth Ann said. "She'll get all upset, and we'll have enough to do dealing with Ashley."

"I'm not stupid," Cassandra said. She slid the door open so she could wake Marvelle and help her out. "Poor thing. I just can't believe it."

Marvelle woke up slowly, blinking and moaning as she tried to get the kink out of her neck. "Can't believe what?" she said.

"Nothing, Mama. Come on, now, we're going in to wait on Ashley. Don't you want some coffee?"

"Not if you're going to make it." Marvelle put her hand on Cassandra's shoulder and stepped onto the pavement. "I'm hungry. When we going to get some dinner?"

"In a little bit, Mama." Ruth Ann took Marvelle's arm while Cassandra locked the van.

"Is it okay if I leave it parked here?" she said, and looked at Chuck.

"No problem." He waved his hand, then held it out to Cassandra. "I'm Charleston Trent. Chuck."

Cassandra shook his hand. "Cassandra Moon."

"Oh, so you're the famous Cassandra I've heard so much about from Ashley."

"Uh-oh. What's she been telling you?"

"Only good things."

Ruth Ann looked back over her shoulder then and snapped, "Cassandra, take Mama's other arm please."

Chuck led them to a small lounge area and promised to come right back with coffee and something to eat.

"I'm hungry," Marvelle said. "Where's Ashley? I want to go to Shoney's."

"Mama, Ashley's upstairs and she'll probably be there awhile." Ruth Ann sat across from Marvelle and crossed her legs.

"She ain't fooling with that boy, is she? She's already got a baby coming, she don't need no more trouble."

"Mama, please," Ruth Ann said. What she needed more than anything was a cigarette, just one cigarette to get her nerves calmed down. "She's not fooling with a boy, she's visiting a friend, that's all."

"Well, you don't have to bite my head off, Ruth Ann."

Ruth Ann took a deep breath and let it out slow. "I'm sorry, Mama," she said.

Chuck come back a few minutes later with a tray and set it in front of them. "We had turkey and dressing for lunch today. The girls in the kitchen are practicing for Thanksgiving. I brought some coffee too. I'll come back in a little while and check on y'all."

"I'm not hungry right now," Ruth Ann said.

"Well, I am," Marvelle said.

Cassandra fixed them both a plate. She took a bite of the turkey. "Not bad," she said. "Maybe a little dry."

"Dressing needs more sage," Marvelle said. She took a big swallow of coffee. "Good coffee though. Better'n yours." She looked at Cassandra.

Ruth Ann stood up. She had to get out of there before she started screaming at them to shut up.

"Where you going?" Cassandra said.

Ruth Ann wondered that herself. Where was the only place she could go? Up there where Ashley was, where Peri used to be. She didn't want to go, but she couldn't just sit still and do nothing either. She wished again that she hadn't quit smoking, that she could take a long, deep drag of nicotine. No going backward though. Too late for that. "Going to find Chuck," she said finally, looking first at Cassandra, then at her mama. "Be back in a little bit." She'd get him to take her upstairs, and maybe by the time she got up there, she'd know what to do next.

It was like walking into a refrigerator, one with the light burned out, when Ruth Ann went in Peri's room to find Ashley. She started to turn the light on, but Ashley laid so still on the bed, she might be asleep, and Ruth Ann didn't want to wake her. She shut the door behind her, then walked across to the window and reached up to shut it. The wind coming in was freezing.

"Don't," Ashley said.

Ruth Ann looked over her shoulder. "I thought you was asleep," she said. She closed the window, then turned and studied the room. Even in shadow, or maybe because of the shadows, it looked just like Ashley's old room there, right down to the posters of rock stars with long hair. Maybe Ashley gave hers to Peri. Typical teenage girl's room. Only Peri was not a typical teen, if there even was such a thing. Ruth Ann didn't know anymore.

"I wanted some fresh air," Ashley said. Ruth Ann could tell her nose was all stopped up from crying.

"It's too cold for fresh air. You'll make yourself and that baby sick."

"Is that all you ever think about? Me and the baby, me and the baby. I'm sick of hearing about it. I guess it'll never be just me again, ever."

Ruth Ann looked sharp at Ashley. "No, it won't, and you might as well get used to that little fact right now."

"You're real big on facing facts all of a sudden, Mama." Ashley sat up and swung her feet to the floor. "You got a Kleenex?" she said.

Ruth Ann dug through her pocketbook, found a pack of Kleenex, and handed one to Ashley. "Your hair's sticking up in ten different directions," she said.

Ashley blew her nose hard, then played with the Kleenex, squeezing it in her hand, then pulling it open again.

"Quit. That's nasty." Ruth Ann took the Kleenex and threw it in the trash can next to the bed. She looked through her pocketbook for a hairbrush. "We need to get on the road pretty soon. Mama and Cassandra's down there waiting. Turn around here now so I can reach the back of your head."

"What are you doing?"

"I'm going to fix this rat's nest you got here."

Ashley tucked one leg under her and faced the front of the bed. Ruth Ann got behind her and started working on her hair.

"These tangles is terrible," Ruth Ann said. "I reckon being out in that wind at Walnut didn't help none either."

"Ow!" Ashley said, and jerked her head away. She looked at Ruth Ann over her shoulder, then scooted away.

"I'm sorry, but I got to get the tangles out."

"Well you don't have to rip my hair out by the roots to do it." Ashley dug an elastic band out of her jeans pocket and put her hair in a ponytail. She looked at Ruth Ann. "There, Mama. All fixed. Everything's fine now. My hair looks good, your hair looks good, the whole fucking world's having a great hair day. Except one, of course. It's hard to have a good hair day when your head's cracked open on the pavement."

"Ashley!"

"Oh, Mama, don't stand there and act like you give a damn. You didn't even know Peri. You didn't know her one bit. Nobody did. Nobody give a fuck about her her whole fucking rotten life."

"Is that any way to talk?" Ruth Ann clenched her hand around the hairbrush and felt like smacking Ashley upside the head with it. She knew better than to talk that way, especially about the dead.

Ashley didn't hear her. She was crying again, rocking back and forth with it, her face screwed up into a knot of pain. All Ruth Ann could do was watch, then she couldn't even do that. She turned away, walked over to the chest of drawers. A birthday card sat on top. Without even thinking about it being private, she picked up the card and read it. *Happy Birthday, Bitch! Can't wait till Saturday. We can talk about what to do then. Love you, Ashley.* Talk about what to do? No telling what they'd been cooking up. Ruth Ann put the card down.

Behind her, Ashley had quieted some, but Ruth Ann could still hear little gasps, snubbing like a child after crying real hard. All she could think about was how much she wanted to turn around and get the hell out of that room, away from the whole place, pack them all up in the van and go home to Davis. But her feet was stuck to the floor, her whole body was stuck, and she didn't know what it would take to unstick her.

"Mama?" Ashley said.

"Huh?"

"Give me some more Kleenex." Ashley walked over to her.

Ruth Ann give her the whole pack, and they stood there together while Ashley blew her nose. For some reason the sound in that quiet room tickled them, and they looked at each other and started giggling. The giggling didn't last but half a minute, then they got quiet again.

"God, Mama," Ashley said. "She dove. Headfirst, like diving in the deep end of the swimming pool. She just started running and dove right over the side."

Ruth Ann didn't want to hear, didn't want to see what Ashley saw. "How do you know that?" she said. "You don't know that."

"Oh, yeah," Ashley said. "I know. I know because I seen her do it."

"You couldn't have."

"I seen her, Mama, right before I left. We snuck up there sometimes, you know, just to get away from everybody else for a little while."

Ruth Ann turned away, went over to the bed, and started smoothing the covers where Ashley had laid down.

"It gets real hot up there. You can smell that tar. The heat comes up and makes everything look all wavy. Sometimes your feet sticks to the floor." Ashley started talking faster. "One time Peri said, Hey, let's pretend like we're on this big raft in the middle of this lake and we're so fucking hot, we're just going to run and dive right off the edge, and that water's going to feel so cool and good, we'll just stay under there and swim and swim and hold our breath for a real long time, and maybe never even come up. We'll just stay down there, live underwater, just you and me, and they'll never find us. We'll be like big fat fish can't nobody catch."

Ruth Ann felt Ashley's voice running up her back, around her neck, nearly choking her. She sat down on the bed.

"They was a big stack of boards they was using to build something on the roof, I don't know what it was. She drug one of them boards over to the wall around the edge of the roof. I bet that board weighed as much as she did. She hollered at me to help her, but I wouldn't do it. She was always doing crazy shit like that. It was too hot to be running around. I just sat and watched her.

"She put one end of that board on top of the wall, then she jumped up on the board and started jumping up and down. She was so skinny, it didn't move much. She said, Look, Ashley, diving board. She jumped up and down on it a few more times. Then she went on the other side of the roof. She said, On your mark, get set, go, and took off running fast as she could toward that board."

Ruth Ann waited for Ashley to finish the story. Finally she turned around and said, "What happened?"

"Nothing," Ashley said. "She was just acting crazy like she always did, making up a story. She was always making up stories for herself. Halfway across the roof she fell down, skinned her knees all to hell. I had to help her downstairs. She laid on my bed so I could put ice on the skinned places. She asked me why I wouldn't play that game with her, just like some little kid."

"What'd you say?"

"I told her I didn't like that game, it was stupid. Guess I'm the one that's stupid. They found that board right where she left it."

Ruth Ann shook her head, then got up and smoothed the bedspread again. What could she say that would do any good at this point? She went around the bed and opened the door. Light fell in the room, across the floor toward Ashley, and the sound of voices in the hall brought the real world back in a rush. Two girls that looked to be about sixteen was coming down the hall, and they quit talking when they seen Ruth Ann standing in the door of Peri's room. They just stared and walked on by. Ruth Ann watched them all the way to the nurses' station. Finally, Ashley come and stood beside her. "I'm ready to go home now," she said.

Somewhere between Oteen and Black Mountain, a hard rain just dropped out of the sky, no sprinkling or nothing to start with, just steady rain that made it hard to see through the windshield. Ruth Ann heard thunder and lightning off in the distance. Oh, great, she thought, after the day they had, and now they had to drive home in a storm. Storms made her nervous. Anything could happen and she didn't have no control over it at all.

At least Cassandra had slowed down and turned the radio off so she could concentrate on driving. Ashley and Marvelle was asleep in the back, and it was a relief not having to talk to anybody. Too much had happened in one day, seemed like. Too much to try and make sense of. The car not starting, then A.J. dropped his little bomb, then the graveyard, then Peri. Ruth Ann knew if it was hard for her, it must be even worse for Ashley. The girl had more on her plate than any nineteen-year-old should have to deal with, but she'd made her choices, they all had, and they wasn't nothing for it now but to go on and live.

If only people knew how hard it was to have children, and how it never gets easier, especially when you have to watch them suffer. If people could only get a taste of what it was really like, then maybe more of them would think a little longer before bringing babies in the world they didn't plan on. Then again, Ashley was an accident, and Ruth Ann couldn't imagine life without her now. A year ago, when she didn't know where Ashley was, or if she was even alive, she felt different. Many times then, Ruth Ann give in to the thought that if Ashley was dead, at least she'd know where she was. Wouldn't be worrying about her being in a bad place or acting crazy.

Funny how young'uns could be both your trial and your salvation all at the same time. She remembered being pregnant with Ashley and so miserable she wouldn't have got out of bed every day if it hadn't been for Angela and Alex. And now here Ashley was pregnant, and seemed like it made a world of difference in her attitude. It had to be due to more than survival of the human race, hormones, or something kicking in to make sure people had babies and took care of them. Not everybody done the right thing because of a baby—you just had to watch the news one night to know that. It wasn't just how you was raised neither, because Lord knows they done the best they could to raise Ashley right. No, it was more than hormones, and more than raising. It had something to do with what kind of person you was born to be. What old folks called character.

Her daddy always said hardship and suffering called out the true character that's already in a body and, depending on how the person acted, either made them stronger or turned them bad for life. That was always part of his grumbling about how none of the generations after his knew nothing about hard work, or doing without, or suffering, and that's why the world was going to hell on a downhill slide. She hoped he was wrong about the going to hell part, but maybe he was right about hardship building character. She hoped he was right, hoped all of this wasn't for nothing.

Things was different already. Not perfect, just different. Her and Ashley still snarled at each other all the time, probably always would. But at least Ashley stayed, and at least they talked to each other sometimes, which was more than Ruth Ann ever counted on, more than she done with her own mama at that age. Ruth Ann always let Marvelle say her piece and never said a word back, not yes or no. She just made up her own mind and done like she wanted when Marvelle wasn't around. It was like she always stayed a child to her mama, and in a way to herself, because she never talked back and told her who she was. The frustrating part was, Marvelle was usually right. But if she'd listened to her mama, she never would've went to work at the mill, and then she never would've met A.J., and then she never would've had her young'uns, and then she never would've ended up sitting in a van going down a mountain in the middle of a thunderstorm.

Marvelle let out a big snort and grunted. Lightning flashed as Ruth Ann turned to look in the back, and it struck her how alike they seemed, Ashley and Marvelle, not in looks but in ways. It was almost scary, both of them sitting there with their cheeks mashed up against the window glass, sound asleep. They looked like bookends.

All her life people had told Ruth Ann she looked like her mama, but she just couldn't see it. She didn't know if she wanted to see it. Not that her mama was a bad-looking woman, but it wasn't easy to turn and see your future snoring at you with her mouth open and big bags under her eyes.

She reckoned she had got her mama's good cheekbones and strong chin and dark hair. Them was all things she appreciated, but she wished she'd got her mama's skin instead of being all pasty and white like her daddy. It was hard to tell now because of the wrinkles and age spots, but her mama's skin used to be like honey, golden and smooth. It hurt now to remember how beautiful it was, hurt to see what time and a hard life could do to a body.

Ruth Ann knew time was taking its toll on her too, and not much she could do about it. Still, she took good care of herself and always had. It wasn't because she was vain, or to get some man, like so many women done. It was for herself alone, maybe the only thing she'd ever done just for herself. She'd always known she was pretty. How could she not, with everybody always commenting on it. But pretty only got you so far. The rest was hard work, and only got harder as she got older.

Ashley, it was clear to see, took after her daddy. She had that square jaw, and them long eyelashes and long arms and legs, and no butt to speak of. Too bad she also got his wandering ways and his flightiness. Maybe, unlike her daddy, Ashley would outgrow it. Ruth Ann hadn't forgot what it was like to be a teenager, and in a lot of ways Ashley on the outside was how Ruth Ann felt on the inside at that age. Maybe that was why she married A.J. His outsides reflected her insides. Too bad the reverse wasn't true. Their marriage might've lasted. But maybe it wasn't all bad that Ashley and her daddy was so much alike. Ruth Ann figured it was easier to learn to control what you let out than to learn to let it out at all. She could count on one hand the number of times in her life she'd let loose without a care for what the rest of the world might think. Usually it involved A.J. when he cheated on her or got her pregnant. She ought to be grateful at least he hadn't got nobody else pregnant, that she knew of.

Ruth Ann jumped when a big crack of lightning shot into the valley off to the right. The rain poured down even harder, like a gray curtain all around them. She looked at Cassandra and said, "Maybe we ought to pull over for a while."

"No," Cassandra said. "I can see."

"Well, at least slow down. I don't want to run off this mountain."

"I'm doing thirty-five now," Cassandra said, but she slowed down to twenty-five anyway.

Ruth Ann pulled the seat belt a little tighter across her chest. It was nearly seven o'clock now, so maybe they'd make it home by eight. She'd be willing to bet a million dollars on A.J. waiting on her at the house, watching her cable and eating her food, impatient for her to get home and give him what he wanted. She still didn't know if she would or not. On one hand, she thought it'd be the stupidest thing she ever done to even consider going into business with that man. After all he put her through? Then on the other hand she thought, what the hell? What exactly did she have to lose, besides money? She didn't have none of that to spare, but she wouldn't have a job after Christmas neither, and whether she liked it or not, she figured she had to start taking chances sometime. What was that thing Chuck Trent always said? If you do what you've always done, you'll get what you've always gotten.

Well, going into the florist business was definitely not what she'd always done, but dang if she wasn't still getting what she'd always gotten—A.J. Payne. Chuck Trent didn't know what the hell he was talking about.

This time, though, this time things was going to be different. There'd be no fooling around of any kind between them. What A.J. done with other women was his own business now, as long as he understood he wouldn't be doing nothing but business with her. He'd have to accept that. So would she. She had to admit sometimes she was tempted, being around him lately, ever since Ashley come home. But all she had to do was keep herself busy, wore out with work and old people and children, and she wouldn't have time to think about A.J., much less let him talk her into the sack. And beyond that point, she wasn't willing to think no more.

I remember it was storming the day we buried Mama, such a contrast to the day she died. Back in them days, you had to get the body in the ground no matter what the weather. We all stood around the grave, thunder and lightning cracking over us and all around, like something wild been cut loose in heaven. I reckon it suited us, all us young'uns. Losing Mama, we felt cut loose ourselves, nothing right in the world, for it was all tilted and changed.

It was me and Tildy got her ready. Should've been Marthy and Kate's job, them being the oldest girls, but every time they seen Mama a-laying there so still and pale, they got the hysterics all over again. Papa and the boys wasn't nowhere to be found. Seemed like the minute Mama let go her last breath, they lit out and didn't come home till way up in the night, all drunk as cooters. By then, me and Tildy was done and Mama was laid out in her coffin in her burying dress. She'd picked out the material months before any of us ever found out she was sick, and made that dress herself, already knowing where she'd wear it.

I tell you what, honey, I can't think of words to describe how it felt to be a-washing Mama's body, getting her ready to be laid out. The first word always comes to mind when I think on it is humble, that's how it made me feel, humble, at least as far as my understanding of that word goes. It was May second, I remember, a fine clear day and the house quiet as church. Like I said, all the men was gone, and the women too. Marthy and Kate went home and took to their beds, and it was too early for neighbors to come calling. Just me and Tildy and Mama.

Mama loved a day like that, just right for flinging open the windows and doors and airing the place out. She loved the way the blue sky looked setting over top of that new green on the mountains. It was a picture. I couldn't help but wish she was there to see it, even though I knowed I oughtn't to wish her back in that body that give her so much torment the last few months of her life. The cancer just eat her up till she wasn't hardly nothing but a shadow there in the bed.

After we got her gown off, me and Tildy looked at each other across the bed, kindly embarrassed to be seeing Mama with no clothes. We never had before. She looked so puny, like letting out that last breath made her whole body go flat somehow. I could tell by the look on Tildy's face she didn't know what to do next. Neither did I. So we just stood there a-looking till this fly come in the window and started buzzing around Mama's head. I flapped it away, but it come right back and landed on Mama's cheek. I flapped it away again and I said, "Shoo, old fly. This is our mama." It kept a-coming back though, so I took and killed it with Mama's shoe, and then I said it again: "This is our mama."

Tildy jumped when I dropped the shoe, the sound it made hitting the floor like a shot. I said, "This is our mama," like it was something both of us had just figured out. She kindly nodded, then went and poured a little hot and a little cold water in the wash pan and brung it over by the bed. I reached in my pocket for the lilac soap Jesse give me for my birthday that year. Mama had lilac growing all around the house, she loved it so. I unwrapped it and held it under my nose and, oh, it did smell so sweet, I about started crying again. Tildy's eyes had got all swimmy too.

"Hand me that washrag," I said. We washed Mama with that lilac soap all over, and once we'd got started, I didn't feel funny about it no more. I was so grateful to be a-doing something for Mama, something she'd done for me many a time until I was old enough to do for myself. But still I kept thinking, it ain't right, it ain't right. But then somehow it was like Mama was there with us, and I knowed it was all right. I started thinking, thank you, thank you, over and over, thank you. And right then, all of a sudden, everything was beautiful: Mama, and Tildy, and that old iron bed, and the ticking of Papa's watch on the table, and the little round cake of soap floating in the wash pan, and the wind blowing the white curtains in, and the way the light come through the room, and my own hands in Mama's hair. I wanted to freeze them things around me and make it last forever.

Now, I know that was silly of me, for I had a husband and a son, and another young'un on the way, though I didn't know it at the time. I had to get on with it. It was a powerful temptation though, that wanting to step outside of the world and outside of hurting. And if I could've seen then what was still to come, no telling what I might've done. That's why I say it's a blessing we don't know from one day to the next what's going to happen.

When we was done, we stood back, admiring Mama, how beautiful she looked even in death, and I felt exactly like after church on Sundays. I felt exactly like Mama looked, with her purple dress and her long dark hair braided and wrapped around her head like a crown. She was free, gone out of this world to a better place, and for just that little time, I was free with her, filled with a peace I'd never known, a feeling I knowed wouldn't come again till the day I left this world myself.

10

People started leaving the cemetery in little groups of two and three and four, and it looked like the rain had quit, because everybody was closing their umbrellas. Keith stuck his hand out to see for himself, then closed the big black umbrella he'd borrowed from Dwight. He was ready to go too, but Ashley just kept standing there, staring at Peri's daddy. All she'd done on the ride up to Brevard was rant and rave about Peri's daddy, how he caused her death, how she was going to give him a piece of her mind.

To Keith, Mr. Morgan looked just exactly like what he was, a little old music teacher at the college. He looked right pathetic, sitting there under the tent next to that open grave, and Keith figured it didn't matter a damn now what he done, because Peri was dead and nothing would change that. He couldn't make Ashley see it that way though.

The doctor about didn't let her come to the funeral, her blood pressure had been so high at her checkup that morning. But she pitched such a fit, and Keith promised to look after her, and now here she was about to have a stroke and no doctor in sight.

Keith reached in his pocket and felt the slip of paper there. He'd written down the phone number to call about Lamaze classes. The doctor told them that morning they needed to be thinking about it, but Ashley just ignored him. All Keith could do was hope that once they got Peri's funeral behind them, Ashley would start thinking more about him and the baby.

A bunch of kids from Appalachian Hall walked by with Chuck Trent behind them. Chuck's nose looked all red and swole up like he'd been crying. Nobody in the group said nothing, just looked at Ashley and kept walking. Chuck stopped and hugged Ashley. She hugged him back, but only for a second. She never made eye contact. Chuck shook hands with Keith and give him a look like what's going on with her? Keith shrugged his shoulders and shook his head. Wasn't nothing he could explain to Chuck, or to anybody. Chuck turned and followed his group over to their van.

Keith kept looking at Ashley out the corner of his eye. He wanted to touch her, hold her arm, but he knew she'd throw his hand off. It'd been months since she let him touch her in any way, shape, or form. Not since before they left Asheville. He'd almost forgot what it was like. If it wasn't for the baby staring him in the face, he might believe they'd never touched each other at all.

The cemetery was nearly empty by the time Mr. Morgan stood up to go. A couple of old ladies got one on either side of him and held his arms as they started walking. Keith realized they was going to walk right by him and Ashley on the way to the limo. He took hold of Ashley's arm. "Come on," he said. "It's over. Let's go home."

She jerked her arm away without looking at him.

"Ashley." Keith stood in front of her to block her view.

"Get out of my way," she said through her teeth.

Keith knew that look, that fuck-with-me-and-die look, and short of dragging her off by her hair, there wasn't no way to move her. He stepped back beside her, his hands folded in front of him. It was up to her now. His job was to get her and the baby home when it was over.

Mr. Morgan and the two old ladies come closer, and Keith seen just how old the guy was. Must be seventy if he was a day. Peri must've been one of them surprise miracle babies that come late in life and their mamas and daddies don't know what to do with them. Her mama had been a lot younger than her daddy and died of breast cancer when Peri was two, so Peri was stuck in that house with her daddy and his two old-maid sisters, two old bats that didn't like men or children. That was her story in group, parts of it anyway. There was only one person heard the whole story.

Ashley kept taking long, deep breaths and blowing them out through her mouth. Keith could see her chest moving up and down, up and down, and he wondered if she was fixing to hyperventilate.

The Morgans finally got up to where they stood. Mr. Morgan was bawling like a baby, and it was all the sisters could do to keep him on his feet. Keith figured if they had let him go, he would've fell on the ground and kept right on bawling, regardless of them or the rest of the world.

Ashley took a step forward and Keith's hand shot out, but he didn't touch her. He watched her watching the old man, her mouth working like words was trying to get out, but her lips got in the way. The Morgans passed and made it to the limo, but Peri's daddy got his foot caught stepping in. He fell forward onto the seat, dragging his sisters with him. Finally they all got in and closed the door so Ashley couldn't see them no more. She kept standing there, couldn't seem to break away from watching that car. As they drove off, she stuck her hand out behind her, waving it around, feeling for something. Keith reached out and grabbed her hand, then stepped up and grabbed the rest of her as she turned into him, crying her heart out against his chest.

"I'm. A. Chickenshit," she said, snubbing between words. "A. Damn. Chickenshit."

"No, you ain't," Keith said, rubbing his cheek against the top of her head. He could feel her belly between them, the place their baby lived. "You ain't no chickenshit. You're the bravest person I know."

She squeezed him so tight around the middle it took his breath. He squeezed back, not quite as hard. As much as he knew she was hurting right then, he couldn't help being happy. It felt so damn good to be close to her again. She could crack his ribs and get snot all over his one good tie, he didn't care. There was no way in hell he was letting go first.

Keith looked over the top of Ashley's head toward Peri's grave and realized they was alone in the cemetery. He could hear the wind moving through them great big hemlocks and spruce pines, and the sound of traffic off in the distance. It was a lonesome damn place to end up all alone.

At the funeral Ashley had stuck a bunch of Kleenex in his pocket because she didn't want to carry her purse to the cemetery. He'd tried to tell her men just didn't carry stuff like that around, but she wouldn't listen. He was glad to have them now and pulled a couple out and held them next to her cheek.

She kept her head bowed as she took the Kleenex and blew her nose and mopped her face. She dabbed at his tie a little bit too. "What time is it?" she said.

Keith pulled his watch out of his pocket. "Three-thirty."

Ashley blew her nose again. "We better be getting home, I guess." She looked back at Peri's grave. "Wait. I want to get a flower." She held Keith's hand and pulled him with her. They stood there quiet for a minute, looking at all the flowers covering the coffin. Finally Ashley picked a yellow rose. "This reminds me of her," she said.

Keith could tell she was heading for another crying spell, and it was starting to rain again too. "Come on," he said. He stepped out from under the tent and opened Dwight's umbrella over them. Ashley kept her arm around his waist all the way to the car. When they got in, she scooted over next to him. Keith wanted to put his arm around her, but because of the rain, he kept both hands on the wheel and concentrated on driving. They stayed quiet, and after a little while Ashley slept. Keith looked at her every once in a while, noticing how she looked a little bit like her granny asleep there with her head throwed back on the seat and her mouth open. There was his future, a long way down the road. Well, he probably wouldn't be no prize himself by then.

Ashley woke up as they was heading down Old Fort Mountain. It was nearly five-thirty by then and starting to get dark. "Look at that," she said, and Keith turned to see where she pointed. The whole valley off to the right was full of white clouds all the way level with the tops of the moun-tains. The rest of the world disappeared, dropped away, nothing left but sky. Keith figured that must be how it looked from an airplane, nothing solid in sight, just clouds all around. That was how he felt just then, like they was in a jet headed who knows where real fast. The rain had stopped, so Keith put his arm around Ashley and she put her hand on his leg. They rode the rest of the way to Davis like that.

As they passed the Food Lion on the way in to Davis, Ashley sat up straight. "Oh, shoot," she said. "Pull in here at the grocery store."

"What for?" Keith said. He put on his turn signal.

"I'll have to buy a cake. Me and Granny was supposed to make one today."

Keith parked the car and turned off the engine. "What are you talking about?"

"We forgot about it being Mama's birthday today." Ashley got out of the car, then looked back in. "You coming?"

Keith got out and went with her, thinking, what's all this we business? It wasn't his mama's birthday. Ashley stopped first at the pay phone beside the entrance. "Give me a quarter," she said. "I'm going to call Betty. Maybe she can get Dwight to come over and all of us eat together. It won't be much of a celebration, but it's better than nothing."

Keith handed her a quarter and waited while she talked to Betty. When she hung up, Ashley said, "Betty's got some chili cooking for supper, and she made a cake, so we're just going to get ice cream."

Great, Keith thought, as he followed her into the store. Quick as that, their day together was over and her family pulled her away from him again. What did she need him for? If her mama would've gone to the funeral with her, she probably wouldn't have cared if he went or not.

But somewhere between buying the ice cream and getting back in the car, it dawned on Keith that Ashley was treating him like a husband, and had been all day. She got him to drive her to Brevard, leaned on him during the funeral, made him carry her Kleenex, ordered him to give her a quarter for a phone call, made him pay for the ice cream, talked his dang ear off about everything and nothing—all things a wife would do. Maybe she didn't realize it yet, and she probably wouldn't admit it, but as far as she was concerned, he was family now. Here he'd been killing himself for months, trying to figure out how to be the man she wanted, and the one day he quit trying so hard and just concentrated on taking care of her, that was what done it. He would never understand women, never never never.

When Ruth Ann got home from work, Betty was in the kitchen stirring something in a pot. Smelled like chili. Ruth Ann was relieved she wouldn't have to worry about making supper. It had been a long day. Seemed like plant management was trying to squeeze a year's worth of work into their last two months. If she'd had any sense, she wouldn't have gone back, but when they called on Sunday, she said okay because at least it was two months less unemployment she'd have to draw, and by the time the plant closed in December, her and A.J. could be well on their way to opening their own business.

"Happy birthday!" Betty said. "What you got there?"

Ruth Ann set her pocketbook and gift bags on the table and took off her coat. "Birthday presents from the girls at work. Where's Mama?"

"Still in the bed. She ain't been out of it all day, except to pee one time."

"What? What's the matter with her?"

"Well, she says she's sick. I don't know. She ain't got no temperature. I made her breakfast and dinner, and she wouldn't eat a bite. The only thing she's had today is a little glass of tomato juice." Betty put the lid on the pot and went to get her coat. "I'm going to run on home now. Will you get Ashley to call me when she gets home?"

"All right," Ruth Ann said. She didn't pay any attention as Betty went out the back door, just stared down the hall toward Marvelle's room. She couldn't remember a time when her mama stayed in the bed all day, not ever.

"Hey!" Marvelle hollered. "Is anybody here?"

Ruth Ann figured she must've heard the back door slam. She went in Marvelle's room and stood by the bed. "Hey, Mama. How you feeling?"

"Who are you?" Marvelle said. She was laying flat on her back, looking right at Ruth Ann. "Where's that other gal? That little short, stout one?"

"Mama, it's Ruth Ann. Betty had to go home. Listen, supper's going to be ready in a little bit. Maybe you can get up and come to the table and eat."

"I don't want nothing to eat. I ain't never getting up out this bed again. I'm going to lay right here and die."

Ruth Ann couldn't think what to say to that. Finally she said, "Mama. You got to eat."

"No, I don't. I don't got to do nothing. Why should I eat when I can't even taste nothing no more? It all tastes like ashes in my mouth." Marvelle turned her head away and looked at the wall. "I'll just be left here to die, and don't nobody care. Don't nobody care if I live or die. Nobody but Jesse. Where did Jesse go? Where did Jesse go? I want him. I want him to come take me out of here."

Ruth Ann tried to talk to her and calm her down, but Marvelle just got louder and louder, started rolling her head back and forth, looking all wild-eyed. Ruth Ann give up and went back to the kitchen. She sat there for a while, then tried to read the paper, but Marvelle kept hollering. Ruth Ann put the paper down, then put her head down on her arms. Who was that crazy woman in there? It wasn't the mama she knew. And where was Ashley? She should be home by now. She was so tired, and nothing was going right, and it was her birthday, dammit. Why couldn't she have a little peace on her damn birthday?

Something woke Ruth Ann up a little while later. What was it? The house was quiet. Marvelle must've gone to sleep. A car door slammed, then another, and a minute later Ruth Ann heard the back door opening. She looked at the clock. Six-thirty. She'd been asleep over an hour. She'd never done that before, fell asleep sitting up in a chair.

Ashley appeared in the door with Keith behind her, looking like a picture of people Ruth Ann didn't know, like some cute young married couple she might see at church or a nice restaurant. Ashley looked so grown up, and she'd never seen Keith in a suit before. She opened her mouth, but before she could say anything, Marvelle started up again, louder than before.

Ashley said, "What's going on?"

"Is she all right?" Keith said.

Ruth Ann shook her head no. "She just keeps hollering. The longer I stayed in there talking to her, the worse it got, so I come in here."

Ashley walked over and run a finger down Ruth Ann's cheek. "You been asleep, Mama? You got a crease in your face."

"I don't know what got into me," Ruth Ann said, and stood up.

Ashley took the ice cream from Keith and put it in the freezer, then took off her coat and hung it up. "I'll go check on her," she said.

Ruth Ann followed, watching as Ashley sat by Marvelle on the bed and waited for her to hush. Marvelle stopped thrashing and looked at Ashley, her eyes still wild.

"Granny, what's got into you? What's the matter?"

Marvelle breathed heavy, like she'd been running. "I can't stand it no more," she said. "I want Jesus to take me. Take me home, Jesus."

"What?" Ashley said.

Marvelle started crying and rolling her head again. "I want to go home. Jesus, Jesus, take me now. I can't stand no more. Take me out of this world. I can't stand no more."

Ashley leaned over Marvelle and spoke in a strong voice, a voice Ruth Ann had never heard her use before. "Granny?" she said. "Listen to me. Listen now. You got to quit this. You got to get ahold of yourself."

"I don't want to live no more. I want Jesus to come get me. I want Jesus to take me away from here."

"Granny. What are you saying? You can't be telling Jesus what to do. You hear me?" Ashley leaned back and waited.

Marvelle held her head still and listened. "What?" she said.

"I said, you can't tell Jesus what to do. You start bossing Jesus around, you're liable to get yourself in trouble with somebody else. Ain't that right?"

Marvelle didn't move for a minute while she got her breathing calmed down. Tears trickled out the corners of her eyes and run down the sides of her face as she nodded at Ashley. "It's hard," she said.

Ashley smoothed the sweaty hair back off Marvelle's forehead. "I know it, Granny. I know it's hard. But wasn't you telling me just the other day how God don't give you no hardship without giving you the strength to bear it? Didn't you tell me that?"

Marvelle nodded again. "It's true," she said. "Lord knows it is, and it's been proved in my life more than once." She pushed the covers down to her waist. "Here, help me sit up," she said.

Ashley raised her up and got some pillows behind her back, then reached in her pocket and pulled out what looked like a picture. She held it out to Marvelle.

"What is that?" Marvelle said.

"It's my baby," Ashley said. "It's a ultrasound picture the doctor took this morning. He was worried because my blood pressure was so high. You was right, Granny. It's a girl."

"I told you that," Marvelle said, and squinted at the picture. "How can you tell from this?"

Ashley pointed. "See? No ding-a-ling."

"Let me see that," Ruth Ann said. She sat on the other side of the bed and reached for the picture. It took half a minute for her to figure out the baby shape. The head was easy, then the body, the hands and feet. She looked at Ashley's belly, then back at the picture. They didn't do that when she was pregnant, let you see inside yourself, see what was going on.

"Are you sure it's a girl?" Ruth Ann said. "This picture's awful fuzzy."

"I'm sure," Marvelle said.

Ashley said, "The doctor's ninety-nine point nine percent sure."

"The important thing is, what you going to name her?" Marvelle said. "You pick the first name, but you know what the second name ought to be."

"I know, don't worry, Granny."

"What are you going to name her?" Ruth Ann said.

"Me and Keith ain't decided yet. He says he don't care, I can pick this one's name, as long as he gets to pick the next one."

"The next one?" Ruth Ann said.

"I know," Ashley said. "I told him we'd just have to wait and see about that. It was stupid of me to get pregnant in the first place. I don't want to make another mistake."

"Oh, honey, don't never call your young'uns mistakes," Marvelle said. "What you done to get them here might've been a mistake, but that don't mean the child is."

"Well, I don't even know what's going to happen between me and Keith, so I can't go planning no more young'uns right now."

"Oh, I can tell you what's going to happen," Marvelle said.

"Is that right?"

"Yes, it is."

"Well," Ashley said. "Are you going to let me in on it?"

"No, ma'am. You'll find out soon enough."

"Granny."

"Don't Granny me. I'm right hungry all of a sudden."

Ruth Ann said, "Well, it ain't no wonder. Betty told me you didn't eat a bite all day."

"You know what Betty's cooking is like. Do you blame me?"

"Mama. Now, you know Betty's a real good cook. It's baking she has trouble with."

"That's right," Marvelle said, then looked at Ruth Ann, her eyes wide. "Oh, Lord, Ruth Ann," she said. "Honey, we was supposed to make you a cake today. It's your birthday."

Ruth Ann smiled at her. "I know, Mama. Don't worry about it. I don't need no cake."

"Don't worry, Granny, Betty made a cake," Ashley said, and got up from the bed. "I'm going to go call her right now."

After Ashley left the room, Marvelle looked at Ruth Ann. "I should've got up and made it myself instead of laying here in this bed all day. It's shameful."

"Mama, don't worry about it," Ruth Ann said. She couldn't remember ever seeing Marvelle look so sad, not even when Jesse died.

After a minute, Marvelle took hold of Ruth Ann's hand. "You know I wouldn't trade you for nothing, don't you?" she said. "Not nothing."

Marvelle stared at her so hard, Ruth Ann felt like she was trying to burn them words into her somehow. She hugged Marvelle and said, "I know, Mama."

When she sat back, she noticed Marvelle staring across the room like she'd seen a ghost. Ruth Ann turned to look and seen their reflection in the dresser mirror. She watched Marvelle's hand come up and touch her own face like she didn't recognize it, like she was trying to see with her fingers. She reached over and touched Ruth Ann's face with her other hand, and Ruth Ann sat real still and let her. Then Marvelle's head jerked around like she'd just caught herself nodding off. "Lordy mercy," she said, and rubbed her eyes. "I look a sight. Ruth Ann, honey, see if you can't do something to my hair. I at least want to look presentable for your birthday."

"Anybody home?" A.J. said as he come in the kitchen unzipping his jacket and stood behind Marvelle's chair.

"Daddy!" Ashley said, and got up to hug him.

Ruth Ann held a napkin over her mouth to keep her smile hid when she seen A.J. go pale at the sight of Ashley's belly. It was about time old A.J. caught on to real life for a change, and there wasn't no mistaking that real life making Ashley's belly stick out.

He hugged Ashley, then said, "Happy birthday, old woman," to Ruth Ann. He looked real quick at Keith, then looked away again. He said hey to Betty and Dwight, and Betty got up and fixed him a bowl of chili and a glass of tea.

Ruth Ann shouldn't have been surprised to see A.J. walk in the door just as they was sitting down to eat. The man knew how to time an entrance to coincide with a meal. Back before they was married, he never picked her up on time when they had a date to go out, but by God he'd get there smack on time whenever her mama invited him to supper. He was a walking garbage disposal. Her daddy used to tease A.J. and say he must have a hollow leg to put all that food in since it never showed anywhere else on him. He stayed lean even when other men his age started getting beer guts. Good genes, that's all it was. Ruth Ann had seen pictures of his parents, and A.J. was the living image of his daddy, big-eyed, curly-headed, tall and lean, with a hungry, lost look about him that made a woman want to take care of him. And his mama wasn't just skinny, she was downright scrawny-looking. A.J. insisted she'd been beautiful once, but that was hard to believe. Both of them was what her mama called poor-looking, and she didn't mean financially.

Ruth Ann's daddy had been a tall, slim drink of water too, but Marvelle was always stout up until the last year or two when she'd really started dropping off. Why, she probably didn't weigh ninety pounds now. Ruth Ann looked across the table at her, watched her pick at her food.

Marvelle hadn't said a word since A.J. come in. It took a minute for his voice to sink in, but the minute it did, she set her spoon down and crossed her arms over her chest. "I'm done," she said.

Nobody heard her at first because everybody was talking at once.

"I said, I'm done!" Marvelle hollered. Everybody stopped and looked at her.

Ashley picked up her napkin and wiped her lips, then held out her chair for A.J. "Here, you take my place, Daddy. Me and Granny's going in yonder."

Ashley stood by Marvelle's chair and waited. Marvelle uncrossed her arms and twisted her wedding ring around and around her finger. Finally, she put her hands flat on the table and pushed herself up, grunting. Marvelle put her hand through Ashley's arm and they walked slowly toward the living room.

"She's getting bad, ain't she?" A.J. said as he sat down and started eating. He burned his mouth on the chili, then blew on it and tried again.

"She has her good days and bad days," Ruth Ann said.

"This morning when I picked Ashley up to take her to the doctor, she said she'd been talking nonsense, something about her sister Velda." Keith got up for another bowl of chili.

Dwight put his spoon down and wiped his mouth. "Well," he said. He looked at Betty. "I reckon it's about time for us to be getting on home."

"No," Betty said, and a long look passed between her and Dwight. "Not till we have Ruth Ann's birthday cake." She called Ashley in from the living room, then got the cake and set it on the table.

Ruth Ann watched Dwight, wondering why he was acting so funny, like he couldn't wait to get out of there.

"It's brown sugar pound cake," Betty said. "I hope it turned out all right."

Ruth Ann looked at the cake. It looked fine, just like when her mama made it every year. If it didn't taste fine, she'd lie and say it did.

"Granny's working a puzzle," Ashley said when she come in. She got a pack of matches and started lighting candles.

"Lord, you didn't put fifty-one on there, did you?" Ruth Ann said.

"Looks like it." Keith grinned at her as he started lighting candles on the other side of the cake.

"Turn the lights out," A.J. said. "I want to see this."

Ashley flipped the lights off, and the cake glowed in the middle of the table like a little campfire. "Okay, Mama," she said. "Blow them out, if you can. But don't forget to make a wish first."

"What do you mean, if I can? I ain't that old." The first wish that come to Ruth Ann's mind was that her mama would never have another spell like she'd had tonight. She knew that was most likely a useless wish, but she wished it just the same. Then she took a deep breath and blew all the candles out, every last one of them.

"What'd you wish for?" Ashley said.

"I ain't telling." Ruth Ann cut everybody a piece of cake, and while they ate, she opened her present from Ashley and Betty. They'd gone in together and got a real nice sweater.

"I love it," Ruth Ann said, and Ashley and Betty both come and hugged her.

"I give you your present early," Keith said.

"I put the mums in my room," Ruth Ann said. "Thank you."

"I got something for you too," A.J. said. "I'll go get it in a minute." A.J. put a big bite of cake in his mouth and said, "This is good cake, Betty."

"Is it?" she said. "I was worried it didn't turn out right, not like Marvelle's. You know how I am with cakes."

"It is good," Ashley said.

Dwight shoved his chair back and got up and carried his dishes to the sink. Ruth Ann had watched him eat his cake, the way he gulped it down in about three bites. Was it that bad? She hadn't had a chance to taste hers yet. He put on his coat, then come over and hugged Ruth Ann. "Happy birthday, little sister," he said. "I got you the same thing I got you last year. I hope you like it."

Ruth Ann laughed. "A little more nothing is just what I need. Thanks."

While Betty put on her coat, Dwight went in and said good night to Marvelle, then him and Betty left.

A.J. finished his second piece of cake, went outside, and come back in with a big rectangular-shaped package wrapped in brown paper. "Go on and open it," he said after he cleared some space and set it on the table in front of her.

"What is it?" Ruth Ann said.

"Open it and see," he said.

Ruth Ann tore the paper and stared. It was a painted wooden sign that said RUTH ANN'S. It had a different kind of flower painted in each corner— a white rose, a pink carnation, a red tulip, and a yellow daisy.

"That's just a little one to go inside, maybe on the counter. We'll have a bigger one just like it made for the outside."

"A.J.," Ruth Ann said.

"Now, don't get mad. I know we ain't talked about a name yet, and if you don't like it, we can change it."

She looked at him standing there like a big old puppy waiting to be petted. "I like it," she said.

"I figured you would, baby."

"I don't get it," Ashley said. "What's going on?"

"Me and your daddy's starting up in business together," Ruth Ann said, putting the emphasis on business. "I didn't mention it before because of what happened to Peri and all. We just decided yesterday."

"What kind of business?"

"A florist. You know Roger Cox? He's retiring and we're going to buy it."

"Didn't y'all almost do that one time before?" Ashley said.

"Back when you was just a little bitty thing," A.J. said.

"Hey, congratulations," Keith said.

"Y'all are going to work together?" Ashley said.

"Every day," A.J. said.

Ashley looked at Ruth Ann, her face a question.

Ruth Ann started pulling the rest of the candles out of the cake. She didn't feel like trying to explain her business to Ashley at this point. She didn't feel like talking about it at all. She was tired of talking.

Keith pushed away from the table and got up. "I need to go on," he said. "I got to be up early in the morning."

Ashley got up too. "I'll walk out with you," she said. "Just let me make sure Granny's all right."

"All right," Keith said. He looked at Ruth Ann and A.J., then said, "I'll wait outside."

It was quiet after Keith left, and Ruth Ann could hear Ashley and Marvelle talking in the living room. Ashley was trying to talk her into going to bed, but Marvelle kept saying she wasn't tired. When Ashley come back in the kitchen, she said, "I guess she'll go to bed when she's ready. I'm going out and talk to Keith for a while, okay?"

"Okay," Ruth Ann said. "Put you a coat on."

When the door closed after Ashley, A.J. said, "You thinking about putting her in a nursing home?"

Ruth Ann sighed. "I can't imagine that," she said. "You know they'd have to tie her down to keep her there, and I just don't think I could stand the thought of Mama being tied like an animal, even if it was for her own safety." She rubbed her hands across the surface of the sign, the raised letters that spelled her name. "I don't know what we'll do, but I intend to keep her home as long as we possibly can. Ashley's so good with her." Ruth Ann stopped speaking, all of a sudden stunned at the words coming out her own mouth. Wasn't it just a couple months ago she told Cassandra she couldn't handle her mama and her daughter both in the same house together? Tonight she'd seen a whole different side of both of them though.

Because of Ashley, Marvelle could stay here where she belonged, where she'd be happiest, where she wouldn't be so intent on running away that she might end up dead on the side of the road or in the woods somewhere.

Seemed like every week, especially in the wintertime, the news had a story about some old person not in their right mind wandering off from a nursing home and being found dead of exposure two or three days later. Of course, Marvelle could just as easily wander off from home, but at least here she was already close to what she was most likely to wander toward—her family.

Keith went out to the driveway to wait on Ashley. He zipped his jacket and pulled his gloves on, then jumped up and down a couple times to warm up. He wished she'd hurry. He couldn't be standing out here all night waiting on her. Them cows would be needing milking in the morning, just like always. Why did she even ask him to wait anyhow? She'd pretty much ignored him ever since they got back.

He felt something warm behind him and turned around. Ashley was just standing there. At least, he hoped it was Ashley. "What are you doing?" he said.

Her teeth showed white in the dark. "Nothing," she said. "Just looking at you."

"You can't hardly even see me, Ashley."

She come closer and leaned against him. "You're right. But I can feel you." She put her hands on his butt and squeezed, and Keith jumped back.

"What the hell are you doing?" he said. He looked toward the house. "Your mama and daddy's right in there."

"So? They ain't coming out here." Ashley come toward him again and he grabbed her arms.

"What are you doing, Ashley?"

"What the hell do you think?" she said, sounding a little pissed off.

Did she do it on purpose, just to mess with his mind? Coming on to him in her mama's driveway when she knew there was nowhere they could go, no way they could be alone, and if that wasn't enough, she was nearly six months pregnant.

"Let's go down to your tent," Ashley said. She pulled a flashlight out of her pocket and turned it on.

"What?"

"God, Keith, are you in a coma? I said, let's go down to your tent." She grabbed his hand and started down the hill. He couldn't think what else to do but follow. About halfway down, she slipped and grabbed his arm to keep from falling. She hung on until they got to the fence, then she found a loose wire, held it down, and stepped over. "Come on," she said. Keith stepped over after her and followed her to the tent. She crawled in first and he kneeled down outside. She was on her knees, unzipping the sleeping bag. When she had it spread out, she sat down and patted the ground beside her. "Get in here," she said.

"I don't think this is a good idea," Keith said.

"Keith," she said.

He crawled in and zipped the tent flap, then sat next to her. She snapped off the flashlight and pushed him down on his back, then pulled the sleeping bag over them. "Scoot closer," she said. She made him move until he was practically laying on top of her, then somehow she got the edges of the sleeping bag together and zipped it up.

She put her hands on his butt, and he knew she could feel his hard-on even through their clothes because she started giggling.

"It ain't funny, Ashley," Keith said.

"What?"

"You know."

She put one hand on his crotch and used her other hand to pull his head down to her. She kissed him until he started kissing back, and then there was no stopping. It'd been too long.

"What about the baby?" Keith said when she'd somehow managed to get both their pants down, then rolled him over and straddled him.

"She won't feel a thing," Ashley said, and started moving on him.

Keith shut up and let it happen, wishing he could see Ashley's face. The sounds she made wasn't like anything he'd heard before. Always before they was somewhere they had to be quiet. Ashley never seemed to have any trouble being quiet, just breathed loud and whimpered a little bit. But tonight she made noise like something wild, and that drove him wild. He hoped to God the sound wasn't carrying up the hill to Ruth Ann and A.J.

Then he couldn't think no more, couldn't do nothing but whatever she wanted.

When they was done, Ashley slid down beside Keith and put her arm across his belly. "Don't let me go to sleep," she said. "I got to go in before Mama wonders where I'm at."

"It ain't been long," Keith said. "She's probably still talking to your daddy." He put one arm out in the cold air. It felt good. They was both sweaty inside the sleeping bag, but that felt good too. He hadn't felt so good in a long damn time. He didn't care if Ashley's daddy walked in on them right now with a shotgun.

"Hey," he said. "When did your mama and daddy decide to buy a business?"

"How should I know? Mama don't tell me nothing."

"You think they'll get back together?"

"I don't want to talk about it," Ashley said, trying to sit up. "Help me."

Keith helped her wiggle out of the sleeping bag and straighten her clothes. She got on her knees and pulled him up on his knees too. She put her hands on his face, then pushed her fingers through his hair and locked them behind his neck and kissed him. Still kissing him, she reached down and zipped his jeans and tucked his shirt in. Then she pulled back and crawled out of the tent. Keith crawled after her and helped her stand up.

"Bye," she said, and headed for the fence. In just a second she was back. She took his hand and put it on her chest. He could feel her heart beating hard under his palm. "Am I a mystery to you?" she said.

Keith wasn't sure what she wanted to hear, so he told the truth. "You're a lot of things to me," he said. "And a mystery's one of them."

"Good," she said. "Do you love me anyway?"

"Yes," he said.

"Good," she said again, and turned away. After she was on the other side of the fence, she stopped and turned back, shining the flashlight toward him. "I'm thinking about making fried chicken for dinner tomorrow." She sounded funny, almost nervous.

"Don't you worry," Keith said. "I'll be there."

"Okay," she said.

He watched her all the way up the hill, and it wasn't until he couldn't see the flashlight anymore that he realized how cold it was. He found his jacket and gloves and put them back on, then zipped up the tent and headed home. He could come back tomorrow and air out the sleeping bag. With any luck, they'd be needing it again.

December
1992

11

Ashley kicked the back door shut behind her, then carried the grocery bags to the kitchen counter. It was cold as hell out there, and she could smell something wet coming, snow or ice, had to be one or the other.

"Oh, that wind's cold! You must be froze," Marvelle said. Her and Cassandra sat at the table looking through recipes Ruth Ann kept in an old Hush Puppies shoe box.

"Where's Mama?" Ashley said.

"Getting ready to go Christmas shopping," Cassandra said. "She said she was going just as soon as you got back with the car. We're hunting Mama's sugar cookie recipe. She can't remember what all goes in them."

"Well I most certainly do," Marvelle said. "Sugar, flour, eggs, milk, shortening, vanilla, baking powder, salt." She picked another recipe out of the box, this one scribbled on a piece of brown paper bag. "Never had no use for recipes myself." She looked at Ashley and tapped the side of her head with her finger. "It's all up here."

Sure it is, Ashley thought. We all know that. It's getting to it that's the hard part. She never used to give it much thought, but ever since Peri died, it made her sad to think of things being lost. At least with Peri, it was unexpected and quick. With her granny, it was something she had to watch every single day. What if, before it was too late, they could hook up some kind of recorder to her granny's brain and take down everything inside? It'd fill up a library.

"That's fine for you, Mama," Cassandra said. "But I need a recipe." She pulled the box over to her side of the table. "Look here," she said, pulling out a yellowed index card. "Here's the recipe for rhubarb cake. Looks like Betty's handwriting. Didn't you say she made that the first Thanksgiving her and Dwight was married?"

"Yes, Lord, and the poor thing never made it again, for nobody eat a bite of it. That cake was bitter as gall."

"What did you get the recipe for, then?" Ashley said.

"I reckon I felt sorry for her. We all did. That was the year she lost that baby and found out she couldn't carry no more children."

"Oh," Ashley said. She'd never thought to wonder why Betty and Dwight didn't have children of their own. She pulled all the groceries out of the bags and put them on the counter. Her mama liked to put things away as she took them out of the bags. Ashley liked to see her stuff spread out in front of her first so she could see what all she had to work with. She put away everything except for the makings for pie crusts.

"What did you leave that stuff out for?" Marvelle said. "That butter's going to melt."

"You're going to help me make some pies today, ain't you, Granny?" Ashley reached in the cabinet for mixing bowls and set them on the counter next to the flour and butter and eggs.

"Well, if y'all going to start on pies, then I'm going home to make my cookies," Cassandra said.

Ashley and Marvelle watched her stuff all the recipes back in the shoe box and tuck it under her arm. Cassandra paused at the kitchen door, swaying side to side in the doorway. "Well. I'll see y'all after while. Tell Ruth Ann I'll bring her recipes back tonight."

After Cassandra left, Marvelle got up from the table and shuffled over to the sink to wash her hands. "Lord, honey," she said. "I ain't made a pie crust since I don't know when. I probably forgot that too."

Ashley hugged Marvelle real quick sideways with one arm. "No, you ain't, Granny. Your hands'll remember even if your brain don't."

"We'll see." Marvelle pushed her sleeves up and looked at Ashley. "What are you fixing to do with that pad?" she said.

"I'm going to write down the recipe so I'll have it," Ashley said.

Marvelle took the paper and pen out of Ashley's hands and laid them on the microwave. "You don't need no paper to learn how to cook," she said. "Practice is what cooking is. I'll show you what to do."

Marvelle opened a bag of flour and dumped some in a big bowl, then sprinkled some salt on top. "Now, Ashley," she said. "They's a plan for everything, and if you'll just foller it, why, you'll have you a nice pie in the end." She slapped a big spoonful of lard on top of the flour and started mashing it into the flour with a fork. "You got to get your flour and lard mixed up good till it makes little balls like, about the size of black-eyed peas, then in a minute we'll add us just a little bit of water to make it hold together."

Ashley watched Marvelle blend the flour and lard. It took a long time because Marvelle's hands kept slipping down the fork as she mashed. While she worked, they talked about what kinds of pies they'd make: sweet potato, pumpkin, custard, and coconut, they decided. They argued about the coconut because Ashley wanted her daddy to have a coconut pie for Christmas, and Marvelle did not. Finally Marvelle give in when Ashley reminded her that Dwight loved coconut pie too.

When the flour and lard was mixed good, Marvelle put in a tablespoon of water and started working the dough. The blue veins in her hands showed even through the flour. They moved continuously, them hands, working, working. Ashley couldn't remember ever seeing them still, except maybe in sleep, and sometimes not even then. Some nights Ashley laid in the bed and watched her granny's hands cook a meal, sew a hem, pet a head, her mouth moving all the while her hands was a-going. Seemed like the woman never rested. It struck Ashley odd that, with all the trouble her granny had with the rest of her body, her beautiful hands still cooperated, still done all the things they'd known to do all her life. Ashley looked down at her own hands, the fingers swollen because she was retaining water, the nails long and painted dark pink. Them hands looked gaudy next to Marvelle's.

Marvelle jabbed her elbow into Ashley's arm suddenly. "You paying attention?" she said.

"Yes, ma'am." Ashley washed her hands, then said, "Okay, Granny, let me get in here and do something now."

Marvelle told her how to sprinkle flour on the counter, make the dough into a ball, and take and slap it on the counter, mash it down, then roll it out thin with the rolling pin.

"If you ain't got no rolling pin, you can use you a glass jar," Marvelle said. "Just make sure it's clean and dry."

While Ashley rolled, Marvelle sprinkled flour on the rolling pin to keep the dough from sticking. Working together like that reminded Ashley of piano lessons when she was little, how she played the song while her teacher turned the pages.

By the time she had four crusts rolled out and set in pie pans to Marvelle's satisfaction, Ashley's hands was caked with dough. She stood a long time at the sink, washing her hands, flexing her clean fingers under the warm water, studying them. The more she looked, the more it seemed like the swelling had gone down some.

Cassandra set the timer for eight minutes and sat down at the kitchen table to wait for her last batch of cookies to bake. Four dozen cookies should be enough, she reckoned, to keep her and Ashley busy. They could make the icing at Ruth Ann's house and decorate the cookies there.

She went back to looking at a *Ladies' Home Journal* she brung from Ruth Ann's house. There was an article on decorating your kitchen for the holidays. She'd never heard tell of decorating a kitchen for Christmas. What kind of person did that? And then what kind of a person paid another person to write an article about it and take pictures of it?

It was bad enough you had to decorate the whole rest of the house. Of course, she hadn't even bothered with a real tree this year. The only decoration was in the kids' part of the house, just that one room. She'd cut a Christmas tree out of a big piece of cardboard from a refrigerator box and tacked it to the wall, then the kids painted it and decorated it with popcorn strings and construction paper chains and things like that. They made one more mess doing it too. Also, in their bathroom, Cassandra had put a Christmas cover on the toilet lid. On top was a picture of Santa Claus waving, and when you lifted the lid, there was Santa Claus with his hands over his eyes. He had on little green mittens. The kids loved it.

For Cassandra, Christmas had got a whole lot less fun, and a whole lot more like work, since she grew up. Besides that, there was nobody to help her decorate, to help her enjoy the results of decorating. When Marvelle lived there, they did make an effort, but it got less and less as the years went on, and Marvelle got to where she couldn't do as much. It just didn't feel like Christmas no more, not like when she was a young'un.

Cassandra didn't know what happened to magic in the world, or at least in her life. Sometime between finding out about Santa Claus and now, magic had disappeared. Was there only magic for young'uns and none for grown-ups? No fair if that was true. No, it wasn't true. She'd seen magic since she got older. It just didn't happen very often, and it didn't have nothing to do with fairies and elves and getting presents. A shooting star on a cold night, birds singing on a spring morning, the wind off the ocean on her face, a perfect sand dollar on the beach, them was magic things, things that made her feel grateful and blessed.

Maybe not having anybody to share it with made Christmas harder. In this world everybody had somebody, seemed like. And if you didn't, they was something wrong. She'd read in some magazine—maybe it was this one—that every person has one other person that matters more to them than anything. That one person could be a husband or a child or a friend, some one special person who was the most special for life. Who was that person for her? She hadn't found him yet, maybe never would, and she had to learn to be all right with that, didn't she? She had to be grateful for her family, a home, a job, a car, being able to breathe and eat and walk.

It was just that times like these—holidays—made the loneliness worse. Made you notice it more, how the whole world was in a couple, or married and having kids.

The timer dinged and Cassandra got up to take the cookies out of the oven. She set them on the counter to cool, turned off the oven, and sat back down. She looked at the magazine again. The picture showed a nice big kitchen with brick walls and a fireplace and a Christmas tree right in the middle of the floor. Well, that was ridiculous. Who had a kitchen with a fireplace and room for a Christmas tree? Nobody she knew.

She did like the wreath with white lights in the middle of the table and the red and green napkins and candles. She could probably do that pretty easy. It was too late this year, but maybe next year. If she felt the need to see Christmas this year, she'd just have to go to Ruth Ann's or to the mall. Lord knows, they had enough Christmas at the mall to decorate a thousand homes.

She turned the page and there was more pictures of Christmas linens and dishes and angels and decorations. Real pretty stuff. Wasn't nothing wrong with maybe decorating just for herself next year. Cassandra tore the pages out of the magazine to save. She'd start a file right now, today. Ruth Ann was done with the magazine, so she wouldn't mind.

That right there made her feel so much better, she got up and dug around in the cabinets until she found some candles—short, fat ones in clear glasses. Ruth Ann had bought a bunch on sale and give Cassandra some for emergencies, for when the lights went out. This wasn't an emergency. Maybe it didn't have to be. It had just started getting dark out. She put the candles on the table and lit them. They looked right pretty against the red tablecloth, even if it was plastic.

She went and put her Carpenters' Christmas album on the record player and turned it up loud. Her stomach was growling. She'd been so busy making cookies she didn't eat no lunch. A tuna sandwich sounded good, so she made one and put it on a real plate. She added some chips and two sweet pickles, then got herself a glass of milk. A green dish towel made a nice place mat, but she had to make do with a paper towel for a napkin. She put the food on the table, turned off the overhead light, and sat down to eat by candlelight. Usually she just ate over the sink. It was quicker and easier to clean up.

While she ate, she hummed along to the music and looked around at her kitchen. She did love Karen Carpenter's singing. What a tragedy, her dying so young like that. Seemed like it had been due to anorexia or something like that. People dying that young scared Cassandra. It was so easy to forget it could happen anytime.

In the dim light, the kitchen looked like a whole different room. The kettle kind of gleamed on top of the stove, and the pine cabinets looked all gold. It really didn't take much, she thought, to make things nice. The hard part for her was appreciating what she had instead of always wishing to be as happy as everybody else looked to be. Dr. Laura on the radio said it was comparing your insides to other people's outsides. It ain't fair to your insides, because other people's outsides is always going to look better. Look to your own insides and let them look to theirs, that's what Dr. Laura would say. She reminded Cassandra of Mama, the way she was so blunt and told it like it was, especially since Mama had got older and quit worrying about hurting people's feelings.

After she finished eating, Cassandra washed her dishes and set them in the drainer. She put the cookies in a big Tupperware container to carry to Ruth Ann's, but then didn't feel like going just yet. She walked around the kitchen, looking at it, thinking how good she felt there, even all by herself. It felt like being with a friend. The kitchen had always been her favorite room, and not just because of the food. It was where a whole lot of the important stuff in life happened.

After a while walking around, she noticed herself starting to feel kind of sleepy. She'd not got much sleep the night before, just restless all night. She stopped and looked down at the floor, her eyes all droopy. The blue and white flowered tile reminded her of Blue Willow, just not as blue. She looked through the door toward the couch. It seemed far away. And the light here in the kitchen was so nice. She looked back at the floor. Why not? It was clean, just swept and mopped that morning. She got on her knees, then sat back on her butt, then laid on her back.

Her back took a minute to ease flat on the floor, which felt a little cold, but pretty soon she got comfortable. The candlelight flickered up on the ceiling, making shadows. The table and chairs, the stove, the refrigerator, the door, everything looked different from this angle. She could see the bottoms of the cabinets and a dust bunny she'd missed under the microwave cart. It was a whole new perspective.

Cassandra rolled on her side and looked at her living room, studying the furniture in there. She needed a new couch bad, or at least a slipcover for the old one. And the legs of the coffee table was all scuffed up. She wished suddenly that she was looking at a Christmas tree in that living room, something green and glowing with lights, something to take attention away from that hand-me-down furniture. A pretty tree, combined with that music, might be magic enough for this Christmas anyway.

Her eyes closed and she decided to pretend there was a tree, a great big one with thousands of colored lights and shiny balls and cute ornaments. And a white angel on top, with gold wings and gold hair and a gold halo. And red and green candles on the coffee table, with evergreen boughs around the edges of the table. And silver garland and Christmas cards tacked around the door. And one of them electric trains running around the tree, and a Christmas village with lights, and a Nativity scene. Oh, she could just see it all, how beautiful it would look.

Right before she fell all the way asleep, Cassandra decided to have a Christmas tree in her bedroom too, a little one all decorated and lit up. It would be so nice to lay in bed and look at the lights until she fell asleep, and wake up to them in the dark of the winter morning.

A.J. hated the mall, hated shopping, hated waiting, hated standing in line. It was mostly men in the other lines at the gift-wrap counter in the middle of the mall, last-minute shopping just like him. Why did they wait? Because shopping did not come naturally to men, that's what it was. A man only went in a store when he needed something specific. A man went in, got it, come out. Malls was invented for women. Store after store with big windows and lots of other women. A.J. figured the mall was to women what the golf course was to men.

The line moved forward a little bit and he pushed his shopping bags up with his foot. Them things was too heavy to stand there holding. He looked at his watch. Nearly six o'clock. The mall closed at six o'clock. It wasn't looking good.

Of course, nothing had gone right since he got here. It started out with running into Ruth Ann coming out of the mall as he was going in, a big surprise since she always made such a big deal about not waiting till the last minute. Everything about her tonight had been surprising. She let him help carry her bags to the car, asked how he was doing, told him Merry Christmas, even smiled at him. He didn't know what to think. It made him nervous, her being so nice. He got so nervous he went right to the jewelry store and bought her some diamond earrings.

Then of course he couldn't find nothing for none of the rest of them, except the boys. He found a lot of stuff for them at the toy store. But even though he went in every store in the mall, he couldn't find the right gifts for the rest of the family. Not even Cassandra, and she was usually easy to buy for. He finally got them all gift certificates at the shoe store. Everybody needed new shoes, some time or other. And now here he was standing in line and the mall about to close, and to top it all off he had to pee.

The man in front of him decided he didn't want to pay two dollars a package, so he grabbed his bag and left. A.J. heaved his bags up on the counter. "Wrap them all," he said. He looked up and down the mall and noticed almost all the stores had pulled their little gates down halfway, getting ready to close. Some was already closed.

The woman behind the gift-wrap counter just stood there, looking at him with dead eyes. "All of these?" she said.

"Yes, ma'am," A.J. said. "If you please."

She give him a real dirty look then and looked at her watch. "We're closing in less than five minutes," she said.

A.J. seen that she was exhausted, had probably been on her feet all day. He wondered what circumstances made it so she had to work this late on Christmas Eve. She looked old enough to be retired by now. Of course, a lot of people had trouble making ends meet once they retired. He was lucky. He squinted and read Stella on her name tag.

"Look here, Miss Stella," A.J. said. "I hate to ask you to stay and do a big job like this. I bet you got family waiting on you at home, don't you?"

She nodded. "My husband," she said. "And my daughter's coming in from Georgia. She's probably there by now with her two kids. Her husband had to work, so he couldn't come." She didn't look at him because she was busy raking leftover pieces of ribbon and wrapping paper in the trash can.

"That's a durn shame." It really was a shame. But he had to get these presents wrapped to take to Ruth Ann's the next day, and he wasn't giving up on Stella without a fight. "It's a shame anybody has to work Christmas Eve. I think it ought to be illegal. I really do. But I got a problem here, ma'am. I can't wrap for shit. Excuse the language. I'm sorry about that. But it's the truth. And it's important to me to make this a nice Christmas for my family. I want them to have a nice Christmas, right down to the wrapping paper." Stella didn't need to know that his family wasn't waiting at home for him like hers was, that he wouldn't see his family till the next day. "Do you think you could help me out here, ma'am?" He let that slow, easy smile of his spread across his face and waited.

She put her scissors and tape in a drawer, looked at her watch again, then looked up at him and smiled back. "I'm sorry, sir, but it's six o'clock and we're closed. Merry Christmas."

The Ray Conniff choral rendition of "O Holy Night" about made Ruth Ann cry every time she heard it. She just hated she wasn't a good enough singer to carry it off. She hummed along with the radio as she wrapped presents. The bedroom door was locked to keep Ashley and Cassandra from peeking. They was just like young'uns that way.

When Ruth Ann got home from shopping, Ashley and Cassandra was in the kitchen decorating sugar cookies while Marvelle worked a puzzle in the living room. They had made a mess with that icing all over the table and the counter, but Ruth Ann didn't let it bother her. She figured baking kept people out of trouble. Maybe that's why her mama was teaching Ashley. Ruth Ann smiled to herself.

"Mama!" Ashley yelled, and knocked on the bedroom door. "What you doing in there?"

"None of your business. Go on, now." Ruth Ann watched the door and waited, scissors in one hand, wrapping paper in the other. She admired the bows she'd tied on the boxes already wrapped as she listened to Ashley walking away from her door. Curiosity had always been that girl's greatest weakness and the root of all her disappointments too. Ruth Ann had seen her experiment with so many things, from the clarinet to tennis, only to get bored and quit once she found out what it was really like. She'd never been able to stick with one thing for very long.

At least Ashley had learned to knock before coming in her room. They must've taught that at rehab, because she sure didn't get it from Marvelle, who still barged right in even if somebody was on the toilet.

Ruth Ann finished wrapping the sweater she'd bought Ashley and reached for the foot massager for Marvelle. The paper rattled as she rolled out enough to cover the big box. That made two rolls she'd used up already, and she still had a pile of things to go and her back ached from bending over the bed.

It wasn't like her to put off her shopping until Christmas Eve like this, but it had been kind of fun. The mall was packed and everybody was in a good mood—even most of the salesclerks still had their sense of humor. The last minute-ness of it made shopping easier too. She clicked right along, picking out presents for everybody in one afternoon. A record for her.

She hadn't even minded running into A.J. at the mall. He sure had been surprised. He even looked a little bit guilty that she caught him shopping at the last minute. Well, hell, she was too old to let something like that bother her, and so was he. After all, he'd caught her last-minute shopping too, only he'd been too flustered to realize it at the time.

Usually she started shopping in August and agonized over every little thing, right down to wrapping paper and bows and the right kind of tape. It took forever to get ready for Christmas and forever to clean up after it was over. This year, she done things different. She picked out one kind of paper, a real pretty green foil with gold angels on it, and bought gold ribbon to go with it. And done all her shopping in one swoop. Simple as that.

Ruth Ann remembered how, when she was little, the first sign of Christmas was the Sears catalog in November. Then, along about the second week of December, there'd be whispering and secrets, giggling and hiding things, knowing looks between Mama and Daddy. They didn't go to town much, they wasn't no mall yet, and they didn't have TV, so they couldn't watch Christmas for weeks and weeks like her grandsons did now. The excitement and anticipation built up just the same though, maybe even more, and she honestly believed they enjoyed Christmas more in her day than Bryan and Jonathan did now. By the standards of forty and fifty years ago, every day was Christmas for them boys.

Ruth Ann felt a shiver of happiness at the thought of seeing them again. They hadn't visited since the weekend in August when Ashley come home, and that had been tense. All Angela had wanted to talk about then was how Ashley was taking advantage of Ruth Ann, and Ruth Ann didn't appreciate being treated like she was incompetent.

She hoped the months since then had given Angela time to calm down. Ruth Ann tried to reassure her whenever they talked on the phone. She told Angela how well Ashley and Marvelle got along, how they worked together, how they would've had to put Marvelle in a nursing home back in the fall if it hadn't been for Ashley. Angela never did sound convinced, much less impressed. Ruth Ann reckoned a big sister just never completely got over being jealous of a little sister.

Angela and David and the boys would have Christmas with David's parents tonight, then get up early, have Santa Claus, and drive to Ruth Ann's from Salisbury. They believed in taking turns between families. They'd get in about dinnertime and then go home early the day after Christmas. Angela said David had to be back at work, and her and the boys had planned some projects at home. To Ruth Ann that meant they just didn't want to stay and had their excuse to leave ready in advance. In a way it was a relief. There was a lot to be said for a nice short visit where everybody got along because they knew they wouldn't have to see each other again for a long time.

Next year the boys would be there, and the baby, and it sure would be nice having young'uns in the house Christmas Eve. Made it more exciting. It'd be something, all right, two little boys and a baby girl. A baby girl. Ruth Ann was just now getting used to the idea of a baby. Would she ever get used to Ashley being a mother?

It was different when Angela was pregnant with her two, partly because she was the oldest and lived so far away, but mainly because Angela didn't seem to need a mama once she got past a certain age, nor during her pregnancies, nor during the whole raising of her children so far. She had her own way of doing things and did not like to be interfered with.

Ruth Ann heard a noise outside her window and froze. It sounded like somebody out there rustling the bushes. She turned and stared at the closed curtains, then walked over to the window. When she pulled the curtain back, she heard giggles, squeals, crashing through the bushes, and running. A minute later she heard the back door slam open and Ashley and Cassandra laughing. Ruth Ann opened her bedroom door and yelled down the hall toward the kitchen. "Next one I catch peeking won't get nothing but a bundle of switches from Santy Claus!" She slammed the bedroom door so they'd think she was mad and went back to her wrapping, singing along with Johnny Mathis on "It's a Marshmallow World."

The manager of the drugstore took some convincing, but A.J. finally talked her into letting him come in and buy some wrapping paper. She locked the door after he come in, and waited behind the cash register. She wasn't bad-looking, and she didn't think he was bad-looking either, he could tell. Sometimes it didn't hurt to have a face that made people open doors for you.

He stood in front of the wrapping paper and his mind went blank. There was too damn much of it. He walked down the whole aisle and nothing popped out and said, here, buy me. Why couldn't that lady at the mall have stayed fifteen more minutes to help him out? Was that too much to ask? He must be losing his touch.

At the end of the aisle, he noticed some bags hanging on hooks, bags with Christmas scenes on them. Gift bags. Now, that was the answer. He got ten of the biggest ones they had for the boys' gifts, and one little bitty one for Ruth Ann's earrings, and headed up front. Only five after six, and he was done. He smiled at the manager as she rung him up, and when she tried to hand him back five dollars change, he told her to keep it for her trouble.

Once he got home, it took him only ten minutes to take off price tags and drop the stuff in bags. Now, that's what he called Christmas shopping. He set the bags by the door so he wouldn't go off and forget them in the morning, then got a frozen dinner and put it in the microwave. He stood in front of the TV flipping channels while the food cooked. Every channel had some kind of Christmas show on, and most of them he'd seen at least once. The only one he really liked was *Miracle on 34th Street*, and that was only because he knew it was Ruth Ann's favorite. She was probably looking at it right now. He ate his dinner standing over the sink, then opened a beer and drained it. He got another beer and settled on the couch, turned off the lamp, then kicked his shoes off and put his feet on the table. The movie was right at the part where the mail guy gets the bright idea to send all the Santy Claus letters to the courthouse. That was Jack Albertson, the guy from that show *Chico and the Man*. Him and Ruth Ann used to watch that show. It was pretty funny, until that Chico guy killed himself. Jack Albertson was dead too, A.J. reckoned. He sure did look young in this movie, but that was him, all right.

While she waited for the popcorn to pop, Ashley looked out the kitchen door window toward the pasture. The only light come from the little scrap of moon and faraway stars. Then she seen another light, one burning low by the creek. What was that? Keith's tent? He did keep a battery-operated lamp in the tent ever since they'd started meeting down there. What in the world could he be doing there after dark on Christmas Eve, especially cold as it was?

The microwave timer dinged and Ashley jumped. She poured the popcorn in a big bowl and carried it to her mama in the living room. Marvelle still sat hunched over a thousand-piece puzzle of the Rocky Mountains, which she liked because of all the snow in the picture. The woman did crave snow. She'd been going around all week wishing for a white Christmas.

Ashley stood by the couch eating a handful of popcorn, watching *Mira-

cle on 34th Street with her mama. It was right at the part near the end where Natalie Wood was in the car saying, I believe, I believe, even though she really didn't.

"Why don't you sit down?" Ruth Ann said.

Ashley wiped her hands on her britches. "I think I'm going for a walk."

Ruth Ann just looked at her.

"Looks like a light on down at Keith's tent. I'm going to see."

"You sure have been going down to that tent a lot lately," Ruth Ann said.

"You put you a coat on, missy," Marvelle said without looking up from her puzzle. "It's cold as a witch's tit outside."

"Mama!" Ruth Ann said.

Going down the hill, Ashley had to lean back a little to keep her balance, and she walked slow to keep from falling. When she was little she used to tear down that hill at a dead run, never worrying about falling or stopping or nothing. Seemed like a million years since then.

Every once in a while she had to stop and bang the flashlight against her leg to keep the light going. Batteries must be about dead. It drove Ashley crazy how her mama wouldn't keep a good supply of things like batteries and lightbulbs around. She just never had that much use for them, Ashley reckoned.

Halfway down the hill she stopped and zipped her coat all the way up to the neck. The wind was vicious cold tonight. She couldn't figure out why Keith would leave his nice warm room. Then again, why did she?

When she got to the fence, she laid the flashlight on the ground so she could hold the barbed wire down with both hands and step over. Gloves, she thought. Gloves would be good. The wire was freezing cold and rough against her hands. She used to could just crawl under the wire to get to the other side, but once she got bigger, Dwight started leaving the wire loose on one post so she could get across easy. Nobody else knew about it but her. And now Keith.

About the time she got on the other side and reached for the flashlight, it went out completely. No amount of banging or shaking would make it come on again.

"Damn," she said. She stood there a minute letting her eyes adjust to the black dark under the trees. With the wind roaring around her, she turned toward the light in Keith's tent and took baby steps with her hands out in front of her, feeling for obstacles. When she reached the tent she went down on her knees and crawled inside.

The tent was empty except for the lamp and sleeping bag. Keith must've gone off and forgot to turn the light out. Well, it was a good thing. She could use it to get back up that hill to the house.

Ashley sat cross-legged on the sleeping bag and looked around. Wasn't much to look around at. The tent was so little she could stretch across and scrape the other side of it with her fingernails. It was kind of cozy though and kept out the cold pretty good once she zipped up the opening. She yawned, then stretched out on the sleeping bag.

The wind in the trees overhead sounded lonesome and made her wish Keith was there with her. She turned on her side and curled up. When she put her hand under the pillow, she felt something hard, plastic, and square. She pulled it out. A ring box? Uh-oh. This must be the present Keith had been hinting about for weeks.

Ashley opened the box and stared. It was a nice little diamond, no more than half a carat, but set real pretty in a platinum band. She tried it on and it fit perfect. Looked good on her hand too. Damn him!

She put the ring back in the box, then snapped it shut and laid there holding it, staring at it, trying to understand. It was like geometry back in high school. Here she had a circle inside a square, and now what was she supposed to do with that? None of it made sense to her, no matter how she concentrated. Why did he have to go and make things so hard? It was Christmas, for God's sake. Here she was having a nice time with her family for a change, and he had to go thinking about the future. It was just too much.

The lamp flickered and Ashley clicked it off to save the batteries. The inside of the tent was real dark at first, then gradually her eyes got used to it and she could make out the shadows of tree limbs over the top of the tent. She laid on her back and set the ring box on her belly. With her arms behind her head, she watched the box quiver as her belly went up and down with her breathing. The tree shadows waved over her in the wind like long arms. Reaching for her, always reaching. Well, what if she didn't want to be reached? What if she didn't want to be had?

She thought about having a baby then, and how that was such a strange way of putting it. Having a baby. I am having you, baby, she thought, and put her hand on her belly. You are mine and I am having you.

Keith wants to get married, but I ain't having none of that. Ashley snatched up the ring box and stuck it back under the pillow.

She laid there a while longer, until the wind started blowing harder against the tent, trying to come in or else trying to jerk it up and carry it off. She sat up and listened. Sounded too wild outside for Christmas Eve. Too dangerous. Anything might happen. This was supposed to be silent night, holy night.

The wind whipped right in when she unzipped the tent, and when she crawled out and stood up, it caught her hair and blew it straight up in the air around her face. It felt like her hair wanted to fly off her head. She looked up at the sky through the trees. Dark dark dark, but for stars and moon. Ashley reached back in the tent for the lamp. A dark night, but not silent. Did holy and silent always have to go together?

She stood holding the lamp without turning it on. The wind kept whipping all over, making her feel nervous. She started humming to take her mind off how dark it was. She hummed "O Holy Night," then started singing louder and louder, as loud as she could. Nobody could hear her in the middle of the cow pasture. "The stars are brightly shining." Funny how she never remembered learning the words to all them Christmas songs. They was just there, like knowing how to breathe or walk. Then again, maybe her mama and granny playing Christmas records since before Thanksgiving had something to do with it too.

She started "O Holy Night" again as she crossed the fence but had to quit about halfway up the hill because she lost her breath. Then she just thought the words. *It is the night of our dear savior's birth.* When the words to the song run out, she thought about Mary, and her having her baby in a stable, and how the Bible only ever told the beauty of the night and the glory of the birth. It never told what all Mary had to go through to get to the glory part. That proved it if nothing else did: The Bible was written by men. That's probably how Keith would write it.

She got up to the door finally and stopped to look back the way she come and wait for her breathing to slow down. The baby kicked, hard, like maybe she'd woke it up with all that walking and it was mad at her. It'd started kicking and poking a lot lately, like a big ball of gas with arms and legs doing cartwheels in her belly. All that moving around made the baby seem so much more real and made Ashley feel like she didn't have any say-so over her own body anymore. It belonged to the baby now.

The doorknob felt like a big ice cube in her hand, but she stopped to look up at the stars one last time. She couldn't get that Bible passage out of her head. And the glory of the Lord shone round about them. Glory. Yeah, right. So far there wasn't nothing glorious about none of it. Then the next part come to her: And they were sore afraid. She turned the knob and the wind pushed the door open for her, wouldn't let her close it for the longest time. Finally she leaned all her weight against the door, slammed it shut. She stood there, listening, waiting. That wind was still out there, restless and wild.

12

Cassandra liked Christmas Day afternoon the best. All the presents had been opened, dinner cooked and eaten, dishes washed, and now everybody was taking a nap—even Angela's boys had fallen asleep in front of the TV. She stepped over them and turned off the set, then the VCR. They'd been watching some kind of a karate movie. Cassandra shook her head. Whatever happened to Lassie and Roy Rogers? Then she figured, well, it must be the same attraction in the karate movies—action and adventure—just in a different, more 90s multicultural way. Although how could you get more multicultural than a collie dog smarter than the people it lived with? Maybe that was multispecies. Whatever it was, she preferred the black and white days to this modern color world where they showed as much blood and guts as possible and the hero killed more people than the bad guys. Now, Roy Rogers had shot his share of folks, but he always regretted the need for killing. None of these ninja things seemed to regret nothing but the fact they didn't get to show their faces all the time. They had to wear some kind of a hood while they was fighting, but then, soon as the trouble was over, they'd rip that sucker off and grin a close-up.

She spread an afghan over the boys' legs and stood looking down at them. Her and Angela had never been all that close once Angela got past the age of five, but Cassandra surely did love her little boys. They was more like their daddy, more easygoing and not so dang picky about the clothes they wore and how everything looked. Jonathan was the image of Angela when she was seven, all tow-headed and skinny, with a round little face and deep brown eyes. Bryan was eleven and already getting tall like his daddy, and he had David's red hair. But his face and expression was A.J., right down to that square jaw and dimpled chin. She bent down and petted Jonathan's head, then pulled the hair out of his eyes. She couldn't understand Angela keeping the boy's hair so long. He was too old for that page-boy that made him look like Little Lord Fauntleroy. He wanted a buzz cut like his brother, and Cassandra figured he'd have one too by summer. He was his mama's match for willfulness, that was certain.

Cassandra put her hands on her knees and pushed herself upright again. The living room was a mess, toy cars and guns and socks and shoes strewed everywhere. A.J. was asleep and snoring in the recliner, and David was stretched out sawing logs on the couch. The males of the family had taken over this room while the females was in the kitchen washing dishes. Every year it was the same. The women cooked the dinner, the men ate it and fell asleep, the women washed dishes, and then they fell asleep. Ashley and Marvelle was in their room, Ruth Ann and Angela was in Ruth Ann's room. Cassandra couldn't figure out why she wasn't asleep too. Usually she headed home right after dinner and conked out for the rest of the day, then her and Marvelle would come back to Ruth Ann's for supper at night. But her mama was already here, and home was so quiet now without her.

She'd even took to listening to talk radio at night. TV just couldn't hold her attention like it used to. Without Mama there to talk through all her favorite shows and drive her crazy, seemed like she'd just lost interest. She learned a lot from the radio, and she could listen and keep busy around the house at the same time. Marvelle used to nag about cleaning, and Cassandra, out of spite, done as little as possible. But now she noticed things that needed doing, things that Marvelle used to do, like sweeping, dusting the furniture, washing the windows, cleaning the lamp shades. Little things that really made a difference when they wasn't done regular.

Cassandra turned off the lamp next to A.J.'s chair and went back to the kitchen. Everything was done that needed doing there, so she put on her jacket and went out the back door. The clouds had been piling up all day, and the weather report was calling for rain or possible freezing rain that night. She hoped the roads would be all right in the morning. Angela and David and the boys was heading back to Salisbury first thing.

Cassandra didn't know why they wouldn't spend more time. Angela didn't have to be back teaching until after the new year, and David was off until the end of December. They just didn't want to spend any more time, at least Angela didn't. She had got real uppity since she graduated college. At least her husband was normal. They'd all been worried she'd bring home some greasy-headed, sandal-wearing granola eater from Chapel Hill.

Ruth Ann never said a word, but Cassandra knew it hurt her that she didn't see her other two young'uns more. Alex wasn't even coming home for Christmas this year. He went to the Bahamas with some friends.

Smoke rose from behind the hill, which meant Dwight and Betty had a fire going in the stove. The homeplace, the house Daddy had brung Mama to all them long years before, the house his granddaddy had built after the War between the States. They still cooked on the wood stove over there and had coal heat. Didn't go in for the modern conveniences at all, and Cassandra had to say it was a comfort to know her old home was still there, still the way she remembered it from childhood. Not that she wanted to move back there, but she liked knowing she could walk in that door any day of the week and Betty would tell her to sit down and ask her what she wanted to eat, just like Mama used to whenever anybody come to the door. Cassandra never thought of it before, but Betty was a lot like Mama used to be, maybe that's why Dwight married her. He'd always been his mama's boy. Hell, all the boys was their mama's boys, no matter how old they got, no matter they had young'uns of their own.

It puzzled her why her and Clark was the only ones, out of them all, never to marry or have children. Now, Clark, she could sort of see why nobody married him. He was too dang mean. As for herself, well, she was still waiting, waiting to be found. And in the meantime, she'd had plenty of crushes on movie stars, but that didn't count for nothing. Jimmy Dean and Elvis in the 60s, David Cassidy in the early 70s, John Travolta in the late 70s—she'd never understand that one—Mel Gibson in the 80s. Until Lance anyway. Once Lance come along, seemed like Mel just faded away. Being in love for real had sort of took all the fun out of having crushes on movie stars. It wasn't fair though, because she didn't get Lance, and now she couldn't enjoy Mel Gibson the same way anymore either. Seemed like the story of her life, always waiting for something to happen and nothing ever did.

Something moved down by the creek and Cassandra seen Keith jump across the water and duck into his little tent. The boy had perseverance going for him if nothing else. Even when he was out of sight, Ashley couldn't miss seeing that blue bubble down there every time she looked out the window. Cassandra smiled and watched Keith come out of the tent. He stuck something in his pocket and headed toward the house. As he climbed over the barbed wire, he looked up and seen her standing there. Cassandra waved and he waved back once he was over the fence. He come up the hill toward her, his hands stuffed deep in his pockets and breath blowing behind him like smoke.

As he got closer, she could see the cold wind had chapped his cheeks red. Dwight must've had him out working. Cows had to be milked even on Christmas Day.

"Hey, Cassandra, how you doing?" Keith stopped in front of her.

"Merry Christmas!" she said, and hugged him. He didn't have time to get his hands out of his pockets to hug her back. "Was Santy Claus good to you this year?" she said.

Keith smiled. "Well, I don't know about Santy Claus, but Dwight and Betty give me this jacket and some money, and Betty made the best ham dinner I ever had."

Cassandra rubbed the tan corduroy on the sleeve covering Keith's arm. "That's a nice blazer, honey, nice enough to wear places. And it looks good and warm. What's that I seen you put in your pocket down there?" She watched him close. It was a good thing his face was already red or she'd swear he was blushing.

He stared right back at her and said, "Nothing. Present for Ashley."

"I know," she said. "Ain't none of my business." She had a pretty good idea what was in that little box though. "Come on in the house. You look froze to death." She put her hand on his back and steered him toward the door. He hesitated, then opened the door and said, "Merry Christmas, Ashley." Cassandra looked around him and seen Ashley standing in the middle of the kitchen, rubbing her eyes.

"Hey, Keith," Ashley said, yawning, and sat down at the table.

Cassandra give him a little push and he went over and kissed Ashley and sat down next to her.

"Oh, your face is cold!" she said, and put her hand on his cheek. "What you been doing outside?"

"Nothing," Keith said. "Working."

Cassandra pulled the door shut and stared at the rectangular glass panes in the top half of the back door. She couldn't see through to the kitchen because of Ruth Ann's red and green Christmas curtain. Still, she could picture the scene, Ashley and Keith at the kitchen table, talking quietly. Further on into the house Ruth Ann and Marvelle and the rest was still laying down. Nobody out here but her. It was a lonely feeling. Reminded her of that dream she had, a dream she felt like she'd had her whole life, it was so familiar.

In the dream, she was a little girl outside a house that looked like the homeplace on the outside and like Ruth Ann's house on the inside. She was about ten or eleven, standing on a crate to see in the kitchen window next to the back door. It was real foggy. All she could make out was shapes and colors and voices. She wiped and wiped the window and gradually the picture got clear enough so she could see her mama and Ruth Ann and A.J. and their kids sitting around the table laughing and talking. Cassandra tapped the windowpane, then beat on the side of the house, but nobody ever looked up or acted like they heard her, so she just learned to stand there quietly, watching and waiting to be seen. Only in this dream she never was. She always woke up from that dream feeling sorry for herself, and mad at the rest of them.

The dream had changed in the last year or so though. First, Cassandra noticed Marvelle wasn't sitting at the table no more. She was always standing at the stove or the sink or wandering around the kitchen. Then one night not long before Ashley come home, Cassandra was having the dream and she couldn't see Marvelle at all, until suddenly Marvelle's face popped up right in front of Cassandra, staring right through the pane, and Cassandra fell backward off the crate and woke up, her heart going like a little bird. Since then the dream had been the same: Marvelle's face at the window, hollering for Cassandra to turn around and look behind her, wasn't nothing to be afraid of, but Cassandra too scared to look. As tired as she was of standing on that crate, she couldn't make herself turn around yet.

She often wondered what it could be, a monster or just darkness or some serial killer maybe. Whatever it was, it was horrifying and dangerous. Marvelle just kept pointing and hollering and Cassandra kept shaking her head no. Sometimes she'd even wake up crying. Maybe she was going through the change, like Ruth Ann. She knew forty-two was young for the change but not impossible. It'd be a relief if that was all it was. Didn't look like she'd be getting married and having children no how, so she didn't need her cycle. Let it go and be done with it forever. Besides, Ruth Ann's children had been enough, and her grandchildren would be too. And she had her own peaceful home to escape to when it all got too much for her. What more could she ask?

Being an old woman would be a relief in a lot of ways. There was too much pressure on young women to look a certain way, get men, have children, be on PTA, and go to beauty parlors. Being a young woman was too damn hard. Better to be past the prime, old and discarded and able to relax and enjoy life. Except they was times Cassandra felt she'd already been living like an old woman her whole life, and that scared her. She never done young-woman things, like date and raise hell, court and get married, and make babies and raise a family. Where did that leave her in the whole scheme of her life? Was she living backward? Or doomed to live the next forty-two years the same way she lived the first?

The word PARALYZED suddenly appeared in her mind like it was wrote in big letters on a chalkboard, and she stumbled forward, headed down the hill, as if to prove she wasn't. She had no idea where she was going or why, just that she had to move. If she'd been in better shape, she'd have run. The cows looked bored with watching her when she reached the bottom of the hill and put her hand on top of a fence post. She was breathing hard and starting to sweat.

She closed her eyes and tried to calm down. The wind moved strong through the trees over her head and she felt her body start to sway. When her breathing slowed to normal, she opened her eyes and focused on Keith's tent. She thought about him up there in the house with Ashley and tried to imagine how it was going.

With any luck the rest of the house would stay asleep a little bit longer, long enough for Keith to do his thing and Ashley to say yes. Cassandra had seen this moment coming on for a long time, from the first time she seen Keith over at Dwight's house and realized he was there to stay. Keith and Ashley was so young, and neither one of them had any sense, but she hoped things would work out anyway. She hoped at least they'd try and see what happened. But mainly she hoped Ashley would realize how lucky she was to have a man willing to speak up, to risk making a fool of himself and having his heart broke. Maybe that was something only young people could do.

Cassandra didn't envy them the hard times ahead, but she knew they was reaching out for something she'd pushed away with both hands all them years ago because she was too afraid to admit she wanted it, too afraid she might actually get it and be disappointed and then not know how to get out of it. Well, where had that got her? Seemed like it might be time for old Cassandra Moon to haul her ass out of the rut she'd been in so long and do something different.

She took a deep breath, and cold air stung the inside of her nose. Her watch read nearly five o'clock; the kids'd be waking up soon and hungry. Come to think of it, she was hungry herself. Time to get the leftovers out and feed that crowd and get on home. She wanted to see the rerun of *It's a Wonderful Life* at eight o'clock, and she knew it'd make her cry, so she couldn't watch it at Ruth Ann's. She turned and looked up the hill toward the house. Damn, that hill hadn't seemed so steep coming down. She'd be sweating and heaving like a mule by the time she got back to the house. She leaned forward and started up.

"I don't know if I want to get married, Keith." Ashley didn't look at him when she said it, just stared down at some salt she'd spilled on the table. When he didn't answer, she looked up and he was staring at her with a curious expression on his face, like she was something he just couldn't figure out and maybe didn't even want to try anymore. Damn, she hated that look—that Indian look, was what she called it. Just sitting there like a rock with his hands on the table and that stupid ring box between them. She never would've pegged him as being so traditional when they first met. She'd fallen for his wildness, and now come to find out he wasn't wild at all. He wanted to get married and settle down. Well, just because he was ready and just because he was the father of this baby, that didn't automatically mean marriage and the rest of their lives. And if he thought it did, well, she was just the woman to set him straight.

"You can quit looking at me like that," Ashley said. He didn't know she'd found the ring last night at the tent and that she'd had time to think about her answer. Not enough time though. "I know what you're thinking. You think we make a nice little equation, you plus me plus baby equals family, and since you never had that you think you want it. Well, you better think again, 'cause it ain't like a TV show. In real life things never work out like that. Look at my mama and daddy if you don't believe me. Hell, your own parents ought to be enough to make you think twice."

She'd noticed before how Keith got little white lines beside his mouth when he was mad, and she could see them now. He didn't like talking about his parents, and he didn't want nobody else talking about them neither. He'd talk about his granny and his uncles all day long, but not his parents. She could understand why, of course. His mama was some whore in Asheville, and nobody knew where his daddy was. His mama taking him away when his daddy left was the worst thing she could've done. She should've left him with his granny from the start, and then maybe it wouldn't hurt him so much that his mama and daddy didn't want nothing to do with him. It was one thing to know it wasn't your fault, it was another thing altogether to make your heart believe it when all the other kids had mamas and daddies.

On visiting day at rehab, when everybody else's family come, Keith would disappear. The only time he ever showed up was when she asked him to meet her mama. She knew it was hard for him. It was hard for her. She saw him as she knew her mama would: a tall, skinny guy with black hair halfway down his back and skin the color of a baseball glove. She'd been pretty impressed with her mama that day though. Ruth Ann hadn't blinked an eye, just said hey and kept on talking. She must've sensed he was special. He was the first boyfriend Ashley had ever wanted her mama to meet. From then on he quit disappearing on visiting day. He joined Ashley and Ruth Ann and sometimes Cassandra, and it wasn't long before it felt natural to have him there. And now, well, there was no denying he was part of the family. Dwight and Betty had practically adopted him, and even her mama asked about him if he didn't show up for a meal.

So why couldn't she just say yes now and be all happy and excited about getting married to this man? Any other girl she knew would already be at the store picking out the dress. But no, she could never do things the easy way. What was wrong with her? As soon as he walked in the door, she got this sick feeling in her belly, this feeling of dread, and it got worse when he pulled that box out of his pocket. What was it, that feeling? She couldn't say, but she knew she had to go with it, at least until she figured out what it was. Now she understood that saying about how this is going to hurt me more that it's going to hurt you. It always sounded like bullshit when her daddy said it before he spanked her. She didn't want to hurt Keith, but that didn't mean she wouldn't do it.

Keith was still sitting there just looking at her when Ruth Ann walked in the kitchen.

"I'm going to make some more tea," she said, and went over to the sink. "We drunk nearly two gallons at dinnertime today." She turned on the water and let it run until it got hot, then filled a kettle and set it on the stove. She turned the burner on high and stood there with her back to Keith and Ashley, who still sat without speaking. Cassandra come in the back door, her face red as a blister.

Ruth Ann turned around. "Where you been?" she said. "You look like you run a mile."

Cassandra shut the door behind her and leaned against it, breathing hard. "I just walked up that durn hill from the cow pasture. Y'all need to install a chairlift or something."

"Oh, that hill ain't that steep. You just out of shape."

"Well, thank you, Miss Olympic Triathlete." Cassandra yanked a paper towel off the roll and wiped her face.

Keith's chair scraped across the floor and he stood up. Ruth Ann and Cassandra looked at him, then at Ashley, then at each other.

"Cassandra, why don't you come help me wake up the boys so we can feed them?" Ruth Ann and Cassandra hurried to the door.

"No, y'all don't leave. I'm leaving," Keith said, but he didn't move, just stood there staring at Ashley.

Ruth Ann turned back. "Why don't you stay and eat some supper with us, Keith? We got turkey and dressing and all kinds of good stuff left over."

He looked at Ruth Ann. "No, thanks, I better get on back. I told Dwight I'd handle the milking tonight 'cause him and Betty want to come over and visit with y'all."

"Well, you come back when you get done. We'll save you something," Ruth Ann said, and her and Cassandra left the room.

Keith opened the back door and the cold air whipped in. He stood there a minute more, waiting.

"You might as well come back and eat with us tonight, Keith, since Dwight and Betty'll be here too." Ashley leaned back in her chair and put her hands on her belly. It was like she was watching herself sit there and act like a cold bitch but couldn't quit.

Keith looked like he wanted to get his hands on her and shake her. "Ashley, would it kill you to say something nice, like you want me to come to supper 'cause you want to see me? Would it kill you?"

When she didn't say nothing, he went out the door and slammed it behind him. She pushed up the sleeves of her new sweater because, in spite of the cold air in the room, she felt suddenly hot, just like one of her mama's hot flashes. The kettle started whistling, and Ashley got up and turned the burner off. She got tea bags and a plastic pitcher out of the cabinet. When she pulled the cap off the kettle spout, steam shot across her wrist and she dropped the cap and the pitcher, which bounced across the kitchen floor.

"Damn, damn, damn!" she said, and run cold water across her wrist. When she turned to see where the pitcher had rolled, she seen Keith's ring box still sitting on the table. "Shit," she said.

Ruth Ann come up behind Ashley. "I heard the door slam," she said. "What happened?"

Ashley turned off the water and leaned over the sink. "Nothing. Just leave me alone, okay?"

"Okay," Ruth Ann said. She picked up the ring box. "You want to put this somewhere? I got to set the table." She held the box out. Ashley stared at it, then took it and went to her room. She'd meant for Keith to take the ring with him. Now she'd just have to stash it somewhere till she could give it back to him. She put it in the drawer between her and Marvelle's beds, then went back to the kitchen.

"We're eating off paper plates tonight," Ruth Ann said. "I'm not washing all them dishes twice in the same day. Here, make yourself useful." She put a pack of paper plates in Ashley's hands, then started pulling food out of the refrigerator. After a minute, she said, "You remember when we all used to get together at the homeplace every year for Christmas, and when we got done eating, Mama'd just leave all the food on the table and pull the edges of the tablecloth up over it? It's a wonder none of us ever got food poisoning. That was back before Saran Wrap and Tupperware, I reckon."

Ashley ripped the plastic off the paper plates and set them on the table. "Betty still does that," she said. "Or else she puts whatever's left in the pots on the back of the stove." She got paper napkins and put one by each plate, then counted out plastic forks, spoons, and knives and set them on the table. "We need a nice centerpiece," she said, looking around the kitchen. "How about this pinecone candle thing?"

Ruth Ann looked at it. "Okay, but don't light the candle or the boys'll have their plates on fire before they get through." She put a plate of turkey slices in the microwave and waited for it to get warm. She leaned against the counter and watched Ashley arrange the table.

She never realized how much time her and A.J. spent just watching the kids until they got to be teenagers and was never around, and when they was around they got mad if they caught you watching them. That had to be one of the greatest pleasures of parenthood, watching your child play and sleep and laugh. Especially when they was little. Ruth Ann couldn't wait to have a baby in the house again. And this one she could spoil all she wanted. It would be up to Ashley to do the hard part. Only now there was this ring that Keith had brought, and even though Ruth Ann suspected that Ashley hadn't told him yes yet, she knew it was just a matter of time before Ashley'd leave home again, to marry Keith or some other man or to get her own place.

The microwave dinged and Ruth Ann jumped, then pulled the steaming turkey out and stuck the plate of dressing in. She found Ashley watching her this time, staring over the pinecone centerpiece. "What?" she said.

"Nothing," Ashley said. "What do you think?" She nodded at the table.

"It looks pretty."

Ashley finished setting the table and Ruth Ann made the tea. They heard the boys' voices from the living room, then the sound of A.J. yawning.

"Go tell them boys to wash up and get in here and eat," Ruth Ann said. She opened the microwave door and the smell of sage filled the kitchen. "Whew! I wish I'd kept Mama away from this dressing."

"She still asleep?" Ashley said.

"She was last time I looked, but that's been a while. I'll go check on her as soon as I finish warming all this food up."

Sage—what a good smell that tickles my nose and makes me sneeze. Papa loved it in his dressing and always snuck in extra when Mama wasn't looking. It makes me think of ever Christmas and Thanksgiving of my life, 'cause that's the only time we put sage in anything. We used to grow our own to dry and put up for winter, and that was the best, so strong it didn't take much. This kind you get in the stores nowadays is weak stuff and you have to dump in half a cup or more.

My young'uns has always been good eaters, except for Ruth Ann. That gal was hard to keep in the house and even harder to feed. Now, Cassandra I didn't never have no trouble with. She's still a big eater, and she needs to cut back some, but you can't tell her nothing. She just gets mad and stomps off. I had the hardest time with the girls.

The boys was easy, practically raised themselves. Of course, once they got to be about ten, Jesse had them outside working and I didn't see them except for meals and on Sundays and when they was sick. But the girls was with me most times, and maybe that's why we had troubles—we was together too much and got tired of one another. Now, when they was little, they was a joy, but once they got to be teenagers and started thinking more for themselves, well, things got kindly strained between us. And with two girls nine years apart, I had to live through it all twice.

Both girls was independent as grizzly bears and just as ornery, and still are. I don't know where they get it from—Jesse, most likely. Now, Mason and Peter and Dwight and Clark and Dean and Frank and Marshall was just as pleasing and sweet as can be. It was always yes, Mama, okay, Mama. With Ruth Ann and Cassandra, it was always leave me alone, Mama, and don't tell me what to do, Mama. What they call teenage rebellion, I reckon.

Course, they wasn't nothing compared to what Velda was at that age. She was a piece of work, and how we ever turned out so different I'll never understand.

Velda was always different from the rest of us, even me, and we was twins. She had something in her mind that kept her from understanding how the world worked and how to get along in it. From the time we was tiny things, I always had to keep my eye on her, and since I loved her so, it wasn't a hardship, not until we got grown, anyhow. Marthy was fifteen when me and Velda was born, and she said Velda was different 'cause Papa held Mama's legs together to keep us from being born till Mama's sisters could get there. Papa didn't believe men ought to have nothing to do with childbirth. He didn't know no better.

Poor Velda was the first, and she pushed and fought and struggled to be born and she pushed and fought and struggled every inch of the rest of her thirty-one years. She wasn't mean about it though. She acted so sweet, but that's all it was, an act. That gal was hardheaded as a brick and sly about getting her way, especially with men. Papa never could tell her no, though he said it to me often enough. Maybe if he'd denied her some things she wouldn't have turned so wild.

She started laying down with boys about the time she started her cycle, about thirteen. She laid down with them a lot, and I just knowed she'd end up in trouble with all her catting around, but she never did. That got me worried about myself, that I couldn't have babies neither. That's why I was so happy when I knowed I was carrying Lena, even though I wasn't married to Jesse yet. I knowed I would be.

When she was sixteen, Velda run off with some feller who come through taking photographs for a dollar apiece. He sweet-talked her, told her she could make him famous with her beauty. She was a beauty, sure enough, and considering we was identical, I should've been one too, but somehow I wasn't. Whatever light in her that drawed the men was lacking in me. I've never understood it, but there come a time when I was grateful not to have it.

We never heard from her for years after she left, and we all wondered if she'd died. I tried to miss her, but to tell the truth, I was relieved I didn't have to watch over her no more. There never was such a girl for getting into trouble, and I felt more like her mama than her sister.

That summer she left, it was the same summer Jesse come to Madison County and, oh, that's something can't never be took from me, that summer I turned sixteen and fell in love. It was the first time I had a feller all to myself and wasn't always being compared with Velda and coming up short. And for the next fourteen years I kept him all to myself, him and the young'uns, and we was happy. We had our troubles, sure, but nothing beyond what we could handle ourselves.

Then Velda come back, and everything changed. It was as if she brung a dark cloud with her. Not that I wasn't relieved to see her alive. I was. And for a while seemed like she might settle down. She was bad sick with pneumonia when she got off the train at Marshall, so me and Jesse took her home to Slatey Knob, where I nursed her and fed her good. It took her a long time to get better. She come in February and it was April before she was strong enough to sit up in a chair by the window.

She wouldn't say a word the whole time she was sick about where she'd been or what'd happened to her. She was puny and had bruises all over her body like she'd been beat regular. I soon learned to quit asking questions, for she never answered and would refuse to eat for a day or two if I didn't leave her be. At first she wouldn't or couldn't sleep. She laid there like a corpse with her eyes wide open even at night. I slipped her some laudanum finally and she slept for a solid week, such a hard, deep sleep I was scared I'd killed her. After that she begun to get better though. When she woke up, I could tell she'd found some of herself again and was glad of it. She still didn't speak but smiled up at me before she went back to sleep, just like she used to when we was young'uns. She was so sweet that way, and I was glad for her to be alive, but it didn't last. I was blind, I reckon, and couldn't see much past right now, couldn't see how things never stay the same, how the bad makes way for the good, the good for the bad, and lots of in between. I learned though, I surely did.

13

Ruth Ann opened the bedroom door and stared through the dim light toward Marvelle's bed, then walked closer. Marvelle slept on her back with one flat pillow under her neck, snoring like a lumberjack.

Ruth Ann sat on the twin bed across from her and smoothed the green bedspread covering the pillow. She didn't know how her mama done it, but somehow or other she'd got Ashley to start making her bed every day. A minor miracle.

And Ashley done other things she'd never done before, like clean house and cook meals and shop and say please and thank you. The greatest miracle, though, was that Ashley had calmed down and didn't go around acting like the first minute the door was open she'd bolt through it and never come back. Marvelle had done that for her, and Ruth Ann wished she knew the secret, for she was afraid that without Marvelle, her and Ashley would go right back the way they was, like strangers. They had Marvelle in common, and maybe they always would, and maybe that was enough of a start that they could make it the rest of the way themselves.

Marvelle snorted and rolled over on her side, facing Ruth Ann. The snoring stopped, but her deep even breathing told Ruth Ann she was still asleep. She had on her Christmas dress, the one she made twenty years ago, and it was hiked up over her knees from all the tossing and turning she done. Ruth Ann leaned over, took hold of the dress tail, and pulled it down over Marvelle's calves. She fingered the rough texture of the fabric and had to admit her mama'd been right about polyester double-knit: It sure held its color. The print—white snowflakes on a red background—was as bright as the day she bought it, and she'd worn it every Christmas since.

Marvelle had bought a whole bolt of the stuff, thinking to make Ruth Ann and Cassandra and Angela identical dresses, even a pair of pants for Alex. Luckily the rest of that bolt mysteriously disappeared not long after Marvelle modeled her dress for them. They hunted all over the house, but it was gone. It hadn't taken Marvelle long to forget about it though, because she always got so caught up in Christmas and decorating and cooking and all.

Back when Ruth Ann and Cassandra was still living at home, their grown brothers and their families would all come stay at Christmas, and the house would be so full of people and laughing and food she couldn't hardly stand it. Her and Cassandra used to go hide over the milking barn, in the place where Keith's apartment was now. Back then it was just bare floorboards and rafters, but it was their hideout. Sometimes they just had to get away by themselves, away from their daddy's and brothers' teasing and picking, away from their mama's fussing. They'd lay up there and listen to the wind coming through the cracks, or the cows being milked below, and sometimes they'd practice dancing, the kind of dances their mama didn't like. Cassandra would sing sometimes and clap while Ruth Ann pretended she was dancing with a fiancé whose name and face she didn't know yet, a man she knew waited in her future as sure as the sun rose.

God, they were naive back then, Ruth Ann thought. Especially her. Everything revolved around a man, first the mysterious Mr. Right, or Prince Charming, then A.J., who didn't turn out to be either. Which was probably a good thing. From her perspective now, Prince Charming seemed pretty dull. She didn't know what she'd want in a man now, or if she'd ever even be interested in men again, but when she did spare a minute to think about it, she figured there must be a happy medium somewhere between Prince Charming and A. J. Payne. Some man who'd put his energy into staying home and pleasing one woman. That seemed like it ought to be challenge enough for any man for life.

She heard shrieks and laughter from the direction of the living room—probably A.J. in there wrestling with the boys. She wished they'd quiet down. Marvelle hadn't slept the night through in weeks. She'd go to bed when Ruth Ann and Ashley did, but then they'd hear her get up in the middle of the night, stomping through the house. She'd go to the kitchen about three o'clock in the morning and start clanking the pots and pans around, pulling food out of the refrigerator, intending to cook breakfast. Usually Ashley woke up first and found Marvelle and talked her into coming back to bed, and Ruth Ann would catch them coming down the hall.

They'd get in bed and Ashley'd go back to sleep and Marvelle would set in to talking. She talked all night long, even after Ashley fell back asleep, telling stories about when she was young in the mountains and married Jesse and lived on Slatey Knob, how in 1942 they come to Davis on the train to run the farm for Jesse's daddy, and on and on like that. All the old stories she kept telling and telling like she couldn't help herself, like she was just going on faith that somebody was listening. Ruth Ann would stand in the door and listen and Marvelle wouldn't even know she was there.

They'd tried to explain to Marvelle what was happening to her, even though they didn't really understand it themselves. The doctor even come out to the car to talk to her about it. But as usual, she just insisted it was old age, it happened to everybody in time, and it was nothing to get upset about. Her granny and her mama went through the same thing, it was just a natural part of living, getting ready to go, nature helping you let go a little bit at a time. And in a way she was right, Ruth Ann thought. Her mama had been letting go a little bit at a time for years, and they'd forgot to pay attention, and now she was nearly gone and what could they do but watch it happen?

Ruth Ann got up and stood by the bed, looking down at Marvelle's face, and it come to her as sudden and unexpected as lightning striking. Her mama was dying. She'd known, of course, all along, but just that hard fact, dying, gone forever, seized her suddenly like a revelation. It was like a door that had been closed in her mind suddenly opened, and she was afraid to step up and look through it, to see what was coming down the road. Death, the unknown, change. Change, oh, how Ruth Ann hated that, and hated the way Marvelle always said the only constant is change. Knowing it was true didn't make it any easier to accept.

Ruth Ann touched her mama's cheekbone, prominent there above the sagging skin of her face. There was dark smudges under Marvelle's eyes, and she slept with her mouth open. Every breath sounded like her last. Ruth Ann realized what a struggle it was for her to stay alive every day, much less get along in the world. How did she do it? How could she stand getting up every morning not knowing if she'd be able to remember where she was or who they all were?

On the night table between the twin beds was Marvelle's diary, a spiral notebook Ashley bought in November after she read somewhere how having old people write things down made them feel better, helped them remember. Every morning Ashley wrote the day of the week and the date at the top of a page and Marvelle kept track of her day there. The handwriting was shaky and paid no attention to the lines on the page, but it was readable. Every little while during the day Marvelle would disappear to her room to write things down or refresh her memory.

Ruth Ann sat down and turned on the lamp between the beds. She picked up the notebook and read what Ashley had written at the top of the page that morning. *Friday, December 25, 1992. Merry Christmas, Granny!* Then Marvelle's notes started.

Breakfast 7:00. Grits, bacon, coffee. Medicine 7:30. Two red, one green tablet with water. Bathroom 7:45, okay. Clark called. Opened presents. From Ruth Ann and Cassandra—new shoes, foot box. From Ashley—puzzle of snowy mountains, 1,000 piece. Angela, husband (?), boys Jonathan & Bryan—nightgown, robe, bedroom shoes. Cash to all. Alex called from beach. Dwight called, him and Betty coming tonight. Put more sage in dressing, made apple salad. Ate dinner. Dressing good, turkey dry. Dean called, coming tomorrow with Frank and Clark. Washed dishes. Marshall called. Can't come till Sunday. Laid down 3:30.

The whole notebook was full of the same stuff. Everything going in and coming out, every phone call, every activity, she'd kept track of it all for the last six weeks. A whole day in one page, a whole life in one notebook. It just wasn't possible to capture a person like that, as much as Ruth Ann wished she could have that to hold on to.

Of course, that bit about the sage in the dressing was pure Marvelle. Ruth Ann had thought that dressing tasted strong. Her mama couldn't taste nothing no more. Ruth Ann could've poured that whole can of sage on her tongue and she'd have said it wasn't enough. Stubborn and sneaky, that's what the woman was. And that crack about the dry turkey. She was just mad because Ruth Ann cooked it in a plastic bag instead of basting it.

She put the diary down and folded her hands in her lap. Someday, probably soon, she'd be glad to have that little book. Marvelle grunted, flopped on her back, and started snoring again. Sounded like a chain saw. Ruth Ann's lips twitched and she thought she might laugh, but just as sudden she felt like crying. She held it in because she had to go out there and see to the rest of the family. She could cry later, when she was in her room and no witnesses.

All of a sudden, Marvelle stopped snoring, turned off the chain saw. She opened her eyes and looked over at Ruth Ann, then rolled on her side and pushed herself up with one hand, reaching for Ruth Ann's hand with the other. Ruth Ann grabbed hold and pulled until Marvelle sat up with her feet on the floor.

"You want some supper, Mama?"

Marvelle opened her mouth, and when she burped long and loud, the smell of sage wafted under Ruth Ann's nose and about made her sick. She fanned her hand in front of her face, then got up and moved away a few steps.

"God, Mama," she said.

"What?" Marvelle looked up at her, sleepy-eyed.

"Nothing."

"What time is it?"

Ruth Ann looked at her watch. "About six o'clock."

"Where's all them young'uns at?" Marvelle yawned and Ruth Ann could see the gaps between what teeth she had left.

"They're all in the kitchen getting some supper by now, I reckon. You hungry?"

"All right. You got to help me up though. I done got stiff a-laying there all that time."

Ruth Ann pulled Marvelle to her feet and waited for her to get steady.

"Thank you, honey. This old back of mine takes a minute to get the kinks out." Slowly Marvelle straightened until her head come level with Ruth Ann's shoulder. She looked up at her. "I think I'll have me some more of that good dressing."

"Did it have enough sage to suit you, Mama?" Ruth Ann fluffed Marvelle's hair in the back where it had got flat from her laying on it.

"Just about," she said.

"Now, Mama, you know you sneaked in more sage when I wasn't looking. That dressing's so strong it could walk in here and eat you."

Marvelle laughed, and Ruth Ann realized it'd been a long time since she heard that sound.

"God, Mama, you are something else," she said.

Marvelle smacked Ruth Ann's hand. "Don't take the Lord's name in vain. It's Christmas!"

"All right, I'm fixing to start putting away this food. Anybody wants any more better get it now while the getting's good." Betty pulled the platter of turkey toward her and started to get up.

Ruth Ann couldn't believe they'd managed to eat so much supper after the big dinner they had. She looked around the table as everybody groaned and said they was too full to eat another bite. Except A.J. He took another bite of dressing, a drink of tea, then wiped his mouth and pulled the waistband of his pants away from his middle. "I'm going to have to unbutton my britches so I can breathe," he said.

Betty got up with a stack of plates and Ruth Ann waved her back down. "Betty, don't do that. We'll clean up later." Ruth Ann relaxed in her chair next to A.J. She felt like sitting awhile.

"All right," Betty said. "Does anybody want any more tea?"

"I want some more pie, please," Jonathan said. He'd climbed on his daddy's lap and was finishing David's coconut pie.

"Me too," Bryan said. "Coconut, not punkin."

"Pump-kin," Angela said.

"What the hell is pump-kin?" Dwight said, and grinned at Angela.

"I wish you'd quit talking like that in front of my children." Angela wiped her lips on a paper napkin, then folded it and tucked it under her plate.

"Talking like what?" Dwight said.

Angela sighed. "Well, cussing, for one thing. And using bad grammar."

"Hell, punkin ain't bad grammar. It's bad pronouncement," Dwight said, and winked at Bryan, who was busy eating his third piece of pie.

"No, it's bad pronounciation," David said, trying not to smile.

Angela's face turned red and her chin went up a little higher. "Y'all go on and laugh. But you cannot underestimate the value of good English."

"We don't underestimate nothing," Betty said. "But you got to admit there's different ways of expressing things. Ain't that right?" Betty looked at Cassandra, then Ruth Ann.

Ruth Ann decided to keep her mouth shut. She was feeling too full and warm and sleepy to get into it with the rest of them, and she had her own little problem to deal with at the table anyway. All the chairs was pushed close together to fit everybody around the kitchen table, and for the past half hour the side of A.J.'s left leg had been pressed against the side of her right leg, and wasn't a thing she could do about it. That wasn't the problem. The problem was, she enjoyed the feel of his leg up against hers. It was making her feel just about hot, and not due to no hot flash. They'd been coming less frequent lately, and this was something entirely different, something that originated in a part of her that had felt cold for too long. She wasn't sure she liked the feeling coming back to her this way, because she didn't know what to do about it. Inconvenient wasn't the word for it.

She couldn't seem to take her eyes off the fine black hairs laying so smooth on top of A.J.'s arm. She thanked God for all the people in the room, or who knows what might've happened. She figured if she could just sit still and be quiet long enough it'd pass and she could get up and forget about it.

David was apologizing for teasing Angela, but she ignored him and told the boys they couldn't have no more pie. Ruth Ann looked at Angela's mad face. Usually she took up for Angela when they picked on her, but she couldn't manage it today, partly because of her preoccupation with A.J.'s arm and leg and partly because she thought it was time Angela learned to do some getting along for a change. She wasn't no better than the rest of them just because she went to college and never worked on the farm or in the mill. Angela thought getting above her raising was a good thing, and Ruth Ann agreed with her up to a point. The rest of the family didn't really want to drag her down from where she'd got to. They was all proud of her for being the first college graduate in the family. But they seen it as their duty to remind her where she come from, and they was good at it.

"Let's change the subject," Cassandra said finally.

She was big on changing subjects and introducing new topics at the supper table lately. Ruth Ann figured she'd been watching Oprah again, or maybe it was all that talk radio.

"Let's talk about what our favorite smells are," Cassandra said.

Everybody looked at her like she'd sprouted antlers, and Bryan and Jonathan giggled.

"Cassandra, you been at that day care too long," Ashley said. "You all the time wanting to go around the circle and tell your favorite color, or what animal you'd like to be."

"Well, I just think it's interesting to get to know things about the people we think we know everything about. I don't have a clue what any of y'all's answers might be."

Ashley and Angela groaned.

Jonathan raised his hand. "Me! Me!"

"Okay, honey. What's your favorite smell?"

"What made you pick smell?" A.J. said.

"I read somewhere that smell is the sense most closely linked with memory," Cassandra said. "And I was thinking about the smell of sage and how much Mama loves it, how it reminds her of Christmastime and family being together. Now hush and let Jonathan talk." Cassandra looked at her nephew. He got suddenly bashful with everybody staring at him and clammed up.

"What, honey?" Cassandra said.

He looked down at his plate and mumbled something, then turned his face in to his daddy's shirt.

"What'd he say?" A.J. said.

"Broccoli," David said, and everybody laughed.

"He loves broccoli," Angela said proudly. "He can be playing across the street and he'll smell that stuff and come running."

"Does he have cheese on it?" Ruth Ann said. "Y'all used to wouldn't touch it without cheese on it."

"No, he likes it plain. I steam it real good with a little butter and he eats it like candy."

"It's good for his digestion," Marvelle said. They all looked at her because she'd not said a word all night, and her eyes had a glazed, faraway look.

"Yeah, it is, Granny," Angela said. "Ever since he had that trouble with his bowels when he was two, he's always liked roughage."

Here we go with the bowels again, Ruth Ann thought.

"Is it my turn yet?" Bryan asked, trying to sound bored.

"Yes, honey, go ahead," Cassandra said.

"Okay, my favorite smell is mowed grass, especially when it's been mowed by somebody besides me." They all laughed, because Jonathan had just started mowing the grass for his daddy the summer before.

"Betty's fried chicken," Dwight said. He scooted his chair closer to Betty and put his arm on the back of her chair.

"Yeah, now, that'd be hard to beat," A.J. said. "They's something about the smell of fried chicken when you hungry calls out to you, makes you feel healthy. That's my favorite, that or steak on a grill. Some kind of meat cooking."

"Watermelon, a big ripe sweet wet watermelon," David said. "I wish I had me one right now."

"Watermelon! Oh, Daddy!" Jonathan said.

"David made himself sick eating watermelon last July at the church dinner," Angela said. "I bet he ate three whole ones all by himself during the course of the day."

"Well, honey, it got hot standing over that Brunswick stew. I was dehydrated."

"Uh-huh." She patted his hand and he held on to her fingers on top of the table.

"Mama?" Angela said.

Ruth Ann looked up and said, "Roses," before she even had time to think. She blinked sleepily.

"Yeah. Roses smell so good," Ashley said. "What is that smell, it's like a clean, pure smell."

"I'd have to go with roses too," Angela said. "They smell like rain."

"Rain? What the hell does rain smell like?" A.J. said.

"I like that smell when rain first hits hot pavement," Dwight said.

"Yeah, me too," Ashley said. "Reminds me of riding the bus home the last day of school."

"Summertime," David said.

"I like the smell of salt air myself," Cassandra said. "Cleans out your nose and lungs, your whole head."

A.J. laughed. "Y'all remember that time Cassandra got stung by a jelly-fish and I got Alex to pee on—"

"Betty!" Cassandra said, louder than she meant to. "You ain't said yet."

Betty looked embarrassed. "All right, now, y'all don't laugh," she said. "But I love the smell of a baby's head."

A.J. and David and the boys did laugh, but Cassandra and Ruth Ann and Angela nodded.

"She's right," Ruth Ann said. "A baby's head has a special smell. Like warm, clean skin and baby powder and something else I can't name."

"Innocence," Angela said.

"You can't smell innocence," Ashley said.

"Well, what is it, then, smarty?" Angela said.

"Creation," Marvelle said. Every head turned toward her. "A baby's head has the smell of the creator's touch still on it, fresh from God, all new and untarnished by this world. It don't last long."

Ruth Ann looked into Marvelle's eyes. She saw for an instant the woman her mama really was, still living behind them eyes, the woman that give birth to twelve children, struggled through the Depression, four wars, and countless unknown personal tragedies to end up here at this table, an eighty-two-year-old widow more out of the world than in it, surrounded by family who loved and cherished her. Ruth Ann saw in her mama's eyes the complete absence of any absolutes in life, no such thing as black or white. Maybe in the beginning of time things had been clear and simple, but now the lines all crossed and wove together so there was no breaking the pattern apart into separate pieces, no beginnings or endings, just a continuing thread.

Ruth Ann saw for just a blink of an eye the creator's touch on her mama's head, on her children, on them all. Maybe the smell went away, just like new-car smell always faded no matter how clean you kept your car. But the mark of what made them stayed, and as she looked around the table, she realized it must be something fine and loving, and definitely something with a sense of humor, out there somewhere sending people into the world. Her nose stung and pressure swelled in her chest as feeling for them all built near to bursting around her heart. Marvelle blinked then and focused on Ruth Ann. For what felt like a long time it was just the two of them, looking at each other, knowing things about each other, not needing any words. It was a going deep into each other, no barriers between them for the first time in a long time. Ruth Ann held her breath, trying to make that moment last.

Then the racket of everybody getting up to clear the table broke in. Ruth Ann looked away from Marvelle when Betty asked what she should do with the leftover dressing. When she looked back, the connection was broken and Marvelle was struggling to her feet. Ruth Ann went around the table to help, but Marvelle pushed her away.

"I can do it," she said.

"You better let her, Mama, or she'll start cussing you," Ashley said.

"Don't talk about me like I ain't in the room, goddammit!" Marvelle snapped a look over her shoulder that was meant to maim if not kill.

"See," Ashley said.

Ruth Ann stood next to Ashley and they stared at Marvelle's back, watching her go away from them.

As soon as Keith heard the weather report on the six o'clock news, he got up and put his coat on. He put on his old one, raggedy as it was, because he didn't want to mess up the nice new one Dwight and Betty give him. Not yet. He wanted it to be new a while longer. He turned Dwight's radio off and made sure the door locked behind him. Dwight and Betty was still over at Ruth Ann's eating supper, but Betty had told him to go on in the house and get him a snack if he got hungry before she got home with his plate.

The weatherman predicted an ice storm later that night, so Keith figured he better get his tent down. Nothing would tear up a tent worse than ice. He could put it back once the weather cleared. Or maybe he'd wait till spring. It was getting too damn cold to stay out there at night, and he was too busy during the day, and since Ashley rejected him, he didn't figure they'd be needing a place to meet anytime soon.

He got his flashlight from his room and headed out through the pasture. At the top of the hill, he stopped and zipped up his coat. Looked like every light in the house was on over at Ruth Ann's. He bet they was having something better than what he had for supper—day-old corn bread and milk. He hoped Betty would remember to bring him some turkey and cranberry sauce.

When he got down to the tent, he propped the flashlight on a stump and pulled his sleeping bag out. He hated rolling up a sleeping bag. It was a job for two people. Finally he got it rolled right and tied a rope around it tight. It took him only five minutes to get the tent down and folded. He laid it on the ground next to the sleeping bag. It was shivering cold, and Keith stuck his hands in his pockets and went over to the fence. He could just barely make out shadows of people's heads in the windows of Ruth Ann's house.

For some reason, that George Jones song his Uncle Bill liked so much, "The Race Is On," kept playing over and over in his head, especially that line about the stab of loneliness, sharp and painful. Was that what it was making him stand in the freezing cold trying to see in the windows up the hill?

He wished he could figure Ashley out. He wished he knew what was going on in her crazy head. But all he could do now was wait. And he hated waiting. He was a man of action, and he was ready now. Hell, he'd jump in the car and drive to South Carolina and get married in the morning if she wanted to.

For months now he'd been going along thinking they both wanted the same things. Now he found out different. What if she kept on saying no? What if she didn't want him, only the baby? What if she didn't want him or the baby? He kicked the fence post, then kicked it again, harder. The hell with it. There was nothing he could do about it tonight.

He turned and picked up the sleeping bag and tent and started up the hill, walking at first, then running, faster and faster until he was so winded he couldn't hardly draw another breath. On the hill back down to the barn, he stepped in a hole and tripped, fell hard and rolled, the tent and sleeping bag flying off in different directions. When he quit rolling, he laid real still, hoping he hadn't rolled through frozen cow shit, glad he'd worn his old coat. He laid there awhile, watching clouds move overhead, smelling moisture in the air. That damn song wouldn't go away. *My heart's out of the running, true love's scratched for another's sake. The race is on and it looks like heartache, and the winner loses all.*

No. He got up, collected his stuff, and kept walking. He would not even think about it anymore tonight. He'd go back to Dwight's and listen to the radio till him and Betty got home, then he'd eat some ham and whatever else they brung him and talk to them awhile. He wouldn't ask them how Ashley acted at supper, but maybe they'd say something anyway, give him some idea how she was feeling now she'd had some time to think. Then he'd go to bed early since he had to be up at four to milk. Then after the milking he'd head over there and try again. He wouldn't quit trying neither. He wasn't no walking-away man like his daddy. He'd prove that no matter how long it took.

Cassandra sat up on the couch and threw the blanket off her. She immediately started shivering. Ruth Ann kept the house like a meat locker at night. That's what blankets are for, she'd say whenever Cassandra complained about the cold. Now, if the weather report had been better and Angela and David and the boys had stayed like they was supposed to, Ruth Ann would've left that heat turned up. But since it was just the four of them, she figured they could all just freeze. Cassandra pulled the blanket around her shoulders, then looked at her watch. Three o'clock in the morning. She'd set the timer to turn the TV off at three, so that's probably what woke her up, the sudden quiet.

Only it wasn't completely quiet. Somebody in the house was crying, sounded like in the kitchen. Cassandra reached for her thick socks on the floor by the couch. She'd kicked them off when she laid down earlier. She couldn't stand nothing on her feet or legs when she was under the covers. She put the socks on, then stood and pulled her nightgown down over her legs and wrapped the blanket around her tight. She tiptoed down the hall to the kitchen and seen somebody standing at the back door with the curtain pulled aside, looking out the window. When her eyes got used to the dark, she seen it was Ashley. In silhouette, her belly looked bigger than it really was.

"Honey, what is it?" she said. Ashley's shoulders shook, she was crying so hard. Cassandra turned on the light over the sink so she could see better, then stood next to Ashley and put a hand on her back. "What's the matter?"

"Nothing," Ashley said, and turned away from the window, just sniffling now.

"It's got to be something for you to cry over it so." Cassandra lifted the curtain and looked out. "What was you looking at?"

"Nothing," Ashley said. She blew her nose hard. After a minute, she said, "Keith's gone."

"What?"

"Keith's gone. The bastard's gone and left me."

"How do you know?" Cassandra said.

"Just look and see for yourself."

Cassandra looked out the window again, then back at Ashley, her face making a question. "It's pitch-black out there. I can't see nothing."

"The tent," Ashley said. "It's gone."

"The tent," Cassandra said.

"Yes, you know, Keith's tent that's been there since August. The blue thing."

"Well, I know that. But what makes you think he's gone?"

"Why else would he take it down? And he must've done it after dark so I wouldn't see, because it was still there at suppertime."

"How do you know it's gone now?"

"Because I went down there to put his lamp back."

"Well, honey, that don't mean nothing. Maybe he took it down just for the winter. It's too dang cold to be out in a tent. He'll probably put it back come spring."

"No, he won't! Don't you get it? I turned him down today when he asked me to marry him." This made Ashley start crying all over again.

Cassandra couldn't think what in the world to say to that. She never imagined Ashley telling the boy no. She already pictured them married and settled down with that baby. Why did people always have to screw things up? Why couldn't they follow the natural course of their life instead of always fighting it?

"What'd you do that for?"

"I don't know." Ashley blew her nose again.

"You got to have a reason," Cassandra said.

"No, I don't. Maybe I just don't feel like getting married. Did you ever think of that?"

"Don't snap my head off. I'm just asking."

"Well, it ain't none of your business, okay? Just leave me alone."

Ashley went over and opened the refrigerator door and stared in. Cassandra could see her little skinny legs right through that thin night-gown. What was she thinking, going out in nothing but that nightgown? Ashley got a Coke and started to shut the refrigerator.

"Wait," Cassandra said. "I might want something out of there." She took Ashley's place, hunting for the ham and potato salad. She put the dishes on the counter and closed the refrigerator. "You want some?"

"No," Ashley said.

Cassandra made herself a plate and sat across from Ashley. "This ham is even better cold," she said, and forked in a mouthful of potato salad on top of the ham. After she swallowed, she said, "Your mama makes the best potato salad."

"How can you eat again after that big supper we had?"

"I couldn't sleep. I had to do something." In between bites, Cassandra took quick looks at Ashley. She didn't want to make her mad again by staring. Ashley's nose and eyes was still red from crying, and her face looked real puffy. Moon-faced was what you called people looked like that. Probably she was retaining water and that made her moody. It was terrible what hormones and water could do to a woman.

"You know what?" Cassandra said. She swallowed the last bite of potato salad and took a drink of Ashley's Coke. "I bet Keith ain't gone nowhere. I don't believe he'd give up that easy. I bet he just took that tent down because of the weather. I bet he's over in his apartment asleep right now. Why, he'll probably be over here in a couple hours looking for some breakfast."

Ashley sat slumped over the table, her chin in one hand, the other hand playing with the Coke can. "I don't know what's wrong with me. Why did I say no? I thought I done the right thing, but now I feel like I screwed everything up."

"You didn't screw up. You just done what you felt like you had to at the time." Cassandra carried her empty plate to the sink. "But that don't mean you can't change your mind." She squirted dish soap on the plate and run hot water over it and left it to soak. Ruth Ann would probably have something smart to say about that in the morning, but Cassandra didn't care.

"What if he changed his mind though?" Ashley said.

"You don't have much faith in him."

Ashley straightened up. "Yes, I do. I love him."

"But do you trust him?"

Ashley stared at her. "Yes," she said. "I do. But he was pretty mad."

"People get over being mad."

"What if he don't? What if I never see him again?"

"Well, it's up to you what happens next. It won't kill you to make the first move, will it?" Cassandra stretched her arms over her head and yawned real big. Suddenly something made a pinging noise on the floor at her feet.

Ashley turned around and looked. "What was that?" she said.

"Lord, I don't know. Oh, it's change." Cassandra bent down and picked up two dimes. "I didn't have no pockets today when I went to the store for your mama, so I dropped the change in my safe." She patted her chest. Sometimes if she didn't have pockets and her hands was full, she'd drop little things like change or keys or notes down in her bra. "Must've stuck to my boobs. They was a quarter in there too." Cassandra put a hand down the neck of her nightgown and felt around. "Oh, well," she said. "No telling where that quarter got to." She handed the dimes to Ashley.

"What am I supposed to do with this?" Ashley said. She laid the money on the table.

"Start you a nest egg," Cassandra said. "Mama always told me and Ruth Ann to keep us a little secret money, even once we got a husband to provide for us. She said a woman should always keep back a little something just for herself, something nobody else knows about. That way, no matter what happens, you always know you got something to fall back on. So this is the start of yours. You just keep adding to it once you and Keith gets married."

"You sure are sure of yourself," Ashley said. She had a little smile on her face that let Cassandra know exactly what was going to happen tomorrow when she talked to Keith, or if not tomorrow, then one day soon.

"You better get your tail back in the bed, young lady," Cassandra said.

"I ain't sleepy. Let's go see if there's any good movies on TV."

They got under the blankets on the couch and channel-surfed until they found *It's a Wonderful Life*. Five minutes later Ashley was asleep, sitting straight up. Cassandra waited five more minutes, then got out from under the blankets. She eased Ashley down on a pillow and swung her legs up on the couch and covered her up good.

She stood swaying in front of the TV, feeling restless for some reason. She went over to the Christmas tree, thinking how empty it looked underneath with all the presents gone. It wasn't much to look at without them. This year Ruth Ann used all silver balls and white lights. She liked all one color on her tree. It was pretty from across the room, but kind of boring close up. Cassandra tapped a ball with her finger and watched it swing. When it stopped, she turned and looked down at the puzzle Marvelle had spread out on the card table. It was another snow scene. This one had a cabin in it and a fence made out of split rails. All that was left to put in was the sky, which, according to the picture on the box, was bright blue with no clouds. Cassandra picked up a few of the blue pieces, then put them down again. She'd never gone in much for puzzles.

She sighed and looked over at Ashley. The girl was dead to the world. It had been a long time since Cassandra slept that hard. The cold in the room had seeped in good and deep, and she started shivering and couldn't quit, so she got a quilt out of the closet and spread it across the recliner. Before she got under it, she went out to the kitchen and got her some Oreos and milk. Cassandra was glad for once that Ruth Ann kept her cookies in a Tupperware box. Made a lot less noise than the plastic package they come in.

She went back to the living room and settled herself in the recliner under the quilt. She used her toes to get the socks off her feet, then pulled her nightgown up to her thighs. The leather of the chair felt cold against her skin, but it didn't take long to warm up. She put an Oreo in her mouth, took a swig of milk, waited a minute, mashed the Oreo against the roof of her mouth with her tongue, swallowed, reached for another cookie. On TV, George and Mary had a big fight, but it wasn't long before they realized they really loved each other and started kissing and hugging. That part always made Cassandra cry.

Ashley laid on her side in the dark, listening to ice hit the window, coming down heavy enough to nearly drown out Marvelle's snoring. The red numbers on the clock said five fifty-eight. She'd woke up on the couch about four-thirty and then come and got in her own bed. Funny how she'd hated going to bed when she was little, and now it was a luxury. She looked across at Marvelle, the little shadowy bundle of her humped up under the covers. This was the first time her granny had slept through the night in weeks. Ashley flopped over on her back and stared up into the darkness.

She stretched her arms out from under the covers, over her head. It was like reaching into a freezer. Her mama turned the heat down before they all went to bed. No wonder her granny was curled up under the covers like that. Ashley put her arms by her sides and scooted down in the bed. It felt so good to lay under heavy covers, the smooth, soft sheet between her and three layers of quilts. It would be hard to name a better sensation than the way her bare legs felt in the warm pocket of air under them quilts. She bent her knees up a little and dropped them down again just to feel the velvety movement of heavy warm cotton against her skin.

The room smelled of cinnamon from the Christmas potpourri her mama bought at the mall, and Ashley sniffed a long deep breath. Cinnamon with the faintest whisper of sage mixed in. The two smells did not go together. She pulled the sheet up over her nose and thought she'd be happy to melt down into that bed, it felt so good. She put her hands on her belly and rubbed, letting her fingers trace the circle of her belly button. She had an outie, even more out since the baby, who laid asleep inside her little mountain. Who'd have thought a year ago she'd be snuggled up in bed with a baby?

Last Christmas, she didn't even know Keith. After she left home that last time, her and her friend Stephanie went to Asheville and moved in with a couple of guys Stephanie knowed. Ashley met a lot of people after that but never really got to know anybody. That was the beginning of what seemed like an endless blur of partying and nightlife, one real long night. She didn't remember much, just flashes of memories that floated in darkness like weird bubbles of experience that belonged to somebody else, that she wished belonged to somebody else.

She thought suddenly of the pickled eggs in the jar at her uncle Clark's store. People actually ate them things, men usually. Women knew better than to reach a hand in that big jar of slime and pull out an egg that had been there for who knew how long. And who knew how many nasty hands had been reaching in that jar before. Them eggs made her think of things best left alone, things that would never go away, but you could get used to them being there without ever having to taste them again.

Clark got her to try one, one time when she was little. He told her it was candy and she believed him, even when the peppery, vinegary smell should've told her he was lying. She held that egg in front of her face and listened to Clark telling her it tasted just like them white chocolate eggs the Easter bunny brought. She listened and believed and took a bite, but she didn't swallow. As soon as her mouth closed around the egg, she realized she'd been tricked, but it was too late. Her teeth had already sunk into soft, wet egg flesh. Half of it laid on her tongue for a second before she gagged and heaved and threw up all over the store. She puked till there was nothing left. She was empty and still suffering dry heaves when Clark called her mama to come get her. Ruth Ann, of course, scolded all the way home, saying, "Why did you do that? You knew it wasn't candy."

Granny always said to ride through the day you can throw a tow sack on a jackass or you can put a silver saddle on a golden palomino. You choose. Ashley had her health, her baby, her family, food, a roof, a bed, and a man that seemed interested in hanging around. Dwelling on past mistakes hadn't done her or her mama or anybody else any good. It didn't matter that she wasn't the good perfect daughter like Angela, or the only son like Alex. She was here, and by God that counted for something when all the rest of them came and went like the seasons. Or at least it ought to.

The ones that stayed had it hardest of all. They done the work of getting along, seeing the dull everyday-ness, watching people through their good and not-so-good times. That was something Angela and Alex would never know about their own family, something they'd probably never even miss. But if Ashley had learned one thing, it was that staying around, toughing out the hard times, asserting your own self in the midst of a bunch of people who'd rather see you be just like them, that was hard. Standing up and saying, "I'm going to live my life my way as best I can without stepping on any toes too much, so you better get used to it. And in return, I'll be understanding of the way you choose to live your lives, and we'll all get along just fine. I'll help you out when you need it, and you'll help me out when I need it. And we'll try to laugh and not kill each other."

She'd never understand her brother and sister. Most of the time when she was around Angela, she felt like one or the other of them must've been adopted, most likely her, not Angela. Her sister was too much like their mama to be adopted—prissy and perfect, both of them. No, that wasn't fair. Her mama wasn't prissy like Angela. She just liked things clean and neat and orderly as much as possible, but she didn't get crazy about it like Angela, who freaked out if her lipstick didn't match her outfit.

Ashley couldn't tell who she was like, wasn't sure she wanted to be compared to any of them. Of them all, she was probably most like her daddy. She had his restlessness and craving for something different all the time. She certainly didn't want to end up like him though, alone and scrambling after whatever bits and pieces of his family he could scrape back together after all his messing around and screwing up. No, she was going to be smarter than that.

She knew her waiting time was coming to an end. Soon she'd have to make hard decisions about the rest of her life and her baby's life, and she just wasn't ready yet. The only way she knew to make Keith give her more time was to run him off, make him mad enough to stay away for a while so she could think. A part of her hunkered down deep inside her chest and hid her face because she knew the future, knew that ahead lay marriage and babies and work, the same life her mama and granny and all the women before them had chosen. But had they chosen? Or had they gone blindly seeking like Ashley and ended up with the first thing they come across? Found themselves married, mothers, widows, grandmothers, divorcées? Was they just as determined to be different in the beginning? She thought of Marvelle and Jesse, Ruth Ann and A.J., Angela and David, how perfectly all right everything seemed between them when she was little. But now she was finding out different. That was parents protecting their children, protecting some kind of security they was trying to hold on to no matter how fragile it was, no matter if it wasn't real.

Well, she was being a big downer laying there thinking too much. She knew she'd never get back to sleep with Marvelle snoring like that, and besides, she had to pee. Oh, it was going to be so cold, but if she hurried to the kitchen, she bet her Mama had coffee made and the kitchen would be warm from the stove being on. The heat was probably on in the rest of the house, she just couldn't feel it in here because the bedroom door was shut. She couldn't lay there all day, no matter how good it felt under the covers. It was time to move. Ashley counted to three, counted to three one more time, then threw the covers back. Marvelle let out a big snore and rolled over on her side with the covers over her head. Ashley left the door open when she went out so it would be warm when Marvelle woke up.

I chose him. Yes, I did, I wanted to stay with Jesse. If I could go back to the beginning, the very beginning, I might change my mind. But I can't go back, and because I can't go all the way back, I can't change what I done, 'cause that'd be like killing my children, killing myself, and I won't do that. I want us all to live on, do better than the ones before. That's the only way our lives has any meaning, any enduring value. That's not to say my life don't matter to me. It does, and it ain't over yet.

It ain't been all bad neither. I have had great joy in my life, great joy. My children, my brothers and sisters, my mama and papa, and Jesse. It just don't make sense to dwell on the hard parts. It's like believing in God. I know they's some folks don't believe God exists, and I can see how the doubt and fear can creep in. But I say, what's the harm in believing? Even if you die and find they ain't nothing there but nothing, you won't know about it. And in the meantime, you can take comfort from faith in a power greater than yourself.

That's what I choose: to believe. I believe they's more to this life and this world than we can ever see or know. The mystery is the greatest joy of all to me, especially at my time of life. We don't know a particle of what there is to know, yet the world keeps on a-spinning somehow. How do you account for it? You can't. It's a mystery, and I leave it to the Lord. I take care of my little bit of business here and that's my part. I ain't afraid.

That's the thing tore me up so bad when Jesse was a-dying. He was so afraid, it like to tore my heart out to see it. And wasn't nothing I could do, nor anyone. I had to stay in that hospital room with him and watch him dread the end of this life with ever breath he drawed. He cried sometimes too, and that man was never one to cry. He was always the one said ain't no point a-crying for the dying, 'cause they going to a better place. I always hated him a-saying that, even if it was true. Knowing my loved ones was in a better place didn't help me get over missing them.

Jesse held his feelings too good all his life, and I reckon maybe they backed up on him and flooded over there at the end. The hardest thing in this life is seeing somebody you love afraid and in pain. They's usually something can be done to ease physical pain, but they's not much for the fear, nothing much a human can do, I reckon. The only help for Jesse was for me to set right by him and watch him cry and scream and holler about it. By getting it off his chest, he relieved some of the pressure and felt better for a while. But it always come back, that fear.

So many times I tried to tell him, Jesse, honey, it's all right. Ain't nothing to be scared of. I'm here with you now. No matter what, you'll not be alone. I'm here with you on this side, and your mama and papa and your brother Dalton and all your kin that's passed before you is waiting on the other side. Mason's there, and Rachel and Rose, and Peter. And Lena, the one we never knew. Our babies, Jesse, they're there too.

I do envy him that, getting to be with our lost children gone from me these many years now. I miss them so. More than I miss Jesse, to tell the truth. It was hard to let go that man, but I done it finally. Them young'uns of mine I have never let go. They live right on in my heart, and not a day passes I don't think of them, trying to imagine what the girls and Peter would've looked like had they lived long enough to grow up, wondering if Mason would've settled down and raised a family with Margaret if he'd come home from the war. What would they've done with their lives, where would they've gone?

Sometimes here lately, my lost children seem more real to me than the ones still here. I reckon that's the pull of the other side getting stronger the older I get. Seems I've about done all I can do here in this life and I'm sort of looking forward to the next, to the adventure of it. I'll be missed, I know, and I'll miss, but I'll not be sad to go, for I know as sure as I know my own name that it's not the last time we'll meet, me and my loved ones left behind. Only the last time here in this world.

I'll go on with the satisfaction of knowing I done my best, and I'm leaving behind a great deal more than when I come into this world eighty-two years ago. Each one of the children—Lena, Mason, Dwight, Peter, Clark, Rachel and Rose, Dean, Frank, Marshall, Ruth Ann, Cassandra—they all do credit to me and everybody who come before and who will come after. Not that any of us is perfect. If I've learned anything, it's that we ain't meant for perfection. We was put here to do our best and love one another, and there is such a thing as good enough. I figure I can give myself credit for having done the best I knowed how at the time, wishing my best had been better, knowing the miracle of forgiveness and mercy waits on us all, even Jesse, even Velda.

Jesse, he told it to me once and I made him swear never to speak of it again. I made him tell me when the nightmares got so bad and he thrashed around in the bed so he split my lip more than once. He was trying to stop her in his dreams. Over and over again he tried to stop her, but she always done what she wanted. She always had her way.

He said the memory of that hour in the woods was like one long bad dream. Even while it was actually happening, it seemed like a dream. He'd gone hunting and come up on Velda squatting in the leaves, her skirt hiked up, pushing and screaming. She was holding on to a little maple sapling, he said, and it was shaking so hard the leaves fell all around Velda, a shower of them, golden yellow in the sunlight.

Lord knows Jesse seen me through childbirth enough times, he knowed just what to do. He caught the baby, poured some white liquor—which he always carried him a little bottle of—over his knife and cut the cord, buried the afterbirth, wrapped the baby in his shirt so she wouldn't get cold in that October air. When he finally got done and looked at Velda, she just squatted there, rocking back and forth in the leaves, staring right through him. He put his hand on her shoulder and spoke her name, and that's when she jumped up and tore off through the woods. He held the baby close to his chest and went after her.

She run to the place we used to play as children, a little grove of hickory nut trees, right close to a cliff. We used to sit up there and play grown-up ladies having a tea party, looking down over our fine property. That day,

Velda run right to the edge of that cliff and stood looking down at the road below. I can see it now like I was there myself. She stood there, and then she turned to face Jesse. He said her eyes was wild and her dress a-flying around in the wind. She looked like a great dark bird a-flapping its wings, ready to fly away. She kept saying go back, go back now, go back I say, screaming the words. He said he couldn't tell if she was a-talking to him or to herself.

Jesse said he didn't believe she understood how near she was to the edge. He said he didn't believe she meant to go over. He took a step toward her, then another, then one more. He held the baby in his left arm and held his right hand out to Velda. The baby begun to cry then, and Velda got real quiet and looked at it. She stared, he said, like she was a-wondering what it was in his arms making all that racket. She didn't seem to know what she'd done.

Well, Jesse was scared to go any closer, scared to death he'd startle her. Finally at last, she looked up at him, crossed her arms over her bosom, took a step backward, and she was gone, flying down to that hard ground below.

Jesse said it was like seeing me go down, watching me die, and the terrible thing was, he felt like he'd killed us both. In a way, I reckon he had.

February
1993

14

Cold seeped through his jeans, into his butt, as Keith sat with his back against a tractor tire, listening to oil run into a bucket. Changing the oil on the two tractors was just the break he needed after a day spreading cow shit. He leaned his head against the tire. Wouldn't take long for the oil to drain, and he'd have to get up, get back to work. Only a minute more to sit quiet and take things in, how blue the sky was over his head, how pretty the cows sounded coming to the barn, how bad Dwight's house needed painting. It was something, the way the whole bunch talked about that house, calling it the homeplace. Made you expect to see some big fine house. It wasn't big or fine, just average, in Keith's opinion. That's what loving a place done for people, he reckoned, made them see more than what was really there. Just like the first time he took Ashley to see his granny and she called the house a shack. He felt like hitting her. Sure it wasn't much, and he could see how it might look to a stranger, but it was home. You don't mess with somebody's home.

His mind went back to the problem that'd been worrying him all day, what to give Ashley for Valentine's Day. He needed something good, meaningful, but not too heavy, not like the engagement ring. She hadn't said a word about it since Christmas, and he hadn't seen her wear the ring, but he wasn't going to be the one to bring it up. The way she'd been acting lately, especially with the baby a week overdue now, he was scared the least little thing might send her off on a shooting spree or something.

He heard footsteps and looked around and the first thing he seen was a shotgun almost right in front of his face. He flattened himself against the tractor tire, then looked up. Dwight, not Ashley. Still, it made him a little nervous being down on the ground, not knowing what Dwight intended doing with that twelve-gauge. He got to his feet quick.

"Boy, you ever do any hunting?" Dwight stood in front of him, wheezing a little bit. He'd had pneumonia in January and still hadn't quite got his strength back.

"Yes, sir," Keith said. "Used to hunt with my uncles all the time." He took a closer look at the gun. "That's a nice weapon you got there, Mr. Moon. What you got it out for?"

"Well, son, I'll tell you. They's a dog got to be killed, and I need you to go out and kill it for me." Dwight looked hard at Keith. "You know the one I mean."

Keith knew. The dog Speed that belonged to Ashley's next-door neighbors, the Spiveys, or the Damn Spiveys, as he'd come to know them. Dwight had tried talking to them, but it was no use. Speed was a Border collie; they said it was in his blood to herd. Which was true. But when Dwight told them his cows didn't need herding, they knew what to do on their own, the Damn Spiveys just told him to get off their property. Dwight then called the law. The law warned the people that Dwight had every right to remove that dog if it come on his property. They all knew what remove meant. That's when the people got real nasty and said if their three-hundred-dollar dog turned up dead, then some of his cows might turn up the same way. It was a mess all right.

Keith looked down at the ground, then up at Dwight. He didn't have to ask if killing the dog was really necessary. He'd worked for Dwight long enough now to know the man didn't enjoy this, but he had a business to run. And trying to break a dog from running cows was like trying to change the course of a river. It was just nature's way. Keith held out his hand and Dwight give him the gun.

"They usually let him loose when they get home from work, you know, so he'll probably be over here 'fore long." Dwight squeezed his eyes shut and pinched the bridge of his nose with his thumb and forefinger. "I hate it's come to this, I truly do." He pulled a box of ammunition from his pocket, handed it to Keith, and turned to go. "You be careful now, boy," he said as he went on toward the house. "Don't shoot one of my cows by mistake."

Keith put the ammunition in his pocket and held the gun in both hands. It was lighter than it looked, and Dwight obviously took good care of it, even though Keith had never seen him use it. Maybe one of these days the two of them could hunt together.

He checked to make sure the gun wasn't loaded, then held it pointed at the ground like his uncles taught him. He went through the gate into the pasture and headed up the hill to look for the dog. The stretch of his leg muscles as he climbed felt good after a day spent on a tractor, and he breathed in deep. It was his favorite time of day, when the sun disappeared but its light lingered, and everything looked all blurry around the edges. He stopped at the top of the hill and studied the red clouds on the horizon. Another clear, cool day coming tomorrow, he'd bet on it. He looked across the pasture toward the woods. Without their leaves, the gray trees looked like pencil drawings with smudges underneath where shadows fell.

Keith had spent a lot of time in the woods growing up, and had shot all kinds of animals, starting with birds and squirrels and moving up to raccoon and possum and deer, even shot at a bear once but missed. He'd never shot a pet before, an animal somebody kept in their house all day and bought Gravy Train for and took to the vet for shots. He shifted the gun to his other hand and stared across the pasture toward the cow path leading from the pond. That's where the cows would be this time of day, heading for the barns, and that's where Speed would be too. Keith prayed for the dog not to come, for it to be home under the kitchen table waiting for supper scraps. The Damn Spiveys should fence in their yard if they was going to have a dog like that, give him a place to run where he wouldn't cause no trouble. Stupid damn people.

They were assholes about everything, not just their dog. They let their kids run wild all over the place, and Keith had to chase them out of the cow pasture several times. They wasn't chasing cows, but Dwight didn't want them getting hurt on his property so their parents could sue him. There was also the big grudge over the leaves, which A.J. told him about last fall. People like that didn't deserve a dog, or kids neither, not if they just threw them outdoors and didn't care what happened to them.

From across the pasture, Keith heard the lowing of a cow, then a single sharp bark. There he was, at the back of a line of cows, circling, nipping their heels. Keith had to laugh. The crazy mutt thought he was keeping the old bitches in line, didn't know they was too stupid to do anything but the same old thing they did every day. Go to the barn, go to the pasture. Eat, drink, shit, make milk.

The dog deserved credit for working hard though. If they had some sheep around here, he'd be amazing.

Speed moved in a little too close to one of the cows and got a kick in the head. He staggered and yelped and the cows kept walking.

"Hey!" Keith hollered. The dog stopped and looked across the pasture toward him, then shook his head and went after the cows again. It was like he had a death wish. Keith started walking toward the herd, keeping the gun down. Damn, he hated to kill a dog. He probably wouldn't be able to enjoy his supper knowing he'd killed a dog. He stopped suddenly, keeping his eyes on Speed. Then again, who said he had to kill it? Maybe he could catch the dog, take it off somewhere. Of course, a dog that smart'd probably find his way right back home again. Unless he had something else to concentrate on besides cows. Keith shook his head. Dwight'd kill him if he come dragging that dog to the house.

The damn dog would not stop barking. Keith turned on his stomach and pulled the pillow over his head. He could still hear it. He should've killed the thing when he had the chance. But, no, he had to try and save it. God.

Finally he couldn't stand it no more and got out of bed. He pulled his jeans on and went to the window. It was pitch-black outside, except for the circle of light around the back porch of Dwight and Betty's house. Keith tightened his ponytail and pulled on a shirt, then stuck his feet in a pair of boots. He seen a pack of crackers on the dresser and grabbed it. Maybe if he took the mutt something to eat it'd shut up. It couldn't really be hungry though, because Betty fed it half a pound of leftover hamburger and some rice and beans for supper. Probably in that barn farting like a wild stallion now, in between barking. Keith bet it never ate that good at home. He knew he never had. His granny had fed him and his uncles fat meat or rabbit and collards and taters. He opened the door, grabbed his jacket, and headed down the steps.

Dwight was pretty pissed when he seen Keith come dragging that dog in the barn, but he got over it real quick when Betty found out what was going on. Apparently he didn't tell her about killing the dog, because he knew she wouldn't allow it. She went and called the SPCA and they give her the name of somebody that took in dogs like Speed and found homes for them.

Border collie rescue, they called it. They also had poodle rescue, St. Bernard rescue, cocker spaniel rescue, and every other kind of rescue in the book. It amazed Keith there was that many people out there interested in rescuing dogs. The only problem was, the Border collie man lived near Murphy, which meant Keith'd have to miss a day of work to drive the dog up there. But once Betty got into her head that was the thing to do, there wasn't no sense arguing. Dwight had to give in.

When Keith opened the barn door, the barking stopped. He waited, felt the dog waiting too. He closed the barn door behind him and felt his way over to the stall where the dog was tied. He couldn't see anything when he leaned over the stall door and shook the crackers onto the straw, but he could hear the dog breathing, then eating, then breathing again.

"You got to hush now, you hear me? Shut up that barking or I'll be too tired to drive your sorry ass to Murphy tomorrow, and then where'll you be? Dead as a hammer, that's where. You won't get no second chances with me." The dog stayed quiet, so Keith turned away and headed out. The minute the barn door closed behind him, the dog started barking again.

He went back in and the dog stopped barking. Keith sighed. So that was his game. He wanted company. He walked to the stall and leaned back against the door. "You're pathetic, you know that? You're a dog. You're not supposed to sit out here and make a fuss just 'cause you don't want to be left alone." Keith slid down until his butt hit sawdust. "I just hope you appreciate this, you mangy mutt."

He stretched his legs out, leaned his head back, and listened to the dog sniffing the boards behind his back. "I have to say I'll be glad to have the chance to see Granny and them again when I take you up to your new home. I guess I owe you one for that. And Betty. She's something, ain't she? How'd she know? You know if it wasn't for her, you and me both'd be in the doghouse. I hope you appreciate all she done for you." The dog scratched the wall, then Keith heard him circling before he laid down with a grunt. In a few minutes, Speed was asleep and snoring and Keith was wide awake, smelling cow and sawdust and hay.

Keith crossed his arms over his chest and put his hands under his arms to warm his fingers. Slowly his eyes adjusted to the dark and he stared up at the rafters. He hoped there wasn't no bats up there. Bats give him the creeps ever since he was little and believed in vampires. They looked like flying rats, and he hated the way they swooped down on you like they did, so unpredictable. He didn't like being swooped on.

He closed his eyes and tried to think about something else—the drive the next day, the best way to go so he could drop the dog off first, then go on to Murphy. He liked picturing Speed on a sheep ranch in the mountains. He could imagine the blue hills, the green pastures, the white sheep, the dog thinking he'd died and gone to heaven. And them Damn Spiveys'd never know. Keith just hoped they wouldn't go out and get a new dog and start the whole thing all over again. If they did, him and Betty'd just have to go into the dog-rescue business themselves, part-time. He wouldn't mind hitting the road every now and again to save a life.

It was weird how he'd been in Davis only about six months, but already it felt like home. Ashley had something to do with it, and Dwight and Betty. But even more than that, it was a feeling he had when he first seen the place, something like he used to feel whenever he was a little boy and waiting for his uncles to come home from work. Him and Granny'd have supper all ready and laid out on the table and here'd come Joe and Bill and Junior from the mill, always laughing and teasing, just like they hadn't spent the last eight hours in a windowless hell turning trees into furniture they'd never be able to afford.

Of course, Keith hadn't known about that then. All he knew was they smelled like sawdust and sweat and called him little man and brung him candy from the canteen. They'd ask him if he kept the wolf from the door while they was gone, and it made him proud they trusted him to watch over Granny and the house all day. Keith figured it was like priming the pump. A little bit of respect up-front drew more of the same. It would be good to see them all again and be able to say he was sober, had a job, was starting a family. Sort of.

It suddenly occurred to him that Ashley might go into labor while he was gone. It'd be just like her to do that. And then get mad at him for not being there. Everything here lately made her mad. A.J. was right. Sometimes all you could do with women was give them a generic apology, because they sure as hell wouldn't tell you what was bothering them.

Keith refused to apologize for going out of town. He had a job to do, and besides, he wanted to go. He'd stop by the shop and see her before he left. Maybe she'd be in a good mood for a change. She'd seemed real excited about helping with the flowers on Valentine's Day. Maybe she'd even like the present he'd decided to give her.

He put his chin on his chest and closed his eyes, determined to get some sleep. The dog shifted in the straw behind him and whimpered a little bit. Must be chasing something in his dreams. Keith smiled. From now on, it wouldn't be cows.

15

"Okay, Granny, close your eyes and hold on to my arm." Ashley helped Marvelle up the ramp and stopped at the entrance. "Okay, now take a deep breath."

"It's cold as a witch's tit in here," Marvelle said, then inhaled deeply once, then again, then again. "Is it a perfume factory?"

"No. Open your eyes."

Marvelle blinked a few times and looked around. "Oh," she said. "Would you look at the flowers."

Ashley led her further toward the back of the truck. Everywhere was color, boxes and boxes of roses, red, pink, yellow, white, lavender. Further on were shiny green ferns, baby's breath, carnations, tulips, irises, freesia, lilies, statice, daisies, daffodils, mums, and other flowers Ashley didn't recognize yet.

"What is this place? Looks like a funeral."

"It's the truck that delivered all of Mama and Daddy's flowers for Valentine's Day. Can you believe it?"

Marvelle put her hand over her nose. "My head's starting to spin from all this perfume. Take me out of here."

Ashley looked at her, disappointed. "I thought you'd like to see all them flowers, Granny."

"I do, honey, but I can't abide all them smells. It's overpowering me."

244 • Pamela Duncan

Marvelle turned toward the open end of the truck. Ashley took her arm and helped her down the ramp and into the car. Marvelle leaned back in the seat and buttoned her sweater.

"You wait right here, Granny. Cassandra'll be out in a minute."

Ashley found Ruth Ann and Cassandra in the workroom, putting long-stemmed roses and ferns in long white boxes. They'd been there since four o'clock that morning. Ashley had come to pitch in so Cassandra could go home and open the day care. Marvelle didn't know it yet, but she was going to the day care with Cassandra. Ashley was thankful she didn't have to be the one to break the news.

It was hard to believe Valentine's Day was here already. Her mama had been going crazy for weeks getting ready. The first big holiday. It didn't seem quite real until yesterday when an eighteen-wheeler backed that re-frigerated car into the lot behind the shop. Ashley hadn't realized until then that a truckload of flowers translated into a whole lot of work. Ruth Ann hired three ladies to help out, and they all worked until after mid-night, unloading and making arrangements. The truck was still half full, but the cooler in the shop couldn't hold another flower.

"What time's them women coming back?" Cassandra said as she put on her coat.

Ruth Ann looked at the clock. "About seven-thirty, I think they said."

"Well, I'm heading on." Cassandra looked at Ashley. "Mama in the car?"

"Yeah, she's all buckled in and ready to go. She just don't know where she's going yet."

"Oh, hell," Cassandra said. She let the door slam behind her.

Ashley sat down at a table with a row of bud vases across the front and looked at Ruth Ann. "Okay, Mama, tell me what to do."

Ruth Ann plopped an armload of pink roses on the table, then a box of ferns. "Okay, stick one rose and one fern in a bud vase. Cut a piece of rib-bon and tie it around the vase like this. That's it."

They didn't say much, just listened to the radio while they worked. Ash-ley couldn't believe her mama was listening to a country station—country love songs, at that. She didn't mind it, she was so glad to be out of the house for a change.

About seven-thirty, Mary Deal, Alma Moser, and Caroldine Cline showed up. They'd all worked at the plant with Ruth Ann since before Ashley was born, and all four of them got laid off at the same time. Ashley remembered hearing their names a lot growing up, but it was weird to be sitting in a room with them, like sitting down with people from a book or a movie. Mary Deal was the oldest, about sixty-five, and everybody called her by her whole name, never just Mary. She had more wrinkles than anybody Ashley had ever seen. A.J. always said if they was to iron Mary Deal's face, it'd be as big as Texas. Ruth Ann said it was all the smoking and her baking herself in the sun or the tanning bed year-round. Mary Deal didn't care though, and she was funny. Her voice always sounded like it was about used up, but that didn't stop her, even when she started out laughing and ended up coughing.

Alma Moser was fat and still wore her hair in a beehive, and she had only one topic of conversation; her daughter Tiffany. Ashley went to school with Tiffany, and she always hated that prissy bitch. She wasn't surprised to hear that Tiffany was in college studying to be an elementary school teacher, or that she was engaged to a chiropractor she met after she hurt her back in a car wreck a year ago. The minute Tiffany graduated college, her and the chiropractor was getting married and moving to Davis, where she'd teach and he'd open Quinn Raeford Chiropractic. Quinn Raeford. What the hell kind of name was that, especially for a man?

Ashley didn't know much about Caroldine, except that she was from Pennsylvania and kind of slutty. Ruth Ann said she had a good heart and didn't mean to be slutty. She just kept getting mixed up with the wrong men and then having their babies. Ashley could understand that. Keith wasn't wrong though, not like the others, and she was not going to end up like Caroldine, all by herself with four young'uns all by different daddies.

"Hey, Ashley honey," Mary Deal said. She had a cigarette hanging out the corner of her mouth and it bobbed up and down while she talked. Her hands was full of pink carnations. "How much overdue are you now?"

"About a week," Ashley said.

"Well, that's normal for the first," Alma said. "I remember Tiffany was nearly four weeks overdue and they had to go in and break my water. I slept through the whole thing, thank the Lord."

"My young'uns was all born at home," Mary Deal said. "Me and my first husband lived way out in the country, didn't have time to get to no hospital."

"How many you got?" Ashley said.

"Seven. All still living. All doing better than me, except my least boy that's in jail for armed robbery. But he's getting straightened out. He's done got religion in there. Ain't nothing like religion for putting men on the straight and narrow. Too bad it makes them boring as hell too." Mary Deal laughed real husky and deep.

"Did you have somebody to help you?" Ashley said.

"What? You mean delivering them young'uns? Yeah, my sister helped me, and my husband. He was pretty good with a knife."

Ashley's eyes got big. "A knife?"

Mary Deal laughed again. "To cut the cord, honey."

"You know," Alma said, "my mama told me to put a knife under the bed to cut the pain. Well, I was in the hospital, so I put the knife under the mattress because I didn't want nobody to see, but it worked, I swear it did."

"Shit, Alma," Mary Deal said. "Didn't you just get through telling us you was asleep the whole time?"

"Well, yeah, but I mean before that."

Caroldine come around the table and got one of Mary Deal's cigarettes. "Honey, you just make sure they give you some drugs. Don't let nobody talk you into doing natural childbirth. They done that to me with my first one, and I thought that thing was going to split me in two."

"Yeah, but you forget all about the pain before you know it," Ruth Ann said.

Caroldine laughed. "Yeah, right. I made sure with the rest of them I got me a epidural the minute I walked through the door."

"I remember when I was pregnant with Angela, I asked Mama what it felt like to have a baby," Ruth Ann said.

Ashley looked up at Ruth Ann. "What'd she say?"

"Well, she thought about it for a minute, and then she said, well, honey, have you ever tried to shit a watermelon?"

They was all still cackling when A.J. strolled in with coffee, orange juice, and a bag of biscuits. "Morning, ladies!" he said, looking at them kind of funny. He didn't ask what the joke was though. He handed out breakfast and they took a ten-minute break to eat. When they finished, they went back to work, and A.J. started loading the van. At nine he headed out to make his first round of deliveries.

Just before the shop opened at ten, Keith knocked on the back door and let himself in. Ruth Ann and the others had gone to the front to open up and Ashley was alone in back. She concentrated on the arrangement in front of her. She was experimenting with roses and tulips, but they didn't seem to go together.

"Hey, Ash," Keith said.

"Hey," she said.

He sat on the edge of the table. "What you making there?" He cocked his head to the side and studied it.

"What does it look like?"

"I don't think you want to know," he said.

Ashley started ripping tulips out of the arrangement and slamming them on the table. "Fine. If you just come in here to insult me, you can get the hell out."

"I didn't come to insult you. I just wanted to give you your Valentine's present."

She looked at his empty hands, then his face.

"Come out to the truck with me."

She hesitated, then followed him outside. The first thing she seen was the dog in the front seat, barking. "Is that it?"

Keith laughed and rubbed the dog's head through the open window. "You recognize old Speed, don't you? I'm kidnapping him to a sheep ranch in the mountains. I'm going to spend the night with Granny and drive back in the morning."

"Does Dwight know about it?"

"It was his idea. Well, Betty's."

"The Damn Spiveys is going to have a cow."

"As long as it ain't one of ours." Keith smiled at her. "Close your eyes and hold out your hands."

She did as he asked and waited. She'd be willing to bet he was trying to give her the ring again. The boy just wouldn't give up. He got major credit for trying, no doubt about that. It was hard to keep the smile off her face, and at that moment she didn't know but that she might just put it on. Give him that much at least. Maybe wear it a while, see how it felt. He laid something in her hand, something flat, square, and smooth. It did not feel like the ring box. She opened her eyes and looked down at what appeared to be a savings book, then looked at Keith, her eyebrows raised in question.

"It's my savings account. I got about two thousand dollars in there now."

"Oh, really." Ashley smiled. "What exactly are you saving for?" Maybe he'd realized she needed a car more than a ring. Maybe he was saving up to buy her one.

"For the baby," Keith said.

Her smile fell. She slapped the book back in his hand. "Oh, great," she said. "Very romantic." The baby again. Was that all he ever thought about anymore? He hadn't touched her since Christmas, and all he ever wanted to talk about was planning for the baby. Well, what about her? She was the one carrying the dang baby, having the baby, the one whose life—not to mention figure—would never be the same again because of the baby. Why didn't anybody think about her for a change? Ashley stomped into the shop and slammed the door behind her.

Keith stared at the closed door for a minute, then got in the truck and looked at Speed. "Do you understand women?" he said. Speed just looked at him, drool dripping off his tongue onto the gearbox. "I didn't think so." Keith cranked the truck, put it in first, and headed for the highway.

It was still light out when Keith got home, and he had got there in time to help with the milking. But instead of getting out and getting to work, he just sat there in the truck, staring. Dwight was probably in the house listening to the news, and Betty was probably in there fixing supper about now. Keith knew he ought to go in and explain why he was back so early, why he hadn't spent the night in Murphy like he planned, but he just couldn't make himself move out of the truck. For one thing, it was cold outside and warm in the truck. For another thing, he didn't think he could go in there and make small talk and act like everything was all hunky-dory when it wasn't, it damn well wasn't.

The screen door squeaked and Keith looked and seen Dwight standing there on the back porch, watching him. He let the door slam shut behind him and started walking real slow toward the truck, picking his teeth with a toothpick. Keith rolled down the window and waited for him. When Dwight got to the truck, he didn't say nothing, just stood there looking off toward the pasture. Finally he said, "You're back early."

"Yes, sir," Keith said.

"Supper'll be ready pretty soon." Dwight stuck the toothpick in his pocket and looked at Keith. "Feel like helping me with the milking, then?"

"Sure," Keith said, and got out of the truck. Maybe it would take his mind off things for a while.

Once they got the cows herded in and hooked the milkers on, they took a few minutes and leaned up against the barn wall, watching the animals, waiting for the machines to finish. It didn't feel as cold here as it had in Murphy, and Keith figured maybe that was due to more than the weather. He liked being with Dwight, felt like this was where he belonged.

"Your people doing all right?" Dwight said.

"Yes, sir, they're all fine," Keith said. All except his daddy. "I got some bad news up there though."

"Is that right?"

"Yes, sir." Keith hesitated. Could he say the words out loud, get them out without choking on them? "It's my daddy." And then the words come out in a rush, like the quicker he said them and got it over with, the better off he'd be. "He's dead. He died in prison in Illinois, got killed in a fight. He was in there for armed robbery, been there nearly ten years. That's why he never come back. Granny and them knowed all about it but they never told me. They said he told them not to. They said he didn't want me to know. And now he's dead."

Dwight was quiet. Keith reckoned neither one of them knew what to say after that.

"They should've told me," Keith said. "My daddy should've told me. People in prison can write letters, can't they? They get to make phone calls. Here I spent my whole life thinking he hated me, and now I find out the sorry son of a bitch has been in prison all this time. He ain't nothing but a criminal. Wasn't nothing. What kind of a daddy is that?" Keith slammed his fist against the wall. "Huh? Tell me, what kind of a daddy is that?" He was fighting hard not to cry.

It was quiet for a long time after that, just the sound of their breathing, the milking machines, and the cows moving their feet every once in a while. Finally Dwight said, "I want to tell you something, son."

He paused, and Keith said, "Yes, sir?"

"Son," he said. "No doubt about it, having a daddy is important to a boy. I have to say, I was lucky myself, had me about the best daddy that ever was." Dwight reached a finger up and wiped under his eye, then cleared his throat. "Seems to me that man wasn't no kind of a daddy to you, and that's a durn shame. I feel bad for you because you deserved better, and I feel sorry for your daddy because he walked away from a fine son like you. I reckon it's too late for him, but it ain't too late for you. Now, you know I ain't got no young'uns of my own. But it looks to me like a man gets two chances when it comes to daddies, to have one and to be one. Son, I believe you're about to get your second chance with Ashley and that baby, and that's a blessing. Trust me, that is truly a blessing."

16

*P*eri *was flying. No wings, but she was flying, floating really, coming closer and closer to where Ashley stood on top of Appalachian Hall. The mountains around them was fuzzy purple in the heat of the day, and Ashley could smell the tar on the roof melting under the sun. Even the bottoms of her feet felt on fire. She squeezed her eyes shut and waited. Something was not right here.*

"It's fucking hot out here today," Peri said.

Ashley opened her eyes and watched Peri float on her back in the dense air, arms behind her head.

"Man, I need a cigarette," Peri said. "You got any on you?"

Ashley shook her head no.

"What the hell's the matter with you? Why ain't you saying nothing?" Peri come upright, treading light as a butterfly. She studied Ashley's face, then looked down at her belly. "Man, you're huge. I mean, that thing's liable to drop any day now."

Ashley looked down too. Jesus, when did she get that big? She looked back at Peri. "Oh, my God," she said.

Peri floated closer and with both hands cupped the air around Ashley's belly. "Hey. Don't panic. It's all right." She put her lips close to Ashley's ear and whispered, "It's a girl."

Ashley reached for Peri's hands and grabbed only air. She let her hands drop back by her sides. "I'm scared, Peri. I feel like hell, my back hurts, my ankles are all swole up, and my face looks like a balloon. And I got to go pee every five minutes, but most of the time nothing comes out."

Peri floated on her side, her head in her hand, long blond hair swinging below her. "You do look pretty rough. But it won't be for long. That's the thing to remember."

"Yeah, but then the baby'll be here and then what'll I do?"

"You sure you ain't got no cigarettes?"

"No, dammit, I quit. I told you that."

"What the hell'd you do that for?"

"For the baby, stupid. Smoking's bad for the baby."

"Bummer." Peri backflipped and her hair whipped over her head, covering her face. "Whoa!" she said as she come upright and wiped hair out of the corners of her grinning mouth. "I'm dizzy." She started to disappear below the edge of the building. Ashley screamed and run up the board and stood on the wall, looking over her belly and down, down, down. Peri drifted like a paper airplane toward the cement below. Ashley hollered for her to stop, to come back, but Peri hollered, "It's okay, Ash, I can fly."

Ashley screamed, "No, you can't!" and Peri disappeared. Not a trace of her remained in the air or on the pavement below. Ashley got dizzy and started swaying, felt herself start to fall, then Marvelle grabbed her arm and pulled hard. Ashley stumbled backward and fell on something soft. Marvelle whispered, "Wake up, honey. You're having a bad dream."

Ashley opened her eyes and the first thing she seen was the baby bed in the corner. She looked around for her granny, but she was alone. She sat up on the bed and stared at the stuffed animals in the crib. They seemed to be watching her with their shiny button eyes. Most of them was gifts from Ruth Ann's friends, since Ashley didn't have no friends in town anymore. They'd also give her a car seat, a high chair, a baby bathtub, and a playpen.

Everything was waiting for the baby, now a week overdue. Despite the fact that only one pair of her maternity pants fit anymore, and despite not being able to tie her own shoes, Ashley didn't feel ready. Her granny and her mama acted like having a young'un was no big deal. Easy for them to say since they'd finished with theirs. They never had all the problems she had neither, like no husband and no job and no money and no prospects.

But then she closed her eyes and remembered the dream, Peri flying and falling and never having the chance to do none of the things she was supposed to do. Ashley told herself she didn't have no business complaining, then realized that sounded just like something Marvelle would say—you ain't got no business complaining, young lady. She put her hands on her belly. The baby was waking up too. She shifted, putting pressure on Ashley's spine and forcing her to stretch her legs out and sit up straighter.

That didn't help much, so Ashley scooted to the edge of the bed and hung her legs over the side. Her ankles looked like tree stumps, and she had to wait a minute before putting her weight on her feet. She reached for a banana clip on the night table and pulled her hair off her face. Her head was soaking wet with sweat and so was her back. Marvelle had been at the thermostat again. Just because it was February she was convinced they was all going to freeze to death if they didn't keep the house hot as a toaster. Ashley looked toward the window, then at the clock. Damn. Five o'clock. She hadn't meant to sleep so long.

It was Marvelle's fault though. She made Ashley go lay down when her back started hurting worse that afternoon. It'd been hurting her all day, probably because of helping out at the shop that morning. The combination of the pain and too many sleepless nights was what kept her napping longer than she intended. Funny how she hadn't been sleeping well at night lately but Marvelle had. She opened the bedroom door and the sound of the early news blared from the living room. Time to pull Marvelle away from her puzzle and the TV and start fixing supper.

"Granny!" Ashley hollered as she headed down the hall. "Granny, you got the TV on too loud again. You know you ain't deaf." She stopped in the doorway, surprised that Marvelle wasn't sitting at her puzzle table in front of the television. Bathroom, she thought, and moved on into the kitchen. She poked at the chicken thawing in the sink, then picked ten good-size potatoes out of the tater box. Her daddy was coming for supper and he loved smashed taters, as he called them.

Before she sat down to peel them, she went back down the hall and stopped in front of the bathroom door. "Granny, you in there? Granny?" She opened the door, but the room was dark and empty. She needed to pee herself, so she went on and did her business, then went to her mama's room to check the bathroom there. No Marvelle. Ashley felt a little shiver of worry, but decided not to panic until she'd checked the whole house.

She went from room to room, checking closets. A couple of weeks before, Marvelle had gone into a closet and shut the door behind her, then couldn't remember the way out. She'd hollered loud enough, though, that

Ashley found her right away. This time the house was too quiet, except for the TV. If Marvelle was anywhere in the place, Ashley would've known it by now.

Her hands was shaking as she went back to the living room and cut the TV off. Where the hell could that crazy old woman have got to? Tears started up in her eyes but she didn't let herself cry. She had to think what to do. First she needed to look around outside. Maybe Marvelle had just gone for a little walk. She pulled her jacket off the hook next to the kitchen door. Marvelle's coat was still hanging there. Oh, God, Ashley thought, please let her be in the yard. Please don't let her be lost. Please let her be okay. Oh please, oh please, oh please.

Compared to the house, the air outside felt good and cool. At least it was a warm day for February, maybe even fifty-five or sixty degrees in the sunshine. Her granny would be okay without her coat for a while. Of course, dark was coming on fast and the temperature would drop way down. Ashley went through the carport and out in the front yard. No sign of Marvelle. She walked all the way around the house, her heart beating faster with every corner she turned.

At the back of the house, she stopped and stared toward the cow pasture. There was nothing moving out there either. What the hell was she going to do now? She could call the police, she could call her mama and daddy at work, she could call Keith.

Keith. Yeah, Keith. He was closest. Marvelle couldn't have got far. Ashley'd only been asleep an hour and a half at the most. How far could one little old woman get in an hour and a half? But Marvelle wasn't no ordinary little old woman. She was a Moon, and her legs was strong as a mule. Ashley run back to the house to call Keith, the baby kicking all the way.

The minute she picked up the phone, she remembered that Keith was still in the mountains, wouldn't be back until the next morning. Ashley had forgot about him going up there to drop off that damn dog and visit his family. Damn him. He was never around when she needed him.

She had to find Marvelle before dark, less than an hour away. She couldn't do it. She needed help. The shop didn't close until six, and her mama and daddy wouldn't get home until seven at the earliest. Cassandra's last kid didn't get picked up until five-thirty. She looked at her watch. Fifteen more minutes and she'd call Cassandra. Fifteen minutes wasn't that bad.

Ashley took a deep breath and sat down on the chair under the kitchen phone. God, she needed a cigarette, but her hands was shaking so bad she probably couldn't light one if she had it. She closed her eyes. Where could Marvelle have got to? What the hell made her run off?

All she could think of was them news stories about old folks wandering off, getting lost in the woods, being found dead of exposure by police dogs. She imagined Marvelle's frozen dead face, her knotty crooked hands with no gloves, her cold cold body curled in a ball and laying stiff by a creek. She didn't have her damn coat on. Why the hell couldn't she at least put her coat on if she was going outside? What was she wearing?

Ashley remembered then that Marvelle had changed clothes after lunch because she spilled tomato soup on her front. She come home from Cassandra's with it all over her, mad as hell because she'd had to stay there all morning while Ashley was working. She'd put on a pantsuit made out of navy polyester with big red hearts on it. For Valentine's Day, she said. It had long sleeves. That was good, and double-knit polyester was one of the warmest fabrics around. Her mama said one time that stuff could be used as insulation in a house. It didn't breathe at all.

Ashley looked at her watch again. Time to call Cassandra. As she started getting up out of the chair, a sharp squeezing pain caught her lower back and she fell against the wall and slid back onto the chair. Her breath wouldn't come, it hurt so bad. She hunched over her belly and waited for it to pass.

Oh, God, she thought. Is this it? Have I been in labor all day and didn't know? Am I going to have this baby here all by myself on the kitchen floor?

She'd never hyperventilated before but she'd seen it happen, and Ashley knew it was happening to her now. It felt like her windpipe had slammed shut and she couldn't suck air in fast enough. Her breathing sounded like she'd been running uphill a long way. She hurried across the kitchen, dizzy and weaving like a drunk, waving her hands in front of her, and opened the drawer where they kept plastic wrap and aluminum foil. She found an old wrinkled paper bag at the back of the drawer, shook it open, and started breathing into it. Quick as she could, she backed over to the chair and sat down again, keeping her eyes closed until the flashing lights went away and she could think again.

Cassandra. She had to get Cassandra over here, then they could decide what to do next. Why did everybody have to be gone the one time she wished they wasn't? Ashley turned sideways in the chair, pulled the receiver onto her shoulder, and reached up to dial Cassandra's number. She leaned her cheek against the cool wall of Ruth Ann's kitchen and waited as the phone rang.

"Hello?"

"Cassandra. This is Ashley. You got to get over here now." Ashley heard a child's voice in the background.

"Honey, I can't right now. I'm still waiting on Brittany's mama to come get her." Cassandra lowered her voice to a whisper. "She was supposed to be here at five-fifteen, but that woman's always late."

"Cassandra!" Ashley breathed into the bag a couple more times.

"What's that noise? Are you all right?"

"I think I'm in labor."

"Oh, my Lord. Did you call your mama? Have you called the doctor?"

"No. There's something else."

"What? Ashley? For heaven's sake."

"Granny's gone. I looked everywhere, the whole house and the yard, and I can't find her. Please. Please come over here and help me." Ashley breathed into the bag.

"I'm putting Brittany in the car with me. I'll be there in two minutes."

Ashley listened to the dial tone for a minute, then hung up. She looked down at the floor. It needed mopping bad. She'd intended to do it today but just didn't have it in her. She got slowly to her feet. Her knees was shaky, but she wanted to get a drink of water and walk around a little bit before Cassandra got there and seen her.

She was pacing back and forth across the kitchen, counting her steps, when she heard tires squeal across cement. That woman was as bad as Keith. A car door slammed, then suddenly Cassandra was in the kitchen, coatless, breathing heavy. They stared at each other while Cassandra caught her breath.

"Where's Brittany?" Ashley said as she put the paper bag back in the drawer.

"Her mama come right as I was backing down the driveway. It's a good thing too or she'd be sitting there now wondering where her child was. Has Mama come back yet?"

"No," she said, not looking at Cassandra. She opened the back door and stared down toward the cow pasture. It was already dark down there under the trees. A tiny star winked on the deep pink of the horizon. It was cold.

"Are you all right?" Cassandra said.

"Yes." The first priority was finding Marvelle. She could fall apart and have a baby later.

There was a moment of silence, then Cassandra said, "How long has she been gone?"

"I don't know. She made me lay down and take a nap about three-thirty, and when I woke up at five she was gone." Ashley turned and looked at Cassandra standing in the middle of the kitchen floor like a big lost child.

"We got to do something," Ashley said.

"Are you sure she ain't in the house?"

"I looked everywhere, even the closets."

"I'm going to look again, then we'll call Ruth Ann, and then we'll call the police. Why don't you sit down? You're white as a sheet."

Ashley shook her head no. "I'm fine," she said.

In less than five minutes Cassandra was back. "Okay," she said, and looked at her watch. "It's nearly six o'clock. I'm calling your mama." Cassandra dialed, then put the phone down. "Busy," she said. She thought for a minute, then picked up the phone again. "Dwight and Betty," she said, looking first at Ashley's belly, then at her face.

When she got no answer, Ashley said, "They're probably milking. Keith's in the mountains till tomorrow morning." She watched Cassandra hang up. "Call the police."

Cassandra dialed 911 and after a long wait explained what'd happened. She listened for a minute, then slammed the phone down. "The hell with them," she said. "We can't wait that long. Come on, let's go."

"Where we going?" Ashley buttoned her jacket and followed Cassandra out the door.

"We going to look for Mama, and we're taking you to the hospital."

Ashley stopped. "I don't need to go to the hospital. I'm not even having pains no more."

"You probably are and you just don't know it."

"Cassandra, I believe I'd know if I was having a pain. Let's go."

They got in Cassandra's van and decided to drive five miles in either direction, looking for Marvelle on the side of the road. Then if they didn't find her they'd come back and call Ruth Ann again. As the van pulled out of the driveway, Ashley felt something hot twisting a knot in her lower back. She couldn't help moaning a little. Cassandra looked over, looked at her watch, then turned back to the road. They didn't say a word. Cassandra looked left and Ashley looked right. Lucky for them, there was a half moon, just enough light to see by.

17

At six o'clock, Ruth Ann locked the door and started closing out the cash register. Even though she took the phone off the hook at five-thirty, there'd still been a steady stream of business, people walking in off the street. It amazed her, the volume of business they'd done in just that one day. Though she'd been on her feet nearly the whole time and should've been exhausted, instead she felt good, better than she'd felt in a long time.

Folks she'd talked to before buying into the business with A.J. had tried to prepare her for what the busy days like Valentine's Day and Mother's Day would be like, but there was no way to know until you actually experienced it. She'd never seen so many frantic people in her life, except maybe at Toys R Us the day before Christmas. And it was all kinds of people, women and men, old and young, everybody loved somebody. Like that Dean Martin song.

Sweat trickled down her neck and she fanned herself with her hand, then with a piece of paper. It didn't help. The hot flash snuck up on her, as usual. She worked a little longer, then put the pencil down and went over to the cooler. As soon as the door opened, cold air washed out over her. If it was just a little bit bigger, she'd be tempted to crawl right in there with the last flower they had left.

She leaned in closer and inhaled that beautiful smell of cold red roses that lingered even after they was gone. They'd sold all but one. She'd put the last one in a bud vase with a sprig of baby's breath and a fern and tied a red ribbon around the vase. It surprised her that some poor fellow hadn't rushed in to buy a last-minute Valentine's Day rose for his wife or girl-friend, or maybe even for his mama.

She reached in and pulled toward her the tub of water that had been full of carnations that morning. She started to lift it out to empty the water but decided to let A.J. handle that when he got back from making deliveries. She looked at her watch. Nearly six-thirty and he wasn't back yet. Still, he'd had a van full of flowers to deliver all over town and a couple outside town, and he hadn't left the shop until just before five. She had to admit he worked his butt off today. Every day, really. The man was not lazy. Of course, driving around was what A.J. was good at. Let him try staying put a little while and see how he done.

Ruth Ann closed the cooler door and went back to her paperwork. For the first time since they opened, she finally felt like they was going to make it. She didn't know why she had such a hard time believing everything was going to be all right. Maybe she'd heard her mama and A.J. and other peo-ple say it too many times when it wasn't all right, when it was awful. But it really was all right this time, at least for today, and that was the most she ever wanted to worry about at one time. Business had been so good today, it didn't matter if they sold another flower all month.

She thought back to January, how it all started, and had to admit a lot of the credit for their success before today was due to the Elvis arrangement. A week before they was supposed to open, a woman that used to work at the plant with Ruth Ann called and asked her to make a special arrange-ment to take to Graceland on the King's birthday, the eighth of January.

Ruth Ann tried to wiggle out of it, mainly because they didn't even have no flowers in yet. But this woman begged and pleaded until Ruth Ann fi-nally give in. She figured it'd be bad for business to turn down a paying cus-tomer at that point.

The woman had no idea what she wanted, just something big with flow-ers, so Ruth Ann designed something special herself. She made a wire frame in the shape of a guitar the size of a coffee table, then went to the greenhouse and bought every blue carnation they had and covered the frame. She made a yellow chrysanthemum heart in the middle of the guitar where the hole was supposed to be, then spelled out *Love Me Tender* underneath in red button mums. She made the guitar strings with black fishing line. It took her half a day to make the thing, but it turned out real good, and Joanne was so happy she cried when she seen it. It embarrassed Ruth Ann to death, her showing that thing all over town before she took it to Tennessee.

When she got to Graceland, the guards almost didn't allow her to carry it on the property, it was so big, but Joanne begged and pleaded until they realized she was just a loyal fan, not a terrorist, and let her in. She set the guitar right up next to the headstone, and the way Ruth Ann heard it, Joanne had to knock some other flowers out of the way to do it. A photographer and reporter from the Memphis *Sun* happened to be there, and they took a picture and wrote a little story about Joanne and her devotion to Elvis, and mentioned Ruth Ann's. The wire service picked it up and run it all over the country the next day. The story had definitely been good for business, so Ruth Ann figured she owed Joanne, and the King, a big one.

The door swung open and A.J. stepped in, then locked the door back behind him. She hadn't even heard him coming.

"Baby, please tell me we're out of flowers," he said. He looked tired, especially around the eyes.

"That's the last one," she said, and tilted her head toward the cooler.

"Good," he said. "Guess how many miles I put on the van today?"

"A hundred."

"A hundred? How about more like five hundred and seventy-six. That's a shitload of flowers, baby." A.J. pushed away from the door and walked behind the counter with Ruth Ann. "How'd we do?" he said, looking over her shoulder.

Ruth Ann didn't turn her head, just kept staring at the paperwork in front of her. A.J. was entirely too close for comfort, his cheek right next to hers, and he smelled good, like sweat and the cologne she always used to buy him for Christmas before the divorce. He would have to pick today to wear that cologne.

"Good," she said, and stepped sideways so he'd be standing beside her instead of behind her. He scooted closer and picked up the pile of twenties.

"Must be a thousand dollars right here alone," he said.

"More like two," she said, and took the money out of his hand.

A.J. put his arm around her shoulders and squeezed her close. "Can you believe it, baby? We're actually making a profit."

She stopped counting. "Did you doubt we would?"

He faced her and put his hands on her hips and she let them stay there for the moment. He cleared his throat. "Well, let's just say profit wasn't the main thing on my mind going into this. But I ain't complaining."

Ruth Ann looked up at the same blue eyes and dimples she seen every time she looked at their children, the rowdy dark hair that still didn't have one streak of gray in it and the man fifty-five years old. The tenderness she felt for A.J. would never go away, she knew that. How could she help but feel tenderness for that little boy inside his man's body? And his body still drew her, still made her feel like a woman, no doubt about that. But she couldn't see herself ever loving him the way she used to, the way she done when she was Ashley's age. They'd traveled too much rough ground together, and then apart, to ever get back to that. What exactly did she feel for him now? Desire? That word made her uncomfortable because she wasn't accustomed to thinking it, or feeling it. But there was something else, something more. They'd grown up together, these long years of their marriage and divorce and children and now grandchildren. Maybe they could be friends finally.

He didn't know that yet, of course. He still wanted to get back that old love, that crazy passion. Every day he struggled to find a way to do it. He was struggling now. She seen it in his face as he leaned closer and kissed her mouth soft, then harder. His tongue tickled her lips open and she thought about giving in just this once. It'd been so long, and she wanted it. She couldn't lie about that. She wanted him. His hands felt so good on her, pulling her into him. She laid the money on the counter and put her hands on his chest.

A.J. leaned back and looked at her. He was breathing fast and his cheeks was pink. "Are you about ready to go?" he said.

"Let me put the money in the bag." Ruth Ann turned away from him to clean up the counter. Her hands was shaking, and she felt young again, like anything could happen.

"Should I put the phone back on the hook?" A.J. said.

"Surely nobody'll be calling for flowers this time of the night."

"We just won't answer it if they do. If they're in the doghouse tonight, they'll need to buy even more flowers tomorrow." A.J. put the receiver back and the phone immediately began to ring.

Ruth Ann finished closing up shop while A.J. parked the van in back and drove his truck around front. Ashley had driven Ruth Ann's car home earlier when she went to get Marvelle. A.J. left the motor running and ran to hold the money pouch while Ruth Ann locked the front door.

"Did you turn the alarm on?" he asked.

"Yes," she said, and took the money pouch from him.

A.J. helped her up in the truck, then slammed the door and ran around to the driver's side. He let the engine warm up a minute, then made a U-turn and headed down Main Street. Town was pretty well deserted by seven, especially in the winter. The only other vehicle was a police car cruising through the business district. A.J. nodded at the policeman as they passed each other. "That's Richard Craven," he said. "His daddy used to work down at the plant."

Ruth Ann didn't say anything, just watched the sidewalks, knowing Marvelle wouldn't be there but watching just the same. What could have possessed her, made her want to wander off? She'd been doing so good lately, hadn't had a bad spell in nearly two weeks. "Don't forget to stop at the bank," she said.

They walked to the night deposit together, and Ruth Ann dropped the money in the bin. Somehow all that money didn't seem to matter now. All she could think about was what if they hadn't put the phone back on the hook? What if her and A.J. had continued carrying on like that, never knowing that Ashley was trying to call them? That's what she got for even thinking about messing with that man again. She knew better. As much as it terrified her to think of her mama lost out there somewhere in the cold, a little part of her was grateful to be spared making the decision of whether or not to spend the night with A.J.

Ruth Ann was grateful to have him with her now though, and especially grateful for him being quiet. They got back in the truck and left the city limits, headed home. The streetlights ended and the dark countryside spread out on either side of the road. Marvelle could be out there any-where. They passed Cassandra's place and Ruth Ann stared at the dark windows, praying to see a light come on there, that it might be Marvelle. It stayed dark.

When they walked in the kitchen, Ashley and Cassandra looked up with scared faces, like young'uns whose parents catch them playing with matches but not in time to stop the house burning down.

"Hey," Ruth Ann said. She glanced around the kitchen, then took off her coat and hung it on a hook next to Marvelle's. She stared at the coats for a minute, hanging there side by side, Marvelle's navy blue and Ruth Ann's tan. She turned her back on them.

"Hey, Daddy," Ashley said when A.J. leaned over to hug her.

"Hey, punkin," he said, and kissed her cheek. He sat at the table next to her, sneaking looks at her belly every few seconds. Finally he said, "How you doing?"

"She's probably in labor," Cassandra said.

Ruth Ann turned from the sink where she'd been filling the coffeepot. She'd forgot about that. "How far apart?"

Ashley looked at her. "No, I'm not. I had a few pains a while ago but they've quit now."

Cassandra looked at her watch. "They was coming every twelve minutes. I timed it."

"Yeah," Ashley said. "All three of them was exactly twelve minutes apart, and now I ain't had one for half an hour. It was my back hurting, that's all."

Ruth Ann studied Ashley's face. She looked like she'd put on white makeup, she was so pale. "Did you call the doctor?"

"No. Even if it is the beginning of labor it'll be a long time before I need to go to the hospital. Granny says the first baby's always the slowest."

"Well," Ruth Ann said. "You just pay attention to the signs. I don't want to be delivering no baby while we're still trying to find Mama."

Ruth Ann went back to making coffee while Cassandra explained how she called the police, and then her and Ashley drove around looking for Marvelle, then when they got back home they called the police again. The guy they talked to said they couldn't do nothing till twenty-four hours passed, or at least till daybreak.

"Did you call the rescue squad?" A.J. said. "They don't care what time of day it is." He went to the phone and dialed a number. "I'm calling J.D. He'll get somebody out here."

After a minute, it became clear nobody from the rescue squad was coming either. When A.J. hung up, he said there'd been a bad wreck on the interstate and all the rescue people was out there working. It'd be morning before anybody could come help them look for Marvelle.

About that time, Dwight and Betty let themselves in the back door. "We had to finish the milking," Dwight said. Ruth Ann had to look away from his face so she wouldn't bust out crying.

Betty carried half a pound cake wrapped in plastic to the table. "Has anybody had any supper?" she said.

"I ain't hungry," Ashley said.

"What's that got to do with it?" Betty said. "And besides, you need to eat something for that baby, and I need to cook something for my sanity."

A.J. and Dwight had a conference by the door, then Dwight spoke up. "Me and A.J. here's going to get some flashlights and look through the woods around here. She can't have got that far."

"Ruth Ann, have you got a flashlight I can use?" A.J. said.

She got her big flashlight out of the cabinet, checked to make sure it worked, and handed it to him.

A.J. looked at Dwight and they went out the door.

"Y'all be careful," Betty hollered after them.

The wind from the back door closing blew across the coats hanging near the door. Ashley watched Marvelle's old navy wool coat swing back and forth, thinking no matter how ugly it was, it was warm and she wished it was wrapped around her granny right now.

Cassandra got up from her chair in a hurry and rushed away down the hall.

"What's the matter with her?" Ruth Ann said.

"I have no idea. She looked sick," Betty said. "Ruth Ann, do you mind me messing in your kitchen? I need to be doing something."

"No, you go on. I'm not sure we got much."

"They's a chicken thawing in the sink and some taters laid out here."

"Me and Granny was going to make supper as soon as I woke up from my nap." Ashley looked at Ruth Ann. "She made me go lay down, Mama. She promised me she'd stay right there in front of the TV."

Water welled up in Ashley's eyes and Ruth Ann stepped behind her chair. She put her hands on Ashley's shoulders and squeezed, not hard enough to hurt. "Ashley," she said. "You have got to stay calm, honey. Nobody's blaming you. Mama's a grown woman, and short of tying her to the couch I don't see how you could've stopped her. You know how she is."

"Yes, Lord," Betty said. "Must've been something needed doing so she went right off and done it, whatever it was."

Cassandra come back in the kitchen. "Stress always gets me in my guts," she said, her nose red in the middle of her red face.

Ruth Ann patted Ashley's back, then got her coat and put it on. "Come on, Cassandra, I want to go over to your place and look around a little bit. Maybe she went there."

"Mama, I want to help look," Ashley said.

"No. You're in no shape to be stumbling around in the dark. You and Betty stay here in case Mama comes back."

"Don't you worry about us," Betty said. She spread some newspaper on the table, then carried over the potatoes and a knife. "Here, Ashley, you get busy on these and I'll work on the chicken," she said.

Ruth Ann opened the door, then looked back at Cassandra. "Where's your coat? It's cold outside."

"I forgot it," Cassandra said. "I don't need a coat anyway. I've got my own insulation."

It was pitch-dark at Cassandra's. She'd run out in such a hurry after Ashley's phone call that she hadn't left any lights on. Ruth Ann had to hold the flashlight while she found her key and unlocked the door.

"Does Mama still have a key to your house?" Ruth Ann said.

"She left here with one. Had it on a cord around her neck. I don't know if she's still got it or not."

Cassandra pushed the door open and switched on the lights. Her answering-machine light was blinking. She pushed the button and waited for the message, hoping it might be about Marvelle.

Instead, a shrill voice she didn't recognize at first squeaked out of the machine. "I want you to know I do not appreciate you taking my baby off the day-care premises. You had no business putting her in your vehicle and leaving without my permission. I will not be bringing her back. My mother will keep her from now on. And I expect a refund for this week. If I don't get it, you'll be hearing from my lawyer."

"Who's that?" Ruth Ann said.

"Stupid bitch." Cassandra pushed rewind and erased the message. "I didn't take her child off the premises. That's Rhonda Bowen. She's been trying to get her mama to take care of Brittany anyway 'cause she'll do it for free. And there ain't no way in hell she can afford a lawyer. What a stupid bitch. I don't know how she got such a sweet child."

"You're getting as bad as Mama cussing." Ruth Ann went down the hall and looked in the bedrooms while Cassandra checked the kitchen, living room, and bathroom. When they met in the living room, Ruth Ann said, "Why'd you have Brittany in the van?"

"Because as usual that woman was twenty minutes late picking up her child when Ashley called about Mama."

"Oh," Ruth Ann said.

"I was going to call her from your house and tell her where to pick Brittany up. Maybe she's learned a lesson."

"Don't sound like it." Ruth Ann picked up a letter laying open beside the phone. "What's this?" she said, then looked at Cassandra. "What are you doing joining a travel club?"

"Nothing. I'm not joining." Cassandra took the letter from her and folded it. "Just something I got in the mail. These people called one night last week. If you join this travel club you get a free hotel night at the hotel of your choice. I been thinking about going to the beach."

"By yourself?"

"You want to go with me? I bet we'd have fun. We could take Mama."

"Cassandra." Ruth Ann looked at her for a minute, then sighed. "Come on, let's go look outside."

A.J. walked behind Dwight along the edge of the woods, and they shined their flashlights against the darkness. It'd be next to impossible to see anybody in there in broad daylight, much less at night. Still they kept on, saying nothing as they walked the fence line around the homeplace. Every now and then Dwight would holler, "Mama!" Once or twice his voice cracked a little, and A.J. didn't know if it was from cold or something else. He hoped Dwight wasn't going to cry. Men crying made A.J. nervous, even when they had every right to be upset. Hell, he was upset himself. Him and Marvelle had their battles, but he hated to think of her out in the woods alone on a cold winter night. He wouldn't want to be out there.

Two hours later they'd circled back to their starting place, no sign of Marvelle.

"Let's go in the house and get warm for a minute," Dwight said. They stopped by the barn to make sure she hadn't wandered in there, then they went up to the house. A.J. followed Dwight into the kitchen, and it was so warm from the wood stove that he took off his coat. Dwight disappeared behind the stove and come out with a bottle of bourbon, half full.

"Put some more wood on that fire for me, will you," Dwight said. "I'll pour us a taste."

A.J. heard glasses clinking as he used the metal hook to lift the stove lid. He picked up two medium-size pieces of wood, shoved them in, then put the lid back down. The fire popped and sputtered a little, then settled down to burning again. The rims of A.J.'s ears started stinging and his fingers and toes tingled. The stove took care of the outsides, and a drink of bourbon would take care of the insides.

Dwight handed A.J. a glass and looked him in the eye. "Appreciate your help," he said, and drank the bourbon fast, coughing a little as it went down.

"Why do you keep it sitting behind the stove?"

"Bourbon tastes better when it's warm," Dwight said. He pointed with the bottle toward the back of the stove and looked at A.J. "That's what me and Betty calls our medicine chest." He held up the bottle. "And this here is the medicine. Every night before bed, me and Betty has us a dose."

A.J. nodded and emptied his glass in one swallow. His eyes watered as the bourbon fired down his throat.

Dwight poured them another. They sipped this time, and A.J. looked at Dwight out the corner of his eye. He didn't feel qualified to offer much in the way of comfort or advice, so they stood quiet together and polished off one more round before Dwight put the bottle away.

As they put on their coats, Dwight turned to A.J. "You know, we might ought to take some of that with us. When we find Mama she'll need something to warm her up quick." Dwight started to go back for the bourbon, then stopped and come back to the door. "What am I thinking. Mama wouldn't touch that liquor no matter how cold she was."

A.J. followed him out the door and tried to quit smiling before Dwight turned around and caught him. If only he knew the number of Christmas Eves old Marvelle matched him drink for drink from the adult-eggnog jug. She always said eggnog was okay since it had only enough liquor in it to add a little zip. He never actually watched her make the stuff, but he'd bet his truck she put at least a fifth of zip in every gallon of that nog.

"Betty's probably got some coffee made. We'll carry us a thermos of that," A.J. said, and put his hand on Dwight's shoulder as they walked to the truck. The old boy felt bony even covered up with all them layers of thermals and flannel shirts he always wore in winter. All the Moons but Cassandra was a scrawny lot.

Ruth Ann got blankets and a pillow for A.J. and left him in the living room. If she hadn't been so worried about her mama and Ashley, she would've had to laugh at the look on A.J.'s face when she told him he might as well spend the night. He looked completely confused, which was a new look for him, and Ruth Ann kind of liked it. Without his usual cocky attitude, he seemed a lot safer and she didn't mind feeding him and putting him up for the night. It was so late when he finally got in, and they'd all be getting up so early to look for Mama again, that she didn't have the heart to send him home. But he had another think coming if he thought he'd be sleeping with her. No, sir, he could stretch out in the recliner and him and Cassandra could have a snoring concert. She'd flaked out on the couch and was already sawing logs.

All Ruth Ann wanted to do now was shut her bedroom door and be by herself for a while. She couldn't remember ever feeling so tired and yet so wide awake. Sleep was probably impossible, but at least she could get some rest. She had made it to the door of her room when Ashley called her. Good Lord, she thought. Would this night never end? She went in and stood over Ashley's bed in the dark. "What?" she said, trying not to sound as impatient as she felt.

"My back's still hurting, Mama." It wasn't like Ashley to whine. She must be hurting pretty bad. Ruth Ann had been through it three times herself, and even though the pain faded, the memory of it never did. "Hang on. I'll get you some Tylenol," she said, and went in her bathroom to get the tablets. When she shut the medicine-cabinet door, her own reflection in the mirror made her jump. She knew Ashley needed her right then, knew she was scared and wanted her mama, and Ruth Ann wanted to be a good mama, but if she didn't get a minute to herself pretty soon, she was going to break into pieces. "Get ahold of yourself now," she said to the mirror. Lord, now she was talking to herself.

After Ashley swallowed the tablets, she laid back down on her side and closed her eyes.

Ruth Ann stood looking down at her for a minute, then said, "Where does it hurt?"

Ashley put her hand on her back. "My lower back's the worst, and it's started wrapping around front, like a squeezing pain."

Back labor, Ruth Ann thought, and sat down on the edge of the bed. It had been the same for her. "Mama always rubbed my back for me when I was in labor," she said. "It'll make you feel better." She rubbed her hands together to warm them, then pulled Ashley's shirt up. "This shirt is soaking wet with sweat. Don't you want to change?"

"No, I'm saving my other shirt for when I go to the hospital."

"You should've let me buy you some more maternity clothes."

"No, I'll be out of them soon enough, and I don't plan on doing this again for a long time."

"I'm glad to hear it." Ruth Ann rubbed hard, pressing Ashley's spine with her thumbs. "How's that?" she said.

"Good. Ow! Now that hurts."

"Okay." Ruth Ann quit pressing and just concentrated on squeezing and releasing, trying to loosen the muscles up. She started rubbing in long strokes, up and down Ashley's back. That's what had always felt the best to her, what always helped her fall asleep. As she worked over Ashley's back, she couldn't help thinking of her mama, of their times together like this, what a comfort it was when she was scared and tired and hurting. And now the thought of her out there somewhere, scared and tired and hurting, was more than she could stand.

It wasn't long before Ashley fell asleep, her breathing deep and even. Ruth Ann pulled her shirt down and patted her back. This girl was going to be all right. She didn't know how she knew it, but she did. It was a relief not to have to worry about her so much anymore. Ruth Ann knew a lot of the credit for that went to her mama.

She stood up a little too fast and got light-headed. She swayed and put her hand down on her mama's bed to steady herself, then leaned over and ran both hands over the bedspread, feeling the nubby texture in the dark. Oh, Mama, she thought, and went down on her knees by the bed. Her hands clutched the bedspread and she rocked back and forth, her breath sobbing in and out of her mouth because it was the only way she could keep from wailing like a banshee and waking the whole house. Please, God, let her be all right, she thought. Please, God, please, God. Her mind couldn't seem to form any other words, just went blank.

Slowly she got up and made her way in the dark to her room. She opened the curtains so she could see out, though she had no idea what she thought she'd see. Nothing out there but the moon. She stared at it, at the yard and the road lit up by moonlight. But what good was it to anybody? They needed daylight to find her mama, and that was hours and hours away. Ruth Ann crawled onto her bed and sat back against the pillows, watching out the window, her mind empty of everything except waiting.

Using Jesse's knife, Marvelle cut the last limb off the little pine and carried it over to the tree where she'd left her walker. She added the limb to the pile she'd collected in the last hour, then waited for her breathing to slow down. While it did, she opened her pocketbook and felt around for the little ball of twine she kept in the bottom. A body never knew when she might need some string. She fished out the twine and reached for a pine bough. She held the cut end up and tied it to the top rail of the walker so the bushy branches hung down to the ground. By the time she'd lined the entire walker with branches, her hands was sticky with sap. She rubbed her hands in the dirt, then rubbed them together to get rid of the sticky. It didn't help much.

The woods around her stood thick and black as pitch, except for a little moonlight sneaking through the bare-limbed oaks. Marvelle hung her pocketbook over one arm and dragged the walker close to the big oak where she'd kicked up a deep pile of leaves. She sat down in the middle of the pile, her back against the oak, and scraped all the leaves she could reach up over her legs, her waist, her chest. She scooted down till leaves covered her up to her neck, then reached up and pulled the walker down over her legs and her middle. She could almost pretend she was in a little bed, all green and brown, even though it was too dark to see colors. She buried her arms back under the leaves and kept them close to her body.

Her papa always said if she ever got lost on the mountain at night, the most important thing was to keep warm and protect yourself from the panthers and the bears. The best way to avoid varmints was to get up in a tree, and Marvelle had looked up the oak and considered trying it, but then she got to doubting her chances of shinnying up there with no low branches to grab on to. So she did the next best thing and built herself a little nest at the foot of the tree. If only she had a hat or a scarf to keep all the heat from running out the top of her head, she'd feel a lot better. If she'd just thought to put on a bra before leaving the house, she could use that to cover her head. She'd had a little bit of an accident in her drawers, so she couldn't use them. She got an idea though. Her shirt was long enough so she could pull the neck of it up over her head in the back and still not leave any of the rest of her uncovered. It pulled up on her arms a little, so she pulled them out of the sleeves and kept them inside her shirt.

She laid still awhile, listening to her stomach growl. It'd been a long time since dinner, and she'd spilled most of that on her clothes. It was no wonder she got shaky and spilled soup on herself, them young'uns making all that racket so she couldn't concentrate. She felt around in her pocketbook for a piece of hard candy, took the wrapper off, and pushed it between her lips. Butterscotch, sweet and warm inside her mouth, took her mind off how cold and tired she was, and it was one thing that still tasted good when everything else seemed to have lost its flavor.

The rough bark of the tree dug in Marvelle's scalp, and she scratched the top of her head against it a little bit. It felt good. A skinny branch way high up cut the half moon in quarters that looked like soft white lightbulbs in the sky. Her head felt clear as that sky and she couldn't understand why they all treated her like she was crazy. Wasn't a thing wrong with her but old age. She closed her eyes and tried to sleep. If only Ashley could hold off having that baby just a little bit longer. Long enough for her to get there.

Honey, I ain't give up on getting to that hospital. I'll get there. I just got to wait till it's light so I can see my way. These dang woods out here, anybody'd get lost they're so thick. That's what I get for taking a shortcut. Mama always told me they ain't no shortcuts in this life, and I should've listened to her. But I never did before and I reckon I'm too old to start now.

Poor Mama. Poor old soul. It ain't no wonder she died young as she did, all she done, fourteen children, running a boardinghouse, helping Papa. And losing so many of her babies too. It ain't no wonder.

My first baby, the one I call Lena, she come too soon and we lost her. She was far enough along so we knowed she was a girl, and she's buried up yonder at Walnut with the others, Rachel and Rose, and Peter. Their graves you can't read no more. Mason's, it's still all right 'cause it's only been there since nineteen and forty-four.

Lord, honey, the things I remember. Some things I remember, would've been a blessing to forget, like losing my young'uns. They ain't no despair in the world matches that, no matter if they's still inside you or if they's grown. It's just a different kind of torment when you watch them grow up and think they're going to be all right and then they're took from you. When Mason got killed in the war, I just wanted to curl up and die too. They never found his body. I still dream sometimes of him a-coming through that door one day and saying, hey, Mama, just like he always done. He was such a handsome feller, that boy, and smart as the devil. He studied for a engineer, and he stayed right down there in the bowels of that ship just a-working. But it blowed up despite him. Some feller that was on board that night and lived to tell about it come to see me, told me the whole thing. Said Mason was a hero. Even if I wasn't his mama, I'd believe that.

Just remember this, honey, when your baby's born, and sometimes cries all night and you got to hold it for hours and hours, and your arms gets so tired you can't feel them no more and you so sleepy you get scared you might fall out the chair and hurt the baby, honey, be grateful. Be grateful you can hold that baby with the sure knowledge that you ain't going to let nothing nor nobody hurt it, 'cause that's about the only time in your life you'll have that luxury. Ever after, you'll always be wondering: Is my baby all right tonight? Is he sleeping peaceful? Is he happy and surrounded by people that cares for him? Is he in pain? Is he lonesome? Does he need something only I can give him, but he ain't got no way to let me know? Lord, please keep my child safe tonight.

That's when I found faith, when my young'uns growed up and I had to let them go. Till then I hadn't give much thought to the Lord. Figured I done it all myself, and done a pretty fair job too. I didn't need no help. But then Mason went off and joined the Navy, and then had to go overseas, and I didn't hear nothing for months at a time. I had to learn to have faith or else go crazy. It's so hard for a mother to trust her young'uns to anybody else, but I had to put mine in God's hands, and then when Mason died, I had to fight to hold on to that faith, even when I wanted to blame God and say why did you fail me? Why did you take that boy of mine?

That's when I learned another lesson about faith. You don't get tested just one time and that's it, everything's pretty and safe from then on. You get tested over and over again, and it's true what they say about what don't kill you only makes you stronger. But being strong don't mean you don't hurt. I feel it ever day of my life for the young'uns I lost, and for Jesse. Ever day I pray for strength to bear that ache that won't never quit, that feeling in my chest and my arms, needing to hold them so bad and not being able to, needing to put my arms around my baby and hold him and pet him and I can't and it hurts me so bad sometimes I want to go out where nobody can hear me and scream and scream.

Sometimes, though, sometimes I feel like they're all a-coming back to me here lately in my mind. I can close my eyes and see Mason as a little boy just like it was yesterday. He used to be always a regular mother's boy, followed me everwhere I went like a little pup. I see him and his white-blond hair lit up by the sun like dandelion fur, and his smile with them little dimples in his cheeks, and him a-chasing after me through a field while we pick flowers for the supper table. And then in a little bit, here'll come Peter, a big boy for his age and always laughing, always hungry. Weighed nearly twelve pounds when he was born. I believe the doctor was right amazed at Peter and me both making it through that delivery without him there to help us.

After Peter, that's when the girls come, and I stop what I'm a-doing and wait for them, my little Rachel and Rose, never one without the other, in death even as in life. I sit on the grass and wait, and they come across the field, picking bouquets of daisies and Queen Anne's lace, giggling like they always done, with their own secret language and secret ways. I watch them close, wondering why me and Velda wasn't never like that.

And so they all come to me, and I gather them up in my lap like vegetables from my garden, thinking ain't nothing in the world could make me any happier than setting there in the sun, warm and young, holding my babies safe. I got everything in the world I need. And that's when I feel Jesse behind me, on his knees, his hands on my shoulders. I can't see his face, but I know it's him, I know his body against mine, the smell of him, the sound of his breathing. He reaches his long arms around me, around us all, wraps us up tight so they ain't nothing will ever part us again.

Ashley, when your young'uns drives you crazy—and they will, they can't help it—just remember they're only little for what seems like a few weeks, then they're grown and gone and you ain't got nothing but memories of their sweetness to hold on to when they don't need you no more. Even if you only get a minute of that sweetness a day, that's what you'll take with you. You won't remember that they said Mama ten thousand times a day, or caused you too many sleepless nights to count, or worried you to death when they didn't come home for supper on time. You'll remember when they hugged your neck so hard it cracked, and the times they come running to you when they was scared, and the way they smiled at you just as they was about to fall asleep, like your face held the light of the world and they didn't want to close their eyes and not see it no more. That's what you'll remember, and it'll be sweet, oh, sweet. Sweet as butterscotch candy in your mouth, honey. Sweet enough to flavor the days when your body hurts all over, and you can't remember what you had for breakfast, and the whole family treats you like a crazy person. In this life, honey, seems like they's just enough sweet to get you through.

18

Ashley woke up all of a sudden and stared into the dark. She'd been dreaming about peeing in the city park swimming pool, which she always used to do as a child even though her mama told her not to. It was too much trouble to get out, dry off, go in, pee, and come back out again. And being in the pool made her have to pee more than usual. That must've been what woke her up, needing to pee. She grunted and rolled out of bed. She was starting to sound like Granny, all the noises she made getting up and down.

She didn't bother to turn on a light, just felt her way down the hall to the bathroom in the dark. When her feet hit the cold tile of the bathroom floor, she reached for the light switch and then felt something warm and wet running down her leg. Damn her bladder, giving out on her like that. She hadn't even felt it coming. Now she'd have to change her panties.

When the bright fluorescent light come on she blinked and glanced down at her feet. They was covered with some kind of bloody, yellow stuff that sure wasn't pee. A puddle spread in a circle over the floor and she nearly slipped when she tried to step back out of it. Good God, she thought. No pains yet, no contractions, but she must be in labor. Her water broke. That meant something was going to happen soon. Things was going to start speeding up. She looked up and seen her reflection, her face like somebody looking down the steepest hill on the roller coaster, about to go down and nothing they could do to stop, no getting off.

She started to run get her mama, then stopped. No, wasn't no sense panicking. No sense waking anybody up yet. Instead, she grabbed towels off the shower door and used them to wipe her feet and legs and mop up the mess. She got her clean outfit from her room, then went back to the bathroom to shower and change.

The warm water beating down over her back felt good, relaxed her some, and she wrapped her arms around herself and leaned into the corner, resting her face against the tile. She felt real floaty, like she might be about to fall asleep, when the muscles in her back started feeling tight all of a sudden, then the tightness spasmed around her middle. She tried to straighten up and couldn't, so she crouched with her hands on her knees to keep from falling. The breath locked in her chest while the pain wrapped around her whole middle for a minute. When it was over, Ashley was shaking so hard she couldn't hardly get the water turned off.

She managed to get herself dried off and dressed, the whole time dreading the next pain, trying to convince herself it wouldn't come, or at least wouldn't be as bad this time. She was wrong. As she combed the tangles out of her wet hair with a vent brush, another pain struck. She leaned over the bathroom sink and puked, dry heaving even after the pain passed. She rinsed her mouth and the sink, brushed her teeth, finished brushing her hair, went to her room, put on shoes and socks, made up the bed, then sat on the end of the bed with the trash can between her knees and a watch in hand. While she waited, she distracted herself wondering where Granny could be, if she was all right, wishing Keith was home, afraid he might not come back to her for some reason. After three contractions come ten minutes apart, Ashley decided it was time to call the doctor, and time to wake her mama.

Ruth Ann was dead to the world. Ashley didn't see how she could sleep sitting up like that with no covers. She must've stayed awake late worrying. Her mouth was open, making little snoring noises. Ashley shook her, then shook her again. Finally Ruth Ann opened her eyes. "What?" she said.

"Mama, I hate to tell you this, but my water broke and my contractions is ten minutes apart." Ashley watched as Ruth Ann took in that information, then swung her legs out of bed. "What time is it?"

"About five-thirty."

"Did you call the doctor?"

"Yeah, I called his beeper and he called me right back. He said he'd call the hospital."

"All right. Let me get my clothes on. Can you go wake up your daddy and make some coffee?"

"Uh-huh."

Ruth Ann watched Ashley shut the door behind her, then went to the window. The sky was getting gray with first light. She leaned her forehead against the cold glass and closed her eyes. Lord help me, she thought, then went and got dressed.

When she come in the kitchen, A.J. was making coffee and Cassandra was holding a watch on Ashley like a gun. She looked up at Ruth Ann. "Nine minutes apart, and getting worse." Cassandra hadn't changed clothes from the night before, and her hair stuck out in twenty directions. She looked halfway crazy, like she was holding them all hostage with that watch.

"We better go, then," Ruth Ann said. She told A.J. to carry Ashley's bag to the car and get the car warmed up, then moved the coffeepot and held her cup under the dripping coffee. When it was full, she replaced the coffeepot, stirred cream into her cup, and leaned against the counter.

A.J. come back rubbing his hands together and blowing smoke. "It's cold out there this morning."

Ashley stared at him, and Ruth Ann stared at Ashley. She looked like a wild animal cornered by hunters, ready to bolt. She was sweating in spite of the cold air A.J. let in, and her hands shook where they rested on her knees. Ruth Ann took a last gulp of coffee, then put on her coat and held Ashley's jacket out to her. "Come on, let's get going," she said. She put her hand in the middle of Ashley's back to steer her out to the car.

A.J. helped Ashley get buckled in the passenger seat while Ruth Ann got behind the wheel. Before he shut the door, he looked in at Ruth Ann. "J.D.'s on his way with the dogs, and I got some more men coming to help us look. We'll get started as soon as they get here. I'll let you know."

Ruth Ann nodded. A.J. kissed Ashley's cheek. "See you soon, honey," he said.

Ashley looked sick. "Bye, Daddy," she said, and pulled the door shut.

As they backed out, Ashley rolled down her window and yelled to A.J., "Daddy! Try to call Keith again. Tell him to get to the hospital. Tell him to hurry!" She rolled the window up before A.J. could answer. Ruth Ann backed into the road, the car rocking as she hit the brakes to put it in drive.

She sat still for just a second as she realized she hadn't even looked first to see if anything was coming. She checked the rearview mirror. Nothing. Maybe all them years of being careful was just a waste. She floored it, leaving a trail of rubber so long it would've made Keith jealous.

Keith woke in the dark of his apartment, not sure where he was at first. The clock by his bed said five-thirty. He didn't need to get up yet. He tried to go back to sleep but couldn't. A strong feeling of urgency kept telling him to get his butt up, something important was happening somewhere in the world, something that mattered to him. Then he remembered Ashley. And the baby. He'd gone to bed and fell into a deep sleep right after milking, too tired to even eat supper. Ashley had no idea he was home already. She could've had that baby, could be having it right now and him not know a thing about it. It was early, but as soon as he got a shower he was going to call over there and see what was happening.

Once he was dressed, he called Ruth Ann's house and A.J. answered.

"Is Ashley up yet?" Keith asked.

"Her and her mama just this minute left for the hospital. I was fixing to call you. Are you going over there now?"

But A.J. got no answer because Keith was already down the stairs, heading for the Camaro.

As he drove toward the hospital, Keith thought about Ashley and how stubborn she was being, taking her sweet time making up her mind. He knew she was scared, but hell, he was too. And that baby wasn't going to go away. That's what it all come back to, the baby, which scared Keith because he didn't want to be marrying Ashley just because of the baby. That's what his mama and daddy done, and look what happened to them. Same thing with Ashley's parents, from what he'd heard. And a lot of other people he knew. A baby was a big thing, but it wasn't a good enough reason to get married. Then again, maybe it was. It was scary as hell to think of spending a lifetime together though. What if they changed their minds? What if they ended up hating each other? There was too many what-ifs in the whole business, so Keith didn't see no other way but to just jump in and do it and see what happened.

That was a big difference between him and Ashley though. He was a jumper; she was a wader. She was a wader that wanted people to think she was a jumper, but Keith knew she liked to test the water with her toe and ease in slow, and that was all right with him. Made for a good balance between them. If he could just convince her of that, he'd be getting some-where.

Though he wasn't as sure about the wife part, Keith figured Ashley would be a good mother, because she was so patient with old people and she loved animals. What she didn't know about babies, she could learn from her granny and her mama. Old Ruth Ann had started softening up a little bit ever since she lost her job and hooked up with A.J. on that flower business. Maybe it took a shock to knock some life back in her. It always seemed a shame to Keith that a good-looking woman like Ruth Ann should be all pinched up and cold and her only fifty-some years old. He was also surprised her and A.J. wasn't still together. They seemed like a good match, another balancing act. You never could tell what went on between two people though.

Keith got to thinking about the baby again and how weird it was that he'd left a part of himself inside Ashley, a part that joined with a part of her to make a baby. It felt like they both belonged to him now, Ashley and the baby, though he reckoned the truth was, it was him belonged to them. Be-cause something went out of him, left him to make that baby. Women was lucky, they got to keep the whole package inside them. The man just had to wait till the package come out. That's why Keith knew he could never think of letting Ashley and the baby go, because it'd be giving up part of himself, just throwing it away. Of course, it might turn out they wouldn't want noth-ing to do with him anyway, and there wasn't much he could do about that. End up like A.J., he supposed. Not without a fight though.

He seen a dead dog on the side of the road and thought about Speed back on that sheep ranch. The man that took him said he was glad the Damn Spiveys would never know what happened to their three-hundred-dollar dog. He said from the sound of it, they didn't deserve to know. The last thing Keith had seen as he drove away was old Speed and three or four other Border collies in a big fenced lot, running back and forth along the fence, barking their fool heads off at some sheep on the other side. Even through a fence they was taking care of business, and they looked happy doing it.

A noise woke Marvelle, but she didn't move, just laid still, curled into herself trying to remember where she was. She opened her eyes. It was a dark place that smelled like dirt. Buried alive? Six feet under? She shifted and heard a rustle, felt something loose slide across her. Too light to be dirt.

Leaves fell from in front of her face, and then she remembered making her bed the night before.

The noise was towhees, scratching in the dirt not ten feet away. It was early morning, the light still soft and gray under the trees. Marvelle watched the little birds dance forward and back as they tried to stir up food. Her stomach growled. She was hungry herself. She rolled on her back and the towhees flew away under another tree close by and started their scratching all over again. Her head was just a-spinning, even laying still, and the sound of the birds faded in and out, far away then close.

Sleeping on the cold ground was something she'd not done since she was a child and used to camp on the mountain with her brothers and sisters. Her bones and joints was a lot younger and more forgiving back then. After the dizzy spell passed, she took a deep breath and scooted up so her back was against the tree. She opened her pocketbook and fished around for something to eat, but wasn't nothing but empty butterscotch candy papers. Her hand closed around her compact and she took it out and opened it. Looked like a big old knot the size of a plum over her left eye where she fell and hit her head on that stump last night. It wasn't bleeding no more, just had blood and dirt and sap stuck on it. She didn't have no way of cleaning it up, so she snapped the compact shut and put it away. Couldn't be worrying about her appearance at a time like this. She had places to go, people to see. Ashley probably done had that baby without her, and it upset Marvelle that she hadn't made it in time to help out. She'd been there for all of Ruth Ann's babies.

She got on her knees, set her walker upright, and held on to it as she pulled herself to her feet. Might be she was wrong. Might be she still had time, if she hurried. She rested a minute, then hooked her pocketbook over her arm and tried to lift the walker. The pine limbs tied to it made it too heavy. She searched out her pocketknife and cut the string so the limbs fell off. Her hands got sticky all over again, and they was already black with dirt from the night before. Well, time enough to worry about washing up when she got to the hospital. She looked behind her to make sure she hadn't forgot nothing, then left the shelter of the trees and walked across a field toward the road in the distance. The grass crackled under her feet. Old Jack Frost done been here last night, she thought. Old Jack Frost paid us a visit. At the edge of the field, she wiggled under a barbed-wire fence, then crawled down into a ditch full of standing water, then crawled up again to the road. When she finally stood on the pavement, she faced east and allowed herself a rest to catch her breath before starting again. Her eyes was acting up—everything looked kindly blurry, and she kept seeing little rainbows flashing in all directions.

She closed her eyes to rest them and the rainbows disappeared. She almost laughed then, remembering how she used to argue with her mama about rainbows. Her mama always marveled at them, recalling how the Bible called them God's promise to mankind. She made her children stand and watch whenever one appeared, like it was God Himself skipping across the sky. But even as a child, Marvelle hadn't been overly impressed with anything as rare and flashy as that, in spite of the story that went with it. A rainbow was fine in its place, but a sunrise—now, that was a promise Marvelle could believe in. Just like that, bam, a new day. The sign of a God that was in it for the long haul and proved it by being regular and predictable as day and night, seasons, stars, living and dying, the moon setting behind her and the sun coming up in front. Now, that was a promise with something to back it up, a generous and loving gift, the gift that kept on giving. It was a circle, was all it was, like most important things in the world, going round and round, no beginning, no end, just moving and changing all the time.

She opened her eyes, and the rim of the world was on fire with deep orange pink, the sun ready to rise up just any second. It near about took her breath away. It was a miracle, it surely was, and no matter how many times she seen it, it never lost its glory. Marvelle stood there in the middle of the road and stared at that sky, waiting to see the sun come up on one more day.

19

Just keep going, Mama! For God's sake." Ashley hung on to the armrest with her right hand and the dash with her left. She'd took her seat belt off to be more comfortable, and Ruth Ann was threatening to stop the car if she didn't put it back on. "I don't care if I do get thrown through the windshield," Ashley said. "It can't hurt no worse than this."

Ruth Ann sped up again, all the way to the speed limit, which was unusual for her. Ashley figured she must really be scared.

"Why don't you do some of that breathing?" Ruth Ann said.

"I am, dammit! I'm breathing. But that sorry-ass husband of mine ain't here to help me." The pain started to ease and Ashley relaxed against the seat.

"What did you just say?"

"What?"

"You said that sorry-ass husband of yours." Ruth Ann glanced at Ashley, then back to the road.

"I did not."

"You most certainly did. Is there something you ain't told me?"

"No, Mama, we have not run off and got married without telling you." Ashley cracked the window to let some fresh air in. "Can you turn off that heat? I'm sweating like a mule."

Ruth Ann turned the heat off.

Ashley stared out the window at pastures full of cows. That's what she felt like, one of them big old cows, udders full to busting, waiting to be milked. "I guess it's just been on my mind a lot lately," she said.

"I'm glad to hear it."

"Mama, that's all you ever say."

"Well. It's the truth."

There was something in the road up ahead, and Ashley leaned forward in her seat to see better.

"Ashley," Ruth Ann said. "I wish you'd put that seat belt back on, honey."

Ashley put both hands on the dash and screamed, "Stop, Mama! Stop the car!"

Ruth Ann stomped on the brakes. The car seemed to take forever to stop rocking, and when it did they both sat there like they was paralyzed, staring at Marvelle's back. It had to be her in that pantsuit, red hearts on blue polyester. Polyester, her fabric of choice.

Ruth Ann was already out of the car running to her while Ashley was still getting her door open. When she finally got up to where they were, Ashley nearly started crying. Marvelle looked awful. Her hair was matted and full of sticks and leaves. The big red hearts on the front of her Valentine pantsuit was shredded, and underneath the rips in the fabric they could see long bloody scratches on her arms and legs. She'd lost her shoes, and her toes stuck out the ends of her soaking-wet socks. The bloody knot on her forehead above her left eye made her look almost deformed.

Ruth Ann kept saying, "Mama? Are you all right?" but Marvelle acted like she didn't even know they was there, just kept staring off in the distance. Ashley looked to see what she was staring at and got blinded as the sun eased up over the horizon.

"Now, ain't that something, girls?" Marvelle said. "That's something worth getting up for, ever living morning of the world." She looked at Ruth Ann, then Ashley. She started to say something else, but Ashley grabbed her belly and crouched down.

"Oh, God! Oh, shit! Mama!"

Ruth Ann went to Ashley and held her elbows to help her balance until the pain passed.

Marvelle left her walker where it was and started walking to the car. "Girl," she said. "You going to drop that baby in the road if you don't get a move on." She got in the backseat and slammed the door shut with no help from Ashley or Ruth Ann.

When she could straighten up again, Ashley went and got in the car while Ruth Ann moved the walker to the side of the road.

"You just going to leave it there?" Ashley said.

"I ain't got time to fool with that thing. Hold on, everybody," Ruth Ann said as she put the car in drive and floored it.

Marvelle bounced back in her seat, then leaned forward again, holding on to the back of Ashley's seat. "Take it easy, lead foot," she said to Ruth Ann. "You going to kill us all. I know what to do if we don't make it to the hospital."

Ashley turned to face Marvelle. "Where in the hell have you been, Granny?"

"Looking for you, trash mouth."

"Granny, I went to my room to take a nap, and you said you was going to sit right there in the living room and do your puzzle."

"And that's exactly what I did do. I was working my puzzle and I looked up and seen somebody loading you in a car to take you to the hospital."

"Huh?"

"It was that Eric, and you and him got in his car. You was in labor. I didn't like the way he was driving neither. Looked like any minute he was going to drive right off a cliff."

Ruth Ann looked at Ashley, and Ashley shrugged.

"What I want to know," Marvelle said, "is what happened to that boy Keith? I thought he was the daddy of your baby."

"What's she talking about?" Ruth Ann said.

"Keith is the daddy, Granny. What are you talking about? Eric who?"

"You know good and well who I'm a-talking about. He's that boy you took up with behind Keith's back, the one claims to be Edward's son 'cause he wants all that money."

"Oh!" Ashley looked at Ruth Ann. "I get it now. There's this girl on one of the soaps named Ashley and she's pregnant and her boyfriend's name's Eric but it ain't his baby but he wants to marry her anyway."

Marvelle tapped Ashley's shoulder. "I know that Eric says he'll take your young'un as his own, but don't you believe it. A woman can do that, raise another's child, but a man has trouble with living proof he ain't the only one his woman's laid down with. Now, I know Eric's a nice-looking feller, but you'd be better off with that Keith. He ain't much to look at, but he's got a job, and he comes by every day, including Saturday and Sunday. You don't never see that Eric on the weekend, now, do you? No, ma'am. He's too busy tomcatting around on the weekend. You take my advice and marry Keith, marry the steady one. Looks and personality ain't everything. I ought to know."

"Granny, Eric ain't a real person. The reason we don't see him on the weekends is 'cause the show don't come on Saturday and Sunday. He's on TV, Granny."

Marvelle looked like she'd been dragged through a hedge backward and still had that I'm-right-and-you-know-it look on her face, and Ashley couldn't help giggling at her. She laughed until her belly hurt, while Ruth Ann drove faster and faster, slinging that Buick around the curves like she was Richard Petty.

Keith blew his horn and waved, trying to get Ruth Ann's attention as she passed him at the intersection, but she didn't notice. She whizzed right on, doing sixty at least. Ruth Ann never drove that fast, even on the interstate.

By the time he caught up with her, she was turning on the road to the community hospital. He was surprised her car didn't go up on two wheels when she took the turn into the hospital parking lot. He honked and waved again, but Ruth Ann kept going until she reached the emergency entrance.

Keith was out of the Camaro and opening Ashley's door before Ruth Ann got the car in park. Ashley looked up at him for a long minute before letting him pull her out of the car.

"Where the hell have you been," she said, then doubled over. Keith picked her up and staggered to the doors, which luckily was electronic and opened right up.

Ruth Ann watched them disappear into the hospital, then told Marvelle to stay put while she cut the engine on Keith's car and got the keys. When she got back, Marvelle was standing next to the car, swaying.

"Mama, where do you think you're going? Stay put and let me get you a wheelchair."

"I don't need no goddamn wheelchair. I'm going to help that girl deliver her baby, and I don't need no help from you."

"Mama." Ruth Ann took hold of Marvelle's shoulders. The knot on her forehead looked like it had got bigger. "Mama, we've got to get a doctor to look at that knot on your head. You might have a concussion." Not to mention loss of blood, exposure, and frostbite, but Ruth Ann kept that much to herself.

She put her arm around Marvelle's back and started walking her toward the emergency entrance, Marvelle grumbling the whole time about how she didn't need no help. An ambulance driver met them at the door and told her he was sorry, but she couldn't leave her vehicles parked there. Ruth Ann's heart beat so hard against the inside of her chest she feared she'd have a heart attack and be no good to anybody. She wished A.J. and Cassandra was there with her. She wished anybody was with her. "You listen to me, buster," Ruth Ann said to the man. "My mama's been out in the woods all night without a coat or shoes or food or water and she needs to see a doctor right now, and my daughter's in there having a baby that's a week overdue. So if you want them cars moved, you going to have to do it yourself." She dropped the keys on the ground at his feet and walked on.

Ruth Ann had to wrap both arms around Marvelle to hold her up. Both their pocketbooks hung from her arm and banged against her leg. Without warning, Marvelle's head fell back and she slumped to her knees like a sack of taters. Ruth Ann went to her knees too and struggled to hold Marvelle up. She looked around and seen several people in the waiting area staring at her, just sitting on their butts like they was watching a TV show. "I need some help!" she said. A second later the man she'd yelled at outside was there, lifting Marvelle, carrying her to an empty gurney in the hallway. He laid her down and called for a nurse and they wheeled Marvelle into a cubicle. Ruth Ann ducked in just as they pulled the curtain closed.

"Are you a relative?" the nurse asked.

"Yes," Ruth Ann said, squeezing the pocketbook straps in her fists.

"What happened?" the nurse said.

The ambulance man looked at Ruth Ann, then turned to the nurse. "I think this lady's mother wandered off from home and has been out all night."

The nurse touched Marvelle's forehead and examined the knot there, then lifted her eyelids and looked at her eyes. She covered Marvelle up to her shoulders with a blanket, then turned to go. "I'll be back with a doctor," she said.

When the doctor got there, he asked Ruth Ann to wait outside. She stood by the cubicle for a minute, then found a pay phone and called home.

"Cassie. This is Ruth Ann."

"Ruth Ann. Are you at the hospital? You sound funny. Did Ashley have the baby already?"

"No."

"Well, we're getting ready to go look for Mama. A.J.'s got J.D. and some other men and a couple of bloodhounds over here. I let them smell

Mama's coat and her bedroom shoes. J.D. says we ought to find her by lunchtime."

"Tell J.D. to take his dogs home. We found Mama on the way to the hospital."

"What? Is she all right? Where was she?"

"Cassandra, just shut up a minute, okay? Now, listen. You need to call all the boys, and all of y'all need to get on over here as soon as you can. You hear me?"

"Oh, my God," Cassandra said.

"Don't get all hysterical now. Just do like I say."

"Is she dead?"

"No, she ain't dead. But I don't know what's going to happen, and I want y'all here."

Ruth Ann hung up and went over and sat on one of the hard plastic chairs in the waiting room. Some people was still staring at her. Why the hell couldn't they have some more comfortable chairs and provide a little bit of privacy for people going through traumatic events? That didn't seem like too much to ask.

20

Keith, I swear to God if you come close enough to this bed for me to reach you, I'm going to strangle you with your own hair! Now, get me some more ice chips!" Ashley threw the Styrofoam cup at him. "And get that goddamn doctor in here now!"

Keith picked up the cup and watched her for a second, then eased closer to the bed. The pains was eight minutes apart but so intense she barely had time to recover from one before the next one started. He could tell her focus was shifting inward, which meant another contraction was coming. Her knuckles turned white as she gripped the bedsheets. He grabbed her left fist and held it in both his hands. "Okay, now, listen to me and breathe like I do," he said. She groaned at him through her teeth and ignored him.

After a few seconds, though, her hand opened and squeezed his back, practically cutting off his circulation. He felt his fingers go numb, but kept on talking to her. After the pain subsided, she flopped back against the pillow, her head wet with sweat, breathing hard.

"Where's my ice chips?" she said without looking at him.

"I'll be right back." He patted her hand and went for ice. When he got back, the doctor was examining Ashley. He looked up at Keith. "She's already dilated eight centimeters. We've still got a little while to go, but you should have a baby by lunchtime."

"Lunchtime!" Ashley looked at the clock across from her bed. It was a little before seven. "I want an epidural."

The doctor smiled. "I'll tell the nurse to fix you up."

Keith set the cup down and stood by the bed. Time for the next contraction, and sure enough her face screwed up and she bent over her belly, moaning. He grabbed her hand and they breathed together until it was over, by which time the nurse come in wheeling some kind of machine. He pulled his hand loose from Ashley's and shook it to get the feeling back. He was beginning to wonder just who this breathing shit was for. It didn't seem to be helping Ashley any.

"A little bird told me somebody in this room wants an epidural," the nurse said.

"Well, it ain't him," Ashley said. "Hook me up."

While the nurse got to work, Keith walked to the middle of the room and started looking around at the walls.

"What you looking at?" Ashley said. She picked up her cup and started sucking ice.

"You're supposed to have something to focus on," he said.

"Oh, please. I've got enough to focus on."

"No, I mean you need something to help you concentrate when you have to push. Remember?"

"That's right," the nurse said. "Like a vase or something." She finished taping the tube to Ashley's arm and checked the needle. "There, honey. That ought to do you for a while. Just holler if you need anything, okay?"

After she left, Ashley said, "What you waiting for, Keith? Go find something. Just make sure you're back here." She looked at the clock. "In five minutes."

Keith stepped into the hall, looked up and down, then decided to go find Ruth Ann. He run down to the maternity waiting room and when he didn't see her there went on to the emergency room where they'd come in. He found her sitting next to the window, staring at the parking lot. When she seen him, she held out his keys. "A man parked your vehicle for you," she said. "I'm not sure where he put it though."

He took the keys and looked over her head. He spotted the Camaro in the third row, right next to Ruth Ann's car. "There it is," he said. "Thanks."

"How's Ashley?"

Keith sat next to Ruth Ann. "Okay. But I need something she can focus on. That's what they told us in Lamaze. You got anything?"

Ruth Ann looked through her purse. "Here's a mirror," she said. "Will that do?"

"No, it needs to be bigger, something she can see across the room while she's pushing."

"Well, I ain't got nothing that big in my purse."

There was a big red pocketbook on the floor by Ruth Ann's feet. "What about that?" he said.

"That's Mama's."

"Where is she?"

"They got her back there checking out the knot on her head."

"What happened to her?"

"She wandered off last night and we didn't find her till this morning. She found us, really." Ruth Ann picked up Marvelle's pocketbook and looked through it, took Marvelle's wallet out, then closed the pocketbook and handed it to Keith. "Here. Take it. Ashley needs it more than Mama right now."

"Thanks." Keith put his hand on her arm, the first time he'd ever really touched the woman on purpose. She looked completely out of it. "Can I do anything for you?" he said.

"You're doing it," she said. "Take care of Ashley. A.J. and Cassandra'll be here any minute."

"Okay, then," Keith said, and stood up. "Doctor said by lunchtime we ought to have us a baby girl. Ashley's got her an epidural, so now all we got to do is wait."

"Don't say that to Ashley."

"What?"

"That all you got to do is wait. She might hit you."

"Right," Keith said. "I get it." He took off running down the hall, hoping nobody mistook him for a purse snatcher and stopped him before he could get to his girl.

Ruth Ann watched the doctor's mouth as he talked. He had the prettiest mouth for a man she'd ever seen, and pretty teeth too. How could he say what he was saying with that pretty mouth of his?

Marvelle was in a coma, and he was very worried about the head injury. He still couldn't get over the fact that she'd walked into the hospital under her own steam, because in addition to the head injury, she was also extremely dehydrated and weak from loss of blood and prolonged exposure.

She must be one tough lady, he said. She must be a fighter, he said. But all they could do for the present was wait. She'd be moved to intensive care as soon as they could get a bed ready for her. His pretty mouth said hang in there, it said try not to worry, but the rest of his face told what he wouldn't say out loud. She's an old woman, she's in a bad way, don't count on her ever waking up again in this world.

The way Betty stood with her arm around Dwight, it looked like she was the only thing holding him up, and Cassandra started crying as soon as the doctor walked away. A.J. put his arm around her and she cried into his shoulder while he stared at Ruth Ann.

"What can I do?" he said.

Ruth Ann stood. "You're doing it," she said, and walked away down the hall after the doctor.

Cassandra looked up. "Where you going?" she said.

"I'm going to find my mama," Ruth Ann said without turning around.

Marvelle was laying on the same gurney in the same cubicle. There was a big white bandage over her left eye, and she was hooked up to several different machines. Her eyes was closed and her mouth open as she breathed deep and slow. There was such a long pause between breaths that each one sounded like it was going to be her last. She looked almost comical, the mess she was in, like a scarecrow that'd fell over in a cornfield and been picked at by crows. Ruth Ann felt tears coming on and squeezed her eyes shut tight. Not now.

A nurse come in with an armload of towels and stopped when she seen Ruth Ann. It was the same nurse from before. She looked at Marvelle, then back to Ruth Ann. "I was just going to clean her up some before we move her. Did the doctor find you?"

"Yes," Ruth Ann said. "If you don't mind, I'll take care of her."

The nurse hesitated. "Well, we're really not supposed to let you back here, you know, the liability and all." She studied Ruth Ann's face. "Of course, we have got her stabilized now, and we're just waiting for a bed in ICU." She hesitated a minute more, then handed Ruth Ann the towels. "If the doctor comes in, just tell him you didn't know you wasn't supposed to be back here, okay? And don't touch anything except to clean her." Then she laid out soap, a pan for water, a hospital gown, antiseptic for the scratches. She checked the monitors attached to Marvelle. "I'll be right outside if you need anything, okay? Just holler. My name's Mary." She pulled the curtain closed behind her as she left the cubicle.

Ruth Ann put the towels beside Marvelle and filled the pan with warm water. She wheeled a small table beside the gurney and set the water, soap, and antiseptic on top. She unstrapped Marvelle's arms and legs and pulled her socks off. They was ruined, so she dropped them in the trash. She reached to unzip the back of Marvelle's top and seen her amber cameo brooch pinned above her heart. She hadn't noticed it earlier. It was a wonder she hadn't lost it out there in the woods. Ruth Ann took the pin off and stood looking at it in the palm of her hand. Marvelle loved that pin because her mama give it to her the day Mason was born. It was the only memento of that day Marvelle had left. She always told Ruth Ann that pin made her happy and sad at the same time, happy because it reminded her of Mason, sad because it was the last thing her mama ever give her before she died. When Ashley was a little girl, Marvelle would tell her that story and she'd cry and cry, and then ask if she could have the pin when Marvelle died. And Marvelle would always say, "Yes, honey, when I die."

Cassandra slipped through the curtain, almost bumping into Ruth Ann. "What's that?" she said.

"Mama's cameo. What should I do with it?"

"Put it in her pocketbook."

"I can't. I give it to Keith for Ashley."

"What?"

"Never mind." Ruth Ann dropped the brooch in the pocket of her sweater. She could put it away later. She reached for Marvelle's arm to try and get the polyester top off, then looked over at Cassandra. "Help me," she said.

Cassandra looked like she was frozen there, staring at Marvelle. Her face was still red from crying, and Ruth Ann hoped she wasn't about to start up again.

"Let's just cut it off," Cassandra said finally. "It's ruined anyway." She pilfered through the drawers of a cabinet until she found a pair of scissors.

"Don't be messing in there," Ruth Ann said, then took the scissors from Cassandra. She cut the polyester right up the middle of Marvelle's body so they could peel it off to the sides. Then she realized she'd have to cut the sleeves too, in order to get them over all the tubes and things hooked into Marvelle's arms. It took her a while because the scissors was small and the material was thick. When she got done cutting the top, she handed the scissors to Cassandra so she could work on the britches. They worked over her together the same way they used to work together making a new dress, quiet, careful, and slow. Only this time, Marvelle wasn't watching over them, telling them how to go.

While Cassandra cut the britches, Ruth Ann pulled the top away from Marvelle's body. It kind of shocked Ruth Ann to see her mama's breasts just laying there on her belly like that, no bra or undershirt or nothing to cover them. She concentrated on getting the shirt out from under Marvelle's back, then wadded it up and threw it in the trash. They done the same with the britches.

"I remember when she made that ugly thing," Cassandra said. "It was the same year she made her Christmas suit. They must've had a sale on double knit that year."

"I think that was about the time most people quit wearing polyester and started wearing cotton again, and rayon. Mama thought she'd died and gone to heaven, getting all that material so cheap."

"Shoo, her panties is nasty," Cassandra said.

They cut the panties off and threw them away, then stood, one on either side of the gurney, looking at Marvelle's body.

"I don't think I've ever seen Mama naked," Ruth Ann said.

"Me neither," Cassandra said.

"I've seen parts of her, but never all the way naked like this."

"That's what we'll look like someday."

Ruth Ann snapped, "Well, you have twelve children and live through what she has and see what you look like."

"Ruth Ann, I didn't mean nothing. Hell, I look like that now."

Ruth Ann put a hand on Marvelle's forehead. "She's burning up."

"Let's wash her off," Cassandra said. "Looks like she's been wallowing in dirt."

Her arms and legs was the worst, dirty and scratched all to pieces like she'd been crawling through barbed wire. Ruth Ann wet a washrag and handed it to Cassandra, then wet one for herself. She squirted some liquid soap on both rags and they washed Marvelle's arms and legs good, then put antiseptic cream on the scratches. After that, they washed her shoulders, under her arms, her neck, around and under her breasts, across her belly, her backside. The skin was so loose it moved with the motion of their hands.

Ruth Ann held Marvelle's knees apart while Cassandra washed between her legs. She was so limp it was like washing a newborn baby, only it wasn't. It was their mama, the same woman who used to wash them that way. How could it feel wrong and yet right at the same time? Wrong because they hated seeing Marvelle so helpless, but right because they was so glad there was something they could do for her.

When she was clean, they laid the hospital gown over top of her. It was impossible to get her arms through the sleeves until the nurse come back and unhooked her. Cassandra covered her with a blanket, and when Ruth Ann went down to tuck it in around Marvelle's feet, she felt how cold they were, like ice. "She needs something on her feet," Ruth Ann said.

Cassandra looked through the cabinets for socks, but didn't find any. She kicked off her shoes and took off her own socks and put them on Marvelle's feet. The socks was thick and red and didn't go with the yellow hospital gown at all.

Ruth Ann looked at the socks, then at Cassandra. "Is them the same socks you've had on since yesterday?"

"Yes."

"They stink."

"Well, what's more important, smelling good or being warm?"

"Fine," Ruth Ann said.

"Her hands has still got all that sticky stuff on them," Cassandra said. "What do you reckon that is?"

"It looks like sap or something, with dirt ground in." Ruth Ann tried to scrub it again with the soapy cloth, but it wouldn't come off. "Reckon she was out there climbing trees?"

"Well, you know how she loves them birds."

They smiled at each other a little bit, then Cassandra said, "I'll see if I can't find some alcohol or something to clean this mess off." She looked through the cabinet again and found alcohol and peroxide. They tried both, and it helped a little, but Marvelle's hands was still sticky.

"Wait," Ruth Ann said. "I think I got some fingernail-polish remover in my pocketbook. I bet that'll cut through the sap." She pulled out a travel-size bottle and put some on a cotton ball.

"I love the smell of that stuff," Cassandra said, and started working on Marvelle's left hand while Ruth Ann did the right.

They worked without talking, concentrating hard on just the fingers and palms of their mama's hands. It wouldn't do to think beyond that little bit of territory that they had some control over. The bottle of nail-polish remover was nearly empty by the time they got most of the sap off. Ruth Ann said, "While we're on her hands, we might as well do her nails too. They're all tore up."

"All right," Cassandra said. "You do the nails and I'll take care of her hair."

Ruth Ann clipped Marvelle's nails short, then smoothed them with an emery board. Cassandra gently lifted her head and, using long, careful strokes, combed her hair as best she could. Finally they could do no more. They put Marvelle's arms under the covers, then pulled up chairs and sat by the gurney. The gurney was so high, their eyes was level with the top of it, level with Marvelle's body, and Ruth Ann felt like a child again, looking up at her mama, watching first her face, then the rise and fall of her chest. She expected any minute Marvelle's eyes would open and she'd ask why was they sitting on their asses staring at her. Ruth Ann hoped for that. She hoped for it more than she'd ever hoped for anything in her life.

The nurse come in a few minutes later. She looked at the monitors and wrote something on a chart, then turned to Ruth Ann and Cassandra. "We'll be moving your mother now," she said. They stood up and moved out of the way as another nurse come in to help the first one. They rolled the gurney to an elevator and all five rode up to the ICU together. When they got out, Cassandra said, "Hey, look, maternity's on the same floor. Don't you want to go check on Ashley? I'll stay with Mama."

Ruth Ann looked down the hall in the direction of the maternity ward. "No," she said. "Keith's with Ashley now and I'd just be in the way."

They followed Marvelle into the ICU, into another cubicle nearly identical to the one she'd been in downstairs, only this one had more monitors and seemed quieter somehow. The nurses put Marvelle in the bed, checked her monitors, and then left them alone. Ruth Ann and Cassandra pulled chairs up next to the bed, one on either side, and sat down.

Ruth Ann closed her eyes, hoping they could just sit quiet for a few minutes. She should've known better though.

"She ain't going to make it, is she?" Cassandra said.

"I don't know," Ruth Ann said.

"She's a tough old woman though. She could surprise everybody. Don't you think?"

"Cassandra!" Ruth Ann's voice cracked a little bit. "Lord," she said. "I can smell them socks all the way over here." She got up and put her hands on Marvelle's feet, feeling how cold they was even through the socks, even through the sheet and the thin blanket. She lifted the covers off Marvelle's feet and took the sock off her right foot and started rubbing. Cassandra got up and took the other sock off. "Put them things in the sink in some soapy water," Ruth Ann said. "I can't stand that smell."

"I'm going to go tell the rest of them where we are," Cassandra said after she put the socks in to soak.

She left the room, and Ruth Ann rubbed Marvelle's feet until they got warm. She kept standing there holding on to her mama's feet even though there was no need. She studied them the way she would a road map, looking at all the little details. They wasn't pretty or dainty or tiny like women's feet was supposed to be. They was big and wide and square and had corns and bunions and rough patches and thick yellow toenails. But it was possible for something to be beautiful because of knowing things about it, not because of the way it looked.

Ruth Ann remembered so many things about her mama's feet. They was the one part of her that went naked just about year-round. Even in winter, with snow a foot deep, she'd run out to get clothes in off the line or gather eggs barefoot and laugh when Jesse told her she was crazy, told her she was going to catch cold. She'd laugh and say, Jesse honey, a little bit of snow never hurt nobody. And it wasn't just snow. She loved the feel of cool grass between her toes in the summertime, or walking barefoot in her garden, mashing big dirt clods under her heels. She loved wading in the creek with her young'uns, kicking water on them to make them squeal. She loved how a clean swept floor felt and the braided rug in the front room. Once she figured out how it worked, she even loved the foot massager they just give her for Christmas. These wasn't things Marvelle ever told anybody, just things that Ruth Ann suddenly realized she knew.

And for now, the only other thing she knew was that holding on to her mama's feet seemed like the only way to hold her in the world. So she held on with both hands, held on tight, because the whole world was spinning too fast, threatening to fling them all off in a heartbeat.

My own life ain't differed so much from my mama's. That seems to be the way of things. It ain't been easy, but looking back now, I wouldn't trade it. Mama felt the same, I'm sure.

We go along wishing for things to be different, but if somebody come up to us and said, okay, here, now, throw away the old and pick something new, how many of us would do it? Could do it? Not me, I don't reckon. There's only one thing I'd change if I could. Really only the one thing, and that would be Velda. I ain't sure how though, if I'd change her nature, or what happened to her, or whether she ever lived at all. I shouldn't even be sitting here thinking such a thing. It ain't my place to make up people's lives. That's the Lord's work, and the individual's. That's why I can't feel too bad for poor Velda. She made her bed and laid in it with my husband and bore his child and what happened to her after that was no more and no less than a natural result of her own actions, hers and Jesse's. I ain't setting him free from blame neither. Nor myself.

We was all selfish, I can see that now. I have to say them two made up a bigger part of it than me though. I was too busy tending young'uns to be thinking about piling up with my man all the time. Maybe that's where my own selfishness come in. I turned away from my husband because my young'uns used up everything I had to give. I didn't set aside nothing for him.

After I found out about him and Velda, I asked him how. How could he go and lay up with my own sister like that? He told me it was only the one time, he was drunk, he didn't know it wasn't me, she tricked him.

Well, that made me madder'n hell, that more'n anything. I said, what makes you think you can take me for a fool, Jesse Moon? We might look alike and sound alike, hell, we might even smell alike and taste alike, but you damn well do know the difference. We ain't just empty shapes nor vessels to lay with and put your seed in and then cast aside when you're done.

Then he got mad and told me how she done things with him I'd never do, things a wife's supposed to do with her husband but I never done with him. But did he ever ask me once? Did he ever tell me what he wanted? No, he just went on and got it somewhere else and never give me the chance.

Then she was carrying his baby and everybody knowed it, and after that it didn't matter if it was once or a hundred times, or if he knew it was her or not. Everything was right out there for the world to see and nothing either one of them said or done could take it back or make it right.

Not that Velda was sorry. No, she never was sorry for nothing. Acted like she couldn't understand me getting all upset, denied she was carrying any baby, much less Jesse's. I sent her away from our house at Slatey Knob, away from all of us, and told her she better not never show her face to me or mine again. He set her up somewhere nearby though, in a little shack somewhere on the mountain. I found out he'd done give her up before he even learned about the baby, but by then he felt bound to care for her and the child.

Jesse asked me one time why I stayed with him. I never knowed how to answer that. All I knowed was I didn't have nowhere to go. By then Mama and Papa both was dead, and none of my brothers and sisters had room for me, they all had their own families. What was I to do? All them young'uns and I wasn't about to go off and leave them behind, though they was times I was sorely tempted. Just get on a train and ride away from

Madison County and North Carolina and never have to account to no-body for nothing ever again. I was tired to death of being the good girl, the one always done right. I'd never wanted to be bad in my life, but for about six weeks after Velda died, that's all I wanted.

I reckon I hurt Jesse and my children, without even knowing I was a-doing it. I reckon I wanted to hurt somebody as bad as I was hurting. I wasn't fit to live with, that's for sure. I hated Jesse and I hated Velda even though she was dead. I purely did hate them both, and I'd never hated be-fore in my life, so it took me a while to recognize what it was. When I did, I took to it with all the might I used to put in tending my family, and I done it all from the middle of my bed. My sister Marthy had to come keep house and feed the children, for I wouldn't move out of that bed nor allow no-body but Marthy to come in the room. I laid there and I could hear that baby of Velda's that Jesse had brung home with him, and I could hear Jesse trying to comfort the children when they cried for me. All I could think about was how I hated the two people I once loved most in the world next to my young'uns.

But they wasn't no room in my heart for that hate, not that and love for my children at the same time. Something had to go, so I asked God to take the hate from me. I prayed and prayed over it, until finally at last it did go, the very day Marthy put Velda's baby in my arms and said, here, you name this young'un, you're her mama now. Then she left me alone with that baby, and her little face looked so like my babies Rachel and Rose. I had never got over the loss of my little girls. Both dead of the diphtheria before their fifth birthday, and me left with that houseful of boys. I loved all my boys, but I had so many hopes for a daughter of mine. Right then I wanted that girl, wanted her more than I wanted to keep on hating Jesse and Velda. It was like she grabbed a hold of my heart with her little hands and un-twisted it and shook it back into its right shape. The hate just run out of me like a long breath I'd been holding since Velda died.

I put my mouth to her ear and whispered real soft, you're mine now, baby girl, you're all mine. I laid my face against her head and it smelled so sweet and felt so tender. I touched the soft spot with my lips and her name come to me then, right out of the air. Ruth, I said. Ruth Ann Moon.

21

It wouldn't leave her alone, the anxious feeling that she'd forgot something, that she ought to be doing something. Ashley opened her eyes. She was in a different room now, not the one where the baby was born. The baby, that was it. Where was the baby?

"Hey, sleepyhead," A.J. said.

"Daddy. Where's the baby? Did you see the baby?" she said.

"I sure did, punkin. You done good."

"Where's Keith?"

"He's down the hall looking at her through the window."

"Where's Mama? Where's Granny?"

A.J. picked up her hand and held it between his, rubbing her cold fingers. "Listen, the doctor said you need to rest. You lost a lot of blood, they said, a hemorrhage or something like that. You go on back to sleep and I'll stay right here with you till Keith comes, all right?"

"Okay, Daddy." She was too tired to listen to the voice that told her something was wrong.

Ashley slapped at the hand trying to shake her awake. "Quit!" she said. "Daddy, quit. You said I could sleep a little bit longer." She didn't feel like going to school. Why couldn't they just let her sleep? Ashley opened her eyes and seen the nurse that had give her the epidural. Another nurse was there too, holding something in her arms. It all come back to her then.

"Honey, it's time for you to meet this young'un of yours," the epidural nurse said. "Can you sit up?"

"I don't know," Ashley said. She pushed herself up and felt her head start spinning. "Whoa," she said.

"Take it easy. The dizziness should pass in a minute." The epidural nurse put a pillow behind her back, then laid another pillow on her legs. "You give us a scare, young lady. But you're going to be fine, and so is this young'un of yours."

The other nurse put the baby on the pillow and said, "Now hold on to her, honey, or she'll roll off."

Ashley put her hands on her daughter for the first time. So tiny, so like a little doll, a little warm, breathing doll. She looked at the red face, the red fingers resting on top of the blanket. She was asleep. "She's all right?" Ashley looked at the nurses.

"As far as we know right now, she's perfect. Now, we're going to leave you alone for a little while. It won't be long before she wakes up hungry, so you just push the button and I'll come help you."

"Where's Keith?"

The nurse looked back from the door. "Would you like me to find him for you?"

Ashley was looking at the baby again. "No, that's all right," she said. She wanted this time alone with her daughter. From here on out she'd have to share her with the world, and she wasn't ready to let go after all the months they'd spent together, just the two of them.

"Hey, baby girl," she said after the nurses left. "Hey there." She put her face close to the baby's, studying her little eyebrows and eyelids and eyelashes and nose and lips and ears and hair. "Hey, baby. You got a name, did you know that? Do you know what your name is? Do you? Your name is Catherine Peri Anne Payne. We might be changing the Payne to Watty later, but don't you worry about that. I'll give you plenty of advance notice if we do so you can get used to the idea."

Ashley pulled the blanket away and looked at the baby's arms and legs, all the parts the right size and in the right place. She touched the baby's cheek and her mouth twitched. Could this really be what had been growing inside of her belly all them months? This little thing that now had a life all its own and didn't need her no more? No, that wasn't true. This baby needed her mama. Ashley stared at her and wondered at her own part in a miracle. Even with all her screwing around and screwing up, she'd been given such a gift. She smelled the baby's head, the smell Betty said she loved best, such a sweet smell. Ashley knew then her granny was right. This was a new beginning, fresh from the creator. She was halfway in love with the baby already and wouldn't let herself think about how scared she was, how she didn't know what to do next. She'd figure it out somehow.

She kissed the baby's head and rubbed her cheek against the fine dark hair. Black-headed just like her mama and daddy. Ashley couldn't wait for her to open her eyes so she could see what color they was, even though she knew they'd probably change color as the years passed. Blue. They'd probably be blue. Deep blue like Keith's, she hoped, instead of light blue like hers. She leaned back against the pillows and held the baby close.

Halfway asleep, she heard the door open and shut, then soft footsteps coming toward the bed. She opened her eyes. "Granny," she said. Her voice sounded sleepy and far away. "I was hoping you'd come."

"Hey, honey," Marvelle said. "Let me see that baby." She lifted her off the pillow and looked into her face. "Lord, ain't she pretty? Looks just like her mama and her granny when they was babies. Yes, you do, sugar," she said, and kissed the top of the baby's head.

Ashley rubbed her eyes and stretched. "What are you doing in a hospital gown, Granny?"

Marvelle looked over the baby at Ashley. "These fools won't leave me alone. They think I'm dying or something. Made me put this thing on and lay down."

"Well, it's probably 'cause you got a great big old knot on your head. What did you do?"

"Fell over and hit my head on a stump. It ain't nothing." Marvelle patted Ashley's hand. "How are you, honey? Are you sore?"

"Yes, I'm sore. Granny, I think I can honestly say I know how it feels to shit a watermelon now, a big one."

Marvelle laughed. She rubbed the baby's head, then leaned down and smelled it. "Oh, honey," she said. "That pain ain't nothing. You'll forget all about it in a week or two."

The baby's eyes opened and then her mouth. She whimpered, then started crying.

"I believe this young'un's hungry," Marvelle said. She put the baby on Ashley's lap and stood back.

Ashley held her and looked at Marvelle. Okay, the baby was hungry. What was she supposed to do about it? "Granny?" she said.

"Why, honey, ain't nothing to it. It's the most natural thing in the world once you get the hang of it. Pull your gown down and flop one of them things out here. Go on, do it. All right, now squeeze the nipple and make sure they's something in there."

Ashley hesitated, feeling her face turn red. It was embarrassing to be squeezing her own titty in front of somebody. But her granny was waiting, and the baby too, so she done it. She squeezed until a drop of thick yellow stuff appeared on the nipple. "What is that? I thought it was supposed to be milk."

"Your milk'll come down in a day or two. This is the stuff your baby needs right now to protect her from sickness. She'll like it good as milk, you'll see. Now, take and rub the nipple against her cheek so she can find you."

In seconds the baby stopped crying as she rooted around, found the nipple, and latched on.

"Ow!" Ashley pulled the nipple out of the baby's mouth. "That hurts!"

"Yes, it does," Marvelle said. "But you'll get used to it."

The baby whimpered, pushing her open mouth against Ashley's breast.

"Give it back to her now. She's hungry."

Ashley done like she was told, and Marvelle laughed as she watched the baby nurse. "You think that hurts, wait till she gets teeth. I still got a mark on me where Dwight 'bout bit mine off one time."

Ashley looked up. "Dwight did?"

"Yes, ma'am. He might be little, but he's a powerful big eater. You just ask Betty."

"God, Granny, seems like everything associated with having children turns out to be painful except sex."

"And sometimes even that," Marvelle said. "Now, you got to remember to switch sides from feeding to feeding or one titty'll be bigger than the other."

"Oh, great. Now I'll be whopsided too. Fat and whopsided."

"Honey, that all passes in time. Don't you worry. What you got to do is concentrate on right now. That'll always keep you plenty busy. Have you give this baby a name yet?"

"Yeah. We decided on Catherine Peri Anne. Anne with a *e*."

"What's her last name?"

"Payne for now."

"I never did like the name Payne."

"Granny, how about giving Daddy a break?"

"Huh," Marvelle grunted.

Ashley said, "How you feel about Watty?"

"Watty? Have you decided to marry the boy?"

"Just about." Ashley ran her finger across the baby's cheek. So soft. "I guess."

"Well, don't look so beat up about it. Keith's a good boy, and you'uns got just as good a chance as anybody. It depends on what you do with what you're give to work with. Lord, look at the head of hair on that young'un."

They watched until Catherine gradually stopped sucking and fell asleep, her mouth still working from time to time. Ashley pulled her loose, then pulled her gown up and sat looking at her.

"You'uns get some sleep now, honey."

"Where you going, Granny?"

"I got to go find my pocketbook. It's got all my valuables in it. My money and my jewelry. I had it when I come in here and now I don't know what they done with it."

"The last time I seen it was in the delivery room. Keith hung it on the wall so I'd have something to look at while I pushed."

"I never heard tell of such a thing."

Ashley yawned. "Well, it did help 'cause I thought of you when I looked at it and I thought, if Granny done this twelve times, surely I can do it once."

"Eleven," Marvelle said. She looked sad all of a sudden.

"Eleven? I could've sworn it was twelve."

Marvelle noticed the TV hanging high on the wall across from the bed. "Oh, Lord," she said. "What time is it?"

"About one o'clock."

"Turn on that TV. I got to watch my story before I go."

Ashley clicked on the TV and found *Days of Our Lives*. "Get up here with me, Granny," she said. She was amazed how much effort it took to move over in the bed a couple of inches to make room. Having a baby really took it out of a body. Marvelle climbed on the bed, and Ashley shifted the baby to her other arm and put a pillow behind Marvelle's back.

The room seemed dark for so early in the afternoon. Ashley looked toward the window and noticed that the sky had got cloudy. "I think it's going to rain," she said.

Marvelle patted her leg. "That's all right. We ain't going nowhere. Now, hush so I can hear."

Ashley managed to stay awake for the first few minutes, then felt herself drifting off. There wasn't nothing exciting on the show this week anyhow, not now the baby was born. When she felt her baby being lifted off her lap, she opened her eyes a crack. "What you doing?" she said.

"You go on to sleep now, honey," Marvelle said. "I'll watch the baby till you wake up."

Ashley closed her eyes again. "All right, Granny," she said.

There was that feeling again, that feeling like something was wrong. Ashley woke up, then sat up quick. "Where's my baby?" she said.

Ruth Ann stood up and come over to her. "She's fine. The nurse took her a little while ago. Y'all was fast asleep."

Ashley laid back against the pillows and rubbed her hand over the spot where Marvelle had been sitting. It still felt warm. Ruth Ann come closer to the bed. Her face was all red, and she had a wad of Kleenex in her hand. "Mama?" Ashley said. "What's the matter? You look like you been crying."

"Ashley. Honey." Ruth Ann sniffed and wiped under her nose with the Kleenex, then looked up. "It's your granny. She passed away a little while ago."

"What?"

Ruth Ann picked up Ashley's hand and squeezed it. "She went in a coma right after we got here and she never woke up again."

Ashley smacked Ruth Ann's hand away. "You're crazy. She was just here, in my room."

"Ashley." Ruth Ann looked at her like she'd said a bad word or something.

"She was. She was right here. She held Catherine. She was fine, except for that knot on her head."

"Honey, she never got up from that bed. Me and Cassandra set by her nearly the whole time."

"Well, it must've been when y'all went to get coffee or to the bathroom or something, 'cause I'm telling you she walked right through that door and stood right where you're standing now, Mama, and she stayed with me for a long time. I told her the baby's name and she helped me feed her and everything. We even watched *Days of Our Lives*."

Ashley started crying then because she knew her mama wasn't lying. Why would she lie about such a thing? It was a long time before she could quit crying. Ruth Ann pulled a chair close to the bed and kept handing her Kleenex.

It got too quiet in the room after she quit crying, so Ashley clicked the TV on and flipped through the channels. They looked at part of a gall bladder operation, then flipped past sitcoms and infomercials, then Ashley turned the TV off. It was even darker in the room than before, the only light coming from the bathroom. "Mama," she said. "Do you believe me? Do you believe she was here?"

"I don't know what to think," Ruth Ann said.

"Did somebody get her pocketbook out of the delivery room? She said she was going to look for it after her story went off."

"Keith brung it to us. I think Cassandra's got it now."

"Granny said all her valuables was in there."

Ruth Ann put her hand in the pocket of her sweater. She had put her mama's billfold and wedding ring back in the pocketbook, but she still had the cameo. She looked up at Ashley and held out her hand, the cameo in her palm.

"Oh!" Ashley said, and her eyes filled up with tears.

"Remember how you used to always ask if you could have it?"

"And she said yes, when she died I could have it." The tears spilled over then and ran down her cheeks. "How could I say that to her, Mama? How could I talk about wanting that pin when she died, like it mattered more than she did?"

"Honey, you was just a little girl." Ruth Ann leaned over and pinned the cameo to the neck of Ashley's gown. She put her hand against Ashley's cheek. "Mama meant for you to have this," she said.

Ashley leaned her face against Ruth Ann's hand. "Oh, Mama," she said.

Ruth Ann smoothed Ashley's hair back from her forehead, then sat on the edge of the bed with her hands folded in her lap. They just sat there quiet for a minute, not looking at each other.

Finally Ashley said, "It's my fault, ain't it? My fault for not watching Granny yesterday."

"Ashley," Ruth Ann said. "I'm going to tell you this one time, and then I don't want to hear no more about it. It is not your fault. I don't blame you, and neither does anybody else. They's things in this life we don't have no control over, and the quicker you accept it, the better off you'll be. Lord knows it took me fifty-one years. Don't let it take you that long."

She handed Ashley another Kleenex. "You're my daughter and I love you and I'll never stop, no matter what. Nothing you ever do or say will change that. That don't mean I don't expect certain things of you. But you've changed since you come home. I've watched it happen." She cleared her throat, patted Ashley's knee, and stood up again. "Now. I'm going to look at my grandchild. I ain't seen her yet. You want to come?"

"Can I?"

"I don't know. Can you?"

Ashley swung her legs over the side of the bed and put her feet down. She jerked them back up again. "That floor's cold," she said. "Will you get me some socks? I think my bag's in that closet."

Ruth Ann carried a pair of thick white socks over and watched as Ashley tried to reach her feet. "Here, let me do that," she said.

Ashley handed her the socks and Ruth Ann sat down by the bed. She put Ashley's feet on her legs and put on one sock, then the other. Ashley tried to pull her feet away, but Ruth Ann held on to them, rubbing them.

"Mama?" Ashley leaned over her, smelling hair spray. Even on a day like today, the woman managed to have perfect hair.

Ruth Ann looked up, her eyes swimmy with tears. She blinked them away, then put Ashley's feet back on the floor. "Come on," she said, and held on to Ashley's knees while she got to her feet.

Ashley eased herself off the bed and held Ruth Ann's arm until she got steady. This time the dizzy spell wasn't as bad and passed pretty quick.

"You all right?" Ruth Ann said.

"Feels like I been kicked in the butt by a mule."

"That sounds about right," Ruth Ann said. They walked real slow, like two old, old women, out of the room, down the hall toward the nursery. Several nurses looked up and smiled as they passed the desk. At the door of the waiting room, they stopped to look for the rest of the family. It was empty except for Keith and A.J., both slouched down in chairs, asleep.

"Look at them two," Ashley said. "You'd think they was the ones just had a baby."

"Get used to it," Ruth Ann said. "Their minds just don't work like ours. If they're tired, they go on and go to sleep, no matter how much there is that still needs doing."

"If me and Keith gets married, I ain't putting up with that. He's going to help me."

Ruth Ann laughed. "Remember me telling you there's some things in this life you ain't got no control over?" She waved her hand at A.J. and

Keith. "Well, there's two of them things right there. Now, come on. I want to see that baby."

Sometimes I look back and I don't see how I lived through it all, losing so much, my mama and papa, my children, my sister, my husband. It's a miracle to me, healing from pain. A miracle to get past it enough to where you're glad to wake up of a morning, to where your young'uns can make you laugh and your husband can warm you. To get past craving death and darkness and be grateful for what you got, that's a blessed miracle.

When I took Ruth Ann to raise, the hate I felt for Velda and Jesse did leave me, and I was able to do my duty by my children, but what took me over where Jesse was concerned was just a feeling of not caring at all, kindly numb like when your leg falls asleep and you stand up to walk and then fall down. You don't know right away what's happened.

When Ruth Ann was about a year old, me and Jesse and the young'uns, we packed up everything and moved down the mountain to Davis. Jesse's daddy had got sick and sent for him, and Jesse took over the running of the place. His brother was dead and wasn't nobody else. I wasn't sorry to go. Too many memories there at Slatey Knob, good and bad. It was easier in Davis.

And so we lived on there together, working hard and raising our young'uns, but between us was nothing more than a great empty place. I know Jesse never lost hope of it filling up again, but it didn't concern me no more than nothing. I kept myself busy making a home and feeding my family. I wore myself out taking care of everybody just so I could sleep nights.

Me and Jesse did sleep in the same bed. It was the only one we had. Used to, when we got in the bed of a night, we'd lay close and tell each other all the things we hadn't had time to tell during the day. That all ended after Velda and Jesse done what they done. They was too much to say and not enough words to say it, and we neither one of us didn't want to hear no more. I turned away from Jesse, turned on my side night after night, listening while he suffered his nightmares and called my name.

Sometimes that first year after Velda died I'd raise up in the bed after Jesse fell asleep and listen to him a-breathing and think how easy, oh, how easy it'd be to lay a pillow over his face and hold it there till he quit breathing. I'd set there a long time, thinking about that. Then I'd get up next morning and go on like nothing happened, like I hadn't thought of murdering him in his sleep. The way he looked at me sometimes, I think he suspected, or maybe he woke up and felt me staring down on him. I reckon the fact he kept on a-sleeping by me was his way of putting his life in my hands, his way of saying, I know I done you wrong and here's all I can do to make it up to you. It won't fair of him to put it all on me like that, but probably it was the only way I could've stood to stay with him, him letting me decide.

Then one day I was a-standing at the clothesline hanging sheets to dry, watching Jesse come up the road from the pasture. It was springtime and the world turning green again. There'd been eight springs since Velda died, but that was the first one felt like the end of a long killing winter. It was one of them vigorous April days, the wind going ever which way, streaking white clouds across that blue sky, a day of changing weather. I looked over that clothesline at Jesse getting closer and closer and still I couldn't leave off looking at him. It was like I recognized him again after a long time apart, like I seen him new again, and him familiar to me as my dress or my hands or my children's faces.

He come up the other side of the clothesline, looking back at me. He stopped and waited, his face red from the wind, sheets flapping and popping around us like great white wings. He waited and I waited, for what seemed like all time. Some sort of an understanding passed between us then, something he'd hoped for and I never expected.

He went in the house directly and washed his hands, then helped me hang out the rest of them sheets. By the time we got done, the young'uns come up the road from school making their usual racket. Even so, that quietness stayed wrapped around me and Jesse all the rest of the day, and that night we put them clean sheets on our bed and laid down again as husband and wife. We didn't do no talking. They's some things can only be said with the body. That night Jesse promised me everlasting faithfulness, and I promised never to leave him alone again.

Then it wasn't long before Cassandra come along. You talk about surprised, honey, surprised ain't the word, me nearly forty years old. She was my last baby and I had a hard time, nearly lost her and me too. But once she got in the world, that little gal fought to stay. She don't think she's strong, but if she'd a knowed herself as a baby, she'd see as I did, from the get-go she was a force in this world, quiet and independent, always with her own way of doing things.

My other young'uns I could always point to me or Jesse to say which one they took after. I believe Cassandra must be a real blending of us both, so much so I can't see neither one of us in her. Appears she is like me in one way though, her life divided in two and now she's ready for the second half of her journey. She thinks 'cause she ain't got no husband nor children she ain't got nothing to show for living this far. I wish I could tell her, you got yourself, honey, and that's all any of us got for sure.

When she was born, Jesse told me he wouldn't mind having ten more young'uns. I just looked at him. This is it, I said, I have a feeling she's the last. And I was right too, but I don't think he was disappointed. I give him more than enough children for any one man.

Me and Jesse, we never did get back that old feeling from our first years together, but we was good companions the rest of his days, like two old mules harnessed together, comfortable plowing our rows, knowing the same steps and enjoying walking them together.

Sometimes people have said to me, Marvelle, have you had a good life? Well, first off I'd tell them, honey, it ain't over yet. And then I'd tell them you can't go putting a whole life in one drawer, good or bad. They's a whole chest full of drawers, and all kinds of things in there, little scraps of happiness, wads of sorrow, every now and then a whole bolt of joy. You can't look at the place where all that's stored up and name it good or bad. They ain't no name for what it is, and that's as it should be. That's part of the mystery.

Eh Lord, all that time, seems it went flashing by, like the sun on the river up at home, the water and light moving so quick and blinding. Before you know it, it's gone, and all that's left here is what endures in them that traveled with you awhile, the ones left behind. You try to leave something to help them on their way, whether they think they need it or not. Chances are they won't till after you're gone. Then they'll be glad of it. They'll be glad and marvel at it and say, how'd she know, that crazy old woman? How did she know?

I tell you what, I'm going to enjoy that. I purely am.

April
1993

22

On the high part of the causeway into Atlantic Beach, Cassandra slowed the van and rolled the window down. She breathed in deep, smelling the salt air, and felt a big smile pull itself across her face. It was too dark to see the water, but she could smell it, feel it in the air. She was here. She was really here, and them lights was so beautiful, like Christmas, white and twinkling as far down Bogue Banks as she could see. She knew then she wasn't crazy for coming.

Somebody behind her honked, and Cassandra looked in the rearview mirror as a pickup truck full of teenage boys pulled around her. The ones in the bed of the truck hollered something as they cut in front. There was three of them, and two pulled their pants down and mooned Cassandra while the third one was still trying to get his belt unbuckled.

"Hey, big mama! Whoooooooooooeeeeeeeeeee, baby!" One almost fell off the truck trying to get his pants back up. His buddies grabbed him just in time, and they all fell down laughing as the driver sped off toward the amusement park.

Wasn't that always the way? Just when you're enjoying yourself, thinking life ain't so bad after all, along comes a truck full of drunk teenage boys hollering obscene things and showing their butts. Well, she wasn't going to let them spoil her vacation. She concentrated on finding the right turn that would put her on the road to the Holiday Inn and her free hotel night.

Ruth Ann thought she was crazy to come down here by herself, and maybe she was. Maybe she was crazy as hell, but so what? Where had being sane got her?

It wasn't even so much the free hotel night that got her. It was the free hotel night of her choice. Her choice. She liked the sound of that now. It was scary, choosing, doing something instead of standing still, and it was hard to remember that excitement felt pretty much the same as fear. Over and over again she had to tell herself to quit worrying about why she shouldn't do things and concentrate on why she should. Quit worrying about running out of time and just enjoy right now.

She just wished Oprah or Phil or Geraldo or Sally Jessy or whoever it was first started all the fuss over stuff like biological clocks, and married people living longer than single people, and women over forty not being able to find husbands, she wished they'd all mind their own business and quit making people feel like something was wrong with them for being different, for living alone without no husband or boyfriend or children, and for living with their mama for forty-some years before that. They should do a show about what people do when they can't sleep at night 'cause they think somebody's trying to break in the house and the police come and it turns out to be just a raccoon in the trash can. They should do a show about what people do when the house is so empty they can hear the quiet squeezing in their ears and they think they're having a heart attack and the emergency room staff looks at them like they're crazy and they go home and pray nobody ever finds out.

As she come around a curve, there was the big Holiday Inn sign right there in green neon, just like it was supposed to be. So far, so good. Cassandra pulled in the driveway in front of the office and glanced around the parking lot. The place appeared to be full of cars, and all the rooms was lit up. She hadn't thought it'd be so busy in April, but maybe it was the warm spell tempting people to the beach even though the water was still cold. She cut the engine, leaned on the steering wheel, and peered through the front window of the hotel. The bald head of the man behind the desk reflected the light so she couldn't see his face, just glasses and a big nose. He was sitting there reading the paper, and she didn't see nobody else in the lobby.

Now all she had to do was take her coupon in there and present it to that man and he'd give her a key and tell her how to get to the room and where the elevator and the ice machine and the drink machine was. Just like when she used to come down with Ruth Ann and A.J. and the kids for vacation. But they always took care of details like hotel reservations and meals and travel. Cassandra just had to show up and play with the kids, like she was one herself.

Well, the hotel man would think she was crazy if she kept sitting there like that. She opened the door and hauled herself out, then reached back in for her pocketbook. The air smelled strong and salty and cool, and Cassandra just leaned against the car and breathed deep for a minute. Then she slammed the car door and walked into the hotel, straight to the front desk, and laid the coupon in front of the man.

He put his paper down and looked up at her. He had what her mama would call a tater nose, and not a hair on his head, slick as a bowling ball. But he had nice twinkly blue eyes behind them big black glasses, and the smoothest golden skin she'd ever seen on a man. He looked like a cross between Kojak and Captain Jean-Luc Picard of the Starship Enterprise. She decided he didn't look like the kind of man who would think she was strange for coming to the beach all by herself for one night.

He looked down at her coupon, then back at her and smiled. White, those teeth against that skin was the whitest things she'd ever seen. She'd always admired perfect teeth, probably since she didn't have them herself, and his smile was downright dazzling.

"Travel club, eh?"

Once again, a smile come across Cassandra's face without her knowing it was coming. She never smiled when she was nervous, but then she realized she wasn't the least bit nervous. Maybe she was having fun.

"Yes, I guess I got suckered, but I thought I'd go ahead and enjoy the free hotel night anyhow." She put her pocketbook on the counter and leaned her elbows next to it.

"Well, good for you." He turned his back to her to find the key, and she admired the broadness of his shoulders. When he turned around, she seen he had a little pot belly, just like all her brothers had by the time they was forty. That's what he looked to be, early forties, judging by the pot and the crinkles around his eyes when he smiled.

"I hope you enjoy your stay, Miss Moon." He smiled again. "What a wonderful name, by the way. Miss Moon." He sounded Canadian, that little bite to his words.

Embarrassment ran up in her face like a hot flash, but she managed to talk back to him. "Thank you. I like it." She took the key, slung her pocketbook over her shoulder, and turned toward the door. She liked her name, she liked him, she liked feeling the way she was feeling.

"Oh, Miss Moon?"

Cassandra turned back. "Huh?"

"Just let me know if you need anything. I'll be right here till eight o'clock in the morning." Then that smile again.

Dang if he wasn't a right nice-looking man once you got up close. "Oh, I reckon I'll be all right. But thank you."

Outside, she smiled to herself. Now, that wasn't a bit hard, was it? She got in the car, drove around to the side of the hotel, and parked. These Holiday Inns all looked pretty much the same: big square buildings with rows of plain white doors, and windows with the curtains closed. But tonight one of them rooms was all hers.

Before she turned off the headlights, she made out the number on the door of her room, then checked the key again to make sure it was the right one. She had asked for an ocean view with a balcony when she called last week to make her reservation, that way she could sit outside at night without going down to the beach by herself. But all they had was a room on the end near the ocean which didn't have a balcony or a view of anything but the parking lot. She had to think positive though. At least she was here, and it wouldn't kill her to walk down to the beach like everybody else.

Cassandra carried her suitcase to the door and unlocked it. As the door swung open and she stared in the dark room, a musty closed-up smell hit her and made her breath stick in her stomach somewhere. A dizzy feeling passed over her and she held on to the door frame to keep from falling. What was she thinking, coming to a hotel in a strange city all by herself, hundreds of miles away from everything and everybody she knew, for no reason other than she wanted to get away? People like her didn't do things like that.

The door of the room next to hers opened and two old ladies stepped out. One of them carried a cane hooked over her arm with her pocketbook. "Hey, honey," the other one said, smiling at her. The lady with the cane smiled too, then asked her if she was all right. She must have looked like a haint or a drunk, standing there swaying outside the door like that.

"Thank you, ma'am, I'm fine." Cassandra smiled at the ladies and they nodded and went and got in their car. If them sweet little old ladies could come down here and stay in a hotel, then why couldn't she? She was young and strong and had fifty dollars cash in her wallet, plus an extra twenty hid in her address book, so what did she have to worry about? She reached for the light switch, and when the lights come on, the room didn't seem so scary anymore. She went in and locked the door behind her, then swung the suitcase up on one of the double beds. She had packed way too much stuff for one night, but she wasn't sure what kind of weather to expect, so she brung everything.

It wasn't a bad room for a hotel. The pink and green flowered curtains and bedspread matched, and she didn't see no stains on the carpet. They'd even put some nice pictures of birds on the walls. She couldn't understand why they wouldn't put up pictures of the ocean in these hotels though. That's what people come here to see.

After she went to the bathroom, she put the TV on, then sat on the bed and went through the channels. They didn't have cable on her road yet, so this TV got a lot more channels than what she was used to. She looked at her watch. Half-past eight. If she was home, she'd have done had supper and now she'd be in the bed, eating ice cream and watching the Friday night lineup on channel two. By ten-thirty she'd be asleep, then wake up at eleven-thirty or twelve, long enough to cut the sound down on the TV and fall back asleep.

A pizza commercial come on and she realized then that in all the excitement of planning and packing and driving down here, she'd forgot to eat. Her mouth about fell open. That had never happened to her before. No matter what else in her life went by the wayside, eating always got priority. Not that she would ever go without food even if she did forget. Marvelle and Ruth Ann never seemed to understand the connection between getting fat and all them Sunday dinners and casseroles and biscuits and cobblers and seven-layer bars they made all the time. Of course, they hadn't held a gun to her head and made her eat. She'd done it herself. Now she was away from all that, it was amazing how having something interesting happen had made her forget food for a while.

She felt silly putting clothes in the drawers for one night, but she might as well use the room since she was here. By the time she unpacked everything and stored her suitcase on the rack next to the bathroom, it was nine o'clock. Time for her favorite show. Cassandra loved *The X-Files* because, deep down inside where she wouldn't admit it to anybody else, she believed in UFOs. Her daddy used to always say there wasn't no such a thing, and as a matter of fact, the whole space program was a trick to get people to pay more taxes. He said he read that Neil Armstrong was really a Hollywood actor and the surface of the moon was really the desert out in California somewhere. Cassandra didn't know where he found such things, and she didn't want to know.

She couldn't help being grateful for what little mystery was left in the world. Everybody acted like they knowed everything, and Cassandra knew that just couldn't be right. Only God knew everything, and sometimes she wasn't so sure about Him. Like Mama, for example. As ornery as she could be, she didn't deserve to lose her mind like that there at the end. That was all she had left after Daddy died and her arthritis made it so she couldn't sew no more. What kind of a God done that to a old woman that hadn't never done nothing worse than gossip behind somebody's back?

But Cassandra just had to write that off as another one of God's mysteries, or else she'd go crazy trying to figure it out. She couldn't be glad and grateful for the good mysteries, like extraterrestrials and weather, and then complain about the things that didn't go her way, things she didn't have no control over.

Right after the opening scene of *X-Files*, a newsman come on and said there was a terrible fire in Morehead City and our Bill Martin is live at the scene. After watching the fire and interviews with the firemen, the spectators, the police, and the other reporters for fifteen minutes, Cassandra got bored and went through all the channels again. Nothing caught her eye, so she made herself turn off the TV. Did she come all the way down here just to do the same old stuff she done at home?

Even though she could hear the traffic from the road and every now and then voices in the parking lot, the room still seemed too quiet. She scooted backward on the bed and leaned against the padded headboard that was screwed onto the wall, not even attached to the bed really. She looked around the room, the pink and green flowers, the hummingbird pictures, the particleboard chest with oak veneer, the framed letter from the Holiday Inn management on the back of the door, her own brush and watch on top of the night table beside her. They was the only things of her own she could see from the bed. Everything else belonged to the hotel, to strangers, and she wasn't responsible for none of it. She didn't have to make payments on it, clean it, cook for it, change its diaper, take it anywhere, repair it, or share it.

Just for one night, what she needed to do was forget all that, which was next to impossible at home because, even when she was by herself, she was surrounded by reminders. Pictures of the family, things they'd give her and Marvelle for Christmas and birthdays, things Cassandra didn't really like but felt obliged to set out. Like that ugly green and gold macramé birdcage with the fake dove in it that Ruth Ann give her last Christmas. Cassandra had never seen anything so tacky, but there it hung over her refrigerator, right where Ruth Ann said she imagined it hanging the minute she seen it at the fall Arts Around Town. Sometimes that house felt like a big junkyard full of everybody's stuff but hers. Everything in it except her clothes was hand-me-downs, and the only reason she had her own clothes was because everybody else in the family was skinny. Maybe it was time to let some of it go, maybe it was time for that yard sale she kept meaning to have. Her mama was gone now. Maybe it was time to move on.

She pushed herself up off the bed and opened the door to the whisper of waves and wind. The beach was down there in the dark somewhere. Sand and salt water and open spaces. She always forgot how good the air smelled at the beach. And how her and Ruth Ann's young'uns had loved to get up early and spend all day on the beach. How they had all loved running on the hard brown sand when the tide went out. Even in the broad, hot daylight they'd run, in bathing suits, their arms flung out wide like flying, laughing and spinning and falling and rolling down the sand, into the water. Cassandra shivered. That was before she'd got so fat though. Now she wouldn't be caught dead in public in a bathing suit, or even shorts. At least not in the daytime.

It was different at night. In the dark she could be invisible and didn't have to worry about what she looked like to other people. Her and the kids used to love going down on the beach at night, after Ruth Ann and A.J. left to go dancing. They'd walk all the way to the Salter Path pier and back if the tide was out. If it was high tide and hard walking, they'd spread a blanket on the sand and lay there listening to the waves, singing songs and watching for shooting stars. Sometimes the kids would fall asleep and Cassandra would lay there all alone in the quiet, feeling like everything holding her inside her body was melting away and she was becoming part of everything that was outside her body, all the things that seemed so big and dark and mysterious in the world, all the things that went into making up the ocean and the sky. Before long, that feeling would start scaring her because it was so big, and that was when she'd feel herself being squeezed back in. At that point, she'd wake the kids up, take them back to the room, put them to bed, and then watch TV until Ruth Ann and A.J. got in.

A car pulled in the space next to hers, and she slammed the door shut so the people wouldn't see her standing there in the door of her room like a fool. It only took her a minute to make up her mind what to do next. She didn't think, just stuck the room key in her pocket and got the extra blanket off the luggage rack. The hotel must be used to sand on their stuff by now. They wouldn't mind her using their blanket.

The wooden walkway to the beach was lit by floodlights that also lit up a little strip of sand in front of the hotel. It looked like an airport runway out there. Cassandra didn't want nobody to see her and wonder if she was dead or crazy, so she walked on down a ways until she found a darker place. She spread the blanket up against a dune, where the sand would make a backrest. Then she took off her shoes and socks and walked down to the water. The first touch was cold, but she got used to it and walked in the shallow water toward Salter Path. She was in no shape to walk that far, but it felt good to move against the wind and have it blow the hair off her face.

The three-quarter moon made a bright white path on the calm water and lit up the beach enough that Cassandra could see if there was jellyfish ahead. She'd stepped on one and been stung once, and A.J. got Alex to pee on the stung place to take away the pain. Alex was only five then, and nobody thought a thing about him whipping it out right there in the middle of the day. So he peed on her leg, with people they didn't even know standing around watching because she was carrying on so. It embarrassed the life out of her. But A.J. was right. It did quit hurting after that. She never did find out how he knew that, but ever since then, she kept a lookout for jellyfish, especially at night when they was just about invisible.

She walked a quarter mile or so, then went back to the blanket, the wind pushing her all the way. After putting her socks and shoes on, she wiggled and pushed at the sand with her butt until she had a kind of seat fixed, then settled down with her legs stretched in front of her so her feet wouldn't fall asleep. The Atlantic Beach pier was only half a mile or so away to her left and lit up so bright she could practically see the faces of all the people fishing on her side. Way in the distance to the right, the lights of the Salter Path pier twinkled like a string of Christmas bulbs. Out on the water, a shrimp boat passed in front of the beach, and it was all lit up too. She could've sworn she seen the tiny moving shapes of men working the nets, or at least she imagined she did. She'd always wanted to go out on one of them boats, just to see what it was like.

When it got cold after a while, she pulled the edges of the blanket around her and laid her head back on the sand. She watched the moon move until her eyes closed once, twice, three times. That feeling of all her edges melting away come over her like syrup pouring over a hot pancake, slow at first, but then faster and faster. This time she decided not to let herself be squeezed back in. Her eyes opened wider and wider until it felt like she was all eyes and nothing else. Something inside her stretched and stretched, then snapped loose and floated. She took deep breaths, in through the nose, out through the mouth, fast at first, then slower and slower as she relaxed down to her very bones. Gradually the steady sound of the waves made her lose track of her breath and her heartbeat so all that was left was the dark and the whoosh and the moon.

She dreamed the dream again, the one where she was a little girl standing on a crate, staring in at her family's life. Only this time they all looked at her and waved and smiled. Cassandra was so shocked, she fell off backward on her butt. She was scared when she seen a shadow leaning over her, but then Marvelle helped her up and brushed her off, then give her a push and said, go on, now, honey. Then all of a sudden there she was on a shrimp boat, and the Holiday Inn man was behind the wheel. It wasn't a regular shrimp boat though. This one had big sails that fluttered white against the blue sky. Dolphins and whales was jumping out of the water all around her, taking her breath away. The Holiday Inn man tied the wheel up and come and stood next to her. When he smiled, his teeth sparkled in the sun so she couldn't see, and next thing she knew she was underwater. She swam and swam and didn't never need to come up for air. The dolphins and the whales and all kinds of fish, and the Holiday Inn man, they all swam with her and it was beautiful, it was like magic, so beautiful she never wanted to go back.

Near daylight, in the cool of the morning, Cassandra woke up feeling better than she had in a long time. She tried to go back to sleep, to grab that dream back, but it was gone. It was the first time she could remember ever dreaming in color. She sat up, stretched, and took deep breaths of salt air, then pulled the blanket around her to keep warm.

The gray light gradually turned yellow, then pink, and Cassandra sat very still, watching and listening. The tide had gone far out during the night and now was slowly starting to push back in. Waves washed shells up and down the sand, and she seen a few big ones she wanted to go pick up. She laughed because that made her think of A.J. and his shell collection, which he kept scattered across the beaches of the world. That was A.J. for you, master of the universe. He tried and failed every year to talk the kids out of carrying home so many shells, since Ruth Ann threw them away along about November. Cassandra kept hers in bowls and baskets in her room. Sometimes she'd take them out and hold them, admire the textures and colors, and try to remember when and where she'd found a particular shell. She didn't remember very many, but she kept them anyway because they reminded her of good days.

A couple of joggers run by with a black Labrador retriever, who come over to sniff her until his people stopped and called him back. Cassandra smiled and they smiled and waved. Probably a married couple. The woman looked over her shoulder as she run on after their dog, then the man looked back too. They probably thought she was loony, a big old forty-two-year-old woman wrapped in a Holiday Inn blanket on the beach at daybreak.

Well, if they did, that was their problem. She couldn't stop smiling at her own nerve for spending the night on the beach all by herself just because she felt like it. There was a lot of things she intended to do from now on just because she felt like it. She yawned and stretched and realized her free hotel night was over and she hadn't even used the bed. That made her smile even more. Shoot, she had enough money to stay a second night if she wanted to. And nobody expecting her nowhere until Monday morning. Marvelle and Ruth Ann and Ashley was in Madison County, and she was free.

EPILOGUE

April was the place winter and spring seemed to get all mixed up in the mountains. Even this late in the month, there was patches of snow in shady places, but the air felt nearly warm as summer. Buds on the trees glowed neon green against that crystal blue sky, and patches of daffodils and even a crocus or two still bloomed in the shade of Walnut cemetery. There was yellow forsythia and pink quince growing together like a hedge around somebody's yard down the road, and it just glowed in the sunshine. At home in Davis, all that stuff had done bloomed and faded, and the new green was already giving over to a darker color.

Ashley knelt down next to Marvelle's grave and put her palm against the ground. It felt cold, and the damp seeped through the knees of her jeans. Still she knelt there, her fingers threading through the grass like it was hair. The sun made the diamond on her finger sparkle, and Ashley turned her hand side to side, looking at it. Of course Keith had got all excited when he seen her wearing it, just like she knew he would, but she told him it didn't mean nothing. She had a lot of thinking to do. He still went around grinning like a monkey about it though.

The sun, sitting high up between two mountains, seemed too far away to do any good, even though sweat was trickling down the back of her neck. It probably got cold as hell when that sun was gone. Ashley shivered and knee-walked closer to Marvelle's headstone. The white marble marker was only a month old, but already it looked as planted and permanent as the others. *Marvelle Dockery Moon*, it said, then below that, *1910–1993*, then below that, *Beloved Wife and Mother*. Sweet new grass covered the grave and eased the memory of that raw red clay and gaping hole in the ground. Ashley pulled some weeds that grew in front of the word *Beloved*, then sat back on her heels and looked over at Catherine. The baby was asleep in her carrier, all wrapped up in flannel footie pajamas and a wool blanket.

There was a melting inside Ashley every time she looked at Catherine, especially when she was asleep. It was like nothing she'd ever known, nothing anybody could explain or prepare you for. It just happened. It was like what her mama said the other day about how she felt when her first grandchild was born, like somebody flipped a switch she didn't even know she had, turned on all this love.

Ashley got to her feet and brushed grass off her knees, then picked up the baby carrier and walked to the edge of the cemetery. She set the carrier down and stared at the blue mountains all around. Had it really been only six months since she last stood there with Marvelle and Cassandra, staring at them same damn mountains? And only a little over two months since they brung her granny home for good? She turned and looked back at Marvelle's resting place, then looked down at Catherine. The baby carrier was sitting on top of a stone. She lifted it and set it over to the side so she could read the marker, blank except for the dates, *1910–1941*. She wondered again if that was just a random rock or if there was a person under there, somebody that didn't want remembering, or somebody people wanted to forget. Ashley sat on the grass and rubbed her hand across the marker. It was icy cold and she pulled her hand away, remembering again that day in October, the look on Marvelle's face when they asked whose stone it was.

She was lucky, her granny was, because she didn't need no marble or granite, or no words written in stone. Her markers walked the earth still, her children and grandchildren and great-grandchildren.

Catherine whimpered a little bit and Ashley put a hand on her feet and patted her until she quieted down. With her other hand, she touched the marker again and felt some of the cold evaporate under her hand. Maybe, like Marvelle, this person left behind something more enduring than words. It didn't really matter though, because nobody'd ever know.

Ashley felt a sudden strong need to hold her daughter. She reached for her, lifted her gently, and held her close against her chest, rocking back and forth, staring at the mountains again. Was this what it all come down to, somebody to carry on what was started way before you yourself were ever born? Ashley rubbed her cheek against Catherine's soft baby hair. Why did it hurt so much to think of them women who come before? She didn't even know all their names, only the ones Marvelle told her, the names she said so many times Ashley couldn't help but remember. Isabel Ann, Elizabeth Ann, Amanda Ann, Dorothy Ann, Sally Ann, Myrtle Ann, Glory Ann, Velda Ann, Marvelle Ann. Why did it feel so tragic, the way they lived and died, here such a short time, and now gone forever? They wasn't so very different from her, was they? They done the best they could with what they had to work with. They lived their lives, no more joy or pain than the next person.

Maybe the tragedy was how they was missed or not, remembered or not. What about Marvelle? It was too soon to forget, but Ashley was scared one day she wouldn't be able to remember the sound of Marvelle's voice, her laugh, or the way she looked when she was talking to the TV, or how she rolled out biscuit dough. What would it take to remember? How could she do justice to that woman? Ashley wanted the world to know, the world needed to know. Marvelle Moon raised her family, loved her man, laughed, cried, worked, played, she done it all, and she give her whole heart doing it. Ashley wanted to say, look here, world, look who this woman was. She was something, by God. How can you people keep on going without her? How do you think your lives can ever be the same without her? You need her. You need her. You need her.

Ashley couldn't see the mountains no more. She leaned over Catherine and cried as quiet as she could. It wasn't the world she worried about. It wasn't the world.

Catherine woke up all of a sudden and started crying and punching her way out of the blanket. Her diaper was dry, she didn't want to nurse, and her little face got redder and redder the harder she cried. Ashley felt so damn helpless that she started crying again too. They sat there like that, staring at each other, watching each other cry, until Ashley felt a hand on her shoulder.

"Want me to take her?" Ruth Ann said. She spread her windbreaker on the ground and sat down on the other side of the marker. "Your butt's probably soaking wet," she said, and handed Ashley a Kleenex. She leaned across and took the baby so Ashley could blow her nose. She held Catherine up and looked into her squalling little red face. "What's the matter with you? Huh? Was your mama pinching you? I bet she was. I bet she was. She better quit pinching my baby girl."

"Mama!" Ashley said. She watched as Ruth Ann jiggled Catherine and made faces at her. Catherine stopped crying and looked back at Ruth Ann. It amazed Ashley, the way her mama had with that baby. She never remembered her doing that with Angela's boys, but maybe she hadn't been paying attention to her mama or anybody else back then.

Ashley blew her nose again, and Catherine waggled her head around to see where the noise come from.

"Hey, honey," Ashley said, and put her face close to Catherine's. "What you doing?" She touched Catherine's nose with the tip of her finger. "Who's got you, girl? Who's got you?"

The baby stared wide-eyed, her face round and sweet, then her mouth opened and for one second Ashley had the crazy notion she was fixing to say something. Instead, she burped, short and sharp, like a firecracker going off. At first she acted like she might cry again, but then she opened her mouth wider in that toothless, irresistible baby grin. Ruth Ann and Ashley turned to each other, laughing, then looked back at Catherine. They couldn't take their eyes off her.

ACKNOWLEDGMENTS

I would like to acknowledge my outstanding teachers for guidance, support, and encouragement over the years: Diane Wright at South Cleveland Junior High School; Frances Kiser at Crest High School; Jan Mitchell-Love at Durham Tech; Daphne Athas, Doris Betts, and Bland Simpson at UNC-Chapel Hill; and Angela Davis-Gardner, William McCranor Henderson, John Kessel, and Lee Smith at NC State University. Thank you all.

I am indebted to Lee Smith for her wisdom, generosity, inspiration, faith, and friendship. Words just don't seem enough. Thank you, Lee.

Thank you, Joelle Delbourgo and Jackie Cantor, for believing in *Moon Women*, and for your enthusiasm, expertise, and hard work. Y'all are amazing, and I will never forget all you've done for me.

I'm grateful to all the folks at Bantam Dell who are so good to me, especially Irwyn Applebaum, Nita Taublib, Barb Burg, Susan Corcoran, Cynthia Lasky, Betsy Hulsebosch, Abby Zidle, A.J. Placke, Anna Forgione, and of course, Jackie Cantor. Thank you all so much. Many thanks also to Jim Plumeri for beautiful cover art, Lynn Newmark for elegant book design, Melody Cassen for lovely jacket design, and Kathy Lord for excellent copyediting.

Thank you, Joy Suzanne Patterson, for being my dearest lifelong sister-friend, confidante, and fellow chocoholic. I'm counting on us still being best friends when both of us are toothless, cackling old rips rocking on the porch of the retirement home. I don't know what I'd ever do without you.

Thank you, Lisa Rogers, for being there at the beginning and for always sharing your stories with me. Without you, I don't know if I would've found my way back to where my own stories started. I wouldn't trade a minute of our friendship, not even all those times you were sick, pregnant, going through menopause, losing your hair, or just in a bad mood.

Thank you, Title Master, a.k.a. Kelly Duncan, for being a great brother, and for naming this novel as well as the next, for a nominal fee.

Thank you, Mary Atkinson, for great photography and even better friendship.

Thank you, Annette Parker-Madden and Susan Baker, for the nudge when I really needed it. I won't forget to pass it on.

Thank you, Darnell Arnoult, for introducing me to The Roger Flourish Writers Group, and thanks to all members past and especially present for your friendship and support. Y'all keep me going.

Thanks to all my bosses at UNC for all kinds of support and office supplies, especially Ralph Henry Boatman, Jr., an ace pilot whose wise advice steered me in the right direction and kept me where I needed to be. I will never forget your kindness, Dude.

I am so blessed to have family and friends who love and support me even when I don't deserve it, and who make the real world outside of novels a wonderful and interesting place to be. Thank you all, especially those of you who got me through graduate school and the writing of this novel: Darnell Arnoult, Debbie and Tim Atkinson, Tamara and Brent Barringer, Virginia Boyd, Renee and Nathan Coppley, Elizabeth Duncan, Kelly Duncan, Pat and Bill Eaton, Becky Hart, Aaron Henderson, Silas House, Jenny Lewis, Cason Lynley, Joy Patterson, Billy Joe Price, Gary Price, Nealie Price, Lisa and Jimmy Rogers, Amy Trester, Nicky and Gilbert Turner, and Lynn York.

And finally but most importantly, thank you, Mama and Nanny, for everything.

The Language of Goodbye

Maribeth Fischer

Annie and Will have both left marriages in order to be together. Their future is fraught with the complications of starting over and both have left pieces of themselves behind. Annie ex-husband is also one of her oldest friends. Will has left behind the five-year-old daughter he adores.

Korean-born Sungae, one of Annie's English-as-a-second-language students, may have left her country behind but she is still searching for the words that will help her resolve the sorrows of her tragic past. As Sungae struggles with the new language and with her memories, her story begins to unravel in ways that will have consequences not only for Sungae, but for Annie and Will as well as their former spouses.

'A strong new voice in women's fiction'

Publisher's Weekly